DRACOHEIM
CONFIDENTIAL

First Printing: 2025

ISBN
eBook: 978-1-960381-44-6
Paperback: 978-1-960381-43-9

Cover & Design: Deranged Doctor

"Lab Day" first appeared in *Fantastic Schools, Volume 2*, October, 2022

"In the Forests of the Night" first appeared in *Sidearm & Sorcery, Volume 1*, December, 2021

"The Last Night of Summer" first appeared in *Fantastic Schools Hols,* October, 2022

"That Summer's Evening Long Ago" first appeared in *StoryHack Action & Adventure, Issue 7*, May 2021

"Better Off Dead" first appeared in *Small Worlds,* August 2023.

"Materials Science" first appeared in *Fantastic Schools Staff,* November 2023

A Brief Guide to the Lords of Nightmare

The Eldest of the Nightmare Lords is called the Grimm
He is the Hunger Wolf and the moreau are subject to him
Nivose, the Empty Quarter, is where he has his throne
In Hunger City in his Fortress made of Bone

Nox is Lord of Air and Darkness in lightless Brumaire
The djinn are his subjects, the people of the air
He has no city or citadel in the endless night
But every shadowed place is his by right

Agni is the Fire Witch, the elder Chaos Twin
Her home is Thermidore, with the aefrit within
The City of Brass is her domain, which no flame can ignite
All humankind must shield their eyes from its infernal light

Chuz is twin to Agni, called the Witch of the Sea
The undines are her people, wild and fierce and free
Pluviose is an open sea, by storms forever tossed
Where Chuz's fleet sails ever, always seeking, always lost

Dreadful Fellmonger rules Messidor, fever-dreamed and cold
His norns comfort the dying, the wounded, and the old
In his City of Dreadful Joy his white tower stands
The Vivisectorium he raised with his bone hands

Heget, the Voluptuous, the Deceiver, and the Fair
Her Garden is called Heart's Desire, her land is Verdemaire
Her people are the incubi, the dreams they grant are warm
Yet in their soft embrace have many men come to harm

Chimiculeon, the Armored King, births the creeping ones
Ventose is his nation, his castle the Malignium
The chigoes are his subjects, insect knights and dames
Who whisper in their silent halls their ancient dusty names.

Eighth is XOR the Clockwork God, master of Ferose's greenless glade
Its people are the forged ones, who are not born, but made
His land is steel and copper, wire and glass and gears
It holds promise for the clever, along with many fears

Lastly, there is Mistigris, Lord and Lady of Bascose,
The rashlings dwell there, rude and bellicose
The Land of Uncertainty, where nothing stays the same
All cards and dice thrown endlessly to suit the endless game

DRACOHEIM CONFIDENTIAL

MISHA BURNETT

CIRSOVA PUBLISHING
©2025

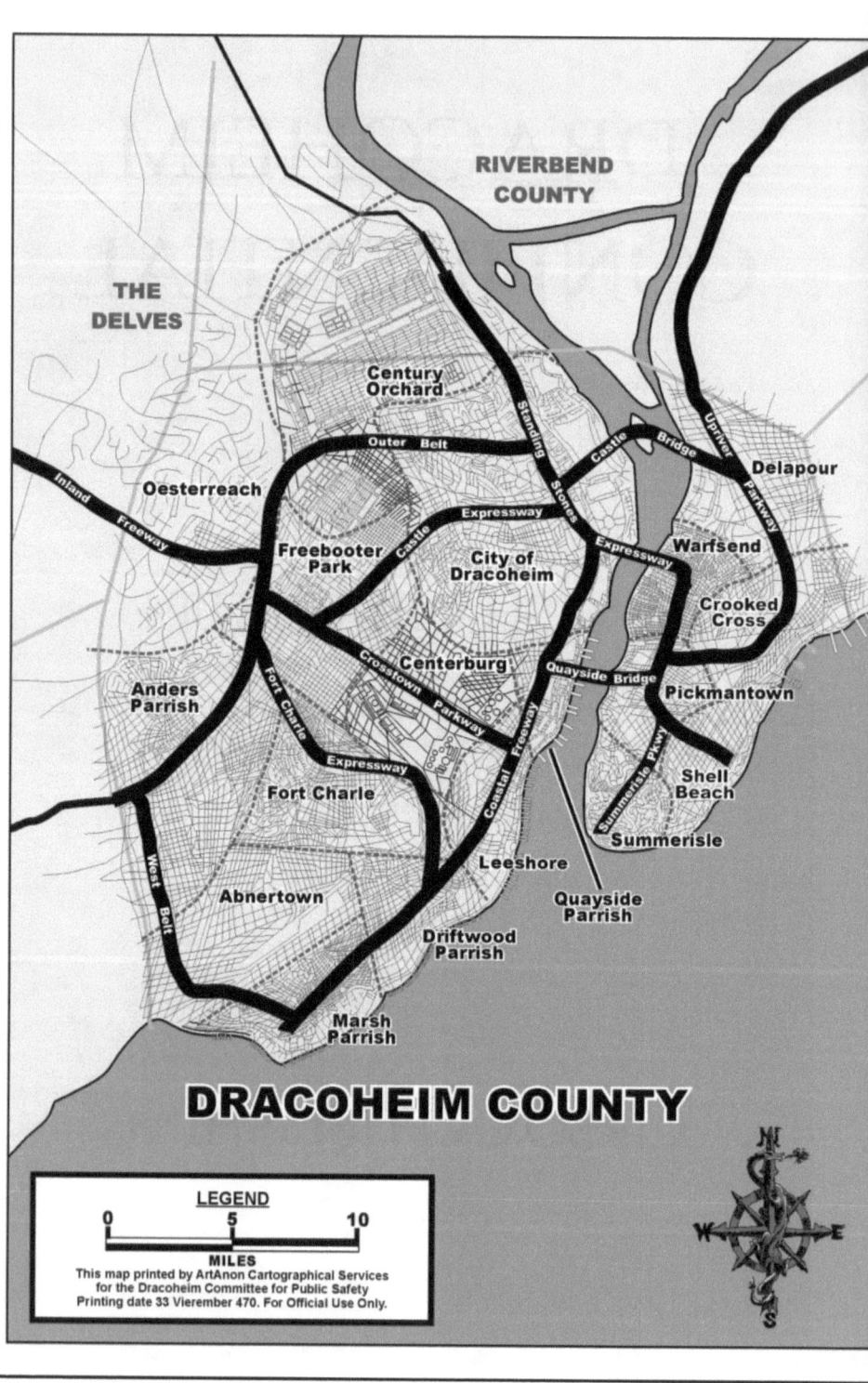

RIVERBEND
COUNTY

THE
DELVES

Century
Orchard

Outer Belt

Inland Freeway

Oesterreach

Stansling

Stones

Castle

Bridge

Upriver Parkway

Delapour

Expressway

Freebooter
Park

Castle

City of
Dracoheim

Expressway

Warfsend

Crooked
Cross

Crosstown

Centerburg

Quayside Bridge

Pickmantown

Anders
Parrish

Fort Charle

Parkway

Expressway

Coastal Freeway

Summerisle Pkwy

Shell
Beach

Fort Charle

Summerisle

West Belt

Leeshore

Abnertown

Quayside
Parrish

Driftwood
Parrish

Marsh
Parrish

DRACOHEIM COUNTY

N
E
S
W

Table of Contents

Introduction: Don't Believe What You Read in the Papers

This is a somewhat chimerical collection. It is, in some ways, a companion to my collection of Erik Rugar stories, *Bad Dreams & Broken Hearts*. In other ways, it's very different.

On the surface, this is a collection of Fantasy stories—there are wizards and dragons and beast-men. In form, however, they most closely resemble a certain type of Science Fiction story that was popular in the 1960s and 1970s. These are stories about technology, and the misuses of new technology.

Tolkien, it is said, based the Shire on his childhood memories of small village life. In the same way, Dracoheim is an idealized version of the world I saw on television and in movies when I was growing up.

As I've said elsewhere, I've never fired a bow or swung a sword. I have ridden a horse exactly once, and it was a miserable experience, probably for the horse as well. The vaguely Medieval, vaguely Northern European setting of most of what is called Fantasy never really appealed to me. When I was a kid I didn't play Knights & Princesses, I played Cops & Robbers.

Dracoheim is the New York of *Barney Miller,* the Los Angeles of *ChiPs,* the Honolulu of *Hawaii 5-0.*

The two characters who alternate stories in this collection, Magus Leonid Vetch and Agent Erik Rugar, are each impacted by technological change, in slightly different ways. Leonid is, by his own estimation, the last of the wizards, an aging practitioner who has watched magic shift from an arcane art to an industry. Erik is a cop who has to deal with a generation of gangsters who have exchanged their guns for magic wands.

In these stories, as too often happens in real life, the good guys are forced to play catch up.

If these stories have a theme, it's that magic is dangerous. The genie promises untold wealth, but once it is out of the bottle it may not obey orders any more. This was the theme of many of the New Wave stories I grew up reading, and I suppose it has colored my outlook on technology in general.

My professional experience in institutional security has only strengthened the lessons of *The Shockwave Rider* and *A Scanner Darkly*. Technology isn't evil, but it *is* amoral. Whether it is a blessing or a curse depends on who is pushing the buttons.

Against the stark cautionary tale theme of the stories, I have the humanity of my protagonists. Leonid and Erik are very different men, but I like them both. They never meet face to face in this collection (I may do that in some later story), but I think if they did, they'd get along.

Of course, Eleanor might have choice words regarding Erik's date for the evening, but she would keep them to herself until she and Leonid were alone. She's a lady.

In any event, I hope you enjoy the following stories. I have some more notes regarding specific details at the end of this volume. As stories, I think they work for the most part, and I'd like to believe that they will leave you with something to think about.

Misha Burnett
28 January 2024

Lab Day

M agus Leonid Vetch only taught one class on Sixdays. *Conjuration 204: Theory and Practice of Major Workings* was a practical lab, 1300 to 1600. Leonid had a demonstration planned and so unlocked the lecture hall at noon to set up the equipment. He flipped on the overhead lights and cranked open the windows a crack to get some of the fresh sea breeze coming from the harbor that could be glimpsed between the buildings across the street.

The conductive plate was a permanent installation in the concrete floor, an eight-foot circular sheet of copper mounted over a thick rubber mat. Leonid checked to see it was clean and the attachment points around the outside edge weren't corroded. Then he unlocked the storage closet and wheeled out the heavy calculating engine and made sure it had a fresh tape. Next came the accumulators, six of them, sturdy wooden bases supporting four-foot poles, wrapped with alternating layers of copper and cloth insulation, the glass accumulators on top looking like oversized light bulbs. He arranged them in a circle around the outside of the plate.

"Need a hand, Magus?"

Leonid looked up. His first students were already coming in. Shotwell and Kent, their bookbags slung over their shoulders, dark blue school uniforms clean and starched.

Leonid glanced at the clock. 12:27. "Did you boys skip lunch?" he asked.

"Slept in and then had a late breakfast at the Dolphin," Shotwell said.

As third year students, they had the privilege of taking meals off campus. Leonid nodded. "Well, if you feel ambitious you could get some number four cables and link the accumulators."

The young men stowed their bags under a lab table and came down to the equipment locker where the heavy cables were stored.

11

While they were doing that, Leonid connected the calculating engine, first to the conductive plate and then to the school's power, supplied by generators in the basement. He verified that the connection was locked out, unable to be energized until he used his key to turn on the power.

He double checked the connections that the boys had made from the accumulators to the attachment points at the edges of the conductive sheet. They were tight, the brass connectors locked into place, so he waved them back to their seats.

Satisfied that the preparations were all in order, he sat at the small desk in the front of the room and lit a cigarette. He reviewed his notes although he could probably have given this lecture from memory. He'd been teaching this class for eleven years.

The rest of the class arrived in ones and twos. At five minutes before the hour, Leonid looked up from his notes and quickly counted heads. Twenty-four. All present.

He ground out his cigarette and stood. "Good afternoon, boys," he said.

"Good afternoon, Magus Vetch," they chorused back.

Leonid walked to windows and looked out. "It's a beautiful Sixday, and I'm sure most of you young men have dates tonight, so I'll try to let you out a little early. I mentioned on Fourday that we were doing a demonstration today—does anyone remember what I said I was going to show you?"

"Apportation, sir," someone spoke up.

Leonid nodded. He didn't bother with raising hands and calling of names; his students were free to speak up, so long as they were polite about it. He ran an informal class. This was not, after all, the Dracoheim Academy for Thaumaturgical Studies, it was Leeshore Technical College.

"Apportation, exactly right."

He gestured at the apparatus set up at the front of the room, then walked to the chalkboard and began writing a complex equation. "Apportation is the act of translating physical objects from one realm to another. It is achieved by establishing an etheric equipotential between the two realms. Remember, it is the frequency of the etheric vibrations that determines the metaphysical constants of a realm's architecture. A containment grid allows us to synchronize a small portion of our universe with another realm. If within this grid we impose a frequency of, say, 9.9 megacycles, which is the native frequency of Ventose, the affected area becomes, in effect, a part of Ventose."

He looked over the equation he had written and nodded to himself. "And so, you just walk across from here to there. Leeshore to the Malignium in three steps."

He turned back to the class. They all had their notebooks out and were dutifully copying down his work on the board. He leaned back against the chalkboard and lit another cigarette.

"Now," he said, "who can tell me the purpose of all those ships out there in the harbor?"

The class was silent, confused at his change of subject.

Leonid smiled, and gestured at the window. "I've just told you that objects can be apported directly into Nightmare by magic. There's the basic equation on the board. Right here, I've got everything you need to dash across to another universe, pick up whatever you want, and bring it back here."

He paused to take a drag on his cigarette, enjoying the moment. "So why all the cargo ships? Why do we sail out onto the dreamsea? Why do the oneiroi come here by ship? Why don't we just apport all the trade between Nightmare and the Midworld?"

"The Navigator's Guild wouldn't allow it." The voice came from the back of the room.

Leonid grinned and nodded, acknowledging the point. "True enough," he said, "but not the answer I was looking for."

He turned back the board and added an equals sign at the end of the equation, then a dollar sign. "Money," he explained. "Apportation is *expensive*."

He quickly circled one part of the equation. "This term right here is what keeps the Navigator's Guild in business. Delta T—the time element."

He ground out his cigarette. "It takes energy to maintain the equipotential, determined by the size of the containment area and the innate distance between the native architecture of the realms. Nivose is our closest neighbor, metaphysically speaking: the frequency is only a few megacycles different from the Midworld. Bascose is on the far end of the spectrum—which is why it's called the Kingdom of Uncertainty. Things are *very* different there.

"No matter where you have an apport field set to go, however, it has to be stabilized by a standing wave signal generated by the containment grid or it will collapse, and the native etheric rhythm will reestablish itself. That, in itself, is not so bad, until you get to the kicker, which is that the instability increases with the *cube* of the duration."

He paused to let that sink in. "Open an apportation link for a minute, and you're looking at a couple of hundred talents to keep it synced, depending on the destination. For two minutes, it's eight times that. For ten minutes, it's a *thousand* times that.

"Now, I know some of you have worked as longshoremen. How long does it take to unload a ship? A couple of hours? Let's say two hours. If we plug 120 minutes into this term we end up with a delta-T multiplier of *one million, seven hundred twenty-eight thousand.*" He punctuated his words by chalking the number on the board and circling it.

He held up a hand. "Ah, you say, don't keep the link active for two hours straight. Just open it for one minute, a hundred and twenty times in a row."

He turned back the board and picked up the chalk. "Nice try, but sadly, it doesn't work like that. Who can tell me why?"

"Samuel's Law?" ventured a voice from the back.

"Are you asking me or telling me?"

"Samuel's Law, Magus," the boy repeated more confidently. "Diminishing efficiency."

Leonid wrote SAMUEL'S LAW on the board. "Curse that Ivor Samuel," he said with a grin. "That man ruins everything."

He turned back to the class and continued. "The math gets a little complicated at this point, but the bottom line is that apportation is a *terrible* way to move cargo. Trade with Nightmare didn't become possible on any large scale until the Lady Chuz's envoy ships made contact with us and sold humans the secret of navigating the dreamsea, back in 228."

"Did you meet the ship, Magus?" a boy asked.

Leonid grinned. Jokes about his age were common enough from his class, and he didn't mind. "No, that was my father," he quipped back, to some amused chuckles.

He got the lecture back on track smoothly. "So why are we covering apportation? Well, there are applications where it makes sense. It is used for traveling to the realms. It's more expensive than passage on a ship, but a lot of companies do business in Nightmare these days, and it's worth it to them to have an executive get to a meeting in a few seconds rather than a week. And some folks are rich enough to take a vacation that way—there are a number of firms in Dracoheim that specialize in transport.

"Also goods that are high in value and low in weight—Ferose clockwork engines, for example, or Nivose metapharmaceuticals. It depends on what's more important—cost or speed."

He stepped to the calculating engine and turned it on. The gears clacked as it reset itself to all zeroes. He looked back to his class. "Some of you will never see an apportation rig outside of this class. Some of you may be prepping one every day of your career. It all depends on where you end up working. When I was in private practice, I don't think I opened one more than a half dozen times. But it's important to understand the principles involved in any event."

He went to the empty side of the chalkboard and wrote *9.9 MC*.

"Today, gentlemen, we are going to Ventose."

He wrote down a series of coordinates, then checked them against his notes. Satisfied, he nodded. "This is a spot in the Stone Forest, about twenty miles north of the Malignium. It should be empty—we don't want to disturb any chigoes. We haven't filed an import plan, so we aren't actually going anywhere. We're just going to open the apport link, verify that it goes where we want it to go, and shut it down."

Lastly, he chalked *180s*. "Three minutes should be enough time to let you all take a look through the window—not that there's going to be much to see."

He turned to face the class. "You'll find the worksheet you need in Appendix C, on page 432. I'm going to give you..." he pulled out his watch and checked it. "...twenty minutes. Work it out separately, and then compare your answers. When I get back I expect you to have settled on one answer. Remember, we need a value for the theta, rho, and lambda axis, an initial charge value, a differential plotted over time, and, of course, the duration." A grin. "That's the easy part—I gave you that one. One hundred eighty seconds."

The students obediently opened their textbooks and got their notebooks and slide-rules out. Leonid checked his watch again as he left the classroom. Two short hallways and a flight of stairs took him to his office. A buff-colored internal mail envelope sat in the wire basket that hung on the outside of his office door; he snagged it as he unlocked the door.

Sitting at the desk in his cluttered little office, Leonid reached behind him to pull an alchemical retort from one of his bookshelves, then a small beaker. He poured himself a neat shot of absinthe from the retort and sipped it as he sorted his mail.

His subscription to the Journal of Gnoetic Materials Science was up for renewal, did he want to the college to renew it? *Yes, please.*

A reminder that midterm marks would be due on Oneday the 34th of Siebenember. No problem, his teaching load was light, and his marks were mostly tabulated already. He made a note to have a chat with one of his first years, Connors, about his performance in Intro to Lab Prep. The young man was eager to learn but tended to be sloppy.

Would he still be willing to act as a chaperon for the Autumn Mixer Dance? *Absolutely! Looking forward to it.*

The minutes from the last Thaumaturgy Department Meeting. *Blah, blah, blah, blah, and in conclusion, blah.*

He polished off his shot and glanced at the wall clock. Time to go back and see how the boys were doing. He set the retort and the beaker back in their places and grabbed a licorice candy from a dish on his desk to suck on.

He heard the low buzz of conversation in the room as he

approached. It cut off neatly when he opened the door.

"All right," he said. "Before I get your numbers for the exercise, I wanted to remind you all that tickets for the Autumn Mixer go on sale next week. This is our year to host, so there's also going to be a signup sheet for volunteers for decorating the gym. I'll be chaperoning again, so I'll expect you to be on your best behavior and treat the young ladies of the Quayside School of Nursing with professionalism and respect."

"Are you going to be dancing, Magus?"

Leonid grinned. "I will. And if Matron Eleanor attends, you might even get to see my tango."

Then he turned serious. "Okay, let's take a look at your data. Mr. Burke, how about you give me the figures?"

As the student read off the numbers, Leonid chalked them on the board. Then, keeping his face and voice neutral, he asked, "Did everyone get the same numbers? Any disagreement?"

Silence greeted his words.

"This is not a trick question," Leonid said kindly. "I want to make sure that you all understand how to do these calculations properly."

"I got one point six E for the rho index," a student spoke up from the back, "but I know what I did wrong."

"Which was?"

"I forgot to renormalize after I divided both sides by negative E."

Leonid nodded. "I threw you boys a curve on the local coordinates. Anybody else forget to renormalize?"

A couple of hands went tentatively up.

"You didn't remember summer," he chided them.

He wrote SUMMER on the board, and then tapped each letter in turn. "Verify your *symbol set*. Check your *units*. Be sure of your *metrics*. Double check your *math*. *Equalize* your terms. And lastly, *renormalize* your terms. If you have any complex numbers, you need to get them out of there."

He turned back to the class and said seriously, "Accuracy, gentlemen. *Accuracy*. You have to get it right. Right the first time, right *every* time. We are dealing with powerful and unforgiving forces here. There are no second chances in magic. If you get nothing else out of this class, I want you to get in the habit of double checking *everything*. It's got to be a habit. A reflex. We all make mistakes, but in this business, mistakes *kill*."

He paused to look over his class. Their faces were grave. He nodded. "You have to catch your mistakes before they become disasters. Once the working has started, it's too late."

Then he lit a cigarette and smiled. "Well, if you're sure this is right, let's get it going. How about you set the engine, Mr. Kent?"

Kent came forward with his notebook and a look of almost comical concentration on his face. While he was inputting the numbers, Leonid said, "And, Mr. Shotwell, if you would be so kind as to ground the accumulators before we begin. They are going to be gathering a wicked charge on this exercise—we want to start them as close to flat as possible."

Shotwell came up and took a short wooden wand with a copper tip from the workbench. Carefully, he touched the tip to each of the glass accumulators in turn. Sparks flew as the wand released the stored energy.

"The rest of you come down here and gather around. During the three minutes that the grid is active, the space directly above the energized copper will be coincident with Ventose. The ceiling of this room is equipped with a dampening grid; otherwise the area of correspondence would extend upwards to the limit of the generator's power—about twenty feet."

Leonid gestured for the students to form a circle around the plate. "Watch the accumulators. *Do not* touch them—they can give you enough of a shock to stop your heart."

He waited until the students had formed a circle around the copper sheet, all of them giving the glass-topped accumulators a wide berth.

"The area that we will be congruent to in Ventose is relatively empty; that's why I chose it. I have done this particular exercise for the last ten years with these coordinates. *However*, remember this is an alien universe. The other realms are collectively called Nightmare for a reason."

He looked over at Kent, who was frowning down at the dials on the calculating engine.

"Are we all set, Mr. Kent?"

"Yes, Magus." He didn't sound sure.

"Someone... you, Mr. Baker. Double check the program."

Baker dutifully looked over the dials and checked them against the figures on the board. "He's got it right."

"Then let's do this thing," Leonid grinned at the students. These boys had grown up in a world shaped by magic. They had lived in houses lit by electricity produced by aefrits, ridden in cars fueled by elixir made by undines, owned toys and tools made by the forged ones of Ferose. They had seen oneiroi walking the streets of their city.

And yet, this would almost certainly be their first look into one of the alien universes that made it all possible. These boys weren't rich kids; they were the sons of commercial fishermen and dockworkers. A generation ago, they would no doubt have followed in their fathers' footsteps, but the new technologies spawned by industrial magic had created a demand for skilled workers.

And if most of them never attained the lofty title of magus, what did that matter? They'd make a good living in the power plant or refineries or as lab workers.

Leonid took out his keys and unlocked the connection to the school's generators. A red light glowed in a caged bulb above the panel. "We are live, gentlemen," he said. "Mr. Kent, begin the program."

Kent pulled the start lever on the calculating engine, and the dials began clicking through their complex movements, regulating the flow of energy into the copper sheet.

The air above the plate grew cloudy, and then, very suddenly, they could see through the mist to another world. It was an impressive view.

The Stone Forest of Ventose was a jagged landscape. Rock spires thrust up through the ground, ranging from a few feet high to enormous monoliths that stretched up until their tops were lost in the mist. The sky was a dull, almost metallic gray, glowing with a sourceless light that made no shadows. Leonid had selected the coordinates to put the point of correspondence at the top of a sharp rise, and the alien world stretched out for miles below them.

The rapt fascination of the class was gratifying. This was Leonid's favorite part of teaching magic—the wonder on the young men's faces as they saw with their own eyes the power of the craft.

"Ventose, gentlemen," Leonid said. "The Realm of Lord Chimiculeon the Many."

He glanced on the time display on the calculating engine. It clicked from 157 seconds to 156, then to 155.

Just then a beetle the size of a large dog swooped out of the mist and into the classroom, its wings clattering as it flew. The students, startled, jerked away from the path of the creature. Leonid saw Shotwell, intent on avoiding the flying thing, about to brush up against one of the accumulators. He reached to pull the boy back and one of the other students bumped into him from behind.

The shock of the stored energy of the accumulator threw Leonid forward onto the conductive sheet, but instead of copper, there was dirt under his feet. His boot caught on a stone, and he staggered forward, still dazed from the jolt. His legs went out from under him, spilling him down the slope. His head hit the base of one of the stone pillars, and the lights went out.

"*Magus!*"

Leonid blinked away tears and looked up into the face of one of his students... Shotwell, it was.

"Is he alive?" someone else asked. Also a student. Mr.... Kent.

His head was clearing. He still felt the tingles from the jolt he'd gotten from the accumulator. He couldn't have been out more than a few minutes.

Minutes.... shit. The contingency field must have collapsed by now and behind Shotwell's head he could see the shifting gray of Ventose's sky.

"It's okay," Leonid said, trying to sit up. His head ached, and he felt nauseated. "They'll send someone for us. Might be an hour or more, they'll need to wait for the interference to—"

"*We don't have an hour, sir,*" Kent whispered.

Leonid turned his head—a bolt of pain lancing down his spine—

and saw Kent. There were figures behind the boy, and Leonid struggled to focus on them.

Smaller than man-sized, with long, thin limbs—far too many limbs.

Chigoes.

"It's okay," Leonid repeated. His voice sounded shaky to his own ears. He made an effort to control it. "A moment, if you please," he called to the crowd of natives. "I hit my head in the transfer, I'm still a bit..."

He started to lever himself to his feet.

The response from the chigoes was immediate. Complicated machines that *had* to be weapons were leveled in his direction. Leonid sat back down, cursing his fuzzy head. Were those... yes, the weapons, the glint of armor on their bodies, the military stance. Warrior caste.

But why? Why would a squad of warriors be out here in the middle of nowhere? And why would they be drawing down on three unarmed humans?

"They say we're smugglers, sir," Shotwell said softly. "I tried to convince them we're not."

"I am Magus Leonid Vetch," Leonid said. "I am bound by oath to the Lord Mayor of Dracoheim, and, through him, I am signatory to the Accords of Nightmare. These men are Thodd Shotwell and Vladimir Kent, my apprentices, and I am guarantor of their obedience to those same accords. We intend no insult to the lands of Ventose or the Court of Lord Chimiculeon. We are here by mistake—a training accident."

One of the chigoes stepped forward. It stood just under four feet tall and was mostly legs—powerful hind limbs like a grasshopper and two sets of long arms. Its body was covered with a jointed carapace. Only its face looked soft, disturbingly human features on its insectile body.

"I am Captain Tethikthik of the Royal Guard. We have been hunting for some time smugglers who bring unlawful goods from Nivose into our realm. We have reports that they apport into this region—just the area where you have appeared."

"We're not moreau," Kent protested. "We're human. From the Midworld."

The captain nodded. "Yes, but it is not uncommon for moreau to hire human magi."

"I see," Leonid said slowly. It made sense. Smugglers would choose the Stone Forest for the same reason he had, because it was uninhabited. "Wrong place at the wrong time."

"We must question you." The captain's voice was firm.

"Can't you do something?" Shotwell whispered.

"Help me up," Leonid said.

With one of the boys on either side he was able to get to his feet. The dizziness and sickness would pass, he knew. It was far from the first time he'd gotten a nasty shock in the lab.

"As visitors—however unintentionally—in your realm we will, of course, cooperate fully with the Royal Guard," Leonid said to the captain, then turned to his students.

"The justice of the Court of Lord Chimiculeon is beyond question," Leonid said, addressing his words to his students but speaking as much for the benefit of the guards. "As innocent men we have nothing to fear." He managed a grin.

"But..." Shotwell gestured uphill, towards where they had apported in.

"My colleagues will send someone looking for us," Leonid said.

"They will be questioned as well," the captain said, "and should you be as innocent as you claim, you will be allowed to leave together."

"But..." Shotwell said again. He seemed unable to say more.

"Mr. Shotwell," Leonid said sternly, "I have pledged my cooperation to Captain Tethikthik"—he only stumbled slightly over the name— "and as my apprentice I have guaranteed your cooperation as well. Do you understand me?"

Shotwell looked to the armed chigoes and then back to Leonid. "Yes, Magus," he said.

Leonid's eyes flicked to the captain and then back to the boy.

Shotwell took the hint. "Your instructions, sir?" he said formally to the captain.

LAB DAY

"Come with us." The captain turned and headed downslope.

Leonid headed after him, noticing that while the captain had turned his back on them, the other guardsmen had not. Shotwell and Kent fell into step beside him.

Leonid turned to Kent. "Do you understand as well?"

Kent nodded. "Our full cooperation with the representatives of the Court." He smiled. "I had nothing planned for the weekend except going crabbing with some of the guys. This is going to be an interesting story to tell."

Leonid smiled back. "That's the spirit."

The chigoes were all different. They ranged in size from knee-high on the humans to nearly as tall as they were. Most had six limbs, but some had eight, and one seemed to have a dozen, all spindly and in constant motion. They had hard carapaces in patterns of dark colors, deep reds, blues, greens, purples. In the gray light, they shone like oiled metal.

Their weapons were as varied as their own bodies, each clearly built to their own requirements. Only the ammunition seemed standardized; they were all loaded with gleaming steel arrows with wicked serrated tips.

Leonid couldn't tell how the bolts would be propelled and didn't want to find out. He didn't know much about chigo technology. Nobody did, really. There wasn't much trade between the Midworld and Ventose. Lord Chimiculeon had accepted the Nightmare accords and agreed to the exchange of embassies but seemed to have little interest in the Midworld or the human race. There was a complicated three-way alliance between Verdemaire, Ventose, and Ferose, but Leonid didn't expect any humans outside of few specialists knew the details.

Nor did humans have much interest in Ventose. The insect-like chigoes were too disturbing. Other oneiroi like norns, rashlings, and even moreau were more or less humanoid, if not human. The djinn, undines, and aefrits were entirely alien, with bodies that weren't physical, living masses of wind or fire or water.

Chigoes looked like giant bugs with human faces. They were inherently horrifying.

Leonid found himself wondering for the first time if chigoes found human beings just as horrible. Perhaps that's why there were so few of them in Dracoheim.

At the bottom of the hill was a clearing of sorts, a wide patch of bare rock without any stone spires. Sitting in the middle of the clearing was an enormous beetle, the size of a cargo van, with metal lockers of some sort hung along its sides.

"We will administer the question, now," the captain said. "Magus, if you please?"

Leonid had no idea what to expect as he walked forward. He tried to keep his stride even, his expression relaxed. His students were looking to him for leadership. He had to maintain calm. If he panicked, the boys were sure to follow.

"What are you going to do?" Leonid asked. His voice was even, despite the ice in his guts.

"You will be searched," the captain said, and opened one of the lockers.

What came out of the locker was a swarm of insects. They buzzed like flies but were larger. The captain whistled, a series of shrill notes like a calliope.

The swarm engulfed Leonid. The small insects buzzed around him, not touching his skin, but flying close enough that he felt the wind from their wings. He forced himself to stay very still.

After what felt like a very long time, he heard another series of whistles, and the swarm retreated, buzzing in a cloud close to the giant beetle.

"You are clean," the captain said. "Now your students."

Leonid looked back at the two young men. They exchanged a worried glance, and then Kent said, "I'll go next."

He walked to where Leonid was standing, a little shakily. Leonid smiled to reassure him. "It's not so bad," he said.

"If you will step back, Magus?"

Leonid walked back to where Shotwell was standing. Together they watched the swarm engulf Kent.

"What are they searching for?" Shotwell whispered nervously.

"Contraband," Leonid whispered back. "I assume. If they are

looking for smugglers from Nivose, probably drugs of some kind."

"What kind of drugs?" Shotwell asked.

Leonid shrugged. "I don't know what would affect a chigo."

The captain whistled his odd tune again and the swarm left Kent, who looked pale. Shakily he walked back to join them. Softly he said, "That was pretty creepy."

Shotwell was staring at the swarm in horror. "I don't think I can do this," he said.

"You have to," Leonid said. "It'll be over quick, and we'll be right here."

Shotwell swallowed hard and walked slowly forward.

The captain whistled, and the swarm engulfed the young man.

Almost at once, Leonid could see that something was different this time. The swarm clustered around Shotwell's left hip, and many of them landed on him, covering his uniform pants to halfway down his left leg. Shotwell started brushing them off in a panic.

The captain whistled, and the swarm retreated back to the giant beetle. Two of the chigo troopers came forward, weapons aimed at Shotwell.

"You will disrobe now," the captain said.

Shotwell threw a terrified look at his teacher and Leonid started forward. Instantly, two more chigoes with weapons aimed came between them.

"Let me help him," Leonid pleaded.

"Allow the magus to assist," the captain said. "Magus, recall your oaths."

Shotwell was trying to unbutton his uniform shirt, but his hands were shaking so badly that he hadn't managed more than a single button.

"Hey," Leonid said softly. "Mr. Shotwell—*Thodd*. Relax. We'll get through this, okay?"

Louder, he addressed the captain. "Why don't we just empty his pockets, first?" Did these chigoes even understand what pockets were? "Maybe whatever you are looking for is one of those items."

Leonid helped Shotwell remove his wallet, watch, pocketknife, a cigarette case, putting them all on the hard ground.

25

The captain gave his whistle, and the swarm came forward. This time, the insects lighted on the ground, and, in moments, they were clustered on the young man's cigarette case.

Leonid had a chilling thought. "What's in there?" he whispered.

"Maiden tears," Shotwell whispered back, his voice a near-inaudible croak.

"Oh, son," Leonid said softly, "how could you?"

"I didn't know I was coming here, now did I?" Shotwell's reply was bitter.

Leonid felt a twinge of guilt at that. The boy had been wrong to have the maiden tears, no doubt about that. It was an unlawful drug imported from Nivose and being caught with it would have meant expulsion. But in Dracoheim, it probably wouldn't have resulted in anything worse, not with a small quantity and a first offense. It was common on the streets. In humans, it produced euphoria and a heightening of physical sensation and—so they said—a lowering of inhibitions.

Here, though...? Leonid didn't know what its effects would be on chigoes, but judging from the captain's reaction, they were probably severe.

As would be the penalty for bringing it into this realm, even unintentionally.

The cigarette case was put inside a very ordinary looking white paper bag, which the captain sealed with tape and a glyph he traced with a steel scribe.

"Thodd Shotwell," he said formally, "you are being charged with the crime of transporting a proscribed substance into the realm of Ventose. You are hereby ordered, upon pain of death, to report with us to the Malignium for trial."

A pause. Then, "Do you understand the charge being brought against you?"

"Yes." The young man's voice was flat, toneless.

There was movement coming down the slope, and Leonid turned to see Kravitz Welsh, the Dean of Magic, along with an armed security guard.

Strike that—a *disarmed* security guard. The man's holster was empty. A trio of chigoes who were very much armed followed the humans downslope.

Leonid took a step in that direction, and the chigoes beside him lifted their weapons. He raised his hands and stepped back.

"After the question, you may meet with your colleagues," the captain said.

The dean and his escort were subjected to the insect swarms, but the bugs didn't signal any contraband. After that, the chigoes allowed Leonid and Kent to join them.

Shotwell stayed back, the guards watching him alertly.

"What's going on here?" Welsh asked.

"Smuggler trap," Leonid explained. "Evidently, some criminals from Nivose have been using this place as a transport site."

"And you just happened to get caught in it," Welsh concluded sourly. "Well, Tucker's going to reactivate the grid every twenty minutes, for two minutes at a time. Let's get back."

"There's a problem," Leonid gestured at Shotwell. "He had maiden tears on him."

"Oh, that poor fool," Welsh said softly. "What are they going to do?"

"Take him to the Malignium," Leonid said. "I need you to get word to the consulate. Maybe they can intervene somehow."

Welsh sighed. "For all the good it'll do."

"You take Mr. Kent back with you," Leonid said. "I'll accompany Mr. Shotwell."

Welsh gave him a long look, then nodded. "It was your screw up," he agreed. "You know there's going to be a full inquiry when you get back."

Leonid nodded. "One thing at a time." He looked back at Shotwell. "Right now, that boy needs me."

"I'll get word to the consulate. They should have someone waiting when you get to the capital," Welsh said, then to Kent, "Come on, let's get back home."

The chigoes returned the security guard's pistol, then waved for them to go back to the transit site.

Leonid walked back towards Shotwell, calling to the captain,

"Will you permit me to accompany my student?"

"Of course," the captain said.

Shotwell was staring down at the bare ground. "I'm dead," he whispered.

"No, you're not," Leonid said firmly. "This is a bad situation, no doubt about it, but help is coming. You're a citizen of Dracoheim, and Lord Chimiculeon isn't going to risk an incident with the Lord Mayor."

"What does the mayor care?" Shotwell asked miserably. "He's not even human."

"Listen to me, Thodd," Leonid said. "*I* care. You are my student, and it's my fault that you're in this mess. I'm going to see this through."

Shotwell looked away and spotted the captain standing by the huge beetle. "Hey!" he shouted. "Can we get moving? Let's get this cursed thing over with!"

The captain looked back. "We will not travel on the walker. I have called a flier, it will be here soon."

"What does he mean, a flier?" Shotwell asked.

Leonid shrugged. They'd find out soon enough.

The flier announced itself with high-pitched engine whine and a sudden wind. It was the size of the cargo beetle but built long and equipped with two sets of gleaming steel wings. It seemed to be partially insect and partially metal, the organic and mechanical parts fused together somehow. Along its back was a line of saddles. The guardsmen ushered them forward.

"Ever ridden on one of these before?" Shotwell asked Leonid.

"I've never even seen one before," Leonid answered. In truth, he had no idea that the Chigoes could manufacture flying machines. "Just hang on and try not to fall off, I guess."

The saddle was adjustable to accommodate the varied bodies of chigoes, and one of the vehicle's pilots moved bits of it around until it was fairly comfortable for a human.

The two humans took their seats, with guardsmen in front and behind them. The high-pitched whine of the motor increased and a hot wind blew from somewhere underneath the vehicle, and then, quite gently, they were airborne.

The Stone Forest dropped away from under them. The view was breathtaking, miles of twisted spires of rock in all directions. The vehicle turned smoothly, rotating in place until it was facing back the way it had come, and then it accelerated away.

Shotwell laughed delightedly. "I need to get me one of these," he shouted over the rushing wind.

"It wouldn't work in the Midworld," Leonid pointed out. "Different cosmological constants."

"Pity."

Under them, the spires of the Stone Forest gave way to rolling hills green with vegetation. From this height, it was impossible to tell what the plants were, but they seemed to be cultivated.

There were buildings, too, wood and stone, ordinary-looking cottages, at least from this height, except that most of them were round or six-sided instead of rectangular. The chigoes seemed to have little use for right angles.

The buildings became both more numerous and larger, and then they were over a city. Here, too, the concept of a right-angled grid seemed to have escaped the locals. The streets were laid out in hexagons, and each hexagonal block was dedicated to a particular purpose. Some were residential, others open parks; some were structures the humans couldn't identify.

There was traffic now, too—chigoes walking or riding beetles of different sizes. Many of the things on the road were constructed like the flying machine, a mixture of organic and mechanical parts. There was traffic in the air, too. An enormous airship drifted by overhead, a dozen or more gasbags supporting a shape of gleaming chitin the size of an ocean liner.

Behind the city, a dome rose up on the horizon, dwarfing the city that sprawled around it. It looked like the polished skull of a titan, half buried. The upper surface was pockmarked with round holes leading into its interior, shadowed like the empty sockets of a hundred blind eyes.

Shotwell's delighted smile faded and his face grew grim. "That's it, isn't it?"

Leonid nodded. He'd never seen it, but from the descriptions he'd heard it couldn't be anything else. "The Malignium."

Traffic streamed around it, both on the ground and in the air. The scale of the thing was hard to gauge. It seemed too large to be real, something that would have collapsed under its own weight in the Midworld.

The flying machine headed for an opening on an upper level that seemed at first comically small, but as they grew nearer the scale resolved itself into a cavern that could have held a dozen fliers. A squad of the warrior class stood in formation on the floor of the hangar. Next to them, looking very small, was a single human figure, a man in a suit.

When the machine landed and the whine of its engines shut off, the man approached, holding out his hand.

"Seth Werner, Parliamentary Diplomatic Corps," he said. "Magus Vetch, Mr. Shotwell, come with me, please."

The warriors formed up around them, Mr. Werner seeming not to notice them. They went through a short, twisting corridor. It was nearly circular in cross-section, flattened on the bottom to form a sort of floor. The walls were a yellowish gray, disturbingly bone-colored. Leonid felt as if he were walking inside the body of some titanic creature.

A circular door led to a small room, hemispherical in shape. There were no windows, but the upper third of the walls glowed with a yellow light. Inside the room was a table and four chairs, very human looking, and Leonid suspected that they were imports provided for the use of human visitors.

The man from the Diplomatic Corps took a seat and waved them to the other chairs. The warriors took up station outside the door, silent and immobile.

"Well, young man," Werner said with a smile, "you've made my day much more interesting."

"I'm sorry for any trouble I've caused, sir," Shotwell said, looking miserable.

Werner shrugged. "It's my job. Cursed bad luck you happened to have maiden tears on you. It's a powerful narcotic for the locals—

they used to use it for an anesthetic, in fact, but it's also highly addictive, so they've switched to other drugs."

"What's going to happen to him?" Leonid asked.

"Well, you are clearly not the smugglers the sweep was intended for," Werner said. "They freely admit that. But on the other hand, you did bring an interdicted substance into the realm. Right now, I'm working on having you remanded into CPS custody for trial in Dracoheim."

"Does the Committee for Public Safety have jurisdiction?" Leonid asked.

"Use of magic to transport a class two controlled substance," Werner said. "You won't be charged, magus, so long as we convince the courts you had no knowledge of the contraband."

"He didn't," Shotwell said firmly. "This is all on me."

"The trip was unintentional, in any event," Werner went on, "the administration backs you on that. So there's no intent to distribute."

Werner paused, then looked at Shotwell, his face grim. "Young man, this is going to go hard for you. You understand that we cannot afford to dismiss the charges—representatives of Lord Chimiculeon's court will be following the case."

Shotwell nodded. "I understand."

Werner stood. "I have a meeting that I must attend. There are certain political ramifications here that I am not at liberty to discuss. Your hearing should take place within a few hours. Do not attempt to leave this room. The warriors will feed you and escort you to the facilities as needed."

Leonid and Shotwell both nodded.

To Shotwell he said, "We'll get you through this. Just try to relax." Then to Leonid. "You're a good man for sticking with him. I'll get you home for dinner tonight."

The hours passed slowly.

At first, Leonid tried to make small talk, but he quickly realized that all he had in common with the young man was the school, and with his expulsion inevitable at this point, that was a sore subject. Shotwell made a few attempts to start a conversation about books, but Leonid didn't really read aside from professional journals.

After a long silence Leonid said, "I'm sorry I got you into this."

Shotwell shook his head. "It's my own damned fault."

There seemed to be nothing more to say after that.

At last, Werner returned, hurrying along the corridor with a squad of warriors. "Come on," he said, "we're being summoned to the presence."

As they moved through the maze of twisting corridors, Werner spoke softly. "I have to warn you, it's going to look bad at first, but I need you to trust me. Don't speak unless you're asked a direct question and give short answers. Don't volunteer any information."

Teacher and student both nodded.

"It's going to be all right," Werner went on, "I promise. Just... trust me."

The corridor quite suddenly opened out into a vast open space, a spherical chamber dozens of stories high, lit by hundreds—no, *thousands*—of lamps affixed to the curving surface of the wall. A railed walkway girdled the chamber at the equator, with a few dozen figures spaced along it, lost in the immensity of the room. In the chamber was...

Lord Chimiculeon. The Seventh Lord of Nightmare, called The Many and The Armored King. It, or *they*, clung to the walls all around. The Nightmare Lord had uncountable bodies, millions certainly, crawling, flying, hopping, a gargantuan swarm of insects of all description. The sound of the swarm was a constant rumble that made the stone walls vibrate. The three humans walked into the presence and were the focus of ten million faceted eyes.

The swarm was in motion, and as they watched, the tiny bodies flowed down the walls of the chamber, pooling in the bottom of the sphere like a liquid and then surging up. A mass of crawling insects, surrounded by swarms of flying creatures that shrouded it like fog, rose up from the bottom of the sphere, taking on shape as more and more of the tiny bodies joined the swelling mass.

Within minutes, it had taken on the semblance of a single form, a jointed body the size of a railway locomotive. A dozen long legs lifted the mass until the front of it—bodies crawling over each other to form a face, huge black eyes above the chasm of an open mouth—

was level with the equatorial walkway.

It—or *they*—spoke. The voice came from all around them, echoing from the walls of the sphere.

"Let the prisoner come forward."

Shotwell swallowed hard. He was shaking, but he walked to the railing unaided.

"Thodd Shotwell, you are charged with bringing into my realm substances that I have forbidden, that are forbidden by the compact your own mayor has sworn with me, substances that are injurious to my people. How do you plead?"

Shotwell cleared his throat. "Guilty, sir," he said in a small, quavering voice.

"By the accords of Nightmare, you are subject to the laws of my realm. I am within my rights as sovereign to sentence you as I would one of my own subjects. There is a petition before me to relinquish my rights and return you to your own world. Can any say why I should do this?"

As Shotwell stood frozen, Leonid started to move forward. Werner grabbed his arm hard and held him back. "Wait," he whispered.

From somewhere down the circular walkway, a voice said, "I will speak to that, with your leave, O Lord of Ventose."

Leonid turned to look. A robed figure stood at the rail, human in outline under the robes, but strange in some way.

"You may speak, child of my sister Heget."

The figure pushed back its cowl. The head that was revealed bore two faces side by side. The one on the left was a woman, on the right a man. This was an incubus, a native of Verdemaire. But what was it doing here?

The male face spoke and gestured with its right hand, also masculine, to indicate where Shotwell stood. "My queen, your sister, asks for clemency for the young human. He admits his fault and takes responsibility for his actions, unwitting as they were. He stands accused by the justice of the Midworld and will not escape punishment for his misdeeds."

"I admit that this is true. Yet why do you speak to it?"

The incubus's female face spoke then. "We believe that the human is best served by human justice. As none of your people were harmed, it seems fitting to us that he be returned."

"Your petition has merit. I will grant it. Is an envoy from the Midworld present?"

Werner stepped to the rail. "I am here, Lord Chimiculeon."

"Are you prepared to take the prisoner to the Midworld to face justice?"

"I am."

"Then let it be so."

The great body in the middle of the sphere collapsed then, the bodies scurrying away from the deflating mass to swarm up the walls of the chamber. Soon there was no trace of the figure, just the swarming motes covering the walls.

Werner took Shotwell by the arm and led him back out into the corridor. The warriors formed up around them again.

Once they were headed down the corridor Leonid asked softly, "What was that all about?"

Werner sighed. "Politics. Now Queen Heget has a marker she can call in the next time Verdemaire has a trade dispute with the Lord Mayor."

He put his arm on Shotwell's shoulder. The young man seemed to be in shock, moving like a sleepwalker. "I told you it would work out. I know that was rough, but you held it together. Good man."

Twenty minutes later, the three of them had been transported back to the Midworld, the grid in the Malignium sending them to the front garden of Government House where agents of the Committee for Public Safety waited to take Shotwell into custody.

Leonid stayed with the boy through the arrest and booking and promised that he would be there for the trial. Then he headed back to his rooming house—not quite in time for dinner—and started to worry about his own upcoming inquest.

The worst they could do was fire him, he knew, and he didn't need the job.

Well, that wasn't quite true. He didn't need the *money*. He'd retired from a lucrative private practice and had invested his money well. He'd initially taken the teaching position as a favor to an old colleague, when the school was starting up, and it was hard to find experienced magi who were willing to spend their days lecturing and their evenings preparing lesson plans. He hadn't planned on making a second career of it, but then his Annalise had died, very suddenly, hit by a laundry van while crossing the street.

The school was all he had. Without it, he'd be just another old widower, spending afternoons feeding pigeons in the park and drinking too much. His students gave him something to look forward to.

Curse Shotwell, anyway, the fool. He had the gift, an intuitive grasp of the principles of spell work. He'd breezed through the mathematics of conjuration while other students struggled. He had so much promise—all gone now, squandered. You couldn't get any kind of license to work in the magic industry with a criminal record. Where would he go now? Back to the docks, to be a stevedore like his old man? Such a stupid waste of talent.

A momentary lapse of reason—a single error in judgment. That's all it took.

Even after several drinks, Leonid was long getting to sleep that night.

In a week, he was back in the classroom.

The inquest found him innocent of all wrongdoing. Just a lab accident, it could happen to anyone. Privately, he was cautioned that the incident might adversely affect his chances with the tenure committee.

Tenure. As if that had ever been a possibility. He wasn't a researcher, with a stack of published papers to his name. He was a middling industrial magus, a man who had made a career with careful, unimaginative work. He knew the job and how to do it safely. Let other people experiment and get themselves torn to bits more likely than not.

On the following Sixday he was back in the lab. He ostentatiously studied his notes, not looking up as the class trickled in. At 1300, he looked up and counted heads. Twenty-three.

The room was silent as he got to his feet.

"Today we are beginning the unit on organic transformations," he began, then fell quiet when he saw a hand upraised.

"Yes, Mr. Kent?" he asked nervously. "What is it?"

"Magus," Kent said, standing. "We just wanted to say... we know you did all you could for Shotwell. You went with him, into the Malignium. You didn't have to do that."

"Well, I..." Leonid shrugged. "I just did my job."

Kent reached into his book bag and pulled out a bottle of a familiar square shape and filled with a green liquid that sparkled in the sunlight. "We wanted to get you something."

He walked down the row between the lab tables and deposited the bottle on Leonid's desk. "We just wanted to say thank you. On Shotwell's behalf."

Leonid looked at the bottle. Absinthe. The good stuff, too, a pricey bottle. There was writing on the label, in black glass marker.

Leonid picked up the bottle and examined it. They'd signed it, looked like the entire class.

"Thank you, gentlemen," Leonid said formally, to cover the lump in his throat. "I don't think I can say how much this means to me."

He felt his eyes filling with tears and turned away to the board to hide his face. A bit shakily, he started writing, then broke off. Without turning around, he said, "I wish I could have done more. I wish... none of that had happened."

He stood silently and got himself back under control, blinked away his tears. When he felt he was ready, he finished chalking the equation he had begun, then turned back to face the class.

"Organic transformations," he began again. "The important thing to remember with organic transformations is that the total value of the humors will always balance out. Understanding the relationships between them is vital to workings of these natures. You must maintain equilibrium."

He sighed, then repeated. "Equilibrium. Really, that's what magic is all about. Maintaining your equilibrium."

In the Forests of the Night

Case:35-ZWI-372//CI#372-0074

It was raining, and some idiot on the Coastal Freeway had run into the back of a 'lix tanker. The Driftwood Parish constable directing traffic didn't even look at the badge I held up for him, he just angrily waved me to join the line of other vehicles merging onto the Crosstown Parkway. It was clear he was in no mood to make an exception and let me slide past on the shoulder.

So much for inter-agency cooperation. I got off the Parkway in Centerburg and started navigating the surface streets.

My destination was in Abnertown. Briefly I considered fighting my way back onto the Coastal downstream of the wreck, but then the storm broke in earnest, buckets of rain and gusts that made it hard for me to keep my sedan on the road. The monsoon that the radio had warned us about all week had finally hit.

So I crawled down Lo Lobey Avenue, peering through a curtain of water and making my best guess as to where the lane markers were, through Centerburg and Fort Charle and finally to the vast glass and concrete dome of the Abnertown Mercantile Expo. I was supposed to meet the local law at the southern entrance. I just looked for where the cruisers were parked, got as close as I could, and stuck my placard in the windshield.

I thought about looking for my rain slicker in the trunk—being a native Dracoheimer I paid no attention to the weather reports—then just sprinted through the downpour to the door.

A uniformed officer started to tell me that this entrance was closed and sorry for the inconvenience, but I talked over him.

"Erik Rugar, CPS Criminal Investigation," I said. "I'm expected."

He nodded and waved me through.

I had been to the Abnertown Expo during its grand opening week last year. It was a huge barn-like affair, with three levels of walkways surrounding a central courtyard with an interior garden.

Dozens of shops under one roof! the advertisements had boasted. Today I could definitely see the appeal of that.

A security officer in the livery of the Expo waved me towards an open stairwell to the upper level. Past him I could see the courtyard, full of shoppers passing by, many of them pausing to gape at the bustling police presence.

The Expo management isn't going to like this, I thought. Part of their sales pitch was the security of the enclosed marketplace.

A section of the second level was roped off. A large storefront was covered with posters of a savage landscape, sharp mountains under a pale blue sky.

Nivose.

High Wilder Excursions the sign above the door read.

I checked out the crowd around the scene. A mix of Abnertown constables and Expo security guards surrounded a smaller knot of suited figures, who in turn surrounded a pair of workmen in coveralls and a small figure, maybe a child. All I could see clearly was a curly mop of bright red hair.

I showed my badge to the nearest constable who then announced, "The CPS man is here."

The uniforms parted to let me through. The first thing I saw was that the small figure wasn't a child—he was a moreau, fox-like and brightly furred.

Then one of the suits detached himself from the others. "I'm Captain Drexel, Abnertown Major Case. You're Rugar?"

I nodded.

"About time you got here," he groused.

I glanced up at the skylights above the courtyard. Rain was still coming down in buckets. "An accident closed down the Coastal," I said. "The weather's got everything tied in knots."

He glared at that but didn't push it. "We've got a missing apport rig," he said.

"Missing?" I asked. "Missing how?"

"Apex Transit delivered the unit three days ago, but they couldn't get installers here until today. Those guys," he gestured at the tradesmen, "open up the crate and, lo and behold, it's empty."

IN THE FORESTS OF THE NIGHT

I looked over at the little fox-like moreau, who was talking animatedly to one of the detectives, and lowered my voice. "How did *he* get cleared for a transit rig?"

"High Wilder Excursions is a Nivose-based company, selling vacation trips to the mountains, but the unit was leased by the Expo management," he explained.

I nodded, getting the picture. Selling or leasing magical equipment to a foreign-owned entity required filing a declaration with the CPS Import/Export division. They'd avoided the paperwork that entailed by keeping the lease in the name of the shopping center instead of the travel agency.

"Where was the crate stored?" I asked.

"In the back of the shop. Our print and picture boys are working the scene now." There was a bit of emphasis on the word "our".

I nodded. If he had his men doing the forensics he must be planning on keeping jurisdiction. "How do we handle it, Captain?"

"Jake Blackwell tells me you're his go-to guy for the shade markets. I want you to find that hardware."

I nodded, thinking it over. "It's tuned for Nivose, I assume?"

"Yeah," he growled. "A drug runner's wet dream."

Tigerberry, maiden tears, and green milk were the top three street drugs in Dracoheim, and all of them were Nivosian in origin. Most of it came in through the docks, smuggled across the dreamsea in the holds of transport liners. Apportation, opening a gateway directly from one realm to another, required both the services of a skilled magus and specialized equipment. Few licensed magi were willing to turn to crime—the risk was too great with CPS keeping a close eye on them.

A rig that was already tuned to a particular realm, on the other hand, could be operated with minimal training. In the wrong hands that rig could be used to flood the city with junk and in the process make somebody a fortune.

Unless we found it first.

I found one of my cards that wasn't too wet and offered it to Drexel and took one of his in return. We promised to keep each other apprised of new developments.

I nodded towards the storefront. "Okay if I use the phone in there?"

"Sure."

A bored constable glanced up to make sure I wasn't trying to cross the crime scene tape that blocked access to the back room, then bent to his *Stage Secrets* magazine again. I called the evening desk officer, who told me that Blackwell wanted me to call him at home. I did, dialing the number from memory and getting it right the first time.

The phone was answered by a little girl who told me with charming gravity that I had reached the Blackwell residence. The grandchildren must be visiting. I told her who I was, and she skipped off to fetch Jake.

While I was waiting, I took a look around. The space itself was very modern, with a polished tile floor and aluminum and glass light fixtures. The furnishings, on the other hand, belonged in a hunting cabin in the woods, table and chairs of wooden planks, irregularly cut but finely polished. Furs and skins adorned the walls, interspersed with big framed pictures of the Nivose wilderness.

"Talk to me, Rugar," Jake's voice came over the line.

I outlined the situation.

"Abnertown can take lead on this," Jake said. "You know the MP is one of the investors in the Expo? I'm sure he's already lighting a fire under Drexel's ass. You beat the bushes and find that rig."

"On it, boss."

"Put together a list of likely suspects, middlemen who would be able to broker a deal for an underground gate. I'll get the locals watching them."

"I'll have it for you in the morning," I promised.

Before I could hang up, he added, "The Nivose embassy is sending their own team. Offer them your full cooperation, but don't let them steer the investigation."

"Right," I said cautiously. If I understood what he wasn't saying, he was worried that they might try a cover up. "I'll send you regular reports."

"See that you do," he said firmly. "I'll forward them to Drexel on this end."

Meaning that he wanted to read the reports before Abnertown got them.

I hung up the phone feeling annoyed.

Politics. Power always brought out the politicians, looking for an angle to drive in a wedge and gain some leverage. Magic was power, money was power, and this case was dripping with both. Rumor had it that constructing the Expo had cost twenty million dollars. If the Abnertown MP had even a small piece of that he would be very interested in making sure the case was wrapped up quickly and cleanly and without threatening the bottom line.

That's above your pay grade, copper, I told myself firmly. *Just do your job and work the case.*

What I needed to do was to figure out where the apport rig had gone when it left here, and—more importantly—where it was now.

Which started with finding out exactly what I was looking for.

The two service techs from Apex Transit were electricians, not magi, but they could provide me the full specs. I wrote down the serial number and model number.

"The thieves didn't take the conductive surfaces, just the transit unit itself," one explained.

"The calculating engine and the modulator and the etheric generator?" I asked.

"In this unit, they are all contained in the same case."

"How big a case?"

"Four and a half feet long, three feet wide, three feet tall."

The size of a steamer trunk. "How much does it weigh?"

"Four hundred and twenty pounds."

Heavy, but not impossible to move with a dolly, or two men.

"What would it take to make it work?" I asked.

"Four number six etheric cables, a conductive plate, and some kind of shielding," he recited. Clearly he had been asked the question several times this evening. "Ideally the whole area should be grounded and warded, but you could make do with rubber mats and a couple of layers of tinfoil."

"And the power connection?"

"A 550 five phase phillips junction."

I glanced towards the shop. "They got that kind of hookup in there?"

A nod. "Yeah, we installed that last week."

"That's a lot of power," I observed.

"It's an extended duration gate," he explained. "It's rated for a seven-minute congruence to Nivose."

Somebody could shift a lot of tigerberry through a door in seven minutes.

"What's the refresh window?" I asked.

"The manual recommends three hours," he said. "But honestly, it'll be ready to reopen in two."

So. An industrial power connection and a couple of hundred dollars' worth of hardware is all it would take to set up a smuggling operation that could drive every other junk dealer in the city out of business.

As I was contemplating this grim scenario, a trio of figures came up from the lower level. The space in front of the shop grew suddenly quiet as the knots of conversations trailed off into silence.

The delegation from the Nivose embassy had arrived.

The one in front was a big ugly thing, some kind of a reptile. He was wearing an absurd suit, trousers and vest of black with pale blue pinstripes, no shirt, knee-high riding boots, and carried a gold-handled walking stick.

The pair behind him were mammals. To the left was a tiger-woman, lean and lethal looking, in a pale blue skirt and blazer and a white blouse. Her face was catlike, with wide green eyes, but her body was very human under a coat of sleek orange and black fur.

The one on the right was grossly fat, with a pig's head, an expression of vacuous stupidity, and a gray woolen suit that made him look like a huge ball of lint.

For a moment we all stood and stared, then Captain Drexel recovered his poise and remembered he was in charge. He made the introductions.

The lizard man was Commissar Apres Lincendie. The tiger was Investigator Joviene Lolo and the pig was Savant Yad Rose. I blinked a little at the last one, and had to remind myself not to judge oneiroi by human standards.

The commissar waved his cane—quite unnecessarily—for attention. "Now, which of you is the agent of the Lord Mayor's office?"

"That's me," I said. "Erik Rugar, Committee for Public Safety, Criminal Investigation Division."

He cocked his head to look at me sideways, with one eye. "Please inform me of your progress with the case."

"Sir," I said, "Captain Drexel is the lead detective. CPS is assisting the Abnertown major case squad. I am here assisting them with locating the stolen property."

"And your progress with that?"

"I am about to get started pulling records as soon as I return to Government House."

"Do that. Lolo, attend Agent Rugar."

I was turning to head towards the stairs, but then his words registered. "Excuse me, sir?"

Investigator Lolo walked quickly over. "I was sent by my Lord Grimm to assist the CPS," she said.

"All I'm doing tonight is pulling files," I protested.

"Then I will assist you in pulling them," she said firmly.

I surrendered. "Do you have a car?"

"We traveled together from the embassy."

"Come on, then," I sighed. "I'm parked out this way."

As she fell into step beside me, I saw that she had a large shoulder bag of high-quality leather, big enough for a weapon. I wondered if she was armed. Firearms were on the interdicted export list to Nivose, but there probably was an exception for agents of the Grimm.

The squall had ended while I'd been inside, and the air was still, cool and fresh. The moreau paused as we exited the shopping center to take a deep breath, nostrils twitching.

"First time in the Midworld, Investigator Lolo?" I asked her.

"Yes," she said, walking briskly to catch up with me. "I spent half a year in Verdemaire, working for the Grimm, and I've been on some brief trips—Bascose, Brumaire, Ventose—a few times, but never here before. And please, call me Jo."

"Then I'm Erik," I responded, quickly shoveling trash over the top of the front seat and into the back, then more carefully stacking the mass of paperwork into a pile. "Sorry about the mess, I work out of my car."

She chuckled. "Don't worry about it."

I saw that she got settled into the seat and helped her fasten the lap belt—help she didn't need, since she'd evidently ridden in human cars before. I couldn't help noticing that her hips and legs were built exactly like a human woman.

A very shapely human woman. I got my eyes back on the road and my hands on the wheel.

"Have you ever been abroad, Erik?"

I shook my head, then had to concentrate on merging onto the Coastal Freeway. When I had my spot in the lane secured—beating out a taxi by intimidation—I glanced over and said, "Honestly, I don't think I've been more than fifty miles outside Dracoheim in my life."

"You should visit Hunger City," Jo said. "It's beautiful. There's the Lord's Opera House, and the Water Gardens, and the Hunting Park."

"Nivose is getting a lot of tourists from the Midworld these days," I said, thinking about the case.

"Not just the Midworld," Jo pointed out. "We get norns and incubi and forged ones—even aefrits and undines."

"That store back there—High Wilder Excursions. They sell trips to the mountains, right? And they were buying that gate to transport tourists?"

"That's the idea, right," she agreed. "It's three days by train from the coast to High Wilder—after a week over the dreamsea by ship. People don't want to spend most of their vacation traveling. With the apportation rig, they could just pop straight to the lodge and go hunting the next day."

"It's pretty expensive, though."

"Well, they worked out a deal with County Power for a reduced rate—I think the Grimm pulled some strings with your Mayor."

I considered that. Slowly I said, "This was an inside job. Someone knew in advance where the rig would be delivered, and had access to the Expo's storage spaces."

"You suspect it was one of our people?"

"A moreau?" I shook my head. "I doubt it. You're watched too closely and you can't hide among humans. But there are plenty of locals who would have known enough to plan this." *Too many,* I thought. IE should have nixed this deal. But since the Expo was technically the lessee, CPS didn't even get read in on it until the deal went south. Politics again.

I got my thoughts back on track. "My point is that they weren't career criminals—at least, not all of them. Either someone in the shade trade heard about the sale and approached one or more working joes who could give them access, or an employee on the inside realized the street value of the rig and reached out to a buyer."

"That makes sense," Jo said slowly.

"Either way, the buyer had to be somebody who looks respectable," I went on.

"Right," Jo said, nodding. "An honest villager from, say, the shipping department of Apex Transit isn't going to just knock on the door of the Blind Joker's clubhouse. We're looking for a fence who operates out of a legitimate business."

"Exactly."

"How much does that narrow down the search?"

I sighed. "Not enough."

The fact was that the Committee for Public Safety was underfunded, and every time the budgets came up for review, Licensing and Import/Export got a bigger piece of the pie at the expense of Criminal Investigation. The public wanted magic, more and better and faster, delivered to their doorstep. Parliament viewed CPS as the Lord Mayor's personal secret police and tried to hamstring us at every opportunity.

Without half trying, I could come up with a dozen shops that I had reason to believe dealt in stolen, bootleg, or counterfeit magic items that we simply didn't have the resources to investigate. In theory, the local constabularies were obligated to give us any assistance we asked for, but in practice doing surveillance or witness interviews for CPS tended to rank dead last in their priority queue.

Until all of a sudden something happened and they needed help. Then everyone demanded to know why we weren't doing more.

I saw the exit for Founder's Park coming up, and I realized that I hadn't eaten since lunch and that was a long time ago.

"I'm going to stop and get dinner before I get to the office," I said. Something occurred to me. "What do you eat?"

"Oh, any small mammal is fine," she said. "Rabbits, shoats, hedgehogs. Your restaurants do serve live food, don't they?"

"Uh," I answered awkwardly, "Well, none that I know of—" I broke off, seeing her grin, a mischievous smile surrounding a mouthful of ivory fangs.

"I'm an omnivore," she said. "And we cook our meals just like you do. Midworld food is very popular in Hunger City, actually."

"Good." I smiled back with my blunt human teeth. "There's a diner across the park from Government House."

The place wasn't busy and we were able to get seats at the counter right away. Jo turned heads, but being in the heart of the city proper, most people were too cosmopolitan to stare openly. I was sure the counterman would have questions for me the next time I came in.

We devoured cheeseburgers and fried onions, and I paid for both of us—making sure to get a receipt—and we headed across the park to Government House. Time to get to work.

The guards at the night entrance checked Jo's ID and asked if she had any weapons. She reached into her bag and surrendered a tightly wrapped bundle of silver chain. The guard put it in a numbered wire cage without comment.

Then down two floors on the elevator to the CI bullpen. It was after hours and empty. I sat at my desk and waved her to my visitor's chair.

"This is going to be dull," I warned her.

"I've got a book," she replied with a smile.

I started digging.

I scribble notes on my desk calendars and I keep all of my old ones in my bottom drawer. I started there, looking for things to jog my memory. As I went through them, a picture grew in my imagination of a particular kind of shop. Not too high end—I could discount the Shell Beach boutiques. Not too low rent, either. The dives in Warfsend wouldn't attract the sort of man I figured the inside guy on this job had to be.

It would be a place where a shipping clerk or civilian desk jockey would feel comfortable. A used appliance dealer that sold scratch and dent items that might have fallen off a truck somewhere along the way, or a pawn shop that specialized in deals that were just a shade too good to be true.

I worked my way through a maze of dead ends, cases that never had quite enough evidence to interest the prosecutors and assembled a list of a dozen names and jackets for incomplete investigations that I could have pulled.

When I looked up from my notes it was a quarter after twenty in the evening. Jo was sitting placidly, hands folded, watching me. I started. She'd been so quiet I'd forgotten she was there.

"Let me run this down to Records," I said, "then we can call it a night."

The clerk on the night desk in Records was a student dozing over a law textbook. I handed him my list of file numbers.

"Supervisor Jakob Blackwell is going to want these on his desk first thing in the morning."

He stretched and yawned, rubbed his eyes. "I'll get right on it," he promised.

At the door, Jo retrieved her chain weapon. I tried to get a look at it unobtrusively, but she caught me and held the thing up for me to examine. A thin leather strap held the chain in a tight coil, with a steel ball the size of a fist on each end.

"What is that?" I asked.

"It's called an enforcer's whip," she said. "It's used to ensure a suspect's compliance."

I nodded. "Looks effective."

"They take a lot of practice," she admitted. "But once you get the hang of it, yeah, it's effective."

I changed the subject. "Am I taking you back to the embassy?"

"I've got a room at the Trainman's Hotel, by the station." She paused to open her bag. "I've got the address here someplace."

"I know where it is," I assured her. "Come on."

I left her at her hotel and said I'd be back to pick her up at seven. She promised to be in the lobby and watching for my car.

She was, bright-eyed and holding two cardboard cups of coffee. Once I'd gotten into traffic she handed one to me.

"Thanks."

"So, what do we do today?" she asked.

"Start knocking on doors," I said. "Ask a lot of stupid questions and get a lot of stupid answers."

"Let me guess," she said with a grin, "I don't know anything, I didn't do anything, why are you bothering me instead of catching thieves and murderers?"

I laughed. "Ah, you've seen this play already."

"Third generation Servant of the Grimm," she said proudly.

A thought struck me. "Is that because you're..." I wasn't sure how to complete the question and already regretting asking it. "...the kind you are?" I finished lamely.

"A predator, you mean?"

"Yeah," I said. "I'm sorry if that's a rude question. I don't know much about Nivose society."

She gave me a smile. I think it was meant to be reassuring, but she had a lot of teeth. "I'm not ashamed of my tribe. It's true, many of the hunting people go into law enforcement—it just makes sense. We're naturally good at it."

"How many... tribes are there?" I asked.

"A few dozen," she said. "It depends on how you want to break them down. Class, order, genera, species."

"But you're all moreau."

"All who contain the spark of reason are kin," she agreed gravely. It seemed to be a quotation.

When we got to my desk, there was a note propped up on my typewriter.

Call me ASAP. —JB

48

IN THE FORESTS OF THE NIGHT

It was never a good sign for the boss to be in this early. Nervously I picked up my desk phone and dialed his extension.

"It's Rugar, I just got in. What's up?"

"Is Investigator Lolo with you?"

"Yes."

"I need both of you in my office. We've got a break in the case." He didn't sound happy about it.

There was a thin nervous man in a good suit in one of Blackwell's visitor's chairs. He got up hastily and handed Jo and me each a business card.

"Axel Janthor, of the Fistingham Agency," he introduced himself. "We underwrite the coverage for both the Abertowne Mercantile Collective and Apex Transit, Limited."

I nodded, guessing what was coming. Jo seemed confused.

"Last night," the insurance man continued, "we received a communication from a person who claims to represent the thieves who took the apportation equipment."

"What do they want?" I asked.

"One hundred seventy thousand dollars in cash," Janthor said. "This represents about a third of our firm's liability should the equipment not be recovered."

"And since it's an Abnertown case..." I prompted.

"The Abnertown Chief of Constables has agreed not to press charges provided the equipment is returned complete and undamaged."

Jo was frowning fiercely. "What's this all about?"

I held up a hand for her to wait, then turned to Blackwell. "Our position?"

"Our position is that we don't want that rig on the streets," my boss said. "If Fistingham is willing to pay the ransom, His Honor says to let them. We will not pursue a conviction—again, on the provision that we get the gear back."

"The Abnertown Expo will take possession, of course," Janthor corrected.

Blackwell looked sour and I knew what he was thinking. But he nodded. "Yes, that's what I meant."

Jo looked from Blackwell to Janthor to me. "So... you'll just let them go?"

"Investigator," Blackwell said calmly, "I don't want to give you the impression that we are in the habit of negotiating deals with criminals. Our primary consideration is preventing that gate being used for smuggling operations—if the best way to do that is to let it be ransomed back to Mr. Janthor's company, then we'll bite the bullet and take the deal."

"I see," she said coolly. "Then I suppose there is no more reason for me to remain here. Agent Rugar, if you will be so kind as to see me back to my hotel?"

"We can at least buy you breakfast before you go," Blackwell said. "Rugar, why don't you take our guest to the commissary before you run her back."

"Sure," I said, standing.

Jo got to her feet. The thought of an institutional omelet and a second cup of coffee clearly didn't thaw her mood.

Once we were outside in the bullpen, with Blackwell's door closed behind us, she said. "Thank you, but I really don't believe..."

"He wants to talk to you without the insurance man listening," I said quietly, cutting her off. "That's why he told me to get you breakfast."

"Oh..." she said, comprehension dawning.

"Let's wait and see what he has to say," I said, and added, "and their pancakes are really pretty good."

She got a plate of bacon and sausage, which reminded me uncomfortably of the pig-like magus who had come with her from Nivose. I knew that moreau weren't the animals they appeared to resemble to human eyes, but... I cut off that line of speculation.

"Are you going to stick around for a while after the job?" I asked, just to be saying something. "Maybe see a show? I've got contacts, I can get good seats."

"They'll probably want me back home right away," she sighed. "We're always short-handed."

I could relate.

She gave a wistful smile. "I'd love to go to the Vespers Radio

Theater."

"Oh?" I was surprised she'd heard of it.

"That's where they record *Days of the Founders*," she said. "They do really have a live audience, don't they?"

"You listen to *Days of the Founders*?" I blinked at her.

"Oh yes," Jo replied seriously. "It's very popular in Hunger City."

"But I thought radio didn't work in Nivose," I objected.

"It doesn't," Jo said. "At least no one has figured out how to make a radio for our metaphysical constants. We get human radio shows on phonograph. They always sell out quickly." A girlish— *kittenish*—grin. "One of my housemates works in a record store, and we always listen to the new shows as soon as they come out. Every two weeks there's a new LP album, and we stay up all weekend catching up."

Her enthusiasm was infectious so I smiled back at her. "I might know somebody who knows somebody," I said slowly. A lot of theater people also worked in radio. "Let me ask around."

She shrugged. "Of course, I probably won't be here that long."

Then my boss came into the commissary, scanning tables. I waved him over.

"Investigator Lolo," he said, extending a hand. "I'm Supervisor Jakob Blackwell of Criminal Investigation."

Jo took his hand and shook it gravely and Blackwell sat beside her.

"Things are moving quickly and I'm still catching up myself, but I'll try to bring you up to speed," he went on. "Commissar Lincendie tells me you're an experienced liaison officer. You worked the consulate in Verdemaire."

She nodded.

"So you know the score. On this case, Abnertown C of C has jurisdiction, and they've asked for our help. I have to let them call the play, whether or not I agree with it."

"I understand the necessity," Jo said without expression.

"But you don't like it," Blackwell concluded for her. "I don't like it either. I hate having someone tell me to back off a case. We *took* the job because we want to *do* the job." That last bit was one of

51

Blackwell's favorite sayings.

Jo nodded slowly. "So how do you propose that we do this particular job, sir?"

Two hours later I was driving into the upper parking lot of the Abnertown Mercantile Expo. Local constables had the lot blocked off with sawhorses; they scrutinized my ID, and then Jo's, before they let us in.

A big black limousine was the only car in the lot. That would be the representatives of Fistingham Surety, with a suitcase full of cash and a couple of armed guards. I parked a few steps away from the limo and got out.

Mr. Janthor got out. The day was overcast and the breeze damp. Janthor and I both wore topcoats. Jo, when she joined us, was in a simple blouse and skirt—but then, she had a coat of fur, and I didn't.

"Who's the contact?" I asked.

"He didn't give a name," Janthor said. "But he shared certain details about the heist that have convinced Detective Captain Drexel that he's legitimate."

I rubbed my hands together, wishing for gloves. "It's got to be almost noon," I said.

Janthor checked his wristwatch. "Two minutes after," he announced.

Making us wait. Classic power game. I sighed.

Soon, though, a stake-bed truck pulled up to the barricade, a big box covered with a tarp tied down in back. The constables waved it through, then replaced the sawhorses.

As the truck approached I saw that it was a rental, from an outfit in Centerburg. It came to a shuddering stop. A pair of armed guards came out of the limo.

The man who slid out of the cab of the truck was fat and balding. He flashed a grin around at everyone. He was wearing a gold watch and worn-down shoes. I recognized him as one of the shyster solicitors who hung around Government House looking for clients among the defendants showing up for court. A born patsy.

"I'm Axel Janthor, junior vice president for special projects,

Fistingham Limited," Janthor said. He didn't offer his hand. "That's Agent Rugar of CPS-CI and Investigator Lolo of the Lord Grimm's Inquirers. Who are you?"

"Now, is that really important?" the solicitor asked.

"Yes." Janthor was firm.

The solicitor looked over at me. "I got immunity, right? That's the deal. You get your gizmo, I get the money, and we both walk away. No reprisals."

"No reprisals," I agreed.

"What about the cat-girl?" he asked.

"I have no jurisdiction here," Jo said. "I am purely offering my assistance as a civilian observer."

He thought it over and said, "Jeffro. Marcus Jeffro."

Janthor nodded. "Very well, Mr. Jeffro, let's get this done before it rains."

He walked to the bed of the truck, Jeffro hustling to keep ahead of him. Jeffro tried to unveil the crate with a theatrical flourish, but the wind caught the tarp and he had to struggle with the folds, which ruined the effect.

Jo and I headed over more slowly, and the guards fell into step behind us. One of them carried a large locking briefcase.

The case matched the dimensions given by the Apex installers.

"Serial number's on the side," Jeffro said. "You can see the case wasn't even opened." He pointed to a red and gold seal.

"Seals can be faked," I said. "We'll need to verify that it's genuine."

Jeffro looked around. "So, where's your wizard?"

"I'll need to see it in operation," Janthor said.

Jeffro gave a strained laugh. "Well, excuse me, but I don't have a commercial power connection in my pocket."

"They do," I said, pointing. An orange Dracoheim County Power truck was being waved through into the lot.

"You're kidding," Jeffro said.

"We have your money," Janthor said. He waved and the guard came up and offered the briefcase to Jeffro. "We simply want to verify what we are buying."

Jeffro sighed and held out his hand for the case. "That works both ways," he muttered.

The guard set the case on the hood of the truck, then Janthor offered Jeffro a small key.

Jeffro unlocked the case, shielding it from the wind with his body. After riffling through the stacks of currency he relocked it. "Looks good to me," he said grudgingly.

The power company truck pulled up beside the stake-bed and uniformed technicians brought out a conductive pad and rolled it out on the tarmac. Then they started running cables to the unit in the back of the truck. A generator—a deeper growl than the truck's engine—started up.

"You're being paranoid," Jeffro growled. "Would I have come out here without the real deal, when I knew you were going to check it?"

"Perhaps," Janthor answered coldly. "You are working for thieves, after all."

The techs worked quickly, and in just a few minutes the board on the case lit up. One of the techs climbed onto the bed of the truck. "We've got a green light," he announced.

"See?" Jeffro said.

Janthor ignored him and looked to the tech. "Give me a forty-five second window."

I stepped up to Jeffro. "Ready to go on a trip?" I asked him.

"Me?" he protested. "Now you're being unreasonable."

"Not at all," Jo said, joining us. "Perhaps the apport regulators have been altered so it sends us to the middle of Pluviose or Thermidore instead of Nivose. You are going with us."

I drew my revolver and handed it back to the guard. "Hold onto this for me," I said.

Then I turned to Jeffro. "You can leave the case here. It'll be safe."

"Oh, no," he said. "I'm not letting go of this."

I shrugged. "Suit yourself."

"Forty-five seconds, ready to engage," the tech said over the roar of the generators.

IN THE FORESTS OF THE NIGHT

I stepped to the edge of the conductive sheet. Jeffro, scowling, joined me, with Jo close behind him.

"Light us up," I told the tech.

The air shimmered and then we were looking at a mountain scene with a bright blue sky. There was a sprawling complex of wood and stone buildings about where the edge of the parking lot was in our world.

Jeffro gestured. "See!" he shouted. "Nivose."

I took his elbow and guided him through the gate between the realms.

Although the sun was bright—a paler gold than the Midworld's sun—the wind was brisk. I wrapped my topcoat around me.

Behind us Dracoheim winked out.

Jeffro hunched up and wrapped his arms around his chest. "It's cold," he complained.

"This?" Jo spread her arms. "This is lovely." She took a deep breath. "Oh, the air is so clear."

We were standing in a large square area like a parking lot, with a surface of fine crushed gravel and surrounded by a wooden rail fence. One side of the lot was the wall of one of the buildings, with an ornate door. I headed towards it.

Jeffro stared at me, then back at the ground where we had appeared. "Wait. When's the return window? We don't want to miss our trip home."

I kept going.

"Return window?" Jo asked innocently, heading after me. "What do you mean?"

"I mean, *lady*," Jeffro growled, "when do we go home?"

She shrugged. "I am home," she said, pointing out over her shoulder.

I paused to wait for her and held the door so that she could go in first. We entered into a lobby of an upscale lodge. There was a desk just inside the door, clearly placed there to greet visitors who had come in through the apport field, but it was unmanned.

Jo crossed to the front desk and we collected some curious looks from the staff. It seemed to be earlier in the day here than in

55

Dracoheim, maybe mid-morning, and although a fire was built up in an enormous stone fireplace, there didn't seem to be any tourists about.

The desk clerk was a massive ape-like moreau who frowned at our approach.

"Did you just come in through that gate?" he asked.

"Yes," Jo answered him. "You can register arrivals here, right?"

The clerk looked over her shoulder at the door we'd come in. "I didn't think they were open until next week," he complained.

"They're not," Jo said. She pulled her ID wallet out of her purse. "We're on the Grimm's business."

Automatically, the clerk took her ID and studied it, then handed it back. "Just a moment, ma'am," he said, his tone apologetic, "We're not quite organized yet."

"Take your time," Jo said kindly.

The clerk dug through drawers and came up with a file folder full of forms. "Here we are." He pulled a form and started writing down information. Unasked, Jo put her ID on the desk for him to copy her personal data.

Then the clerk looked over at me. "And you are, sir?"

I laid my own ID on the desk and the clerk started a form for me. "Is this your first visit to Nivose, Mr.... uh, Agent Rugar?"

"Yes," I said.

"He'll be traveling with me," Jo said. "I can give him the orientation."

"Very good, ma'am," the clerk said absently, writing. To me he said, "I need a home address."

I flipped over my ID wallet to the side with my driver's license and showed him.

"Leeshore," he said, writing it down. "That's on the beach, isn't it?"

"I can see the ocean from my front window," I said.

"Very nice."

Jeffro came stomping up behind me. "Okay, Rugar," he said angrily. "You've had your little joke. Ha, ha. Very funny. *Now get me back to Dracoheim.*"

IN THE FORESTS OF THE NIGHT

I turned. "You've got your ID on you, I hope?"

He glared at me, then at Jo, then at the clerk, and then slammed his wallet down on the counter.

The clerk raised one massive simian eyebrow and began filling in the next form, peering at the information on Jeffro's license.

Once that was complete, the clerk looked to the door. "Is there anyone else in your party?"

"No, just us," I said. "Shouldn't be anyone else coming through there."

The clerk collected the forms and shuffled through the pages. He pulled a carbon from two of them and, after a glance at the names, handed one flimsy sheet to me and one to Jeffro.

"These are preliminary visitor visas. They are good for fifteen days. If you intend to stay longer, you will have to file an intent to reside at an Alien Registry Office—there is an office in the High Wilder town hall, down in the village. Please keep these papers on you at all times."

I nodded to show I understood. Jeffro angrily stuffed his sheet into his pants pocket, provoking another lifted eyebrow from the clerk. "May I register you for the lodge?"

"We're not staying," Jo said. "Where's the train station from here?"

The clerk gestured at the front doors. "Just across the quadrangle. You can't miss it."

I reached into my wallet and realized that I didn't have any local currency for a tip. "Is there someplace I can change money?" I asked.

"I can do that here, sir," the clerk said helpfully.

I changed a hundred bucks of Midworld cash into a stack of thin gold coins, and handed one back to him. He accepted it with a smile.

I looked over at Jeffro's suitcase. "He probably can't do all of that."

Jeffro glared back. "You think you're so funny. When I get back to Dracoheim I'll have your badge, and I'll sue everyone in your department, up to the Mayor himself."

"And here I was going to offer to pay your ticket to Hunger City,"

I said, heading towards the front doors.

"Hunger City?" Jeffro stopped in his tracks.

I kept going. "From there we can get on a liner back to the Midworld. We'll be back in Dracoheim in a week, a week and a half."

Jeffro hurried to catch up. "Listen, you, I'm not going to Hunger City."

I waved him back to the desk clerk. "Then you'd better get a room. It gets cold here at night."

Fuming, he followed me, banging the door open with his suitcase.

Vendors pushed carts selling everything from sausages on sticks to wooden swords. This early, only a few tourists were around, mostly from abroad but a few moreau as well, tourists from one of the cities. Jo had stopped to buy three cups of hot spiced cider from a short but very broad moreau with a head like a bear. She handed one to me and I sipped it. Very nice.

Jeffro looked like he was going to refuse his, but changed his mind and wrapped his hand around the hot paper cup. He set down his suitcase gingerly to warm both hands.

"Thank you," he muttered grudgingly.

"We should be able to get berths on the afternoon train," Jo told me. "Hunting season is just beginning, so it shouldn't be too crowded going back to the city."

"Or," Jeffro said pointedly, "you could open the cursed gate back up, and we could all have dinner at the Opera Club tonight. My treat. How 'bout it?"

"I can't do that from here," I pointed out.

"You've got some kind of backup plan," he shot back. "You wouldn't be here if you didn't."

"Opening a commercial gate is expensive," I reminded him. "Of course, you do have a lot of money on you."

"It's not his money, though," Jo said, as if the thought had just occurred to her. "Say, I hope his partners don't get impatient waiting for it."

"Yeah, that could get sticky," I agreed. "Him disappearing with all their cash. I mean, we know that it wasn't his idea, but they don't."

"And they are thieves," Jo added. "Probably dangerous customers."

Jeffro was looking back and forth from me to Jo. "What are you saying?"

"When were you going to meet your contacts?" I asked casually.

He lifted his wrist to study his watch. Time in Nivose passes at the same rate as the Midworld, or close enough, so it was keeping Dracoheim time. I could see him realizing that he was going to miss his meeting.

"This ain't my fault," he said, glaring at me.

"Oh, I don't know that they'll care about that," I said and took another sip of cider. "They probably had someone watching the handoff through binoculars. You take the money, go through the gate, don't come back out? That's going to look suspicious."

"Oh, no, no, no," Jeffro said. "You're not going to set me up."

I finished my cider. "They're your partners," I said with a shrug. "You'd know."

Jo clapped Jeffro on the back. "I wouldn't worry about it. You owe that money to a Dracoheim gang, right? They can't get you in Nivose."

Jeffro sighed deeply. "Okay," he said. "Okay. You win. Let's talk."

"Sure, chum," I smiled. "But we'll talk in the station. It's cold out here."

I started walking, and he snatched up the suitcase to hurry after me.

The waiting area inside the train station was outfitted with chairs and couches arranged in conversational groupings. There seemed to be something wrong with the perspective, though, and for a moment I thought my eyes were playing tricks on me. There I realized that the furniture was of different sizes.

Of course it would be—moreau themselves came in a wide range of sizes. But the furniture was identical except for scale. A couch, a coffee table, and two armchairs, all in dark green leather and polished mahogany, the same set repeated a dozen times. Some were tiny, the backs of the couches coming up to my knees, while others would have seated giants.

It gave the impression of a surrealist painting to my human eyes.

Jo led us unerringly to seating sized for humans. We parked Jeffro on the couch and took the armchairs, flanking him.

"Now talk," I told him.

"The immunity deal is still good, right?" Jeffro asked.

"Not my department," I said. "That's between you and the Abnertown prosecutors."

He looked around the lobby. A trio of incubi were talking softly over an unfolded map a few tables over. Aside from them, we had the waiting room to ourselves.

"I'm going to need some guarantees before I say anything," Jeffro's voice was low, nearly a whisper. "From both of you."

Jo leaned forward. "There were moreau involved in the theft, then?"

"I'm going to need protection."

"Protection?" I asked. "From whom?"

"Promise me," Jeffro said. "My name is never going to come up. I'm not going to sign anything and if you list me as a source I will sue your asses off. This conversation never happened. Everything I say is off the record. Promise me. Both of you."

I sat back and considered. Before he had just been belligerent, now he was frightened. He knew something about his contacts that scared him. Something that he didn't want them to know that he knew.

"My department makes provisions for confidential informants," Jo said.

The solicitor shook his head. "That's not good enough. I don't want be in some file as a CI. No record of me *anywhere*. Ever. Or I don't say a word. I'll take my chances."

"We can keep your name out of it," I assured him, then looked over at Jo. "Right? No notes, no files."

Jo grimaced—a very fierce expression on her catlike face—but then nodded. "Off the record entirely," she said.

"And we go back *tonight,"* Jeffro insisted. "Get a gate open one way or another. I need to be back in Dracoheim before midnight."

"Sure," I said. "I can arrange that. *If* your information is worth it."

"You're a bastard, Rugar," Jeffro snarled. "You know that?"

I shrugged. And waited.

He took one last look around, then started talking in a low voice. "About two weeks ago I got a call from a man who said he wanted to talk about a job, but he wouldn't give me his name and he didn't want to meet in my office. He tells me he'll give me three hundred for a half hour consultation in this diner just off the Standing Stones Expressway, near the Castle Bridge. In my business that's not unusual, so I show. There's a buddy of mine on the constables in Delapour that does odd jobs when he's off duty; I got him to keep on eye on me from the lunch counter, just in case."

Jeffro paused, took another look around. No one was nearby, and none of the staff seemed to be looking in our direction.

"When I get there," he went on, "I can tell right away it's not the guy who was on the phone. This is a kid, and he's got fingernails about an inch long, and his eyes are as big as half-dollars—"

I glanced to Jo and saw a confused frown. "Symptoms of tigerberry use in humans," I explained.

"Right," Jeffro said. "I see a lot of junkies in my line of work. This kid is dosed. But he's got an envelope with three bills in it, so I take it and ask him what he needs fixed."

A frown. "He rambles for a while about his sister being in jail for soliciting, but he's not sure where she was arrested and doesn't know where she's being held, and at first her name is Sasha then halfway through his story it changes to Sally. Still, I took his money so I write it all down and promise I'll look into it. He still doesn't want to give a name or a phone number and he says he'll call me in a day or two."

I nod and gesture for him to get on with it.

"So, I get back to my office," he says, "and there's this character waiting in my office. *Inside* my office, sitting at my desk—and believe me, my building has good security. This is the guy who called me."

"They wanted you out of the office so they could break in," Jo said.

"Obviously," Jeffro agreed. "And my first impulse was to tell him to take a walk off the pier, because I don't appreciate those kinds of games. But something tells me that this gentleman was somebody I shouldn't antagonize. For one thing, getting into my office wouldn't have been easy. And he's wearing a suit that put him back half a grand, with imported shoes and all. Serious money. And the way he talked, like he was used to giving orders and having them obeyed."

"What were his orders to you?" I asked.

He bristled at that, then shrugged. "He paid me a retainer and told me to be available yesterday and today. I got the call last night about midnight with the information I needed to set up the deal with Fistingham."

I nodded slowly. "Good to know, but that doesn't add up to a trip home by apportation."

Jo started to stand up, "I'll get the train tickets."

"Wait," Jeffro said quickly. "I'm not done yet."

Jo sat back down. "Go on," she said, sounding bored.

"I got my buddy from Delapour to track down that junkie for me—the one who had the three bills in the diner. It wasn't hard." Jeffro leaned forward. "I scare this kid a little and he folds right away. He says he got that envelope and his instructions from his dealer, who works out of a pushcart on the Warfsend river walk, selling fruit ices. The dealer's a moreau, a little red fox type."

I nodded, thinking of the little fox who had been the counterman at High Wilder Excursions. Coincidence? I doubted it.

"This kid tells me that his dealer has a scar on his shoulder." Jeffro was nearly whispering now. "And I ask, like a knife scar, or a bullet? But he says no—it's a burn. Like a brand. And it's in the shape of this funny kind of ax with a short handle."

I felt Jo stiffen beside me. I glanced over and her eyes were wide.

Jeffro nodded, looking smug. "Yeah, I figured you'd know something about that. Some kind of gang mark, right? A Nivose gang?"

"You could say that," Jo said softly.

IN THE FORESTS OF THE NIGHT

"Two days later," Jeffro said, his voice still low but gaining in intensity, "I get a call from my buddy in Delapour. He tells me that they found this junkie in an alley off the docks. He couldn't get the path report, but this kid was cut up bad. In pieces. He wasn't just killed, he was—"

"Butchered," Jo finished for him.

"What do you know?" I asked her.

"Go send your telegram," she said. She looked grim.

I got up and asked the ticket clerk—a cheerful squirrel-tailed fellow so tiny that he stood on the counter, not behind it—where to find a telegraph office. It turned out that there was one inside the station.

I wrote: *Communications Secretary, Office of Midworld Consulate, Hunger City, Nivose* on the recipient line of the form and *Eric Rugar, Mayor's Committee for Public Safety* for the sender. In the blank for the message I wrote: *Please Forward To Jakob Blackwell, Supervisor CPS-CI, Government House, Dracoheim, Midworld. Urgent. Message Follows: Karianne will be ready at—*I looked up to check the local time on the huge clock mounted above the exit to the train platforms. It was just short of noon now. I did some figuring in my head, guessed at how long the message would spend on each step of the journey—*1400 today. Please respond.*

I paid the cost for the telegram and added a healthy tip from my stack of gold coins. A disturbingly attractive female—despite her coat of gleaming red and black scales—smiled and assured me it would be sent at once.

"I'll be expecting a return reply," I said, then pointed to where Jo and Jeffro sat. "I'll be right over there."

Karianne was the name of the Jake's little granddaughter who had answered the phone last night. We had decided to use her name as code for "reopen the gate" and 1400 local time was when I wanted it open.

I joined the others at the table. "Two hours," I said.

Jeffro visibly relaxed. "Okay, good."

I turned to Jo. "Now, tell me about this gang with the brands."

"They call themselves buck-cutters. 'Gang' isn't the right word

63

for them—they're a cult. They have a ritual..." She looked down at her hands and flexed her claws nervously. Without looking up she said in a small voice, "They're cannibals."

"They eat... other moreau?" I asked.

She nodded. She still couldn't meet my eyes. "There aren't many of them. When we catch them, we kill them. I hadn't thought there were any in the Midworld. Or anywhere abroad."

"That's a pretty serious crime here, then," Jeffro hazarded.

Jo looked up to glare at him. "It is a violation of the Law of Blood."

A quote from my middle school History of The Realms textbook came to mind. "When the Grimm uplifted the beasts of Nivose he commanded them not to taste the blood of their kin..."

"Not to drink the blood, not to eat the flesh," Jo clarified, "for all who contain the spark of reason are kin."

I nodded. "So these buck-cutters deny the authority of the Grimm."

"The Law of Blood is what civilization in Nivose is based on. Without that... we're just animals." Jo's voice was low, but I could hear the passion behind her words.

I checked my watch. An hour and a half to kill. There was a diner in the terminal. "Let's get some lunch," I suggested.

On the way I stopped by the telegraph office and the clerk told me that my reply had just arrived. I scanned past the header from the consulate office to Blackwell's message.

Will pick up Karianne at 1400.

I thanked the telegraph clerk and tipped her again. Her answering smile was wide and her tongue flickered out, long and forked.

In the diner, over bowls of boiled ham and rice—bland, to my taste, but filling—I tried to reconstruct the timeline.

"That clerk at the travel agency—the fox. What was his name?"

"Anthor Graham," Jo said.

I paused, thinking over how to word my next question.

Jo beat me to it. "You're wondering about a connection between him and that dealer in Warfsend," she said, then leaned back to consider it. "Graham's only been in the Midworld for a month, and he wouldn't have gotten a work visa if he'd had any evident connection with criminals. On the other hand, tribe bonds are strong—particularly in the smaller people. A single male, alone in a strange land, would be drawn to seek out his own kind."

I nodded. "He could have been recruited by the buck-cutters after he arrived in Dracoheim."

"We should look into it," Jo agreed.

"Hey, now," Jeffro spoke up, "remember that you're leaving me off the record."

I sighed. "Yes, I remember. I think we can pick up a tigerberry dealer on the riverside docks without mentioning you."

It looked like Anthor Graham was going to be the key to this investigation—if, I reminded myself, there was going to be any investigation. Blackwell hadn't been sure this morning. There was that immunity deal that Abnertown worked out with Jeffro, but it applied only to charges brought by the Abnertown constabulary relating to the theft from the Expo. The thieves had no immunity from charges brought by CPS, and our legal team was working on that.

Of course I couldn't say any of that in front of Jeffro. But I was going to continue under the assumption that there was a case and I was still on it until somebody told me different.

I changed the subject. "You said that you didn't think any of these buck-cutters were abroad. Why?"

She winced and had involuntarily glanced around when I used that term, but while a few other tables were occupied, no one was close.

"They're separatists," she said. "Radicals. They oppose the Treaty of Nightmare, say the Grimm sold out Nivose to foreign interests."

I nodded. "We've got groups like that," I admitted. "Isolationists."

"So, what's a Nivose separatist doing selling junk in Warfsend?" Jeffro asked.

I looked to Jo. "He's got a good question," I said.

"I don't know," she said. She looked away when she said it. She had a theory, but she didn't want to discuss it in front of Jeffro.

I checked my watch. "Okay," I said, "let's get back over to the lodge."

Jeffro stood up quickly, leaving his food unfinished. "I'm ready—let's go."

"You know," I said, getting to my feet more slowly, "there are people who pay a lot of money for a vacation here."

"People are stupid," he shot back.

The lobby of the lodge was busier now. Groups of tourists were clustered around native guides dressed in traditional furs and leather negotiating prices for trips up the mountain trails. Some of the vendors from the plaza had come inside, too, and seemed to be doing brisk business.

The ape-like clerk had a line in front of him, but Jo stepped right up to the counter, flashed her badge, and said, "We're leaving now. Through the gate."

He gave her a comical look of surprise, then recovered and said, "I'll need their visas," indicating Jeffro and me with a nod of his massive head.

I handed mine over, and Jeffro dragged his considerably more crumpled one from his pocket.

Then Jo marched us over to the door to the transit lot while the clerk was still fussing with his stamps and folders.

"Being on the Grimm's business sure streamlines the paperwork, doesn't it?" I said softly to her.

She flashed me a needle-toothed grin. "Sometimes," she admitted. "Other times it makes it worse."

It had gotten warmer when we'd been inside, and the lot had a beautiful view of the mountains over the top of the lodge. *This would be a pleasant spot for a vacation*, I thought as I waited for the gate to open. Not for hunting—I did my hunting with a rod and reel—but they had ski slopes, and I always wanted to try skiing. It would be nice to take a girl up here and spend the day on the slopes, followed by hot chocolate with brandy in front of a fireplace.

Then there was a rush of warm air and the gate to Dracoheim opened. What I saw through it wasn't the parking lot of the Expo, but the inside of High Wilder Excursions. They must have moved the transit unit. Jeffro hurried forward, lugging the heavy suitcase. Jo and I followed him through.

I noticed Commissar Lincendie first, gaudy and angular. Beside him was my boss, and constables were scattered around the room. I stepped off the conductive pad of the transit unit and a moment later Nivose winked out of existence behind me.

"Well?" Jeffro said belligerently.

"Thank you for your cooperation, Mr. Jeffro," Blackwell said. "You are free to go."

He glanced around at the waiting constables as if suspecting a trap, then turned and started towards the front door. After a few steps he stopped. "Where's my truck?"

"In the parking lot where you left it," Blackwell called.

Another man—after a moment I recognized him as Captain Drexel—added, "Detective Vetch will give you a hand with that suitcase."

After Vetch escorted the grumbling Jeffro out, we retired to the employee break room. Jo and I took seats on one side of the table, with Blackwell, Drexel, and Lincendie on the other.

"Report," Blackwell said curtly.

I filled them in on everything that Jeffro had told us in Nivose. When I got to the part about the junkie butchered in Delapour the three of them exchanged glances.

I finished up the last few details.

Captain Drexel got out a cigar, looked around the break room and reluctantly put it back in his pocket. "Anthor Graham didn't show up for work this morning," he said. "I sent a couple of uniforms over to his place to check on him and they found him in his kitchen. Somebody strung him up by the heels, cut his throat, and cut him open. The ME says his liver and kidneys are missing."

I looked to Lincendie. "It's these buck-cutters, isn't it, sir? They're here."

He nodded, a savage jerk of his head. "They're here. I've sent word to the consulate and called for some of the Grimm's guard."

Blackwell looked uncomfortable at that. "We've sent a request to the OEA for liaison."

I nodded. The Office for External Affairs handled—among other things—extradition of foreign nationals and jurisdictional disputes between signatories of the Treaty of Nightmare. This whole mess seemed to me to be squarely in their yard.

Drexel was more direct. "Graham was murdered in my city. It's my case. I don't care where the killer came from. This is where he did the killing, and this is where he's going to be hanged."

"Of course, Captain," Lincendie said. "I did not mean to imply otherwise. The Grimm's guard will be at your disposal and under your orders. They are simply here to assist your officers."

I gave Jo a sidelong glance. She looked down at her hands and flexed her claws.

"Where does that leave us, sir?" I asked Blackwell.

He shrugged. "Our interest in the case was the transit unit. That's been recovered."

I stood. "Well, I've got paperwork back at Government House."

Blackwell looked at his watch. "It's late, Rugar. I'll see you in the morning."

He laid my service revolver on the table and I picked it up, returned it to my holster.

"Thanks, boss," I said, then turned to Jo. "It was a pleasure working with you, Investigator."

"Agent, could I impose on you to give Joviene a ride back to the hotel?" Lincendie asked.

"Sure," I said.

Jo stood. "And from there, Commissar?"

"I'll let you know," he said. "We may need to continue to act as liaison with the external affairs office. We're still hammering out details."

Drexel gave the moreau a dark look, but didn't comment.

Once we were out of the store and into the crush of the Expo I asked her, "Want to stop for a drink on the way?"

She gave a heroic sigh. "Absolutely. Maybe two."

We walked out of the Expo into twilight. Transiting to Nivose and back in one day had left me with no sense of what time it was. I checked my watch. 17:30. The Coastal would be jammed with rush hour commuters. Couldn't be helped.

We had a long walk to the upper parking lot where I'd left my sedan. Jo fell into step beside me, matching my stride easily with long-legged grace.

"That's a nice lodge there at High Wilder," I said. "I might want to take a vacation there myself someday."

She laughed. "It certainly has changed since I was a kid."

"You've been there before?"

"A long time ago. My mother's family was very traditional. My grandmother insisted on taking me up there to be blooded—it's a big thing with the traditionalists."

"What was that like?"

"Oh, you know how kids are," she laughed. "It was fun at first, but after a couple of days I wanted to go home. At the time there was nothing except some stone huts—no library, no other kids, no museums." A chuckle. "I'm a child of the Treaty—I like the city."

I nodded. "Me, too."

We'd reached my car. I opened her door, and as I was walking around to get in the driver's side she said softly, "I'm glad I did it. When I have children of my own, I'll take them up to the mountains for their first kill. Running down your prey, tearing it open with your teeth, feeding on blood still hot from the chase...there's nothing like it."

I started the car, thinking about my uncle building a fire on the beach for me to grill the first fish I'd ever caught all by myself. "I can imagine."

Then she laughed. "But we'll stay at the lodge, and not build a lean-to in the snow to huddle under. There are limits to tradition."

"That lodge is new," I remarked. "What was there when you went with your grandmother?"

"Not a whole lot," she said. "Not even a train station. The tracks ended at Fosterpoint back then and you had to take a carriage the rest of the way."

The Coastal Freeway was flowing pretty well. The night was clear, and as the coastline faded into blackness, the lights of the city came up, glimmering. I wondered what this view—so familiar to me that I scarcely saw it—looked like through Jo's captivating green eyes. A cat's eyes, but also a woman's eyes. I wondered how she saw me. As a man? Or an animal that could talk? An animal that, if not for the legal fiction of the Treaty of Nightmare, she would see as prey?

I turned on the radio.

"Oh!" Jo said. "Can I...?"

I showed her how to work the tuner. She found Dima's Madcap Ballroom and we listened to a sketch full of spicy innuendos. Jo giggled like a schoolgirl. When that was over and Dima struck up the band, she dialed away to a wrestling match. Madam Moth against Lady Feral.

"I met her," I remarked. "Madam Moth, I mean. I interviewed her when her manager was killed."

Jo was listening to the play-by-play with an expression of confused concentration, and it occurred to me that moreau probably didn't have sporting competitions. How could they, when the range of physical capabilities was so broad?

She moved on without comment and found a torch singer. I took the Founder's Way exit and busied myself with local traffic to the Trainman's Hotel. It turned out the hotel bar was reserved for a wedding reception, though.

"Still want that drink?" I asked. She might have just been being polite and I wanted to give her an out.

"Please," she said, and I saw she really meant it.

"Follow me."

Founder's Way was full of the kind of places that served two-dollar cocktails, but I knew the neighborhood and took us down a side street to a dive better suited to working folks. Peeling paint on the wide plate glass window told us we were at Pietr's Place and there were open parking spots. It looked good to me.

Inside it was about half full, mostly men in dungarees, stopping to hoist a few after a day's work before heading home to empty flats and quiet rooming houses. Most of the space was taken up by the bar, which stretched parallel to the street. A jukebox played a swing tune from one corner.

We found seats at the bar and I ordered the house cider.

"I want gin," Jo announced. "Warchief Smith drinks gin. I want to try it."

The bartender gave her a carefully neutral look and produced a shot glass full of clear liquid. I laid a bill on the bar and took a drink of my cider. It wasn't bad.

Jo lifted her shot glass and took a careful sip. After a moment of careful contemplation, she rendered her verdict. "This is terrible."

"Usually people mix it with something," I suggested.

"I don't think that would help," Jo said. "I don't suppose you have any mead?"

The bartender frowned. "No, but I do have a honey cordial."

"Hit me," Jo said.

She reached for her purse, and I put my hand on her wrist. "Allow me," I said. "You're my guest."

She gave me a warm smile. "Thank you."

She received a small glass of amber fluid and lifted it to her lips. Soft, pink lips, surrounded by orange fur that looked so soft. I felt an impulse to pet her, like a house cat, and suppressed it. The jukebox clicked to itself and then started playing a cool, smoky jazz number. I wanted to ask her to dance. I suppressed that, too.

Instead I laid another bill on the bar. When the bartender brought back a handful of silver, I pushed it to him and waved my hand. He scooped up the coins with a grateful nod.

"What happens now?" I asked Jo.

She knocked back her drink before replying, and her pink tongue darted out to lick the last drops from the glass. I looked away.

"The Grimm's guard are good at what they do," she said. "If the criminals are still in the city, they'll find them."

"Drexel is going to want them brought in alive," I said.

She shrugged. "Everybody wants something." She pushed her empty glass towards the barman. "Me, I want another one of those."

A car's headlights suddenly lit up the bar, and I turned on my seat to see what was going on. An engine revved. I had just enough time to realize that the car was going to hit the window before it did, and

I got my hands over my face before a shower of glass hit me. Then a table. Then the floor.

I lay on the floor, struggling to get my wind back and make sense of what had just happened. I heard the car's engine, very close, and somebody was cursing, loudly. Car doors opened.

A confused babble of shouting voices. Running feet.

I managed to sit up, shaking glass out of my hair, and opened my eyes. The front grill of an old beat-up sedan was a foot from my face, the headlamps blinding me.

Bodies struggled close beside me, and something gave a shriek of rage, a terrifying, inhuman sound.

Jo.

I shoved back against the bar and used it to get my legs under me. I tried to get my gun out, but my right arm wasn't working.

Then the car backed up, furniture splintering under the wheels.

I had just enough time to think, stupidly, *Someone just drove into the bar. Isn't that peculiar?* when the car jounced back onto the street, dragging bits of wrecked tables and chairs under it.

Then, more urgently, *They've got Jo!*

I was standing and my legs held me up. My arm was starting to wake up and it hurt like fire, but I could make it move.

I took a look around. The front window was shattered, and the tables that had been in front of it were kindling. One man was down on the floor, curled into a ball and cursing. Another stared blankly into the street, blood running down his face.

I needed to call this in.

But they had Jo, and if they were crazy enough to use a car as a weapon to get her, who knew what they might be capable of?

I made a choice. The barman was already on the phone. I fumbled one of my cards out with my left hand and dropped it on the counter.

"When the cops get here, give them that," I said. Then I staggered out to my sedan.

The trail of broken furniture showed me which way they'd gone. I hadn't gotten a good look at the car, but I thought it was black, or maybe dark blue, and old. I remembered the grill was dented and spotted with rust.

IN THE FORESTS OF THE NIGHT

My arm was working well enough to turn the key and work the shifter, but I hoped I wouldn't have to shoot at anybody. There wasn't much traffic on the road. Most of the office workers had gone home, and the theater crowd wasn't out yet. I studied the backs of the cars ahead of me, cursing myself for not getting a good look at the taillights as it pulled away. My head was starting to clear, and I was beginning to second-guess my actions. Protocol demanded that I secure the scene and wait for backup.

Then there was a spray of sparks from under a dark sedan half a block ahead.

Bingo. It had picked up something on its crash through the window and whatever it was had worked loose enough to drag on the ground. As I accelerated to catch up, it fell free. A chunk of the window frame, I guessed, but I didn't take my eyes off the car to check.

A Cataphract, ten to fifteen years old, original color black, probably, but so filthy that it was hard to tell. Three occupants, or maybe four. I crept up closer. Three heads, all human and male. Jo might be down on the floor, or in the trunk. If the driver had noticed me, he wasn't reacting.

I got my notebook out and managed to scrawl down the license number. In the process I weaved all over the road. Good. If they saw my headlights behind them they'd probably think I was just a drunk.

I drifted back a bit and let them get half a block ahead. They were driving very carefully, staying under the speed limit and signaling far in advance for turns. They didn't want to get pulled over for a traffic violation with a kidnapped agent of a foreign government. That might get awkward.

Who *were* these thugs, anyway? There was no way for them to know that I would take Jo to that bar, since I didn't know it myself until I saw it. Had they followed us from the Expo? Maybe—I hadn't really been looking for a tail.

More likely they had staked out the Trainman's Hotel, waiting for Jo to come back. Maybe they'd been planning on grabbing her from her room, and when they saw us go through the lobby and right back out again they panicked.

DRACOHEIM CONFIDENTIAL

That stunt with the Cataphract was ballsy, but stupid. It was just dumb luck that they didn't end up with a couple of flat tires and a busted axle. Probably junkies, like the cutout they'd used to set up Jeffro. Which would make sense, if the buck-cutters were mixed up in the tigerberry trade—but why ransom back the transit unit instead of keeping it for themselves? And who was the mysterious well-dressed human who had braced Jeffro to set up the exchange? They'd wanted the hundred and seventy grand in cash more than they wanted the unit. From Jeffro's timeline, they put him on retainer before the theft—even before the unit had been delivered to the Expo.

This gang was a weird mix of brilliant and incompetent. They'd gotten the transit unit out of the Expo storeroom and they'd done it without anyone even knowing it was gone. They'd had Jeffro lined up in advance. Everything they'd done to set up the heist had been methodically planned out in advance.

Killing Anthor Graham like that, though, and leaving his body to be found—that was both brutal and stupid. It just confirmed his involvement in the theft. Cops all over the city would be tracking down his contacts, now, interviewing every member of the Nivose expatriate community to see who he talked to.

And why take Jo? She was here to work with me, and I was off the case. Even if she was being reassigned to liaison between the Grimm's Guard and the local law, did they think that kidnapping her would somehow keep the Guard from being able to work in the city?

The black Cataphract had been lazily cruising down surface streets between empty office blocks, moving in the general direction of the riverside docks. Then it made a quick right turn into an alley that ran under the Standing Stones Expressway. I made a split-second decision and kept going down Division Avenue. This time of night, the docks would be dead empty and even a stoned driver couldn't help noticing following headlights.

I went half a block and made a U-turn in the middle of Division, snapped off my lights, and turned to creep down the alley after them. I kept their taillights just in view, navigating by what the owners of the warehouses left on to discourage burglars.

IN THE FORESTS OF THE NIGHT

The car pulled up to a loading dock, and I pulled in behind a dumpster half a block away and shut off the engine. I crept out and left the door open behind me. Three men got out of the car.

I didn't like my odds, but maybe if I got the drop on them...

Then the loading dock rolled up and there were three more. One of them turned to say something to somebody still inside the warehouse.

Seven to one. At least. They were likely to be hopped up on tigerberry, and my arm still ached like a broken tooth. It would be suicide.

I melted into the black shadow of the dumpster and watched.

One of the men opened the trunk, three others standing around him. They pulled out a thrashing bundle. Jo was still alive and fighting. One of the men went down, shouting curses. Another one bent double with a groan.

But there were too many of them. They managed to cart her up the stairs and through the dock door. The door rolled down behind them with a clang and the street was dark again.

I crept forward to read the address, then went back to my car. Finding a working payphone in this neighborhood was an outside longshot, but there was a 24 hour 'lix station on Division.

"Night desk."

"This is Erik Rugar. I've got—"

"Rugar! Blackwell wants you."

"I haven't got time"—but I was already on hold. I fumed and waited.

"Talk to me, Rugar." Blackwell's voice was icily calm.

"Investigator Lolo was taken out of a bar in the city financial district called Pietr's Place by persons in a black Cataphract," I gave him the license number. "They are currently in a warehouse in the city docks." I gave him the address.

"Do you have them under observation?"

"Not at the moment," I said. "I had to break visual to call in."

"How many?"

"At least seven. I wasn't able to see inside."

He set down the phone and I could hear him giving orders. Then back to me, "I'm rolling City Tactical to that location. Get back there, observe, and direct the tacticals when they arrive."

"Yes, sir."

"Get moving."

I got moving.

I parked in the shadow of a different dumpster and kept to the shadows. Along the way I swung my arm to limber it up. It wasn't broken, but I was starting to suspect a couple of ribs might be.

I did a circuit around the place. The ground floor windows were dark, but the second floor glowed faintly. The black Cataphract was still at the loading dock, looking like an abandoned vehicle. Other vehicles on the street looked as bad or worse, except for one. A new red ragtop Stanhope parked by the front doors. I wrote down the license number.

Marcus Jeffro's car? Was this where he was making his delivery of the cash?

Headlights came down the street. A passenger car, by the shape. I faded back around a corner. The city tacticals would arrive in vans, and not just one.

It pulled up and parked behind the Stanhope. A big black sedan, new and clean. All the doors opened and five men got out. The boss was obvious at a glance, well-dressed and with an air of command. The other four were bruisers, big men in dungarees with the look of stevedores. They took up position in a square around their boss, their eyes alert and their hands close to their jackets.

I froze and tried to pretend I was part of the pavement.

One of the bodyguards rapped hard on the front door, echoes drifting down the empty streets. The boss waited with ill grace, clearly not happy about the meeting place.

The front door opened and the five men went inside.

I crouched in the dark, thinking furiously. City tacticals would need to know the situation before they breached. There was a fire escape in the alley; I took it as quietly as possible, wincing every time the ancient metal squeaked.

The ground floor was as dark as midnight. Through a dirty second floor window I could see light and movement, but not enough of

76

either to tell what was going on. Voices were raised in anger, indistinct.

I kept going up.

The third floor was dark. I tried the window, but it was solidly painted over. A ladder led up to the roof. I went up, hoping for skylights. There weren't any, but there was a penthouse shack, probably for the elevator machinery. I was able to slip the latch with my penknife.

I paused, listening. Voices from inside, arguing. Traffic hurtled by on the Standing Stones Expressway, four blocks over.

Inside the shack I could dimly see huge spools of thick cable and behind them a square patch of light on the floor, the hatch leading down. I managed to get there without breaking an ankle and headed down the ladder into the shaft of the freight elevator. Light was coming in from the opening to the second floor, but I swung out onto the third and started feeling my way, looking for a stairwell.

I could hear the argument clearly enough to distinguish two voices, but I still couldn't understand their words. I headed towards the sound and found an open stairway. At the landing, I crouched in a patch of shadow and could see into the second floor.

"You're crazy, you know that?" the man from the black sedan shouted. "You are absolutely bug nuts."

It was a broad open space, mostly empty. A few stacks of crates were against the wall, looking forgotten. Light came from flames emerging from a pair of oil drums.

"You have your priorities, I have mine," the fox-like moreau said calmly.

In the circle of light, the two figures, one much smaller than the other, stood together between the improvised braziers. The four bodyguards were behind their boss, tense, alert, ready for things to go south.

"Priorities? What possible priority is kidnapping an agent of the Grimm?"

At the edge of the darkness behind the fox-man, figures lounged, some seated, some leaning against pillars. I counted nine of them.

"I wouldn't expect you to understand."

DRACOHEIM CONFIDENTIAL

The suitcase containing the cash from the insurance company lay on the floor between the oil drums.

"Good. I'm glad to hear that. Because I don't understand. You know why I don't understand? *Because it makes no sense!"*

On the far side of the circle of light from me were two heavy wooden chairs. Marcus Jeffro was tied to one. Jo was tied to the other.

"Captain, what's done is done. I take responsibility for this, and I will see it through. It need not concern you."

Captain? Captain of what, I wondered.

"You know what? We're done here. I can't work with you anymore. You're just too unstable. Find someone else to move your cargo. I'll just take my share and get out." He gestured to one of his guards who moved towards the suitcase.

"Then I no longer have any need of you."

It was the small moreau's tone as much as his words that made the captain's men reach for their guns. It didn't save them.

I heard two quick gunshots, and then a third. Then there was only a mass of struggling bodies. The gang of tigerberry junkies swarmed like a pack of feral dogs.

Two more shots, both reports muffled.

And then it was over.

The captain and his four men were crumpled on the cement floor. There was a lot of blood, black in the flickering firelight. The junkies backed slowly away, staring at what they had done.

Jeffro was the first one to break the silence. "Just let me go," he breathed. "Take the money, I don't care. I won't say a word to anyone. Just let me go." The last word became a sob.

The moreau glanced at him, then deliberately walked to the mess of bodies on the floor. He looked over the blood-soaked floor and bent to pick something up. A gun.

He opened the cylinder, nodded to himself, snapped it closed.

"No," Jeffro sobbed. "No, no, no. *I'll do whatever you want."*

The moreau lifted the gun. "Then die," he said.

Fired two shots into Jeffro's head.

Tossed the revolver back onto the pile of the dead.

"Savant?" one of junkies said hesitantly. "Mackie's hurt. I think he's hurt bad."

"He got shot in the belly," one of the others piped up. "He's really bleeding a lot."

The moreau looked annoyed at the interruption and I could see him thinking it over.

"All right," he decided. "Take him to Angel Street. Don't bother coming back here—we'll be done soon."

Two of the men got the wounded Mackie up on his feet and supported him. His shirt and pants were soaked with blood. I doubted that he would last to Angel Street Hospital. Long term tigerberry use resulted in a number of medical problems including high blood pressure and rapid heart rate. The man was bleeding out as he walked.

The moreau surveyed the scene. "Captain Clarke has been very generous tonight," he said. He gestured at the bodies. "Dinner." Then at the suitcase. "And drinks."

He grinned at the remaining junkies, and they produced an obedient round of chuckles. Then he turned to look at Jo. "Just one last job and we'll be on our way."

"If you lay one greasy paw on me, I'll see you girding a tree in Telegraph Park," Jo said. Her voice was very calm, very confident.

"Oh, I don't think so," the fox said. He reached behind his back and produced a long blade. A butcher knife.

"The Grimm's Guard is here," Jo said. "There is nowhere you can hide from them."

The fox chuckled, but it sounded forced to me. To his waiting followers, he said, "She's bluffing."

"Actually, she's not." I didn't know I was going to speak until I heard my own words echoing through the big empty space.

Every eye turned outwards to the darkness, seeking me.

"Who's there?" the moreau demanded.

"Commissar Lincendie requested permission from the OEA for a detachment of the Grimm's Guard to operate in the city. It was granted, and they're on their way here," I said.

The junkies were spreading out, looking for me. I stood, my gun in my hand, and walked slowly towards the light.

"I'm Erik Rugar of the CPS. You can surrender to me and face the Dracoheim courts, or you can wait for the Grimm's Guards and go back to Nivose. Your choice."

The moreau lifted his knife. "Come and get me, then."

The moment stretched.

Then an amplified voice rang through the building. "THIS IS THE POLICE. WE ARE COMING IN. RESISTANCE WILL BE MET WITH LETHAL FORCE."

I lowered my gun. "Time's up," I said.

Then the building was filled with the sound of doors being smashed open and boots stamping.

"This is Rugar," I shouted down the stairs. "They are up here! They are armed!"

The moreau threw down his knife, and at that the junkies lost their nerve. No one else died when the city tacticals came up in force.

The moreau and his minions got cuffed. I showed my badge— very carefully—and when they were satisfied they'd swept the building, they let me go to Jo. They'd used a lot of rope on her, but I'm a fisherman's son. I know knots.

When she was free of the chair, she put her arms around me, pulled me close, and started licking my face. Her tongue was rough, like a cat's tongue.

At my reaction, she pulled away and looked down, embarrassed. "I'm sorry," she said. "Humans don't do that, do they?"

I resisted the urge to scrub my face with my hand. "Not usually, no," I admitted.

She stepped back away and stuck out her right hand. "Well, thank you, Agent Rugar."

I shook her hand. "You are welcome, Investigator Lolo."

Captain Clarke, it turned out, was the master of a cruise ship that ran passenger cruises. He had been supplementing his income with smuggling.

The moreau was Isner Kelt. He was in the Midworld unlawfully and transported back to Nivose. I heard that he was sentenced and beheaded.

Seven humans were charged with the murders of Captain Clarke and his crew members. All were eventually convicted. The two that had taken their wounded comrade to Angel Street Hospital were among them. Mackie didn't make it.

I ended up with a commendation for exemplary cooperation with an allied agency. I stuck it in the desk drawer along with the rest of my souvenirs.

High Wilder Excursions got to keep the transit unit, under the oversight of Import/Export. I think the Expo ended up paying some nominal fines.

Jo went back to Hunger City. Mail service is slow between the realms, but we kept in touch with the occasional postcard.

It was about a year later when I took a cab to the Abnertown Expo with my suitcases. High Wilder Excursions was doing good business, and I shared my transit window with a family with two serious-faced teenage girls who carried brand new bow cases.

When we blinked into the field, I led the way confidently to the lodge. This time the desk was occupied by a huge bear, and I surrendered my ID meekly in exchange for the flimsy temporary residence permit. Then I went to the lodge desk and registered for my room.

I had time for a mug of mulled cider before I spotted a long-legged orange furred figure among the crowd coming in from the train station. I waved her over.

She smiled when she saw me, her teeth very white and very sharp.

I never did get around to learning how to ski, but Jo and I went together to the community ice rink, me tottering along on rented skates, her strong and confident, the two us scandalizing the locals by skating hand in hand under Nivose's clear, cold, pale blue sky.

The Last Night of Summer

Graduation

"**M**agus Vetch, may I have a word?"

Leonid Vetch, OccD, Master Magus, and Full (though non-tenured) Professor of Industrial Magic at Leeshore Technical College, looked up from the stack of lab reports he was grading.

At first, he took the figure standing in the door of his small, cramped office for a student, and then placed him as a junior faculty member, not long out of the Dracoheim Academy for Thaumaturgical Studies. His name was... Tanner? No. Tillman? *Tellman*, that was it.

"Magus Tellman, right?" Leonid waved the young man in. "What can I do for you?"

Tellman took a step, which brought him nearly to the edge of Leonid's desk. "Dr. Bink said I should talk to you. You've heard that Magus Winter is ailing?"

"I handled several of his lectures last semester," Leonid said with a sigh. "He really should retire. We'll miss him, of course, but his health must come first."

"Well, he's not going to be able to attend the Autumn Mixer, and Dr. Bink wants me to chaperone in his place. He said I should see you about the details."

"Oh dear," Leonid said. "Abe must be doing poorly indeed. He hasn't missed a dance in years."

"What do I need to do?" Tellman sounded very young, and Leonid reflected again that the teacher wasn't that much older than his charges. Given the intensive nature of the instruction at the Academy, he was likely less experienced in social matters than the working-class boys who attended Leeshore College.

Leonid leaned back in his chair and favored Tellman with the relaxed smile of a veteran. "We'll open up the school at 1400 to let the volunteers decorate the cafeteria. The caterers usually show up about 1600. They'll take care of all the food and drinks, and they know where everything is, we just need to unlock the kitchen for them. At 1800, the band will start up and they play until 2400. Then everyone staggers home."

"A lot of drinking?" Tellman asked nervously.

Leonid shrugged. "They're kids at the end of the term. As long as no one gets behind the wheel who shouldn't—and most of these boys don't have their own cars anyway—I don't see a problem."

"And the young ladies?"

"The matrons bring them on a rented bus and take them home the same way," Leonid said. "Relax. It's not a drunken orgy; it's just a dance. Oh, somebody will end up getting sick in the bushes, certainly; but we've been doing this since the school opened, and we've never had a problem."

The young teacher looked unconvinced but nodded. "1400, you say?"

"That's when I'll be there. You don't need to show up until about 1600 or so." Leonid frowned. The young man was acting like the Autumn Mixer was some kind of administrative punishment rather than the high point of the school year. "Relax," he repeated. "It'll be fine."

Tellman nodded, not looking at all relaxed, and left.

Leonid watched the boy go, troubled. He'd known Abram Winter for... twenty years? More. They had both been independent operators, one-man shops in a field that was increasingly being taken over by the large firms with their stables of freshly-scrubbed graduates. Industrial magic had become a trade no different than engineering or accounting.

You and me, Abe, he thought. *We're the last of the wizards.*

And where had they ended up? Teaching magecraft to boys who would work in factories, punching a timeclock. The time of magic being the province of secret masters of the hermetic wisdoms was gone—the drab men in gray flannel suits had taken over, with nary a shot being fired.

Leonid turned back to his stack of lab reports. One couldn't stop progress, of course, but at times, one wanted to kick it in the balls.

He reached for the next exercise book in the stack and was

surprised to find that he had finished. He totaled the semester grades and smiled. All of his students had passed—true, some had barely squeaked by, but he wouldn't have to issue any deficiency reports.

He went back over the grading sheets automatically, scanning for errors. Satisfied, he squared the edges of the stack and slid it into an inter-office mail envelope. Time to call it a day.

He stopped to drop the grades off with Mrs. Barden, Dr. Bink's secretary, and noticed the door to the president's inner office was open. He jerked his head at the door, and she nodded that it was okay for him to enter.

"Leo," the president said with a smile. "How is the end of the term treating you?"

"I just dropped off the reports," Leonid said. "I wanted to ask you about Abe Winter."

The president gave a frown of professional concern. He was a plump man, an able administrator and good with the juggling act of keeping the college running, soothing the faculty's feathers and sweet-talking investors—a political animal who, to his credit, never claimed to be anything but.

Leonid had never warmed to the man. Didn't dislike him particularly, but he wasn't a mage—his degree was in business administration.

"Magus Winter is leaving the faculty," Dr. Bink said. "We're sorry to see him go, of course, a brilliant man. Not up to a teaching load, I'm afraid. He gave notice during the semester."

Leonid nodded sadly. "I can take over his labs if you need me to, at least until you can find a replacement. I'm not on his level in Conjuration & Evocation, though."

"That's good to know. The registrar is working on the new catalog," Dr. Bink said noncommittally. "He'll be in touch to finalize your schedule. And we're interviewing candidates."

"Abe's still living with his niece, isn't he?" Leonid asked. "I was thinking about dropping by for a visit."

Dr. Bink's smile seemed almost genuine. "I'm sure he'd like that."

THE LAST NIGHT OF SUMMER

"You left me in the lurch, Abe," Leonid said. "Dr. Bink is giving me some baby-faced apprentice for the mixer. He'll probably report me to the board for dancing with Eleanor."

Abe laughed weakly. In truth, he looked very sick. The two men were in the back garden of Abe's niece's Shell Beach townhouse. Although the day was warm, Abe was wrapped in a quilt, and his hands shook when he sipped his glass of coffee.

"Tellman's a good boy," Abe said. "Has the makings of a first-class C&E man, once he gets some seasoning. Top quarter of his class. We're cursed lucky to have him."

"Why *do* we have him?" Leonid wondered.

Abe shrugged. Even that gesture seemed shrunken. "He's not a company man, I guess." But he was looking away when he said it.

"You know something," Leonid accused.

Abe's lips twitched, and there was a gleam in his eye. For the first time he looked like his old self. "I might have heard something."

"Spill it."

"I really shouldn't say."

"Abe..."

Abe's shoulders hunched forward slightly, and his already weak voice dropped to a near-whisper. "After graduation, he did the usual interviews and got an offer with one of the little firms. Apprentice, but with a verbal commitment to make him a junior partner in a year. Then, that firm was bought by Blackstone-Tate."

Abe paused, and Leonid gestured for him to continue, already suspecting what was next.

"So, the kid puts in his year as an apprentice, lab prep and sweeping floors, and then goes to the advancement committee to ask about getting his sash, and they say, 'Oh, that agreement was with the old firm—we're not bound by it. Maybe in a couple of years, kid, if there's an opening.'"

"So he quit," Leonid suggested.

Abe chuckled. "Not just quit. He stormed out. The way I heard it, he did some property damage along the way. Melted a statue in the lobby."

85

"Melted?"

A shrug. "That's what I hear. Blackstone didn't want to make a formal complaint and look bad in court, so they hushed it up. But like I say, the kid's a first class evocator."

Leonid laughed. It was a good story, but he suspected that it was exaggerated. The Magus Tellman that he'd met didn't strike him as someone who would throw fireballs around the lobby of an office building.

The next week was taken up with the usual cheerful chaos of graduation, with the thousand last-minute glitches that were exactly the same as last year's last-minute glitches, but nonetheless took everyone in the administration by surprise.

Leonid weathered it with a smile and a sigh. Despite everything, the students managed to line up for their places and march across the stage to receive their certificates. It lacked the pomp and gravitas of the Academy for Thaumaturgical Studies' graduation, but Leonid couldn't stop grinning as his watched his boys claim their scrolls. They were good kids, and they worked hard; and they had every right to be proud and know that he was proud of them.

Underneath his excitement, though, there was a dark mood waiting. The upcoming Autumn Mixer was the final event of the school year. Sevenday night, the 32nd of Siebenember and then he was at leisure until the beginning of the spring term, Einsember the 12th. Lab classes—the only part of being a teacher that he truly enjoyed—wouldn't resume until the 20th. A month and a half—sixty days of aimless wandering through the city that dear, dead, Annalise had loved, looking for something to distract him from the long empty nights with no companion but the bottle.

He needed a research project. The administration would support him, provided it was something neither too expensive nor too dangerous. Something in materials science would be good. There were half a million gnoetic alloys of orelchium coming out of Ferose these days, and only a fraction of them had complete properties graphs. He could pick one of the obscure ones and run a series of tests, measure the changes in the etheric potential in response to environmental factors. Time consuming, boring, and almost certain to return nothing of interest to anyone except a handful of specialists.

He made a mental note to make an appointment with his department head, and the dark mood chuckled at him. He made the same resolution at the end of every term and never followed through on it.

On the day of the mixer, he spent the morning cleaning his small, cluttered office. Too many books and far too many journals, and he hated to part with anything. A crate of active metal samples from one of the school's suppliers proved too heavy for him to lift, so he shoved it into a corner for use as an improvised end table.

He found himself thinking of the Quayside School of Nursing. The two schools had a good relationship, sharing resources and lab space where the disciplines overlapped. The overlap was increasing, not just as medicine found more uses for magic, but also as the long-term effects of practicing magic on the human body were better understood. The spinal palsy that was slowly killing Abe was a malady found exclusively in mages. No one had yet pinpointed the exact mechanism, but it seemed related to the neurological damage caused by the street drug called seventy-seven.

He'd miss Abe at the mixer. It had been Abe who'd goaded him into asking Matron Eleanor to dance, after Annalise had died. Eleanor was a handsome woman, tall and elegant, with a stern, no-nonsense bearing that could turn disarmingly kittenish after a few drinks.

He resolved to find a way to see her during the intersession, morbidly aware that, like his resolution to secure a research grant, it was a promise he made to himself and broke every year. Like his resolutions to renew his membership in the athletic club and get back into shape, lose these extra pounds and regain the wind that he once had. Once, thirty years and twice that many pounds ago, he had been a fair tennis player. Today, he got out of breath from watching a match.

Enough with the self-pity already. It was close enough to 1400 to head over to the cafeteria and unlock it. The boys would be showing up soon, and he didn't want to bring his black cloud to the party. Let the boys and girls have their fun.

Automatically, Leonid unlocked the doors and flipped the switches to warm up the overhead lights. He pulled out the big carts that would hold the folded chairs and tables to free the floor for dancing. Then he went out into the parking lot to smoke and wait for the boys. A dozen of them piled out of the city bus together, carrying parcels containing paper decorations. Leonid went to meet them, his mood already brightening.

The students had decided on "A Clockwork Music Box" as the theme. They started stringing silver and gold streamers and hanging paper gears. Leonid watched and offered suggestions, which the boys cheerfully ignored.

"Magus, do you know where we could find some bricks?" one of the boys asked him suddenly.

Leonid glanced over at the boy. Was it a joke? He patted his pockets. "Sorry, I seem to have left my masonry in my other jacket. Dare I ask what you want bricks for?"

The boy—Baker, his name was, and Leonid remembered him as both serious and studious—gestured at the corner of the room that would serve as the stage. Several other boys were wrestling with some sort of construction of poles and brightly colored cloth. "We made a music box, sir, but it keeps falling over. We need something heavy to stabilize the bases."

"Let me think," Leonid said, strolling in that direction. It was a clever construction, fabric panels decorated with gears and pulleys. The poles that were intended to hold the panels upright leaned crazily in all directions, unable to support the weight.

After a moment's study, Leonid decided the boy was right—weights on the base of the poles should work. But what?

"We tried books, but they're not heavy enough. Foster got a little carried away."

Foster—red-haired and plump—grimaced at that. "You said you wanted it to look like a music box," he said sulkily.

It was an impressive bit of work, and it would be a shame not to use it. Leonid remembered the box of metal samples in his office.

"I think I have something that might work," he admitted. "Come with me."

The samples were cast in cylinders six inches high and four across, each one stamped with numbers that identified the precise alloy. Two of them, taped to the base of each pole, made the entire structure stable. Well, stable enough.

Magus Tellman arrived as they were finishing up. He glanced at the work, then gave the metal cylinders a hard look. "What are those?"

"I got a case of test metals from Grimtooth's," Leonid said. "They needed something heavy to put up this tent."

Tellman frowned. "Non-active, I hope."

Leonid shrugged. "Active, but with a very low resonance. They aren't dangerous."

"Any active material has the potential to be dangerous," Tellman said pedantically.

"So does having a tent fall on you," Leonid replied. "Relax, no one is doing any magic tonight."

"Hey," objected a young man who was unpacking his saxophone, "Give us a chance, brother."

Leonid laughed, and after a moment, Tellman's face relaxed into a smile.

"Come on, it looks like the caterers are here," Leonid said.

"Do they need help?"

"No, but we need drinks."

The boys were trickling in, scrubbed and shaved and in their best suits. Leonid circulated, offering his congratulations all around. He was a popular instructor, and nearly all the boys had been in one of his labs during their three years at the college. The boys asked about Magus Winter, and Leonid said that, yes, Abe was retiring; they had spoken recently, and the elder magus was in good spirits, if not good health.

The word came that the bus from Quayside had been spotted coming down the road, and Leonid clapped his hands for attention.

"Gentlemen!" he called. "It's time."

The boys quickly lined up across the floor, facing the door, quickly and with a minimum of jostling. Leonid walked a few steps in advance of the line and looked around for Tellman, annoyed. There he was, gossiping with the band.

"Magus, if you will attend, please," Leonid called, his voice echoing in the suddenly still cafeteria. "We have guests to greet."

Flustered, Tellman rushed to join the older instructor. "Sorry," he muttered.

Leonid strode to the door to the parking lot, Tellman following nervously.

The bus was parked by the time they got outside. The doors swung open, and the matrons climbed out, three of them. Handsome women in formal gowns, Eleanor in the lead in a deep green that complemented her auburn hair.

Leonid bowed to her. "Looks like we made it through another term," he said with a smile.

Eleanor smiled back warmly and offered her arm.

Flustered and unsure, Tellman approached the others. "I'm Magus Oskar Tellman, ma'am," he said stiffly. "Magus Winter was unable to attend."

"Elizabet Vance," the younger one smiled at him, offering her arm. "And that's Viktoria Throckmorton. Don't worry, you're only obligated to one dance, and I promise I won't step on your toes."

He chuckled nervously and took her arm.

Behind them, Matron Viktoria signaled to her flock, and they came out in a flood of color. They were working class girls, the daughters of longshoremen and fishermen. Their gowns were from thrift stores, painstakingly home-tailored, shoes and jewelry borrowed from aunts and older sisters, makeup applied inexpertly with hands more accustomed to scrubbing floors than faces.

Pride in their accomplishments and hope for the future gave them a radiance that their breeding denied them, though, and tonight they were princesses, every one.

Leonid opened the doors to the cafeteria with a flourish. By tradition, the first dance was ladies' choice, and the young men stood straight and tall, smiling nervously. This year, there were more boys than girls, and the newly minted nurses made a show of making their selections. A few stern looks from the matrons hurried the process along, and soon, the girls were all paired off, the surplus boys slinking off to the bar.

Eleanor came into Leonid's arms, graceful and long. Viktoria, he noticed, had taken Tellman, who looked uncomfortable. With a smile, Leonid nodded to the band, trusting that they were watching him through the openings in the music box tent.

The band started up with a long smoky note from the saxophone, and the year's Autumn Mixer had begun. Leonid scanned the floor during the first few measures to ensure that things were going smoothly, then turned his attention to Eleanor.

"You look lovely tonight," he said with honest admiration.

She acknowledged his words with a smile. "You're wearing the same suit as last year. And the year before. And, I think, the year before that."

Leonid looked down at himself, suddenly self-conscious. It was an old suit, he had to admit, but in good repair. It wasn't as if he wore it often.

"Somebody should take you shopping," Eleanor went on, her eyes laughing. "Put you into something modern."

"I'm not a modern man," Leonid objected.

"Nor am I a modern woman," Eleanor left his arms and then spun back to him, momentarily displaying long, lean legs. "But I can look the part."

"It's different for men," Leonid complained, looking around at the young graduates in their loud checks and stripes. "I'd just look silly in a mod get up."

"I can't imagine you ever looking silly," Eleanor said softly. And then the song was over.

By unspoken agreement, they separated, going off to police their respective charges, making sure that no one was sneaking off or hitting the bar too hard.

So far, the night was going well. This year's band was good, sticking to old standards but giving them enough swing to keep the kids on the dance floor. Leonid nursed a cider carefully, wishing for a shot of absinthe but knowing it would be a bad idea. He was working up the guts to ask Eleanor for another dance when word of the disaster reached him.

"Magus Vetch," a breathless voice got his attention. It was Foster, the pudgy redhead who had made the music box tent for the band. "I think the Summerisle ferry is on fire."

"What?"

The boy jerked his head towards the parking lot. "You'd better come see."

Vetch walked quickly outside. As soon as he reached the lot, he could see the glow of the fire. A dozen boys and girls stood solemnly at the edge of the lot, looking out across the river to where the ferry sat dead in the water. On the upper deck, cars were burning, at least three or four, maybe a half dozen of them.

"When did this start?" Leonid asked.

"It just happened," one of the boys said. "We were out here, you know, just having a smoke, and... boom! They all went up together."

Leonid stared. He could see the crowd on the ferry, milling about in panic. As he watched, one of the small figures went into the water with a splash, either jumping to escape the fire or pushed by the crush of bodies.

More people were coming out onto the lot, the kids watching, frozen in horror. Eleanor was at his shoulder.

"We have to do something," she said urgently.

"What?" Leonid wondered aloud.

The harbor patrol had to be mobilizing already. All that a gang of students could accomplish would be to get in the way and slow down the rescue.

Then Tellman hurried up, his arms full, pushing his way through the students and to the water's edge. Leonid rushed to catch him.

"What are you doing?"

Tellman dropped his burden, the metal cylinders thumping into the soft soil of the riverbank. "Start scribing those," he ordered. "Open thetas."

Leonid reached to pick up the first of the cylinders automatically. "Open thetas?" he asked. That was the root for an energy transfer. "Why?"

In answer, Tellman reached down to slap the water's edge. Where his hand struck the water it crystallized, freezing instantly.

Leonid got it then. He fumbled his pocketknife out, turning over his shoulder to shout, "We need help here."

He started scribing the metal cylinders. The alloys were low yield; they wouldn't provide much power. He looked out at the stretch of water that separated the shore from the burning ferry. Maybe...

He held up the sample cylinder. "I need the rest of these from the bandstand. And the crate; it's behind the bar someplace."

The boys hurried back to the school.

Tellman exhausted the first cylinder and held out his hand for another. Already, the ice bridge extended yards into the river. Abe had been right: the man really was a top evocator.

Leonid handed over another activated chunk of metal and went back to scribing the others.

Eleanor led a group of students to the water's edge. The boys had discarded their jackets. "How soon can we walk on this?"

Tellman looked back at the question. "Not yet," he said grimly. His face was pale and covered with sweat. "It's too thin. Give me a few minutes."

Eleanor nodded.

"You should be getting the girls ready to treat the wounded," Leonid said.

"Viktoria's doing that," Eleanor said. She had another pair of metal samples. "You need me here."

Leonid took the cylinders. "I'll take the boys to the ferry," he said.

"You can't," Eleanor argued. "You need to stay here and support the bridge."

Tellman reached back for the next sample, and Leonid handed it to him automatically, thinking furiously. He didn't want Eleanor to take the boys across the ice bridge, but she was right. He was needed here, with Tellman, and the boys needed a leader.

Tellman stood and slammed his foot down on the ice bridge. It held. It was five yards wide and extended more than halfway to the ferry.

"It'll hold," he said. "Get moving."

Other boys came up with more sample cylinders, and Leonid scribed, his hands cutting the soft metal with deft strokes born of long practice. When he looked up, Eleanor was halfway down the ice causeway, a group of his graduates close behind.

Tellman was ready for more activated metal. The strain showed on his face as he siphoned the heat out of the water. Talented or not, it was a desperate task he'd set himself. Under ordinary circumstances, a working like this would call for at least four evocators and a dozen apprentices.

"They made it!" somebody shouted, and Leonid looked up. The ice bridge now surrounded the ferry, trapping it place. Figures were scrambling down from the deck onto the ice and headed towards shore.

Spotlights announced the arrival of the fireboats, spraying the top deck with river water even as passengers scrambled to safety.

Leonid looked back to Tellman, who had dropped to sit on the bank, exhausted. "Can you hold it?"

"Don't have to," Tellman gasped. "It's passed critical. It's stable now—for a couple of hours at least. Plenty of time."

The ice bridge stretched from shore to the ferry, as wide and solid as a highway bridge. It was the most impressive feat of spellcrafting he had ever seen.

"Son of a bitch," he murmured. "You did it."

"*We* did it, Magus," Tellman corrected him. "Without you doing the prep, I would never have gotten it stabilized."

The first of the passengers reached the shore and were met by the young nurses who started checking them for injuries. Some were burned; others had been trampled in the panic.

Eleanor was not among them. He looked back to the ferry, but it was obscured by steam. In the center of the roiling cloud firelight still blazed. After another quick glance at Tellman, he headed down the ice bridge, slowly, against the flow of passengers.

The ice wasn't as slick as he expected. It crunched under his shoes like packed snow. Still, it was slow going, even when the stream of wounded trickled to a stop. Three of the students came out of the fog. The one in the middle was badly burned, the other two supporting him.

"Matron Eleanor!" Leonid demanded. "Where is she? Did she get off the boat?"

One of the boys tried to answer and started coughing. The other just pointed back along the ice causeway before staggering on towards shore. The air was opaque with smoke and steam. Leonid only found the hull of the ferry by running into it.

"Eleanor!" he called. "Where are you? Can you hear me?"

There was no answer. He pulled himself up and struggled onto the deck. It was frozen in place at an angle and slick with water and ice. Visibility was only a few feet in any direction.

"*Eleanor!*" he called again.

It seemed that all the cars on the upper deck were burning now, the elixir in the tanks producing clouds of oily black smoke to mix with the white steam and paint the world in shades of muddy gray. He could hardly hear his own voice when he tried to shout over the roar of fire and water.

He slid into the bumper of a car—a big black sedan. It had broken free of the vehicular deck and rolled into one of the benches. Under the rear wheel was a still figure, draped in forest green.

"*No,*" he breathed, dropping to the deck. It was Eleanor, still breathing but in shock. Her leg had to be broken under the wheel.

He shoved against the car, and it rocked forward but then rolled back before he could pull Eleanor free.

"*I've got a wounded woman here!*" he shouted, hoping a fire boat was close enough to hear. "*I need help!*"

Light blossomed in the cloud of smoke, followed by a wave of heat. The fire was still spreading, igniting the elixir in the car's tanks.

They didn't have time to wait for rescue, Leonid realized. If he didn't get Eleanor free, she'd burn to death when the fire spread to the sedan that trapped her. He braced himself against the bench and shoved the car forward. It rolled just enough to free her leg.

"*I am so sorry, but there's no other way,*" he whispered, then kicked her leg.

Eleanor screamed.

The sound made Leonid sick, but when he eased the car back it didn't roll onto her. He dropped down beside her and lifted her shoulders. Her eyes were open, and she focused on his face.

"We have to get away from the cars," he told her. "It's not safe."

"I can't," she gasped. "Just leave me."

"Not going to happen." He got under and lifted. She groaned in pain, but he managed to drag her a few feet before he had to stop, fighting for breath. He was too old and too fat—*too cursed useless!*

If only Tellman were here. The situation called for an evocator.

Instead of an artificer. What could Leonid do, build a way out? Out of what?

Another 'lix tank blossomed into flame.

Elixir was an exothermic alchemical compound. A car engine converted the energy into a usable form. Open thetas, just like he'd prepped for Tellman. He didn't have to build a way out, the way out was already built for him.

He'd just have to modify it a little.

He turned his body and started pulling Eleanor back towards the car.

"What are you doing?" she gasped.

"Just trust me."

He got to the black sedan and opened the back door. Wincing, he manhandled Eleanor into the back seat, as gently as he could but knowing time was short. Every cry she made tore at his heart.

Then he slid into the front, getting out his pocketknife. He looked around the cab for metal, but it was a luxury model with a leather interior.

Going to have to do this the old-fashioned way.

He tore off his jacket and ripped his shirt to expose his left forearm. He cut deeply, careful not to get close to either the veins or tendons. Fortunately, he had plenty of extra meat.

He dipped the fingers of his right hand into the blood running down his arm and tried to clear his mind. Another tank went up, far too close, and he felt the heat on his face.

Keep it simple, he told himself. Don't worry about optimizing the sequence. It only has to last long enough to get us to shore. He closed his eyes and visualized the symbols.

You can do this.

The fire was close enough that the cab felt like he'd been running the heater full blast. He took a deep breath and opened his eyes. With one smooth motion, he painted six symbols on the windscreen in his blood.

The car lifted into the air. He turned the wheel, and the car slewed around, then straightened as he shoved down on the accelerator. At first, all he could see was smoke and steam, then he was out of the cloud.

There was the school parking lot, flashing lights of emergency vehicles painting the sky in red and blue. He headed that way.

As he grew closer, he slapped the horn. Nothing happened, and he felt foolish. Of course, the accessories wouldn't be working—the car wasn't actually running. He'd just tapped into the power plant for his working.

No lights, no horn. He'd just have to hope they saw him coming.

They did, the students pointing and yelling. They cleared a place for him, and he brought the car down hard enough to bounce on its springs. He winced again, thinking of Eleanor's broken leg.

But they were back.

He opened the car door to a circle of staring faces. "Matron Eleanor's in the back," he shouted. "Her leg's broken. Get her to the ambulance."

Then he sagged against the car, shaking. He was too exhausted to object when they took him to the ambulance, too.

The papers got it all wrong, of course. They used words like "heroic" and "fantastic" to describe what was just basic applied thaumaturgy and failed to realize that Tellman's working was far more impressive, from a technical standpoint.

Laymen never understood magecraft.

Dr. Bink visited him at home the next day with the news that the board had unanimously voted to extend tenure. Evidently the publicity was good for the school. Leonid asked if they made the same offer to Tellman.

"He's still very young," Dr. Bink hedged. "But his actions will be taken into account, when the time comes."

Leonid accepted tenure, which came with a research stipend. He'd think of some way to spend it.

He brought flowers to Eleanor when he visited her. Her leg was in a massive cast, which made him feel guilty.

"I'm sorry I was so rough with you," he said. "Time was short."

"You saved my life, Leo."

"Well..." he trailed off, embarrassed. "Yeah, I guess I did."

She looked down at her leg. "They say it's a clean break. It should heal just fine, and I'll be able to dance again."

"That's good," Leonid said. It sounded silly, but he didn't know what else to say.

The silence stretched, uncomfortably.

Then Eleanor laughed. "You really are impossible, aren't you?"

"I'm sorry?"

"Come here and kiss me, silly man," she said. "And when I get out of here, you can take me dancing—but first you'll have to let me buy you a new suit."

That Summer's Evening Long Ago

Case:16-DRM-373//CI#373-0195

It's not easy for a private citizen to get into the offices of the Criminal Investigation division of the Committee for Public Safety. It can be done, though, if you are patient and determined.

Being a pretty girl doesn't hurt, and Mikki was a very pretty girl. I knew her from Miss Kitten's Dating Service.

I had just finished up a report for a case that was on its way to trial—a magus who was using his practice to launder money from the tigerberry trade—and looked up at a sudden silence in the squad room.

Mikki had just walked through the door, wearing a blue and green summer frock, her hair in tight red-gold braids down her back. She was being escorted by a uniformed constable sergeant named Sterenko, a cigar-chewing bruiser who had come up through the ranks from Marsh Parish. Sterenko waved in my direction, and Mikki headed towards my desk, smiling like Midsummer morning.

I got up to meet her halfway.

"What are you doing here?" I asked her.

Her face grew serious. "I need to talk to you, Erik. Can we go someplace?"

I grabbed my jacket off the back of my chair. "Sure, I was about to go for lunch. Give me a minute."

I went and stuck my head in Blackwell's office. "I'm going to lunch, boss."

He glared at me. "You're not going anywhere until I get the Bledik report, Rugar," he growled.

"I gave it to Agnes ten minutes ago," I countered.

He waved his hand. "Then shoo." He looked past me and saw Mikki standing there. His eyebrows rose. "Take the rest of the day if you want."

DRACOHEIM CONFIDENTIAL

Mikki continued to collect admiring glances as we headed up the elevator to the ground floor and out through the bustling hallways of Government House. I enjoyed walking with her, being seen with her, but at the same time I was worried. Something was bothering her, something important enough to come downtown and find me at work.

I got us a pair of pork sandwiches from a cart and found a bench that no one else was using.

"What's up, kid?" I asked once she was settled in.

"I think there's been a crime," she said. "A crime done with magic."

"You think?" I asked.

"It's Ilse, my roommate," she said. "She has—*had*—a necklace, with a watch built into it. She wore it all the time. It looked great on her, and she's had it forever. Then, a couple of days ago, I noticed she wasn't wearing it, so I asked her about it, and she didn't remember it."

"She didn't remember losing it?" I asked.

"She didn't remember ever owning it. She didn't remember it *at all*," Mikki's voice was low and intense. "She thought I was making a joke. At first, I thought maybe she'd pawned it, and was too embarrassed to admit it, but I know she doesn't need money, not like that. And I'm sure she's not lying. She really doesn't remember it."

Mikki took a bite of her sandwich and I waited while she chewed. Then she said. "Can somebody do that? Steal a memory?"

I nodded. "Yeah. It's not easy, and it's illegal, except for medical reasons like a treatment for trauma, but it can be done."

"I think somebody did that to Ilse. They took her necklace, and then they made her forget that she ever had it."

I considered that. "Have you noticed any other changes in her personality? Is she acting differently in any other ways?"

"She ate my strawberries. That was strange," she said slowly.

"She doesn't like strawberries?"

"Not like I do," a flash of a grin. "I bought a pint and was going to pig out on them, but when I got home from rehearsal she'd eaten the whole pint. She bought me another one, the next day, but that's

100

not like her."

I nodded. Changes in dietary habits could be a sign of mental tampering. "Can you come back to the office and write out a complaint?" I asked.

She smiled brilliantly. "You'll take the case, then?"

"I think it might be worth investigating," I hedged. I didn't want to get her hopes up. "What's the estimated value of the necklace?"

She looked blank. "I don't know. It's silver, and it had little diamonds on the face of the watch."

"Write down over a hundred dollars," I told her. "If magic was used in the theft, that'll make it a CPS case in any jurisdiction."

I walked Mikki back to Government House and showed her the window for citizen complaints. After the clerk typed up the form, I ran it down to records and pulled a case number, then ducked back into Blackwell's office to give him the rundown.

"Mental tampering is bad medicine," I concluded. "This is a party that we want off our streets."

He raised a skeptical eyebrow. "You figure this is on the level?"

"Why wouldn't it be?" I asked. "What's she got to gain?"

"Attention?" he suggested. "Maybe it's an insurance scam?"

I shook my head. "Mikki's not like that. Maybe this Ilse's got a scam, but I'd know if Mikki was trying to run a number on me."

He didn't look any less skeptical, but he nodded. "Just watch your back, okay? Personal connections make for bad police work."

I took the rebuke meekly and headed back up to collect Mikki from the lobby.

On the way to Mikki's rooming house in Centerburg I quizzed her about the necklace. From her description it was well over a hundred bucks, almost certainly Ferose made. She was less able to fix its origin.

"Ilse used to be a taxi dancer in Pickmantown, years ago. One of her customers gave her that necklace." A shrug. "That's what she said, anyway. She had it when I met her."

"Kind of a pricey gift for a dance partner," I observed.

Mikki looked out the window at the city going by. "I don't know the details. She just said a rich customer gave it to her."

101

"Got any pictures of it?" I asked.

She looked surprised at the question. "Why would I?"

"Any pictures of Ilse wearing it?" I clarified.

"Oh, yeah, sure. Like I say, she always had it on."

"When we get back to your place, see if you can find one, but just slide to me on the QT. I don't want Ilse seeing it until she's ready." Confronting a victim of mental tampering with physical evidence was a tricky business. They reacted in unpredictable ways.

"Can they cure her?" Mikki asked me suddenly.

"You mean, restore her memory?" I shook my head. "Probably not. Depending on how much damage was done to her mind, there's a chance that the memory will come back over time, as she heals. A forensic mage can do some tests, but in my experience this kind of tampering tends to be permanent."

"That's just... wicked," she said angrily. "To do that to somebody."

I nodded. "That's why it's illegal."

It was also rare. I knew of a couple of ways to erase memories. Usually it was done alchemically, which involved getting the victim to ingest the magical infusion somehow, then activating it, then specifying what to forget via a verbal or written command. That took time to set up, and privacy to accomplish. In most of the cases involving mental manipulation that came to mind, the perpetrator had a personal connection to the victim: a spouse, a coworker, a friend.

A roommate.

Glumly I realized that if I had been handed this case cold, my first suspect would be Mikki herself. I'd have to make sure I had evidence that eliminated her before I sent this up the chain—hard evidence, something more than my personal conviction that the girl was innocent. And ideally, I'd get it without tipping her off that she was a suspect.

Blackwell was right; personal connections did make for bad police work. Blackwell was usually right, curse him.

"What are you thinking?" Mikki blurted suddenly into a silence that had grown uncomfortable.

THAT SUMMER'S EVENING LONG AGO

"This isn't a random theft," I said slowly. "Somebody went to a lot of trouble to set this up, and that means it was somebody who saw Ilse regularly, knew the value of the necklace, and had the opportunity to get her alone to do the working. Does Ilse go on dates for Miss Kitten's?"

"No," Mikki said. "She works full time for Golden Mermaid Revue."

I knew of the show, although I'd never been there. It was an aquatic burlesque, one of the better ones, supposedly. Girls in bikinis doing synchronized swimming, very popular with longshoremen.

"She's a dancer?" I asked. "Or, swimmer, I guess?"

"No, she does their music," Mikki said proudly. "She plays the calliope and writes the arrangements. She's real good."

"Oh," I said. I had just assumed that Mikki's roommate would also be a chorus girl. "Interesting."

Centerburg used to an agricultural community, back in my great-grandfather's day, and there were still some of the old farmhouses scattered around, in among the modern businesses and apartments. Mikki's place turned out to be one of those, a sprawling three story edifice that had once housed an extended family of farmers.

The last of the line was a cold-eyed matriarch with iron-gray hair and an inflexible attitude concerning gentleman callers. She was unimpressed with my badge.

"Do you have a warrant?" she asked.

"No," I said, trying out my winning smile, "this is just a preliminary interview."

She sniffed. "Then you may use the library." She gestured.

I glanced at Mikki, who shrugged. "I'll get Ilse," she said.

I liked conducting victim interviews in the victim's homes—people were more at ease, more likely to tell the truth in familiar surroundings. Trying to strongarm the landlady into letting me upstairs would start things out on the wrong foot, though—if I even could. I'd make do with the library.

It was a cozy room, lined with shelves and fitted out with a half-dozen overstuffed chairs. I chose one and killed time by looking over the shelves. A lot of poetry and plays, battered, well-read books, probably collected from secondhand shops.

"Mr. Rugar? I'm Ilse Vecker. Mikki said you wanted to see me?"

She was a tall, handsome woman, with a lean, athletic build, in her mid-thirties. She was in a dark blue skirt and a white blouse, very simple, which suited her lines. Her hair was very dark and cut in a smart pageboy bob.

I decided on a casual approach. "Mikki asked me to talk to you about some missing property. I'm with the CPS—"

She cut me off. "Is this about that cursed diamond necklace?"

I nodded. "She's worried about you."

An exasperated sigh. "I don't know where she got that idea, but I assure you that if I had a diamond necklace stolen from me, I would be aware of it. Mikki has a good heart, but she's not the brightest girl. She's confused."

Mikki herself walked in at the end of that. If she was offended by Ilse's remark she gave no sign. Instead she went to me and passed me a photograph. I took it without looking at it.

"We do live in a time where mental manipulation is possible," I pointed out reasonably. "There may be nothing to it, but it's my job to check these things out." I waved her to a seat and took the one opposite. Mikki took a third, off to one side.

For a moment I thought Ilse was going to leave, but she sighed and sat down. "Go ahead."

"Mikki tells me that you used to work at a dance hall," I said.

"The Purple Room in Pickmantown," she agreed.

"And that you received the item as a gift from a client," I said and then went on before she could object. "The Purple Room did allow girls to accept gifts from men?"

"Sure," she said. "Even jewelry, sometimes. That's not illegal. But I never got a necklace with a watch in it like Mikki says."

I smiled and nodded. She was starting to get defensive. Something was bothering her, something that she couldn't put her finger on.

"Men can be very generous to a pretty girl," I said easily. "I'm sure you had many admirers."

"Some, sure. It's why we work there," she said. There was an edge in her voice. "Believe me, mister, fifty-cent dance tickets don't pay the rent."

I glanced quickly down at the photograph I held in my lap, out of her view. It was a good picture, maybe a publicity still, and it showed Ilse sitting on the calliope bench, hands on the keys, her head turned to grin at the camera. Around her neck was a silver chain with a jeweled pendant, the face of the watch clearly visible.

I looked back up at Ilse. "Do you have anything from those days?" I asked. "Any keepsakes?"

She started to snap back at me, then shut her mouth and I could see her thinking it over. At last she said, "No, I don't think so. Most of it went straight to the pawn shop."

I lifted the photograph, looked it over, then handed it across to her. "So you don't recognize that piece?"

I watched her reaction carefully as she looked at the picture. She frowned, then cocked her head, studying it. After a moment, her hand crept up to touch her neck, as if feeling for the necklace. Very slowly she lowered the picture, then looked over at Mikki.

"Is this what you saw me wearing?" she asked slowly.

Mikki nodded seriously. "You always had it on."

Again her hand touched her neck, searching. That convinced me. Her body remembered the feel of the necklace, the weight of it. Her fingers knew that something was missing, even though her brain denied it.

She looked back to me. "You think someone took my necklace and tampered with my memory to cover it up?"

I nodded. "That's the theory I'm working with now, yeah."

She looked back at the photograph for a long moment. "I can't..." she said softly, touching the image of the necklace. Then she looked up. "So how do we catch this bastard?"

The next day I pondered that question while I paged through a very slim file. The victim complaint was, by necessity, almost blank. She didn't know when the item was stolen, couldn't describe it, didn't know anyone who might have shown any particular interest in it. Even the history was second-hand.

105

Mikki had tried, but she only knew what Ilse had told her, and I had to take that as hearsay. Ilse was able to fill in the exact dates she'd worked for The Purple Room, so if she had actually gotten it from a client there then it would have been given to her between six and eight years ago.

I'd need to swing by the Golden Mermaid Review and talk to the staff. There was a good chance the thief worked there, and if nothing else I might be able to nail down exactly when it went missing. The dining hall opened at 1600 on weekdays, though, and the first curtain was at 1900. I'd want to make sure all the staff was there, so I'd hit them in the afternoon.

I got the boys in the photo lab to make me a couple of blowups of the necklace itself, working from photos of Ilse. It was beautiful, a braided silver chain with a watch the size of a fifty-cent piece hanging from it. It sure looked like Ferose work to me.

If it was an import, the trail was going to end there, but I figured there was a good chance it had been a special order and made in the city. If I could find the maker, then maybe I could get an inscription or a maker's serial number, something I could put on a hot sheet for circulation to pawn shops and dodgy jewelers. The forged ones have long memories.

I'd start there.

It took me two hours to track down the shop where it was made. I started with a forged one I knew in the jewelry business and showed him the blowup.

It shook its little metal head. Forged ones come in a variety of shapes and sizes. This one was small and delicate, and went by the name of Little Hammers.

"I do not recognize this artisan," it said.

"But it was one of your people, right?" I pressed.

"Oh, certainly." It lifted the photo to catch the light. Its hand was like a bundle of jointed knitting needles. "The form is harmonious." It lowered its voice, which in this case was a matter of reducing the airflow through the bellows that fed the reeds it used to speak. "No offense meant, Agent Rugar, but your brothers have little instinct for form."

THAT SUMMER'S EVENING LONG AGO

"None taken," I said easily. "Who knows more about timepieces in the city?"

"Inquire at the shop of Weaver of Brass," it told me, and gave me an address in Shell Beach.

Weaver of Brass said the watch was pedestrian and uninspired, and tried to sell me a pocket watch that reported the phases of the moon and the state of the tides as well as the time.

I explained that I didn't want a *new* timepiece, I wanted to find the maker of *that* timepiece. It eventually gave me three shops to try, after lecturing me on the importance of something called "omnidirectional halo." I assured it that all of my halos were omnidirectional and headed off.

The second shop I went to was a dingy little place in Delapour with a sign in the window that said "Timepieces Sold Repaired And Bought." The proprietor introduced itself simply as Counter.

"Oh, yes, that's one of mine," Counter said with a glance at the photo. "Would you like to buy one? I can have it assembled and engraved in a day."

"I'm not looking for one like it," I said. "I'm trying to track down this particular one. It's been stolen."

"Stolen?" It brought its hands together and tapped its copper fingertips together in a complex rhythm. "That is most confusing. The human who wished to sell it to me is the same one who commissioned me to make it."

"Wait," I said. "Someone tried to sell you this watch? Recently?"

It nodded. "Yes. Five days ago. The human came into my shop and said he wanted to sell the watch back. Of course, I couldn't give him the full price for it since it was a personalized piece and I would have to rework it in order to sell it again. He refused my offer. He was most upset."

"How can you be sure it's this one?" I asked, tapping the photograph. "You do make others like it, right?"

Counter swiveled to look at me. This one hadn't been given a human face; its head was a polished metal sphere with a half-dozen lenses of different sizes mounted to it. Tiny gears whirred as it focused the lenses one at a time. Was it rolling its eyes at me?

"The numeric indicators on the face of the piece."

I peered at the picture. There was a tiny diamond where each number would be on a regular watch face.

"King, trilliant, pear, trilliant, pear, heart, marquise, oval, king, king, oval, trilliant, oval, trilliant, trilliant, marquise," it recited.

I looked up at it, confused.

"The cuts of the diamonds from one to twelve," it said slowly. "I use a different pattern for each timepiece. Each one is unique."

"You can tell the cuts from this picture?" I asked, dubious. It was a good picture, but the diamonds were tiny, just chips.

"That is my business," it said. Those mechanical eyes could focus like microscopes, I realized, and its brain recalled what it saw photographically. If it said it was the same watch, it was the same watch.

I got out my notebook. "Tell me everything."

The watch had been ordered on Zweiember 34, 367, towards the end of Ilse's employment at The Purple Room. The man had paid cash and not left a name, but had returned on the first of Dreiember—the day before Midsummer. The inscription read, "For my Beautiful Ilse, on a Summer's Evening."

The total purchase price had been two hundred and eighty-five dollars, which had included the inscription and a fine presentation box, Counter said.

The next time Counter saw that man was Dreiember 12, 373—five days ago. He brought in the piece and demanded a refund. Counter had offered him a hundred and fifty.

"The human became quite belligerent," Counter said sadly. "I found it necessary to call the authorities."

"Did the Delapour constables arrest him?" I asked eagerly.

"No, he left the premises before they arrived."

Pity. That might have wrapped up the whole case right there.

"You're sure that it was the same human that commissioned the piece originally?" I asked.

"Quite certain," it said.

If the shopkeeper had been human—or a moreau, or an incubus—

THAT SUMMER'S EVENING LONG AGO

I would have considered the possibility that the thief was a rashling under a veil. But rashling illusions don't work on the forged ones.

Counter was able to provide me with drawings of the human. Full face and profile as detailed as a photograph.

I studied them while waiting for the ink to dry. I was looking at a scowling, pinched face. It was lined, but they weren't laugh lines. He didn't seem to be a man who often laughed or took much joy in anything. Maybe fifty, with buzzcut hair short enough that his scalp showed. A hard customer, I thought.

I thanked the forged one and headed to Centerburg. I needed to talk to Ilse again. Along the way, I tried to fix the timeline in my head.

Six years ago, a young woman was dancing for tips in Pickmantown. She catches the eye of a customer, and he buys her an extravagant Midsummer gift. Half a month's wages for a dockworker, more or less.

She moves on, leaving The Purple Room behind but keeping the necklace. She becomes the music director for a popular stage show.

Then—six years later, almost to the day—her mysterious benefactor returns to take back the gift and, in the process, erased her memories of having ever owned it. Anyone who knew enough to perform that conjuration had to know it was a serious crime. Getting that piece of jewelry back meant enough to him to risk prison time.

Then, try to sell it back to the shop where he originally bought it? And throw a fit when the owner wouldn't give him what he'd paid for it new?

It didn't make sense.

Or rather, it didn't make sense to me. It made sense to someone, the grim-looking man that the forged one had drawn for me. Once I found him, I could ask him.

The next step was figuring out who he was, and I really hoped Ilse would be able to tell me. Assuming that he hadn't erased the memory of his own identity when he took away the necklace.

The landlady called up to the girls and had me wait in the library again. Mikki came down in a green leotard covered with sequins and gave me a big hug.

"I'm a dryad," she explained.

Ilse was in a denim jumper. "I'm the dryad's seamstress," she said with a sigh. "We've been trying to get that mess to fit all morning."

I gave Mikki the once over. "It looks fine to me," I opined.

Mikki smiled and twirled.

Ilse sighed. "You should see the floorwork they've got blocked for her numbers. She's got to be able to do the splits in that thing—more than once."

I considered that for a moment, then changed the subject. "I've got a picture here that I'd like you to try to identify," I said, and handed Ilse Counter's sketch.

She took it, and I could see her thinking hard. After a moment she said. "That's Ivan. He looks older here, but I knew him."

"A client from The Purple Room," I suggested.

"Yeah..." she looked up at me. "This is who gave me the necklace? Or the one who took it?"

"Both, evidently," I said. "What can you tell me about him?"

She frowned. "Well, he's no magus. He managed one of those canneries up the river in Warfsend or Delapour."

"A regular?"

"Oh, yeah. Fiveday and Sixday nights, like clockwork," she said slowly. "A nice enough guy, I guess. He never got pushy like some of the regulars."

"Generous?"

She nodded. "He always tipped big at the end of the night, told me to take a cab home because the streets weren't safe."

"Any big gifts you can think of?" I asked the question in as casual a tone as I could manage.

"Yeah, he, uh..." She trailed off. Her hand crept to her throat in an unconscious gesture. "I can't remember."

I nodded. Out of the corner of my eye, I saw Mikki start to say something, then shut her mouth.

"When was the last time you saw him?" I went on.

"I'm not sure," she said. "He stopped coming in. It was maybe a month or so before I quit that place. I figured he'd just found some other girl to dance with, at some other club."

"Ivan," I repeated. "I don't suppose you remember his last name?"

"No. I don't know that I ever knew it," she said.

I held out my hand, and she gave me the sketch. "Anything else you can think of that might help me find him?"

After a moment she shook her head. "I'm sorry," she said. "It's been years."

"Well, if you think of anything, call my office and leave a message, okay?" I handed her my card.

"Sure," she said, then shrugged. "Honestly, though, I never really paid much attention to the men. They all want to talk, and after a while you learn how to smile without really listening."

I gave Mikki another hug, and she whispered to me, "Let's go out when this is all over. We won't tell Miss Kitten." I promised her that I would and then headed upriver to the cannery district.

My father worked on a fishing boat, and I grew up making pocket money cleaning fish for a local market. The smell of seafood doesn't bother me.

But the stink of canneries is something else altogether. The day was hot and after half an hour of quizzing workers and showing the sketch of Ivan, I fancied I could smell that stench coming out in my sweat. It clung to you. Pushing through the hanging canvas curtains into the canning floor was like wading through fish guts.

After two hours, I was ready to burn my suit and scrub my skin with bleach.

But at last I found someone who recognized my target. Kaletsky Fine Foods, the sign above the parking lot announced.

"Black Ivan," a big man smoking a pungent cigar exclaimed with a chuckle. "Yeah, I knew him. I haven't thought of that guy in years."

"Black Ivan?" I asked.

The big man grinned. "That's what we called him after he got arrested. You know, like on the radio?"

DRACOHEIM CONFIDENTIAL

The nemesis of Warchief Smith on *Days of the Founders*. I nodded to let him know I caught the reference. "What can you tell me about him?"

A frown. "Kind of a quiet guy," he said. "Dependable. Everyone was really shocked when it turned out he was stealing from the company. It's always the last guys you expect, you know?"

"So, he was arrested for theft, then? How long ago was that?"

"Ahhh, I don't know. Ten years ago, maybe?" Another frown. "No, less than ten years. It was after they remodeled the office. Five years maybe?"

"You remember his last name?"

A head shake. "Naw, sorry. They might know in the office."

"He was a manager here?"

"A shift lead is all," the man said, shaking his head. "He put in the timesheets for the line. That's what he got busted for—screwing with the payroll."

The office girl turned out to be singularly unhelpful. She was the kind who panics at the sight of a badge and wouldn't say anything without approval from the boss—who was unavailable.

I tried explaining that all I wanted was information on Black Ivan for a case that had nothing to do with the cannery or any current employee of the cannery, but she clammed up and answered all of my questions with a tight-lipped shake of her head.

I sighed and thanked her for her time. I knew what and where and approximately when. The Delapour Township constables could fill in the details. An hour later, I had the whole depressing story.

Ivan Winston Drake was arrested on Dreiember 8th, 367 on a charge of theft by fraud of approximately 300 dollars, charges filed by Jon Kaletsky, the owner. Drake was sentenced to seven months at Debtor's Island, plus restitution to be made upon release.

In Actember of that year, he was involved in an altercation with another prisoner named Konstantine. It turned violent, and Konstantine went over the railing from third level of the cell-block. He suffered broken ribs and a collapsed lung and subsequently died in the prison infirmary.

Drake was charged with manslaughter. Sentenced to five years and transferred to Oesterreach.

I called the offender's registry and found that he was released Actember of 372. Two months ago. I got an address in Warfsend and a phone number for his current employer, a liquor distributor called Happy Hour Spirits.

Happy Hour Spirits was able to confirm his employment over the phone. He was a delivery driver and had shown up for his regular shift that morning, 700 to 1400. I checked my watch and was surprised to see it was almost 1700.

I called the office and caught Blackwell before he left for the day. I filled him in.

"We've got to assume he's a freecaster," my boss said when I was finished. "Tactical support. I'll set it up with Warfsend. You say his shift starts at 700?"

"That's right."

"I'll set it up for 600. Box him when he leaves for work."

"Sounds good to me," I agreed.

"You head on home," he said. "I'll have the night desk call you in an hour to confirm the details."

B efore dawn the next day I was drinking coffee with a gang of rough customers in a parking lot a couple of blocks from Drake's rooming house. I outlined what I knew of the suspect and stressed that he—or someone working for him—had already used high level unlawful magic.

"We don't know what we'll be walking into here," I said. "He might just surrender when he sees the tin."

"Yeah, like that ever happens," one of the tacticals muttered.

I acknowledged his point with nod. "You're here in case he doesn't."

At quarter of 600, we headed out to surround the place. I stood leaning against a lamppost across the street; the Warfsend men took up stations out of sight, behind cars and around corners.

We waited.

And waited.

700 came and went. 715.

113

Traffic, both vehicles and on foot, was starting to trickle around us, the locals staring with wide eyes and then moving along, asking no questions.

"He ain't coming out," I said to the captain. "Maybe I spooked him. We'll have to go in."

"Roger that. Which one is his place?"

"The basement," I said.

"Figures."

Three men, including the captain, came with me through the front door. The others waited in the street or in the alley behind the place. There was a basement level door that led to the alley, but no way to tell if it connected with Drake's apartment.

The building door wasn't locked, nor the door to the stairs leading down. A dank stone hallway below street level led us to a solid looking door marked with a brass letter A.

"That's it," I whispered.

The captain knocked, hard. "*Warfsend Police!*" he shouted. "*Ivan Drake! Open up!*"

No answer.

I nodded to him and he pounded again, repeated his command to open up.

No answer.

I jerked my head at the door. "Break it down."

One of the constables gave the door a critical look, then nodded. He raised an armored boot and snapped a kick just below the doorknob. The door slammed open and hit the wall with a crash.

I went through the door in a crouch, my hand on my gun.

The room was a cluttered mess, bottles scattered all over a pair of big tables. My eyes scanned past the junk, looking for human figures and places a man could hide.

The tactical constables went past me. One jerked open a closet and announced, "Clear."

The other went through a door that opened on a tiny bathroom. "Clear," he echoed after a moment.

Drake wasn't home, and there weren't any other exits. There wasn't even a bed he could have been under, just a mattress on the floor.

"Agent!" the captain called. "You'd better look at this."

I looked back at the bottles and saw that it wasn't just the empties from somebody's month-long binge. The bottles were arranged carefully, and the table was laid out with lengths of wire stapled to the wood, making a containment grid. The bottles were filled with a variety of colored fluids, some of them glowing, others bubbling as if at a slow boil.

"Evacuate the building," I said, and backed slowly away from the table.

The captain nodded and started barking orders into his radio.

I called the office from the radio in one of the cruisers. Blackwell was in and they patched me straight through.

"What's the story?"

I took a deep breath. "Boss, we need a cleanup team. He's got an alchemical laboratory, and it's hot. Warfsend is evacuating the building now."

"I'll get Tengu's boys moving," he said. "Have you got Drake?"

"He wasn't there," I said. "He left before we showed up. Something tipped him."

Blackwell cursed. Then, "Find him. I'll put him on the citywide."

"We have to assume he's got active materials, wherever he is."

"Right. I'll flag it as 'observe and do not approach.' Has he got a car?"

"Not according to—" I broke off. "Shit. He drives a delivery van. Call his job, make sure they don't let him get it."

I ran for my car.

We were hours too late. Sometime in the night, Drake had broken into the lot and taken out his van. I called Blackwell and added the description and number plate of the van to the citywide alert.

There were a million delivery vans on the streets of Dracoheim. The one we needed wasn't even marked with a company logo—no sense in advertising that it was full of booze. One unmarked white van in a very big haystack.

I called Blackwell back and told him to send somebody around to watch Kaletsky's Fine Foods. "If he's looking for revenge," I said, "he might still hold them a grudge."

"Yeah, we've got Delapour constables there. So far no sign."

"Might be a good idea to have a witchfinder make a sweep."

"When we've got one freed up."

I hung up and looked around the office. I needed to get moving, to do *something*, but without some idea of what he'd do next, I was just flailing around blindly. I saw a line of hooks on the wall. One of them still held a clipboard.

"This Drake's?" I asked the dispatcher.

She looked up. "Yeah, daily route log."

I picked it and paged through it, just to give my hands something to do. They were liquor invoices, so many cases of this and that. Bars, restaurants, nightclubs...

The Golden Mermaid was buried in the middle of the stack.

Shit. Of course. That was how he'd known where to find Ilse. I was an idiot not to think of that sooner.

I called Blackwell back.

"Boss, it's the Golden Mermaid. Where Ilse works. *It's on his cursed delivery route!"*

"I'll call Quayside Parish. Get over there."

The morning traffic was crawling and the Quayside bridge was a parking lot. I fumed and told myself that honking wouldn't make anybody go any faster. They all wanted to get across the river as much as I did.

So. A lonely guy working a dead-end job in a fish packing plant starts going to a two-bits-a-dance club in the evenings. He falls for one of the club dancers, starts tipping her big in the hopes that she'll fall for him back. He even talks up his job, calling himself a manager instead of a shift lead to try to impress her.

That's not working, so he goes for a big gamble, ordering a piece of high-end jewelry and then fudging a pay slip to cover the cost.

The boss finds out and presses charges. He gets sent up and then, two months before he's going to get out, gets in a fight and is suddenly looking at serious time for manslaughter.

At long last, he gets out and starts trying to put some kind of life together. The parole board gets him an apartment, sends him making the rounds of companies willing to hire a felon.

He gets work and then, *bam,* he sees the girl of his dreams. She probably never noticed him. Who sees the guy who delivers the booze except for the bartender?

No wonder he went over the edge. I could almost feel sorry for him.

But he crossed a line. It's not hard to find black books of magic if you have the right contacts, and he'd just spent six years in prison. Alchemy isn't hard—dangerous, yes, but not all that complicated.

When I finally got to the Golden Mermaid, there were a pair of Quayside cruisers parked across the entrance to the lot and a white delivery van pulled up to the front door. I didn't have to check the number plate.

"We haven't been inside," one of the constables said. "They said to wait for you."

"This all you've got?" I asked.

"More on the way," he assured me. "There's a ten-car pile-up on the Coastal Freeway, it's got traffic in knots."

"Tell me about it." I looked around the lot. This early, there was only one other car, an old surrey.

"Is somebody else in there?" I asked.

He shrugged. "Like I say, we haven't been inside. That car was here when we got here."

I considered. "You cover the building," I decided. "One of you get to where you can watch the back. I'm going in."

They didn't like that, and I had a feeling that Blackwell wouldn't like it either, once he found out. But if someone was in that building with Drake, we needed to know.

The front door was unlocked. I pushed it open slowly, my hand on my gun. Inside, there was a dim hallway. The lights were on, but they were small brass sconces made to look like candles, providing mood lighting. I would have swapped the lot of them for a floodlight just then.

Wrought iron benches lined the hallway, for the convenience of guests waiting for a table. I passed a door for the Gents and then one for the Ladies. At each one I paused, listening.

DRACOHEIM CONFIDENTIAL

A splash sounded from up ahead, something big falling into a lot of water.

There was a hostess station. I looked behind the counter to make sure nobody was hiding in there. Nothing but stacks of menus.

A wide pair of swinging doors led to the main hall. I paused and listened.

Voices on the other side. At least two, a man and a woman.

I crouched down and pulled the doors apart, opening them only enough to duckwalk through.

Then I moved slowly around the outer wall, trying to get a feel for the space.

There were maybe a couple of dozen round tables spread around the room, each with chairs upended atop them, making my view a forest of chair legs. What light there was came from the front of the room.

I eased up to stand against the back wall so I could see the stage.

It was a complicated affair, built around an enormous glass-fronted pool, like an aquarium. There was a stage in front of the pool, illuminated by colored lights shining through the water, and a smaller stage at the top, a platform for divers to enter the pool.

On the upper platform a man stood, gazing into the pool. Beside him stood a woman. Her posture was awkward, a little bent, and I saw her arm was tied to the railing around the diving platform.

"Ivan Drake!" I called. "We've got the building surrounded. Let the woman go."

His head snapped up and he scanned around the room, looking for me. "Who's that?"

"I'm Erik Rugar," I said. I was pitching my voice low, hoping the acoustics of the place would keep him from fixing my position. "I'm from the Committee for Public Safety. Don't make things any worse for yourself. Come down here and we can get this sorted."

His head kept moving. The glow from the pool would be in his eyes, and the dining room was dim. I was betting he wouldn't see me unless I flashed a light. "I don't think so, Mr. Rugar. Do you know what I've got here?"

"Suppose you tell me," I said. I wasn't sure what he was talking about, his hands seemed to be empty. The important thing was to keep him talking until I could get him away from his hostage.

"Sanguinem flumine," he said, and cackled. "I've got enough to poison this whole rotten city."

That's when I realized the tank wasn't lit by underwater lights. The water was glowing, colors shifting in a slow pattern. He'd activated the entire tank. I couldn't estimate how much that thing held—fifty thousand gallons? A hundred thousand?

"What's your plan, Ivan?" I tried to keep my voice calm.

"A hundred grand in cash and a boat," he said. He was still searching the darkness, looking for me. "Or I dump this in the river."

"There's no way I can authorize that kind of deal," I said.

"*Then call whoever can and get his ass down here!*" Ivan screamed.

"Relax," I said. I was sweating bullets, but I hoped my voice was still calm. "Quayside has officers all around the building by now. How about you send the woman to explain the situation to them. I'll stay in here with you. You've got a whole city of hostages, you don't need her."

He thought that over. Nodded slowly and turned to the woman tied to the railing. He started to loosen the rope, then turned back to me. "Come out where I can see you," he demanded.

"After she's free," I said. "Let her go and I'll come out in the open."

"Why should I trust you?" he shot back.

"Think it over," I replied. "What choice have you got?"

He turned back to the woman and yanked at the rope. He had some trouble getting the knots untied, then shoved her towards the ladder that led off the platform. "Get out of here!" he snarled at her. "Make sure you tell them what I said. I want that money and that boat now."

She stumbled up the center of the dining room to the door, passing about ten feet from me. I didn't recognize her. She was in slacks and a tuxedo shirt—probably the bartender.

She hit the doors and went through. I heard her steps retreating down the hallway.

I took a deep breath and stood up slowly, holding my hands away from my body.

"Here I am," I said. "I'll come closer. Let's not do anything rash, okay?"

As I walked slowly towards the stage, he pulled a pint liquor bottle out of his pocket. Whatever was in it glowed green. He held it up, and I could see his hand trembling.

"That's close enough," he said.

I froze in my tracks.

We stood looking at each other for a long moment. I was considering the angles. I had a lousy position. I might be able to shoot him from where I stood, if he was distracted, but I'd hate to bet on it.

To buy time, I asked, "So I guess this tank is piped to the river, then. To drain it?"

"That's right."

"And if you don't get what you want, you open the valves?" I looked around the edges of the pool. There were bunches of thick pipes in the back, painted to match the walls and designed to be unobtrusive to the audience.

"Oh, no, no, no," he laughed. "I already opened them. That's what that nosy bitch caught me doing, opening the spill valves."

I looked at the level of fluid in the tank. It was constant, no sign that the stuff was draining out.

He caught my look and grinned. "Right now the spill pipes are full of ice. Changes of state in matter are easy—it's almost not magic at all. And I needed the heat for the working. I just took it from there," he pointed at the pipes, "and put it in there." A gesture at the pool.

I got it then. "When the ice melts..."

"Yes. When the ice melts this city dies."

Ingenious. Timer and dead-man switch in one package. I was sure that the Quayside Sewer Department could try to isolate the building, but finding the right outflow pipes and figuring ways to block them would take time, and the odds were good that even if the shutoffs worked, there would be enough leakage in the pipes to contaminate the ground water for blocks around.

Time. It all came down to time, and we didn't have enough of it.

"What's the status, Rugar?" a voice called from just behind the dining room doors.

I turned my head without moving the rest of my body. "I'm here with Mr. Drake. He's filled the performance pool with poison and opened the spill pipes. Right now, the pipes are blocked with ice, but when that melts, the poison will drain into the river."

"It's sanguinem flumine," Drake shouted. "Look it up. Give me what I want or start digging a shitload of graves."

"Understood, Rugar," the voice called back. "Mr. Drake, your request is going to take some time to get together."

"You've got until the ice melts! Work fast!" Drake shouted.

"That may not be possible," the voice called.

"Until the ice melts, assholes!" Drake screamed it.

There wasn't any response from the hallway. After a moment I asked, "Okay if I sit down?"

He glowered at me, but nodded. "Don't get cute," he warned.

I moved slowly and carefully, took one of the upended chairs and sat it facing the stage, then sat down on it.

"What happens now?" I asked.

"You tell me."

"They'll have to contact the mayor," I hedged.

"That monster," Drake growled. "Like he'd give a shit if humans die."

"He takes the safety of the city very seriously," I said mildly.

"I'm not asking for much," he said. Suddenly he looked very sad, and very old. "I could have asked for a million dollars, you know." A sigh. "The bad guys on the radio always ask for a million dollars when they do something like this. But I don't need that much."

"A hundred thousand dollars," I said slowly.

"I want my life back!" he roared. Then the sudden burst of rage evaporated as quickly as it had blown up. The next moment he spoke calmly and reasonably, just as if we weren't having the conversation with a pool full of death between us.

"You know how long six years is?" he asked conversationally. "If

121

I'd had son on the day I got arrested, he'd be starting school this fall."

"This isn't the way," I said.

"No?" He held up the bottle and looked into it. His hand shook and the green fluid jiggled. I hoped it wasn't too volatile. "Maybe not, but it's the only way I've got left."

"You're doing a lot of seventy-seven, aren't you?" I asked. "To help with the magic. I can see the shakes from here."

"Yeah," he admitted absently. "Yeah, it makes everything so clear."

"It also tears up your nervous system, you know," I pointed out. "There's a reason it's illegal."

He had only been out of the joint for two months. To have gotten the shakes that bad so quickly he had to be doing massive doses, every day probably. It also explained his mood swings. That stuff was eating up his brain.

"I gave her a choice," he said softly.

"Ilse?" I asked.

He nodded. "There's a little deli down the road. I met her for dinner. If she'd been willing to give me a chance—*just a chance*—I wouldn't be doing...this. But she wouldn't."

"So, you took back the necklace and her memory."

"Why shouldn't I?" he asked bitterly. "I gave them to her in the first place. And she never gave me anything in return."

"Mr. Drake," I said. "We should talk about how to get you out of this mess."

"There is no way out," he said miserably. "I'm not going back to the box."

"They've got the building surrounded," I said. "They are putting a breach team together now. Why don't you save us all a lot of trouble and just surrender? We can walk out together and let the wizards get to work on neutralizing—" I gestured, "—*that.*"

"I'm not asking for much," he said, looking down at the bottle in his trembling hand.

"I really don't think you want to kill all those people, Mr. Drake."

"You don't know me!" he roared. "You don't know anything

about me." His breathing was rapid and the shakes were worse. His eyes were twitching now. Then his rage faded away again, leaving him looking exhausted.

"Why can't they just let me go?" His tone was plaintive. "Why does everything in my life turn to shit?"

I waited without speaking. He was breaking down. The man's mind was unraveling as I watched.

"I expected her to be married when I got out," Drake said suddenly, and his voice was calm and even. He sounded perfectly reasonable, but I knew it wouldn't last long.

"After six years, sure," I said, matching his tone. "Makes sense."

"But that... that's not what she told me." His voice was starting to shake again, and I braced myself. He laughed, a bitter, near-hysterical sound. "She's a butch. She's shacking up with some showgirl." That ugly laugh again. "I went to prison for six years 'cause I was chasing after a butch, and I didn't know it."

I nodded, putting as much sympathy into the gesture as I could.

"It's funny, huh?" The shakes were coming back, harder than ever. "I mean, you could just *die* laughing."

"*Ivan Drake!*" boomed an amplified voice from the hallway. "*We are coming in. You will be taken into custody. If you resist, we will shoot. This is your only warning!*"

Drake looked at the door, then down at me. "I'm not going to get my money."

"No," I agreed.

"Or a boat," he went on, suddenly calm again. "They're not going to let me go."

"No. They won't."

"*We are coming in now!*"

The door burst open, and armored figures poured into the room. I got up and hurried to one side to get out of the line of fire, weaving between the tables.

Drake looked down at me and nodded, coming to a decision. He tossed the bottle he'd been holding over the side of the platform, not at the squad coming in, but at the tangle of pipes at the base of the pool.

Then he turned his back on all of us and stepped off the platform, into the poison of the pool.

Green light flared where the bottle had smashed, and I realized what he'd done.

"Fire!" I shouted. *"It's melting the ice!"*

The tacticals were already on it, though, rushing forward to smother the flames. Their own magus was on the scene, refreezing the ice and ensuring the block was solid while a team of alchemists began unraveling the conjuration that had changed the water in the tank into liquid death.

By the time it was safe to pull out Drake's body, he was nothing more than a partially dissolved skeleton. They could have buried him in a suitcase. Quayside Constables handled that, though, with assistance from the City Major Case squad.

There was nothing left for me to do but paperwork.

Ilse's necklace showed up eventually in a pawnshop in Warfsend. The owner verified that it had been Drake who brought it in. He said he'd given Drake a hundred for it. Ilse got it back and started wearing it again. It's a beautiful piece, no matter how she got it.

I saw Mikki a couple of times, dates to the Empire for dinner and dancing. She admitted that she and Ilse were more than just friends, but claimed that Ilse didn't mind her going out with men. All the same, it felt awkward, and I stopped seeing her. I heard she quit Miss Kitten's not long after.

That was okay. There are plenty of other girls who would be nice to a generous man as long as there are men who will pay for the illusion that somebody loves them.

Better Off Dead

Case:36-FMF-373//CI#373-0422

The Pickmantown Necromantic Control Office isn't in the main Water Street Station, it's in a suite of rooms in an old office building near the upriver docks, tucked under the Quayside Bridge. It's not easy to find, but fortunately I had been there before.

It was early enough that it might as well have been still night in the shadow of the bridge and the surrounding buildings. I parked, stuck my placard in the windshield, locked my cruiser, and took a freight elevator to four. The NCO takes up the whole floor. I showed my badge to the constable at the desk and said I was there to see Captain Kent.

The constable—a burly bruiser with a scarred face—pointed me to an office in the back.

I had to cross a space like a cafeteria to get there. Rows of tables, old, mismatched, and probably scavenged from other government offices. A crew of dangerous-looking customers occupied one group of tables in a corner. Pickmantown maintains the only police unit in Dracoheim County specifically for the hunting of ghouls. They were proud and tough and gave me sideways looks as I passed, no doubt wondering what a CPS agent was doing on their turf.

I was wondering that myself. Chief Blackwell hadn't briefed me on the situation, just told me to report to Captain Kent.

The door to Kent's office was open. There were two men in there, but it was obvious at a glance which one was the captain. He looked like an older—but no less fit—version of the bruisers in the bullpen. He wore a tactical police uniform, not a suit and tie like I did.

The other man was thin and tanned like a chunk of old leather. He was wearing shirtsleeves and a red apron and looked nervous.

I held up my badge. "Erik Rugar, CPS. You wanted to see me, sir?"

He waved me at a chair. "Agent Rugar, this is Anton Quinn. Mr. Quinn has a story that might interest you."

I gave Mr. Quinn my most reassuring smile. It didn't work. If anything, he looked more nervous.

"I got a pushcart in Quayside," he said, speaking softly, almost a whisper. "I sell hot pretzels and ices on the boardwalk, you know?"

I nodded.

"I been there thirty years," he went on. "Since I was a kid. I seen a lot of stuff."

He fell silent for a moment, looking down at the floor.

"What did you see that brought you here?" I prompted.

"I got my patch, see," he said. "We've all got our spots—nothing official or anything. Just the place we set up. Kind of an agreement." He looked up to me.

I nodded again. "I used to work the Leeshore boardwalk," I told him. "I know how it works."

That seemed to reassure him a bit. "My patch is upriver, not far from the carousel. It's a good location."

Again the man seemed to lose the thread of his story. I glanced over at Kent.

"Tell the agent about last night," Kent suggested. "What you saw at the photo studio."

"Taduz is a good guy," Quinn said. "Been there almost as long as me. He's got a little shop at the end of the walk, just short of the city limits. A lot of young guys come in with their girls, get their pictures, then pick up the prints on the way back to their cars. You know?"

I nodded and restrained myself from saying more. Whatever he had seen had spooked him bad. He'd get it out in his own way, at his own pace.

"Last night I'm headed up Palmetto, heading home, and I see that Taduz has still got his lights on. I figure he's just doing some prints, maybe he got a big order, or maybe he's just cleaning up the shop. He stays late some nights—he's like me, he's got nobody to come home to. His wife died, oh, I guess ten years now. Me, I never got married."

I suppressed a sigh, wondering if he was ever going to say something that would explain why I was here.

The pushcart man seemed to sense my impatience. "I look in the window, and I see these three guys at the counter. The guy in the middle was in this long black coat, like a rain slicker almost, and he's got this big black hat on. The other two guys were ghouls. They was standing there, like bodyguards or something. But they were ghouls, sure as anything. Dead as coffin nails, the two of them."

That got my attention.

"You're sure?" I asked automatically.

He nodded vigorously. "Yeah, I'm sure. Like I say, I worked the boardwalk twenty years. They weren't the first ghouls I ever saw. Taduz's shop ain't that big, and he keeps his windows clean so as folks can see inside. His lights are real bright, too, for taking pictures. I was maybe six feet away from them."

"And the man in the middle?"

"I never saw his face or much of anything except that big coat. He was talking to Taduz. I couldn't hear what they were saying, but they were arguing."

"What did you do?" I asked.

"I went on down the street," he said. "Quick-like." Then, as if he expected me to argue with him he went on, "What was I gonna do?"

I smiled reassuringly. "You did right. Then you reported it this morning?"

He shook his head. "Last night. The night bull on my patch ain't hard to find, he always walks the same route."

Captain Kent cleared his throat. Referring to a notepad on his desk, he said, "Constable Piscal interviewed Taduz Thelk at his place of business, Beachside Portraits and Prints. Mr. Thelk reported that he'd had no suspicious visitors that evening and had not seen any ghouls. The constable reported no evidence of a disturbance at the studio."

Quinn looked me square in the face for the first time. "I know what I saw, mister."

"So this morning you came here and made a report as well," I prompted.

"Sure," he said. "These are the ghoul experts, right?"

"That's right," Captain Kent agreed, standing. "Thanks for sticking around to talk to the agent. I know you're losing business by being here—I can have one of my men run you back over the bridge."

Quinn stood, but shook his head. "I'll get a cab," he said. "I don't want to be any trouble."

He smiled, but then looked away nervously. The old pushcart man didn't want to be seen with the cops.

After he left, Captain Kent said softly, "You figure we got another Bloody Jake?"

I winced. I had been trying very hard not to think about that name. He was the reason why Pickmantown had formed the Ghoul Squad.

"I hope not," I said. "Maybe he was just mistaken."

Fifty years ago, a necromancer named Jakob Kranzovitch had terrorized the waterfront with a gang of ghouls he had managed to bind to his service. It had taken near five years to run him down. I'd seen photographs of the warehouse where the final showdown had taken place. He'd made sure they couldn't take him alive.

To this day, no one knew how the gang had been controlled. A ghoul itself had no mind—it was dead, an inanimate object. The metafungal infection that caused the muscles to move exhibited vitaltropism, moving in the direction of living things, but wasn't intelligent in any way that could be measured. Necromantic and psychomantic theory agreed that there was no way to bind an infected corpse—all you could do was put it down.

But somehow Bloody Jake had managed to train ghouls to obey commands, and there were creditable eyewitness accounts of his undead soldiers opening doors and carrying objects to use as weapons—things no natural ghoul could do.

"So what now?" Kent asked.

I put away my notebook. "I'll go talk to this Mr. Thelk, and some of his neighbors. If someone is running a shakedown, then they're sure to have hit more shops than just one portrait studio."

"And if you can't get anyone to talk?"

"That will tell me something, too."

An early weekday morning during the school session is a good time to interview boardwalk vendors. I was able to park right outside Beachside Portraits and Prints.

BETTER OFF DEAD

The shop was small and cluttered. The walls were covered with framed pictures, mostly pretty girls either on the boardwalk or with a variety of fanciful backdrops. Taduz Thelk had a camera disassembled for cleaning on his counter. He smiled big when he saw me come in, then his eyes got cold when he made me for a cop.

"Help you?" he asked gruffly. He was short, with a bad wig of coal black hair that clashed with his white eyebrows.

I walked up and laid my badge on his counter. "I'd like to ask you a few questions."

He sighed. "Go ahead."

I turned away from the counter to study the walls. The photographs spanned decades, and I could see a number of local celebrities, including Madame Dragonfly. That one had been taken recently, after she left the ring, but she was grinning and camping for the camera.

"How long have you been in this shop?"

"Twenty..." he paused, considering. "Twenty-four years now."

"Good location," I observed.

"I do okay, I guess," he said. He was nervous, waiting for me to get to the point.

I took a few leisurely steps, still studying the wall of photographs. He was a good photographer, I decided. The people in the pictures looked natural, not stiff and posed. "I hear you had a visitor last night."

"No, no," he said quickly. "No visitors."

I turned to look at him, raising my eyebrows in mock surprise. "I have a report from Constable Piscal that he interviewed you at a quarter to twenty-two last evening."

"Oh," he nodded. "Yeah. Him. I guess he came by about then. He's a good cop, he checks in on us a lot."

I met his eyes and held them. "Who did you think I meant?"

"Nobody," he said too quickly.

I waited, giving him a cold stare.

He looked away. "Uh, well, Piscal asked me about some guys that somebody thought they saw in my shop. I thought you were talking about them."

"You told the constable you hadn't seen any such people."

"That's right."

I turned back to look at the pictures on the wall. "But you were lying."

"No, I—"

I spun around and cut him off. "Who is he?"

"I don't know what you're talking about!"

He was scared. Scared green, and not of me. It was time to back off.

I made a show of looking through my notebook, then closed it and put it away. "I understand," I said gently. I got out one of my cards and put it on the counter. "If you decide you've got something to tell me, call this number. Any time. It's always answered."

Then I left the shop.

Like I told Captain Kent, people can tell you a lot by what they refuse to say, and over the next three hours, I learned enough to worry me.

Quayside Parrish is a quiet little town, full of docks and warehouses and housing for the longshoremen who shift goods from one to the other. The shops on the boardwalk catered mostly to the locals, places for working men to take their families on the weekends to relax. There was a nickelodeon full of mechanical games, run by a silent forged one. Shops that sold pretty and sometimes useful things for longshoremen's wives' kitchens. Clothes of the sort that you bought for a day on the beach and discovered years later in your closet and wondered what you had been thinking. Amusements for the kids, cheap toys, a puppet theater—shuttered now, so early in the day—a bandstand for local boys to practice their riffs and impress the girls.

And everywhere the subtle stink of fear.

There was a certain edge to the way the shop owners and pushcart vendors looked at me. It reminded me of what an old watch captain used to call "blue fever"—that over-polite nervousness of petty criminals when the cops show up. They had something to hide, but in this case, it wasn't anything they were doing, it was something being done to them. Like Taduz Thelk, they weren't scared of me, they were scared to be seen with me.

There was a Quayside Constables Substation on Driftwood Avenue, just a few blocks from where I'd parked. After my interviews—and a brief pause for frybread and a lime fizzy—I headed there and asked politely if the precinct captain might be available.

After a while, he was, and I introduced myself.

"So what can we do for the Mayor's Office?" he asked.

He was a battered campaigner by the name of Ed Morgan, and I'd bet good money that he had started out walking a beat and worked his way through the ranks.

"I got a report of someone using ghouls to shake down shop owners on your boardwalk," I said. "I did some interviews, and I think there might be something to it. They're scared."

He reached into a desk drawer and pulled out a half-smoked cigar and struck a match on his battered desk, puffed the rope into light before replying. Around a cloud of foul vapors, he asked, "Is this an official CPS investigation?"

"Not yet," I said. "I'm gathering evidence to open one."

He puffed. "This is about that pushcart man, right? Quinn?"

"That's right."

"He filed a report with CPS?" A long pull on his cigar followed by a prodigious cloud of smoke. I started to wish I had a gas mask.

"He contacted the Pickmantown Necromantic Control Office. They called CPS."

Captain Morgan looked at his cigar like it had just suddenly appeared in his hand, stubbed it out, and dropped it back in his desk drawer. "I won't lie to you, agent, we get shakedown artists from time to time, leaning on the shops for a cut of their take. Sometimes it takes some time to run them down, but we always do. Maybe we got one now. But... Bloody Jake, risen from his grave? Naw, I'm not buying it."

"I'd like to follow this up," I said.

He considered this for a long time. Then he said, "Well, it's your time, but I think you'll be wasting it. You'll share anything you find with my office?"

131

"Of course."

"Feel free."

"Thank you, captain," I said, and turned to go. On the way out the door I said, "By the way, Bloody Jake doesn't have a grave. He was cremated."

He opened his desk drawer and got out his cigar again, looked at it suspiciously. "I didn't know that."

I headed back to Government House and took the elevator down to Chief Blackwell's office. He listened to me run down the day's activities.

"You think this Captain Morgan is in on it," he said when I had finished.

I winced. "I didn't say that."

"But you think his attitude is suspicious," he pressed.

"He was awful quick to dismiss it," I agreed.

He leaned back in his chair and looked at the ceiling. "Let me ask around," he said. "If this Morgan is bent, somebody will have a line on him already."

"I don't think he believes there are ghouls involved," I said. "Whether or not he is."

"Do you think there are ghouls involved?"

I thought that over. "People are scared," I said. "This wasn't just the usual brushoff. Maybe they're scared because the local law is in the pocket of the gang... but I think it's something more."

"So what's your plan?"

I had been chewing that over on the drive. "I'd like to go home and get a couple of hours sleep, then come back after dark."

"If something really is going on, you'll need backup."

"Captain Kent is taking this seriously. I'm sure he'll loan us some muscle if we ask him nicely."

The chief nodded approvingly. "I'll call him. You scoot—I'll have the night desk call you with the details at twenty."

I nodded and scooted.

By twenty, I'd gotten my sleep, a shower, and a couple of cups of coffee. The night desk called to tell me that a Sergeant Bale of the Pickmantown NCO would meet me at an all-night 'lix station just off the Central Expressway in half an hour.

Bale was in plainclothes, a suit which he'd have to have had custom tailored. He was one of the biggest men I'd ever met, over six and a half feet tall and built like a bull. I felt like a shrimp beside him.

"What's the play, Agent Rugar?" he asked. We left both our cars on the street and walked down Market Street.

"I want to interview some shop owners," I said. "Watch the streets after dark. Keep our eyes open. You're read in on the complaint?"

He nodded ponderously. "I'm not sure I believe it, but I've read it."

"You think Quinn was mistaken?"

"I think he saw what he was supposed to see," Bale said. "Suppose someone was running fake ghouls. Makeup and costumes and betting that no one was going to get close enough to see through it."

I considered that. "It would take some pretty heavy stones to pull off a scam like that."

"More than working with real ghouls?"

"Good point." It did make sense. The stories of Bloody Jake were horrific, and an enterprising con man could have decided to cash in on the fear that still lingered along the riverfront. "The pushcart man did say that he'd seen the ghouls only through a shop window. And no one else will talk at all."

Then he grinned down at me and patted his jacket to check his weapon. Whatever he had in there was bigger than a pistol. "Of course, I'm prepared to be wrong about that."

"Good."

We walked along in silence. Ahead, the lights of the carousel painted the street in cheery colors. Then, very casually, without looking at me, he said, "If it is fake, then it's more likely the local law is in on it. Your chief said this Captain Morgan seemed suspicious, and Quayside law hasn't got the best reputation."

I looked out onto the dark streets before replying. "I don't like accusing cops without hard evidence."

"Nobody does," he said. "But it happens."

I nodded. Yeah, it happened all right. Way too often.

We reached the carousel just as they started shutting it down. The last children—cranky and over-tired—were being pulled, protesting, from the wooden horses and leaping fish by their equally cranky parents. The ticket window was already shuttered, and as we watched, the strings of colored lights were switched off one by one.

We went by Beachside Portraits and Prints and glanced in. Mr. Thelk was engaged with a trio of Merchant Marine Academy cadets, almost glowing in their new white uniforms. I paused by the window long enough for him to notice us, then nodded politely and we went down onto the boardwalk proper.

On the corner, a man in a bartender's white apron took down a sign that read "Dinner Specials" and replaced it with one advertising "Dancing Nitely." Past him, inside the restaurant, I saw a pair of busboys stacking chairs to clear the floor as musicians unpacked their cases.

It was that transitional time I remembered well from my years walking a beat in Leeshore. The closing of the carousel was a signal. Now the families were heading home and the young bucks with their long-legged does were coming out.

A pair of constables had stationed themselves by the bandstand where a trio of nervous kids were setting up for a gig. I got my wallet out slowly and showed them my badge.

"Rugar, CPS," I said. "That's Bale from Pickmantown NCO. We're doing a sweep tonight."

Both were tall, beefy men with cold eyes that didn't thaw when they saw the tin.

"Yeah, the captain said you might come by," one of them allowed. His name tag said Piscal. He'd been the one to interview Thelk last night, then.

The other one just glared. Stanton, I read. I met his glare with a grin and jerked my head for Bale to follow me down the walk.

Bale was frowning. Softly, he said, "And here I thought we were entering a new era of efficient inter-departmental cooperation." He was quoting from a recent speech from Castor Tak, the MP of Shell

Beach.

I chuckled. "Maybe they didn't get the memo."

He glanced back at the constables. "Scared we'll screw up their collections."

I bristled at that. "Nobody's happy to see outside law on their patch. It doesn't mean they're bent."

He looked back to me. "You've walked a beat." It wasn't a question.

"Leeshore," I admitted. "Six years. You?"

He gestured across the river. "Pickmantown, my whole career. Constable, detective for a few years, then ghoul squad."

"How many ghouls do you put down a year, anyway?" I asked. "A half-dozen?"

"Eleven last year," he answered quickly. "But that was a bad year. Eight is average."

"So what do you do the rest of the time?"

"Take a lot of long lunches," he said, and laughed. "I wish. No, we do overflow work for other municipalities. Last week, I worked a burglary in Shell Beach; before that, I helped set up a dope bust in Warfsend."

"They keep you busy."

"Only about a quarter of our funding comes from the town—we have to hustle up the rest."

"I didn't know that." I glanced at him. "So you bill the other jurisdictions? Are you going to bill the CPS for tonight?"

He shook his head. "Naw, this is part of our regular work." Then he gave me a wry look. "Unless it turns out you're going after a tigerberry dealer and the ghouls are just a ruse to get me here."

"Anton Quinn came to you," I pointed out.

"True," he agreed. Then he frowned. "Have you seen him?"

"No. Maybe he called it a night," I shrugged. "He was out this morning."

"Yeah, maybe." He was still frowning. "Most of those pushcart soldiers work pretty long hours, though. Go home for a nap in the afternoon, then back out again to catch the dinner crowd."

"Think we ought to call for a welfare check?" I asked.

He shook. "Not yet. He doesn't come out tomorrow, I'm gonna be concerned."

I took us into a tiny coffee shop. I had interviewed the owner that morning, and he looked nervous to see me returning, but all I asked him for was a couple of coffees and a couple of slices of cheese and apple pie.

When we came out of the shop I scanned the crowd automatically and caught a face I recognized.

"Down there by the lamppost," I murmured to Bale. "That beanpole in the green coat. I want to talk to him."

"Copy that."

We headed that way. I saw the skinny man in the long green coat—far too warm for a sultry night—stiffen when he saw me. For a moment, I thought he was going to run, and I could feel Bale get ready to drop his coffee and go after him. Then the skinny man decided he was going to brazen it out, just walk on past and hope I was looking for someone else.

I caught his arm when he got near. "Kenny Tsing," I said with a smile. "Fancy meeting you here."

"Agent Rugar," he said. "I'm just out catching some air. I ain't doing nothing."

"Nobody said you were," I answered, still smiling. "I just wanted to introduce you to my friend from Pickmantown. Kenny, this is Sergeant Bale. Sarge, this here is Kenny Tsing. Kenny's got a shop in Freebooter Park. He sells alchemical reagents."

"Is that right?" Bale asked with a smile.

"Yeah," Kenny said nervously. "I got an alchemy shop. Clyde Street Wet & Dry."

"The thing is," I went on, "I've investigated that little shop. Several times. For some odd reason, people keep spreading malicious rumors that he's trading in proscribed necromantic compounds."

"Huh," Bale said. "That's interesting."

"Of course, there's nothing to it," I said. "Well, there were a couple of times that we found a few things on the premises that weren't *entirely* legit, and Kenny had to go to court, but nothing was ever proven. Good legal representation, you understand."

Bale nodded sagely. "Having a good solicitor is important," he agreed.

Kenny was sweating, and his eyes kept darting back and forth. His smile showed too many teeth, making his thin face look like a skull.

Bale turned his head to me, but kept his eyes on Kenny. "You figure this guy is connected to, uh, what we're here for?"

I shook my head and let go of Kenny's arm. "Mr. Tsing here? Naw, he couldn't be. He's a legitimate businessman. Right?"

"That's right, Agent Rugar," Kenny said, too quickly and nodding like a metronome. "Just here, you know, taking the air is all."

I gestured for him to go on down the walk. He shot a nervous glance at Bale, as if suspecting a trap, then hustled away, head down, almost running.

Bale watched him go, frowning. Softly he said, "We could've searched him."

I shook my head. "Even if he was carrying it wouldn't stick. He's connected, that one. Powerful friends."

"Then why was he sweating bullets?"

I turned to glance back. Kenny had already vanished into the sparse weekday crowd. "I wish I knew."

I stopped at the next payphone and called the night desk.

"I want you to call Freebooter Park, Lantern Street Station, and leave a message for Captain Jakob Braz. See if he can free up a watch detail for the Clyde Street Wet & Dry. The owner's a party called Kenneth Tsing."

The dispatcher read back the information, then asked, "Have we got an open complaint on this Mr. Tsing?"

"At least one," I assured him. "He's a regular customer. Braz will have a file on him."

"I'll pass the message along."

I went back to Bale. "Maybe we can spook him. He's not scared of the law, but I bet he's scared of what might happen to him if the law starts sniffing around. He might turn evidence to save his hide

137

from..." I waved my hand at the boardwalk, unwilling to give a name to my growing suspicions.

Bale nodded. "It's happened before."

We talked shop until we reached the end of the walk. Ahead were the Cattail Street docks, and behind them we could just see the Leeshore riverfront. I pointed out the general direction of my building, and he waved vaguely across the river and explained where he lived. We compared rooming houses for a while—his place was bigger, but I had a view of the water.

That led naturally to talk about women as we headed back into Quayside. He'd told me about his ex-wife, concluding sadly, "Some women just aren't cut out to be cop's wives."

We passed back by the bandstand where the trio was jamming— the trumpet was really hot and the others were competent, so we paused there to listen for a while. I dropped a buck in their hat and Bale tossed in a handful of coins. When we moved on we talked music for a while, and I learned that he worked security at the Thomist Arena regularly, so I quizzed him on the celebrities he'd met—nearly everyone, it turned out. In self-defense I had to tell him about dating Lana Z.

Then a dance club—the bouncer breathing a sigh of relief as we passed him by—got us back to the topic of women and, with one thing and another, four hours passed.

The evening joints were closing up and the last of the weekday drunks staggering home when we took a seat on a bench overlooking the Steamboat Street pier for a rest. He didn't look like he needed it, but I did—my legs were starting to ache. I'd been spending too much time behind a desk.

"Well?" I asked.

"Customers are thin tonight," he said. He got a cigarette out, and I got out my lighter. I lit his, then one of my own.

"Fine night like this, even in the middle of the week, I'd expect more," he went on. "And did you notice how stag the crowd was? Not a lot of couples, almost no hen parties. Just men."

I nodded. I had noticed that.

"Not a lot of pushcarts, either," he said slowly, considering. "It's not just this Quinn—most of the carts stayed home tonight. Okay, so a thin crowd to work means less business, but..." He trailed off.

"There were plenty this morning," I said. "But they're not out tonight. It's like they're scared of the dark."

Bale took a deep drag on his cigarette, let the smoke out slowly. Then he said, "Couldn't say any of this in court, of course."

"No," I agreed. "But you feel it, don't you? Something's... wrong."

Bale looked out at the dark beach beyond the lights of the boardwalk, and the dark water of the river, and up to the lights of Pickmantown on the other shore. "Yeah. Something's wrong. And there's your friend Tsing. He wasn't here for the two-drink special."

"Stick around awhile?"

He shrugged. "You got me all night. I got no one to go home to."

He started to get up, and I waved him back down. "Let me finish my smoke."

Piscal and Stanton strode up while we were sitting there. Stanton had his nightstick out and was twirling it idly, as if he was hoping for a chance to use it.

"Evening, gents," I said cheerfully.

"Closing time," Piscal said. "Guess you'll be shoving off soon?"

I stretched out my legs. "It's a nice night," I said. "Maybe I'll soak the city for another couple of hours of overtime."

I glanced over at Bale.

"I've been on time and a half since twenty-three," he said. "I got bills to pay."

Stanton looked out across the river. "Not enough work in Pickmantown to keep you busy?"

"You know us," Bale said easily. "We go where the ghouls are."

"There aren't any here," Piscal shot back angrily, "no matter what that crazy old man said."

"Even better," Bale said. "Money for nothing."

"Yeah, that's what you ghost busters get, isn't it?" Stanton said angrily. "Money for nothing."

Bale smiled at him. "What was the take for the band?" he asked. "They were pretty good."

Stanton stopped twirling his stick and brandished it. "What are you saying?"

Piscal put his arm on Stanton's arm, holding him back. To Bale, he said, "We wouldn't know how they did. Donations received for performances on the public bandstand aren't subject to city oversight." His voice was cold.

To Stanton he said, "Come on, we've got real work to do."

The two of them stalked off.

Bale watched them go. "Yeah, *sure* they're not bent," he muttered.

I ground out my cigarette and got up, "Come on, let's make another round."

I led Bale away from Piscal and Stanton, back towards Leeshore.

The lights were off in the shops, and we walked down a wooden river of darkness from one streetlit island to the next. The breeze from the river had finally cooled off, and under the stink of the city, I could catch the clean salt smell of the sea.

"It's the brackish water, right?" I asked Bale. "Where the ghoul fungus grows?"

Bale nodded and waved his hands to indicate the buildings to our left. "This was all salt marsh when we came to this land. If you look at old maps, from the founding, they called this the Dead Swamps. You know, when you think about just how hostile this land was when we first arrived, it's amazing that we survived."

"We had the Mayor to help us," I pointed out.

"Not at first," he replied. "It was nine years between the founding of the first colony and the accords of Dracoheim. You ever study the history of the city?"

I shrugged. "Sometimes I listen to *Days of the Founders*."

That earned me an eyeroll. "You were a surfer in school, weren't you?"

"Wrestler," I grinned at him. "Does it show?"

He laughed. "I thought all you CPS agents were college boys."

"Not me," I said. "I'm just a street cop with neat handwriting."

"Well—" he began, then broke off suddenly, his face growing serious. "Wait, do you hear that?"

BETTER OFF DEAD

I held still and listened. A dull thump sounded from somewhere low to the ground. I scanned the shadows looking for the source, and there was a second one.

Bale was moving in a slow circle, eyes wide. Nothing happened for a while and then it started again.

Thump.

Thump.

Thump.

A sound like a fist on wood, as if someone was knocking hard on a heavy door. I looked to the line of shops, but all the doors had glass panels in them and nothing was moving behind them.

After a pause, it came again.

Thump.

Thump.

Thump.

Bale looked down at his big feet, then pointed.

I nodded and tried to fix the location in my mind. I pointed at Bale, then at a spot a few feet downstream, then at myself, and a spot an equal distance upstream. He nodded and we moved to the railing on the beach side.

I pulled out my flashlight—small, but very powerful. He nodded and got out his weapon—a short-barreled shotgun with a pistol grip. He held up three fingers on his free hand, then two, and then together we vaulted over the rail. I landed in a crouch and clicked on my light.

A man lay under the boardwalk, bound in ropes and covered with blood. I started crabwalking towards him.

"Stop!" Bale roared. "Don't touch him."

I froze in place. Bale was too big to crouch under the walk. Instead he came slowly forward on his hands and knees. I saw that he had put away his gun and put on a pair of brown rubber gloves that reached to his elbows.

He glanced back at me. "Call University Hospital and get their infection unit. And let my night desk know what we've found."

I set my flashlight on the sand so that its beam illuminated the cramped space. What *had* we found? The man, I saw, had been cut

141

in patterns, angles and curves carved into his skin. It was a wonder he'd remained conscious long enough to signal us.

Then I climbed back onto the boardwalk. I remembered passing a pay phone not long ago. I ran to it.

I called my night desk and had them relay the information to the hospital and the Pickmantown NCO. Then I hurried back to where I'd left Bale and the bound man. Bale was dragging the man out onto the beach, his gloves smeared with blood that looked black in the shadows. I noticed those gloves had wide canvas cuffs stitched with the silver thread of a magical containment ward.

"On their way," I told him. "What is it?"

"Necromancy," he grunted. "But he's still alive. Tough old buzzard."

I took a look at his face. "That's Anton Quinn," I said.

"Thought it might be," he muttered. To the figure at his feet he said, "We've got the ambulance coming, Mr. Quinn. Once the doctors have looked you over, we can talk about who did this to you."

"...pale...king..." Quinn gasped.

"Hush," Bale told him. "Save your strength. You're going to be okay, but you have to rest now."

Then he shot me a worried look that gave lie to his comforting words.

"I'll watch for the ambulance," I said, letting my tone make it a question.

Bale nodded. "I've got Mr. Quinn."

I made my way through an alley between the closed shops and out onto Ocean Avenue. The most direct route from Parrish Metro would be down Ocean.

Movement caught my eye, and I looked to see a dark figure in a long black coat cross the pool of light from a streetlamp and back into the shadows again. He moved slowly, deliberately, and I had an uncanny feeling that he had wanted me to see him. A wide hat covered his head, and his face was turned away from me.

I stared after him, and he melted away into the shadows. There was something... *wrong* about him, something that made me want to pull my pistol and give chase, but I could already hear the sirens tearing down the empty streets.

A moment later, blue lights strobed across the brick, and I was directing the medics down the alley to the boardwalk and their waiting patient.

Quinn was still alive when they loaded him onto the stretcher, but the men's faces were grim as they worked. The thin figure was paper-pale from loss of blood. I caught a glimpse of tubes and bags for a transfusion as they slammed the doors and roared off towards the hospital.

By then, the rest of the crew was arriving. Quayside Parrish had two cars, one uniformed, one plainclothes. Then the ghoul squad in a tactical van, and at last Supervisor Glynn, who was the night duty officer at Government House this month. Glynn had a sleepy-looking staff magus with him.

A lot of bodies for the boardwalk in the middle of the night. I sat down and got my notebook in order and waited to see who was going to end up with the case.

Pickmantown won the jurisdictional pissing match, exiling the locals to secure the perimeter of the scene and grudgingly allowing the CPS mage to take recordings of the area. Whatever his instruments showed made him frown and briskly order a twenty-foot length of the boardwalk closed to all traffic.

"For how long?" one of the Quayside plainclothes officers wanted to know.

"Until I say otherwise," the magus shot back.

I gave my verbal report to Glynn and the Pickmantown night watch commander and promised both of them written copies in the morning. Then I stared out over the river and fought off the stink of the salt marsh with cigarettes while Bale did the same.

It was somewhere between too late and too early when they let Bale and me head back to our cars.

"So what was that all about?" I asked him softly as we walked together down the silent street.

"What do you mean?"

"What they did to Quinn."

"I don't know."

"You said it was necromancy," I reminded him.

He was quiet for several long strides, and I thought he wasn't going to answer. Then he said, "It stands to reason, right?"

I waited.

He sighed. "There's a theory that whatever Bloody Jake did to make his ghouls controllable was a ritual performed on the victim before death. Those were runes carved on Mr. Quinn. Then he was left to die next to brackish water."

"You think that's how he does it?"

A ponderous nod. "We've got to take down this bastard."

"The pale king."

That earned me a sharp glance. "What was that?"

"What Quinn said," I explained. "When you were talking to him on the beach. It sounded like he said, 'pale king'."

"I didn't catch that," he admitted. "I was just trying to keep him calm."

"Do you think he'll make it?"

A shrug. "Hard to say. He lost a lot of blood."

"If he doesn't...?" I couldn't finish the question.

"They'll pump him full of the anti-venom," Bale assured me. "No matter what, he's not going to reanimate."

We'd reached the cars and said goodbye, and then I headed to Government House. There was no point in going home. Maybe I could get away for a nap later.

For the moment, I settled for a large cardboard cup of coffee and settled down at my typewriter to document the night's events. I made four carbons.

Chief Blackwell came in early and passed by my desk on the way to his office. I handed him the original of my report then went to the mailroom and had one copy messengered to Pickmantown and another to Quayside. I filed the last two in my desk—the way this case was shaping up, I figured somebody would be asking for them sooner or later.

My phone rang, and Blackwell asked me to come to his office.

The magus who had been on the boardwalk last night was there, looking as worn out as I felt.

"Dr. Bari, why don't you go first," Blackwell said.

"The thaumic flux was in the six-to-seven-hundred-talent range," he said, "about what you'd find in a commercial lab."

I digested that. "Did you find the foci?"

"As near as we can determine," Bari said slowly, "Mr. Quinn was the sole focus."

"That's not possible," I said automatically. Then, "Is it?"

"I don't—" he broke off and scrubbed his face in his hands. "I don't know. If you had asked me yesterday, I would have told you that a living human being can be the focus of *maybe* three hundred talents maximum. I've worked industrial accidents where men were killed by half that."

He sighed. "But I know what my instruments read, and University Hospital's own magi confirmed it. We are dealing with something... unprecedented here."

Unprecedented, I thought, *except for Bloody Jake.*

Blackwell turned to me. "Captain Kent has requested that you be attached to his command as an adjunct for the duration of this investigation. Do you have any objections?"

"No."

Blackwell nodded, expecting that answer. "Go home and get some sleep. You've got a mission briefing at the PNCO at 1900."

I stood. "Yes, sir."

Then I headed home. I checked my calendar and saw that I had a date scheduled, so I called Miss Kitten's service to cancel. Pity. I was supposed to be seeing a new girl, Darla, and I liked her pictures a lot. I made a mental note to bring her something nice as an apology when I had a chance to reschedule.

Then I hit my bed and let the lights go out.

At a quarter to nineteen, I was back in the Ghoul Squad, in a fresh suit, shaved and showered and with a belly full of diner food. Captain Kent waved me into his office. Bale was already there, in civvies but with his shooting iron in a hip holster rather than under his coat.

Kent spoke without preamble. "I just got back from University

Hospital. Mr. Quinn is in intensive care, but he's expected to pull through. He'd lost a lot of blood and had an advanced stage one infection, but thanks to you two, the docs think they caught it in time."

I breathed a sigh of relief and nodded for him to continue.

"He hasn't been conscious much and he's delirious when he is, but they've got a recorder going in his room just in case he does say something significant. Maybe he can identify who did this to him. Maybe not."

He paused to let that sink in, then continued. "I've also been talking to Captain Morgan of the Quayside constables." A frown. "He assures me that they will cooperate fully with our investigation but has asked that we keep our presence to plainclothes officers unless we have proof of an active outbreak."

"Proof?" Bale asked incredulously. "What do they call Quinn's condition?"

"He says it's inconclusive."

Bale started to speak and Kent cut him off. "I got a call from Crawfish's office. Evidently the MP got an earful from across the river about us being on their turf last night. Rugar—you met with Captain Morgan and got a verbal okay to run your investigation, right?"

"That's right," I said.

"And Blackwell will back you on that?"

"Absolutely."

"This whole thing is starting to really stink. Make sure you document every interaction with the local laws." Kent lowered his voice. "I have *also* spoken, informally, with a buddy of mine at Parliamentary Oversight. There are going to be a lot of eyes on the Quayside cops—we need to focus on the person or persons who did this to Mr. Quinn."

Kent then pulled out a bundle of papers from his jacket. I recognized the green-bordered pages of a magus's official report. "Now, you know how much I love reading technical documents,"— a dry chuckle from Bale—"so I got one of their staff wizards to break it down for me in words of one syllable. This is, at a minimum, attempted murder by means of magic and unlawful experimentation on a human subject, plus assault and kidnapping. It's enough to get this guy the gas chamber if he goes to trial."

He glanced at the sheaf of notes in his hand, and I was sure that he had read it and understood it at least as well as I would. The big dumb bruiser pose was an act.

"The experts say that we can't be sure what the invocations carved into Mr. Quinn's body were intended to do, but I think we can make a pretty good guess, and what's more, I think we have to assume he can actually do it."

He extended the magus's report to me. "You can read these things, right?"

"Sure," I told him.

"Give it a look-see when you've got a minute. I'd like to know what you think."

I took the papers and stuck them in my jacket pocket. "What's the play, Captain?"

"You heard about your buddy Tsing?" he asked.

"No," I said. The report from Freebooter Park must have come in while I was asleep.

"He scampered," Kent said. "Didn't show up at his shop, and when they checked his place he was gone. Looked like he moved out in a hurry."

I frowned. "That's on me. I wanted him spooked, but not so spooked he'd run out."

Kent shrugged. "It happens. They don't have enough for a warrant, but he's listed as a person of interest. If he shows up, he'll be detained for questioning."

"He won't," I said. "He's probably abroad by now."

"That leaves us with one victim, who might or might not be able to talk anytime soon. Our description of the suspect is straight out of a penny opera." He gave me a sharp glance. "I think you were right not to go after him, if that was him. We'd be hauling your body out from under the boardwalk today if you had."

I nodded, but I had my doubts. *Curse it,* I thought, *I almost had him last night.*

Kent seemed to sense my reservations. "There are no heroes in this business, agent. I don't like going to cop funerals. It's bad for my digestion. We operate in teams—you stick with Bale. Nobody goes off alone."

"Yes, sir," I said. "What's our play?"

"Hunt ghouls," Kent said. "We need a cold body for the ME's office. Get me that, and we'll hit the boardwalk in force."

"Where we found Quinn," I suggested. "They had to get him there with nobody seeing anything."

"Obviously," Kent agreed.

I shuddered. Crawling under the boardwalk was not my idea of a good time. But it was where the evidence led. I looked over at Bale.

Bale was looking out the window, and for the first time I realized it faced west. Past the bulk of the bridge was a stretch of river, and past that was the Quayside docks. Without looking at the captain he asked softly, "How far up you figure this to go, sir?"

Kent turned to follow his gaze. For a long time I thought he wasn't going to answer, but then he said, "This isn't like some night shift watch desk taking a few bucks to lose the booking records of a Blind Joker, here. This is serious black magic. Necromancy."

He sighed and went on. "Is Quayside bent? Some are, some aren't, just like cops everywhere. You were on the streets long enough to know how it works. And yeah, that station house has got a reputation. But... in the pocket of some new Bloody Jake? No—I work with those guys all the time. *That* bent, they're not."

"Look," I put in. "Whatever is going on is something that can only happen in the dark. As soon as we break it open, Parliament and the Mayor are going to come down on that town like a demolition charge. This can't be swept under the rug, it's too big and too ugly. We just need to shine a light on it, and it'll be out of our hands."

Bale nodded. "Yeah. Yeah, I see your point."

I left my cruiser in the PNCO lot, and Bale drove us across the bridge in a massive panel van that gave him room to sit comfortably behind the wheel. We didn't talk on the way, both of us thinking our own thoughts.

BETTER OFF DEAD

The damage control has already begun. News of Mr. Quinn's condition couldn't be contained. Hospital workers talked, and this case was too sensational. Stories—carefully phrased as "unconfirmed reports claim"—of human necromantic rituals on the Quayside boardwalk would be in tomorrow's paper. Bloody Jake would be rehashed on the radio talk shows. By the weekend, we would have a circus on the streets. For every honest citizen that would wisely keep his distance there would be three who come crowding down to the river, hoping to catch a glimpse of the new monster.

Pity Quinn would be in the hospital for a long stay. He could make a killing on the streets.

And in locked offices and the back rooms of private clubs, there would be a quieter, more dignified kind of hysteria going on, if not tonight, then soon. Bale was right, of course, a racket of this magnitude needed friends in high places. Those kinds of friends were very fickle, though. Men in those positions didn't get into those positions without knowing when it was time to wash up and present themselves to the press and the people with clean hands. Captain Morgan might get caught up in the storm—he had street smarts, but I didn't peg him as a high-level political operator. Above him?

I could hear it now—heck, I could write those speeches. *We are shocked—absolutely shocked, I tell you—to learn of such nefarious dealings in this fine city. My office is working tirelessly to [conduct an investigation]/[produce legislation]/[install additional safeguards]/[strike out as required] to prevent any such thing from ever happening again...*

Bale's thoughts must have paralleled my own. After he parked his behemoth, he turned to me.

"We hunt ghouls," he said.

"That's the plan," I agreed.

"Let's get this corpse-fucker off the streets." With that, he got out of the truck, and I followed him into the twilight.

The mood was even worse than last night—a lot worse. The streets were almost empty. The only time I'd seen the boardwalk so deserted was during a typhoon warning. The few that remained had the same attitude as those who went out during a storm, too. Tough guys looking to prove that they weren't afraid.

One of the tough guys swaggered up to stand in front of us, sneering. Stanton, the patrol bull who had been with Piscal the other night. He had his nightstick in his hand again, swinging it idly. I wondered if he slept with it, like a security blanket.

I looked around. "Evening, officer. Where's your partner?"

"He's out sick," Stanton sneered.

"You want to be careful out here," Bale said. "It can be rough with no one to watch your back."

"I got plenty of backup," Stanton shot back. "It's you that should be worried."

"Naw," Bale glanced around with deliberate casualness. "I ain't worried. You worried, agent Rugar?"

I shook my head. "I'm just here for a beer and some crabs. Who's got the best crabs in this town?"

"Vlad's. Out by the causeway. But they close early—why don't you come back tomorrow when they're open?"

I was tired of playing games. "You saw that man Quinn when he pulled him out from under the boards, right? If you know anything about that, now's the time to come clean. Tomorrow could be too late."

He looked away, uncomfortable, but he held his ground. "Got nothing to come clean about, *Agent* Rugar. There's nothing going on here that the Mayor needs to get involved with." He shot Bale a quick glance. "Or Pickmantown bulls either."

Bale gave Stanton a long look and seemed about to speak, then just shrugged and headed down the boardwalk. I followed, leaving Stanton twirling his baton. Half a block later, I glanced back over my shoulder and he was still there, gazing out over the river.

"How long do you figure Quinn was under there?" I asked.

"A couple of hours."

I considered the timeline. "So he was put there before midnight."

Bale nodded slowly. "Yeah. Earlier, even. I'd guess he was there no later than twenty-two."

"Plenty of traffic here, then." I thought about it. "We passed through here a couple of times before we found him."

"It had to get quiet," Bale said. "So we could hear him."

I thought about how close I had come to calling it a night when they shut down the bandstand and shuddered.

The warning barricades were still blocking off that section of the boardwalk. We ignored them and studied the businesses. They were all closed now, and I tried to remember which ones had been open last night, and when. We'd made two trips down this way during the evening, before we found Quinn on our last lap.

The fried fish shop had been open on our first pass, around twenty, but had been closed the second time around—I remembered that, because I had been considering a snack. The tattoo parlor, Ghastly Thomas's, had been open on both trips. There had been some unsavory citizens in there, and I kept one eye on the door as we went past. Beside that was a newsstand that had been closed before we arrived, although I recalled them doing brisk business during the day.

Bale was frowning at the window of the tattoo shop. There was an official notice posted in the window saying that the business was closed by order of the Quayside constabulary. Below it was a sign hand-written on cardboard that said, "Moving to New location," but didn't say where the new location was. He turned and looked at the riverside railing, measuring distances with his eyes. I caught his meaning.

I vaulted the rail and shone my light under the boards. Quayside had assured us that their crime scene techs would investigate the scene, but it didn't look to me that anyone had been down there since Bale pulled Quinn out. On the far side of the patch of disturbed sand, I could see the base of the buildings.

"Let me get closer," I said.

"Careful," he cautioned. "I don't want to have to go in there after you."

I crept forward on hands and knees with my light in my teeth. The tracks where Bale drug Quinn out were easy to see, along with smears of dried blood. Beyond that...

"Coming out!" I called.

"Well?" he asked once I was back up, brushing the sand off my suit.

I nodded and pointed. "Yeah, they came through the ink parlor. There's a basement window level with the sand. He was dragged through there."

"You're sure?" he pressed me. "You'll testify to that?"

"Sure enough to get a warrant—" I began, but then the big man smashed the window with his elbow and reached in to unlock the door.

"Or... we could just let ourselves in," I concluded. I could imagine Blackwell's pained expression when he found out about this. There had better be something inside that shop.

Just inside the door, a couple of mismatched couches sat flanked by ashtrays and tables full of photography magazines, and then a waist-high railing with a swinging half door in the middle. I got out my flashlight, but Bale just flipped on the switch by the door.

"I was absent the day they taught subtle," he told me with a tight grin. His gun was out.

I drew mine.

Behind the rail, there were half a dozen makeshift booths with reclining chairs for the clients. Each booth was hung with displays of the artist's work. There was a lot of what the more conservative papers would call "violent imagery." Skulls wreathed in flames, striking snakes, wolves, swords, and battleaxes. The booths were messy, with tools and bottles of ink left out, overflowing ashtrays and empty bottles scattered around.

We swept the place quickly, scanning any space that could have held something close to man-sized. It was empty.

Bale headed to the back, and I followed.

A door led into an office. In sharp contrast to the chaotic clutter of the front room, the office was nearly empty. Too empty.

"Moved out," I suggested.

Bale sifted through the leavings of a spilled ashtray with his shoe. "In a hurry," he added.

Then he kicked savagely, sending up a cloud of ash. "He was *here!* The whole time we were speculating about whether or not he existed, he was *right here.* Probably watching us."

He headed to a door in the back that looked as if it led to the basement.

"Hold up," I said. "Let's call this in first."

He frowned, then nodded.

I called the night desk from the office phone and put in a request for a full background on the Ghastly Thomas Tattoo Shop, and the owner of the building in which it was housed.

"Any employees should be considered persons of interest in the Quinn case," I added. "Get me a list if you can."

"Roger that," the duty constable said. "Do you have the location under observation?"

I paused, considering, then decided to come clean. "We're in the property now, conducting a search. There was compelling evidence."

Drag marks by the window, and a stripped office. That should be enough, but it would be nice if we found something more in the basement.

As soon as I was off the phone, Bale jerked his head towards the back door. I nodded and got in position to cover him when he went through it.

Bale tried the knob and then slammed the door open and stepped back around the corner. I could see a narrow brick shaft with a wooden staircase. No one was in view.

"Pickmantown police," Bale announced. "We *are* coming down there!"

And then he headed down at a trot, his gun up. I gave him a few steps and followed.

There was a bend in the stairwell, so we couldn't see the basement until we reached the bottom. It was dark, only the light that filtered in from upstairs. I clicked on my flashlight with my left hand and held it away from my body, just in case anyone was down there and felt like shooting at cops.

Bale swept the space, with me trying to keep the light ahead of him and not on him. For such a big guy, he moved fast.

"Clear!" he announced, sounding a lot more relaxed and

confident than I felt. Then he added, "I think you need to check this out."

I found a switch beside the door and clicked on some dim overheads, bare bulbs and not enough of them. But it was enough that I could turn off my flash. I looked at what he was pointing at.

"Let me do a hazard assessment," I told him. "Don't touch anything."

My first impression was a hobbyist's lab. A homemade bookcase against one wall held the usual paperback grimoires, *The Red Book, Keys and Windows, The Witch's Dictionary*—books that were illegal because they were dangerous to anyone fool enough to try to use them, as well as anyone in the vicinity. Cheaply printed, full of errors, the kind of trash that was sold wrapped in brown paper out of the back rooms of sleazy bars and gaming clubs.

One table held a makeshift alchemical grid, but the few bottles on it only had dried sludge in the bottoms of them. Copied on one brick wall—in peeling red paint and a very crude style—was a diagram showing the relationship between the Midworld and the Realms of Nightmare. It was accurate, as far as it went, but nothing that you couldn't find in a public library.

A closer look was more disturbing.

There was a calculating engine, a solid commercial model. It was a few years old, but in good condition and wouldn't have looked out of place in a legitimate practitioner's workroom. It would have taken two strong men—and a fair amount of sweat—to get it down those stairs. No doubt whoever had moved out in such a hurry hadn't the time and manpower to get it back up.

Many of the shelves were empty, dust showing where books or tools had stood. The good stuff, I guessed, unlike the junk that had been left behind.

There was a degaussing rack for arthames that was of industrial quality. The blades themselves were gone, but the rack had been properly bolted to the floor with copper bolts for discharging accumulated energy to earth.

"I've seen enough," I said. "Let me call the crime lab."

"What do you make of this?" he asked, gesturing.

154

BETTER OFF DEAD

In the center of the room was one of the big leather chairs the artists upstairs used to seat their clients in for decoration. With some additions.

There were heavy belts bolted to it, affixed in positions to hold someone securely. The leather was black, but still showed darker stains and drips of wax in a variety of colors.

"Out," I told him firmly. "Now."

He obeyed, but slowly, and asked as he plodded up the stairs, "That's where they did the work on Quinn, right? And the others?"

I went up the stairs, shooing him along to get him moving. "Maybe," I admitted. "But we need to get some containment on this whole place, pronto. Then the lab boys can figure out what it's for."

He sped up and I made a beeline for the phone as soon as we were upstairs.

We went outside to wait for the techs. I pulled out the mage's report on Quinn's condition and tried to determine if it could have been done in the basement lab. Assuming the empty shelves had held the right gear, I didn't see any reason that it couldn't. But there were too many unknowns to be sure of anything.

Bale paced and smoked and glared out at the river.

In ten minutes, the first van full of techs from Government House arrived and headed downstairs in white canvas safety suits covered with anti-magic silver stitching. Ten minutes after that, the circus came to town.

Captain Kent was there, along with a half-dozen of his bruisers. A pair of mean-looking characters in expensive suits who identified themselves as agents of the Quayside branch of the Parliamentary Guard. The Quayside Chief of Constables and a cadre of uniforms, although Captain Morgan was conspicuous by his absence. A boatload of armed response officers from the Department of Waterways. A fellow from something called the Riverfront Merchant's Collective Association, which I had never heard of.

And Chief Blackwell, of course, giving me his *I'm not angry, I'm just disappointed* look.

"Talk to me, Rugar," he said, not sounding at all like he wanted to hear what I had to say.

155

I didn't waste time apologizing for getting him out of bed—*again*—I just gave him a fast rundown of what we'd found in Ghastly Thomas's.

He nodded wearily. "Okay, report to Captain Kent. Don't talk to anybody else—especially not the press."

I glanced around quickly. Everyone I saw looked like a cop. "Are they here?"

"They will be." Blackwell rubbed his eyes, looking very old. "Quayside C of C called them."

"At this time of night?"

"He's trying to get ahead of this thing. It's going to blow up in a lot of faces. He wants his spin in the morning editions."

I nodded, then went looking for Captain Kent. Bale had already made his report, of course, so all that I could add was my opinion that the procedures outlined in the report on Mr. Quinn could have been performed in the basement of the tattoo shop, assuming some materials that had subsequently been removed.

It was clear from his reaction that I wasn't telling him anything that he hadn't already guessed.

After that, I kept my head down and used the ghoul squad as cover. They were in full contagion armor—what they called "lizard suits" because the overlapping plates looked like scales. They accepted me, more or less. I wasn't one of their own, but Bale vouched for me, which made me a provisional meat eater as long as I didn't disgrace myself by doing something stupid.

The press arrived, clustering around the Quayside Chief and pestering anyone else who looked important. Then—with timing that couldn't be accidental—the Quayside MP arrived with two limos full of staff and started his own impromptu press conference.

"All we need are acrobats," I told Bale, watching the explosion of flashbulbs ruining everyone's night vision and waking up any of the locals who had slept through the rest. "The clowns are already here."

Then a worried CPS tech in a white lab suit hurried up to talk to Captain Kent. He listened and then waved me over. Bale tagged along.

"Chief Blackwell told me to tell you," the tech said to me, evidently repeating what he'd just told the captain, "that we found a tunnel out of the basement."

"Show me," Kent said. He motioned for all of us—me and the ghoul squad—to follow him. The front entrance was being used as a stage for the C of C and the MP to share the limelight uneasily. There was no way to get inside that way.

"There's a back door," the tech added helpfully and led us down the boardwalk and into an alley. A few of the reporters clustered in front watched us curiously, but their attention was on the bigwigs, who were starting to accuse each other.

The door from the alley was easy to miss, and our attention had been on the office and the basement. One of the CPS staff magi met us as we entered.

"I've isolated the hot spots," he said. "There's nothing active, but a lot of residual."

"Felony unlicensed casting?" I asked.

"Well beyond that," he said. "Class one, easily. Don't touch anything I've got taped."

There was a lot of red and silver tape down in the basement. It might have been easier for the magus to just mark what *wasn't* dangerous. Another tech—sweating in his heavy isolation suit—showed us the tunnel.

It was the bookcase, the one that had been filled with the cheap grimoires and other junk.

Kent shook his head disgustedly. "Secret passage behind the bookcase. This guy really is a penny opera villain."

Then he looked at me. "You up for this?"

I took a deep breath and nodded. "Blackwell told me I'm under your orders, and he told the tech to inform you of the existence of the tunnel. If you want me with you, I'm with you."

"Good man," Kent said. "Bale, make sure we get the agent back to his boss in one piece."

The tunnel was narrow and lined with old brick, probably an old smuggler's tunnel, left over from the days when Quayside was a major port of entry. We had to go single file. Two of Kent's men went first, then Kent, then two more lizard-suited constables, then Bale, then me, then two more covering the rear. I was in the middle of a crowd of armed and armored men, but that didn't make me feel safe.

What had happened here was exactly what the Committee for Public Safety had been formed to prevent—an outlaw magician developing a new technique that we couldn't understand or counter. Necromancy had always been the most heavily regulated and most nearly suppressed branch of the art. For much of our history, it had been outlawed entirely, but it was impossible to prevent criminal research and many of the techniques were too useful. So, it was permitted but discouraged. Necromantic workings were subject to far more regulation and oversight than any other.

It was a necessary policy, but the unintended consequence was that when an underground lab made a breakthrough, the legitimate practitioners worked at a disadvantage playing catch up.

I didn't know the answer. Policy wasn't my department. My department was finding whoever was making citizens into ghoul-slaves and stopping him, by any means necessary.

The tunnel had walls and floor of ancient brick, worn smooth, and stunk of the sea. No doubt it flooded regularly during monsoons. It was more or less straight, and I tried to guess where it was taking us. I didn't know Quayside that well, and all I was sure of was that we were going inland.

Up ahead the tunnel entered a wider space, a natural cavern of some kind.

Light flared then, blue-white and brilliant. Someone had thrown a flare. The first rank charged in to take advantage of the dazzling light, and the rest of us followed more slowly.

It was wide and low, like a parking garage. The walls were mostly dirt, and the ends of roots hung from the ceiling. Only the floor seemed artificial, stone flags cracked and heaved from generations.

Shapes around the walls resolved themselves into trash from the harbor, washed in by floods and caught. Driftwood, bits of sailcloth, rope, shattered barrels. The ghoul hunters fanned out slowly, weapons at the ready.

BETTER OFF DEAD

"Bellville," the captain called to one of his men. "Are we where I think we are?"

Bellville nodded slowly. "Yeah," he said, and pointed at the dirt above our heads. "That's the Morgan Street Cemetery."

I looked up and shivered. In the harsh light of the phlogiston flare, I could see all too clearly and could imagine the thick pale roots above me belonging to the century-old trees that shaded the boneyard. It was an old cemetery, full of mausoleums bearing the names of venerable shipping dynasties.

After the ship my father was working on went down in a hurricane, the main service was held in the Morgan Street Chapel, where the captain's family was laid to rest. The empty casket for the captain was carried into a marble tomb the size of my mother's house.

My father got a plaque on the wall of the Theosophical Reading Room in Leeshore. No matter. The ocean was his headstone.

Bale touched my arm. "You okay?" he asked softly.

"Sure," I said. "I was just thinking. When I was a kid I wanted to be a fisherman like my old man. But my mom convinced me it was too dangerous. So I became a cop instead."

He grinned at that. "Let's find a way out of here."

The others were already working on it. In two-man teams, they moved to the walls, carefully picking their way through the stinking piles of junk.

We found three ways out. Along with the way we came in, they were set at the cardinal points of the compass. The captain chewed it over. I could see he didn't like the idea of leaving unexplored passages behind us, but neither was he willing to split his scant forces.

While he was still considering his options, the dead came out of the walls all around us.

I heard a shout. *"I got cold here—northwest!"*

I looked that way and saw shapes pulling free of the earth, shaking off clods of stinking graveyard mud. They were so caked with filth that they were only vaguely human in outline.

Then more shouts.

"Cold, north!"

They seemed suddenly to be everywhere. A second before, the room had been empty except for us, and now it was teeming with the things.

"Cold, west!"

Waves of stench came off the things, like a fish market dumpster in midsummer.

"COLD!"

"Hold your fire and be sure of your target!" Kent shouted back. "Bale—get the agent clear!"

Bale grabbed my arm and ran for a tunnel—not the one we came in, but the one to the west. It was closer.

I followed, stumbling over the trash. As we entered the tunnel, I heard Kent shout, "Check your zone... and *fire!*"

I went deaf. Those shotguns going off in the little cave was like being punched in the ear. The pain staggered me. My head was ringing—and I didn't even get the worst of it, being a few yards down the tunnel. Bale dragged me on, pointing down the tunnel, which was old brick like the first one.

A blast of stinking air hit me in the back and nearly knocked me off my feet. I tried to turn to look, but Bale hauled me on, mouthing words I couldn't hear and making me scramble to keep up.

We went around a bend in the tunnel and Bale leaned back against the wall, catching his breath. It had gotten very dark, and I got out my flashlight to get a look around. The ringing in my ears still drowned out any noise from behind us.

I leaned around the corner and shone my light back to the cave. It was gone—there was nothing but dirt and mud, scattered here and there with what I hoped were bits of white rock.

Bale saw it, too, and headed back down that way. I grabbed his arm and got dragged a pace before he turned to glare at me.

"There is nothing that you can do," I enunciated very clearly and hoped he could at least read my lips. "We need to get help." I pointed. "That is going to take a work crew to clear. Not two guys with their hands."

He seemed about to shake me off and head down there anyway,

but then the sense of what I was saying penetrated. He gave an exaggerated nod and pointed down the tunnel, away from the collapse.

I nodded back and we hurried that way. We needed to get to the surface and a phone.

The tunnel kept curving, and for a while I was afraid that it was just going to lead back to the collapsed cave under the cemetery, but then I saw light ahead. Red light. Fire light.

A few more yards and I smelled the fire, too. Greasy, smokey, like burned barbecue. The hallway opened up ahead to a big space, lit by some kind of fire pit.

My hearing was better, but still not good enough for whispering, so Bale and I had a quick conversation in gestures—he was going to go straight in, I'd cut to the side once we were through the doorway and cover him.

This cavern had been reinforced with brick pillars and looked as if it had once been a storeroom, probably for illicit goods. Those pillars were the source of both the light and the stench. Human bodies had been chained to the pillars and set alight as grisly torches.

They were still moving, struggling against the chains that bound them and the flames that consumed their bodies.

I made myself look past the macabre display. At the end of the row of burning ghouls was a figure in black. Beneath his broad hat, his face was white. He stood with his back to a mass of red draperies that concealed the far wall of the cave.

The Pale King, I assumed.

Bale advanced, his gun out and pointed at the figure. "I'm going to say this *once*. Get down on the ground, face down, hands behind your back."

The figure threw back his head and gave out with a theatrical cackle.

"Do you think I fear your toys, mortal man? I have traveled beyond life and—"

Bale shot him in the face and his head exploded. The Pale King fell straight back and Bale walked up, fired a second charge into the body's chest and stepped over it to the drapes. He grabbed a handful and pulled, and the rotted cloth came down, revealing a set of wooden stairs leading up.

I stood there stunned.

"I wanted him alive!" I shouted after Bale.

"Oh, we were way too late for that," he told me without turning around. And then he was up the stairs and gone.

I checked the rest of the room, moving slow, gun out. When I got to the Pale King, he had stopped twitching. Bale was right, he had been dead for a long time, months at least. His body was covered with a network of runes carved into his flesh, and under them old tattoos. I turned away from the corpse and to the back of the room. It was time to get out of this hole. Past time.

The stairs led out into an alley, between the back door of a liquor store and the tradesman's entrance of a cheap hotel. There was a payphone in the alley, and Bale was just hanging up when I got to him.

"Search and rescue is already on site at the graveyard. I'm headed there now."

I nodded and he scurried off.

I looked at the phone, considering how to call this in. In the end, I gave dispatch the location of the back door to the crypt and requested a crime scene team for multiple homicides. They told me that Blackwell was still on-site at Ghastly Thomas's, and that he would like to hear from me, soonest. I assured them I was on my way to him.

Walking back to the boardwalk, I wondered how this would all shake out.

Maybe Pickmantown had an opening for a constable. Or a dogcatcher. Or maybe I could buy a pushcart somewhere.

Blackwell didn't want a report. He just took my gun and badge, locked them in the truck of his car, and told me not to talk to anyone until I saw the mayor's solicitors.

One of Kent's men—Thadd Gren—died before they could get him dug out. Two others left the force on disability retirement. The rest, including Kent himself, escaped with minor injuries and are all back on duty.

BETTER OFF DEAD

They were able to identify the self-styled Pale King by his old tattoos, the ones he got before he started using his own body for necromantic research. He turned out to be Helmut Venner, a graduate student in Advanced Alchemy at the Dracoheim Academy. About two years ago he had shown up at an emergency room showing signs of a ghoul attack. He'd been treated and told to come back for the antitoxin, but had missed the appointment. The clinic had been unable to reach him, and had closed the file.

Investigators weren't able to find out much about Venner. He'd been a loner, without any friends that we could locate. One of his instructors admitted, "I didn't even realize he'd dropped out of my class until I was totaling the end-of-term grades. He just... wasn't somebody you noticed."

Kind of sad really. Nobody paid attention to him until after he died.

CPS techs dug through the rubble of the cave-in and the tunnels around it for months. When they were finished, the Lord Mayor ordered two buildings condemned, at once, and wasn't taking no for an answer.

Whatever they found, they locked in a vault and threw away the key. I never even heard a whisper.

Kenny Tsing was picked up in Hunger City for unlawful entry into Nivose and deported. He was interrogated by CPS when he returned to Dracoheim and made some kind of deal—sealed testimony in exchange for reinstating his import/export license. We keep a very close eye on him these days.

As for me, I got a week off—which stretched into two—for an investigation into my part in the mess. In the end I was cleared, and I went back to work with a nice tan.

Bale's investigation was a lot rougher than mine, but in the end he was not only cleared, but given a commendation.

Captain Morgan of the Quayside Constables disappeared. Even money whether he's laying low in the Territories or in a concrete-filled barrel in the bay.

No one else was publicly implicated. Quayside constables had a "personnel restructuring" that involved a couple of watch commanders being invited to pursue careers in the private sector, but they closed ranks and kept the press out of their dirty laundry.

The press had plenty to say about the case. Dracoheim went ghoul-crazy for weeks. A couple of old plays about Bloody Jake were revived to sellout crowds. A full-orchestra musical about the Pale King is in production. I don't know if they have anyone lined up to play me.

It died down in time. It always does. This is a big city, and easily distracted. Nothing stays sensational for long. Even the tattoo shop reopened, under new management. The artists who rented space there were cleared of any involvement in Venner's activities. Privately, I had my doubts, and kept my eye on the place.

Just in case.

Anton Quinn was released from the hospital and is back on the boardwalk. I stop by when I'm in the area.

After we were both back at work, I called Bale and we checked our duty rosters and eventually came up with a night when we both were free to get together for a few drinks.

I steered Bale through the bar at the Empire Hotel like I was a tugboat towing a barge until I spotted the booth I wanted. The girls were already there, glasses of something sparkling on the table, looking like a pair of dreams—the good kind that people with clear consciences have.

"Ladies," I said. "I'm Erik Rugar, and this is..." I paused, trying to remember if I'd ever heard his first name. "...Officer Bale, of the Pickmantown Ghoul Squad."

Bale shot me a look that told me I would pay for this later. "Josef," he said. "Josef Bale. Call me Joe."

"Hi, Joe," the tall one said. I had told Miss Kitten's that I wanted a date for a big man, and they had sent a blonde amazon in a blue cocktail dress. She offered an elegant hand with silver nails. "I'm Audrey."

"And you're Darla," I said to the curvy little redhead sitting beside her. She was even cuter in person. "I'm glad to finally meet you."

She smiled at me, and we took our seats.

BETTER OFF DEAD

"Ladies," I announced, "this is the man who took down the Pale King of Quayside in single combat. A genuine hero—a necromancer slayer."

The girls looked impressed.

Bale sighed deeply. "It wasn't like that—"

I cut him off. "Shut up, I'm telling this story."

"If I have to listen to you telling lies, I'm going to need a cider," Bale said, getting up.

"Get a pitcher," I suggested.

Then I turned back to the lovely ladies. "See, it all started with this pushcart man named Quinn..."

Materials Science

Intersession

"Magus, I think I must be doing this wrong."

Leonid looked up from his daydreaming. He had plans with Eleanor that evening. He'd managed to secure reservations for The Satrap's Yacht. Technically, of course, it wasn't a yacht, it was a motor launch, which Eleanor pointed out pedantically when he'd shown her the tickets.

But she'd been smiling when she said it. The six-hour evening cruises—Summerisle to Blackrock Island and back—on the elegantly appointed vessel were the season's hottest attraction. Dinner and dancing under the stars, champagne at midnight, a respite from Dracoheim's oppressive heat and humidity. Scoring the tickets had been a coup, made possible by a former student who was now a managing director at one of the larger refineries.

Reluctantly, Leonid pulled his mind away from reveries of Eleanor's long-limbed frame clutched close to his as the music played, and turned his attention to his student. At the moment, the two of them were the only ones in the lab.

"Let's take a look, shall we?" he said.

The student—a third-year young man named Garner—had his bench well organized. The material sample was mounted in the pressure rig properly, with the stamped numbers facing outward. The graph sheets that Garner was using to record changes in flux were neatly lettered and the sample numbers matched. The three thaumic resonators were arranged in an equilateral triangle around the pressure rig. The young man's personal items—book bag, coffee cup, jacket—were neatly stowed on the next bench over, not cluttering up his workspace.

"Everything seems to be in order," Leonid said approvingly.

"But these numbers are impossible," Garner objected.

"'Impossible' is word we don't use in the craft," Leonid said automatically, then looked at the proffered chart. "Oh," he said, once

166

the figures had registered. "That *can't* be right."

Leonid—Magus Vetch to his students—had been awarded tenure last year, and with tenure came a stipend for research. He had arranged to test a collection of new orelchium alloys for thaumic properties. The Ferose embassy provided the alloy samples, in exchange for graphs of the data. Leonid would be able to publish his findings in the Journal of Gnoetic Materials Science. His students— six of them had applied for positions, and he took all of them— would get a pittance for their work but end the term with paid lab experience, which would help in getting their first jobs in the industry.

The work itself was spectacularly dull. The alloys were all mildly reactive, and their task was to determine how the reactivity changed in response to environmental factors. At the moment, they were testing tensile stress. The samples were placed in calibrated vises and squeezed.

Write down the numbers on all three thaumic resonators in the spaces provided on the chart.

Tighten the vise on the material to five pounds.

Write down the new numbers from the thaumic resonators.

Tighten the vise to ten pounds.

Write down those numbers.

Tighten the vise to fifteen pounds... and so on.

At one hundred pounds, the students would slowly release the tension, remove the material and replace it in its numbered box, get a new sample, write the sample number on a new set of forms, and begin again, generally after a short break for a cigarette, a cup of coffee, and a walk around the lab.

The flux numbers were calculated by comparing the readings from the resonators. Applying that formula was the most demanding part of the process. The resulting graphs were nearly flat, with a change of two to five percent across the bottom axis.

This chart was different.

At fifty pounds, the flux jumped from .035 (t) to 2.85 (t). Then at fifty-five, it jumped again, to 7.35 (t). At sixty, it went to 22.65 (t). At sixty-five, it registered 47.85 (t), which was well out of the "mildly reactive" category. If these numbers were accurate, then this particular alloy became a usable magical source when subjected to pressure.

But those numbers *couldn't* be right.

Leonid examined the thaumic resonators. The scale was set properly, and they read what Garner had written down.

"Crank it back down to zero," Leonid told the young man.

The dials on the resonators dropped precipitously as the student turned the crank.

They ran through the procedure, and the numbers matched. At forty-five pounds, Leonid said, "Take it to forty-six."

They increased at one-pound intervals. The increase in flux was slow at first but then began to rise. By the time they reached sixty-eight pounds, they were reading a flux of 77.40 (t).

Leonid stopped Garner and went to his briefcase to fetch his ocular. 75 (t) was the lower limit of visual detection.

Sure enough, viewed through the ocular, the sample was surrounded by a faint blue halo.

"Crank it down and give me that sample," Leonid said. "You can get started with the next one in the series."

The sample was a metal cylinder the size of a soup can. The designation stamped across the face of it read "OR/MHL/FE/028874".

He glanced at it through the ocular. Without the pressure, it was inert. He stuck it in his jacket pocket. "I'll be back in a few," he told Garner.

He headed for the door, then stopped and went back to collect the boy's charts for the material.

Two eighty-eight seventy-four, he thought. *You are going to make somebody very wealthy. Pity it's not likely to be me.*

Kravitz Welsh, the dean of magic, wasn't in his office. Leonid found him in the office of Dr. Bink, the president. Good, both of them should know about this, and it would save time to go over it once.

"Leo," Dr. Bink said brightly. "We were just going over the catalog for the fall term. You wouldn't mind an evening lecture, would you?"

"No, of course not," Leonid said distractedly. Then added, "What is it?"

"Intro to Notation," Welsh said. "Twodays and Fourdays, nineteen to twenty-one. Basic stuff, just symbol set and graphing. I'll get you the book, and the syllabus is already worked out. I had it down for Schuyler, but he's got a new baby and doesn't want to be out in the evenings if he doesn't have to be."

"Sure, that's fine," Leonid said. "Look, I've run across something peculiar in my materials study I wanted to show you."

He laid the chart out on the president's desk. Magus Welsh studied it for a moment.

"He changed the setting," Welsh suggested. "Turned the scale up. It's easy to do, he probably just bumped it."

"That's what I thought," Leonid said. "But I reran the sequence with him." He pointed to the second chart. "We're looking at a significant change in potential across the pressure spectrum."

Welsh frowned down at the paper. "Where's the sample now?"

Leonid pulled it from his pocket. "I have it. I'm going to run a full workup on it, pressure, temperature, light."

Welsh nodded slowly. "Use the high energy lab," he said. "And lock that sample in your office when you don't have it on the bench. Just in case."

Dr. Bink looked from Leonid to Welsh and back again. "I'm missing something," he said. "Remember, I'm not a wizard."

"It might be nothing," Leonid said. "Like Dean Welsh says, it's probably an instrumentation error."

"Okay," Dr. Bink said patiently. "But suppose it isn't." He waved his hand at the chart. "What's significant about this?"

"It could turn out to be a very valuable alloy," Leonid said.

Welsh picked up the explanation. "What these numbers suggest is that one of the alloys that Leo is testing is strongly transitive, which means that it can be used to convert mechanical energy to thaumic flux, or vice versa. That's what makes orelchium so valuable. Now, the alloys you're testing are what, five percent active materials?"

169

"This series is three percent," Leonid said.

"As opposed to...?" Dr. Bink asked.

"Most of the strong transitives are around seventy-five percent orelchium," Leonid said. "There are some usable alloys for certain application as low as sixty."

Dr. Bink chewed this over. "So... what we have here—*potentially*—is a material that can do that with one-twentieth of the orelchium?"

"*Potentially,* yes," Welsh agreed.

"What would something like that be worth, do you suppose?" Dr. Bink asked.

"Millions," Leonid answered quickly. "The cost of transitive materials is a significant percentage of the cost of any metaclockwork mechanism. It would revolutionize the industry."

Dr. Bink stared at him, as if he suspected he was being put on. "Yes, you better keep that locked up," he said at last. "And do a full materials test right away."

"We'll want to see that data," Welsh added quickly, "but don't share it with anyone else."

Leonid nodded. He'd expected that.

"This isn't our material, technically," Dr. Bink said. "It's on loan from the embassy, for purposes of research. We'll have to inform them of our findings."

"Not until it's complete," Welsh said. "At the moment, we have nothing definite to share."

"But why would they send us something like that?" Dr. Bink wondered aloud. "They must know what it's worth."

"Because it's not valuable over there," Leonid explained. "Ferose has different cosmological constants, and materials have different properties. That's why they have to be tested in the Midworld, to find out how they operate here."

"Ah." A light went on behind the president's confused expression. "So, it would only work in export items."

"Which is a huge chunk of Ferose's production," Welsh pointed out. A thought struck him. "Leo, can you extrapolate the properties of the material for Nivose constants?"

"Not accurately," Leonid said. "I mean, I can give you a projection, but it's only an educated guess until we can test a sample under native conditions."

Welsh considered that. "Well, run your sequence and let us know how it turns out, okay?"

Leonid picked up the papers and left.

He stopped to check in with Garner.

"This one's coming out right," the student said without looking up from his papers. "The graph looks like all the others."

"I'm going to run this sample again," Leonid told him. "It may be contaminated with impurities."

"From Ferose?"

"It happens," Leonid assured him. "Even the forged ones can make mistakes."

"As long as it's not me," Garner said.

"No, you're doing fine. I'm going to run this down to another lab. If you need anything, the dean's in the office."

"I'm good," Garner said. "I think Stackhouse is coming in later."

Leonid checked the posted schedule. "He should be in already. Tell him to write in what time he actually gets here, okay?"

"Will do, magus."

The High Energy Evocation Facility—which students and faculty alike nicknamed "the Boom Room"—was kept secured at all times when it was not in use. The lock was not on the building master key, and keys were issued only to the qualified magi on the staff. Leonid had one, because he occasionally had assisted magus Winter with evocation labs, but didn't use it often.

Evocation was flashy, fireballs and lightning bolts. It was the kind of magic that impressed the students—what they expected from listening to the exploits of Magus Crimson, Warchief Smith's lieutenant on *Days of the Founders*.

Leonid found it vulgar, but that might have been jealousy. Artificers built the infrastructure that made industrial magic possible. They were responsible for the power that lit the city, the fuel that kept the trucks moving and food in the supermarkets, the machines that did the work.

171

But it wasn't *sexy*. No one ever said, "Oh, you're a wizard? Let me see you plot a thaumic flux decay curve for resonance over time—that's so cool!"

No matter. The high energy lab did have a perfectly serviceable test bench, and it was the most secure location on the campus. Leonid grabbed what he'd need from his office and set up the experiment.

Before he began work, he checked the accumulators and frowned. There was a charge he couldn't account for. After a moment's thought, he went to the back of the room and examined the sandboxes. Three four-foot square areas, filled with sand, six inches deep. Two were properly raked smooth, but the third was partially covered by a dozen symbols.

Another reason to dislike evocators—they had a reputation for being sloppy. That should have been discharged and erased at the end of the last term.

He squatted by the pit, examining the symbols left in the sand. Open kefs and a spiral theta with an inverted rho. The beginning of an energy transference invocation. Even inactivated, it had been left long enough to gather a vicious charge. He got up and fetched a long wooden pole wrapped in insulating wire. Carefully, he drew the last few symbols in the sand and completed the circuit.

The sand erupted into flame, and he stepped back quickly, watching the power burn itself out. When the flames died down the sand was perfectly smooth and level.

He replaced the pole and made a mental note to tell the dean about this. Then he got to work.

Over the next two hours, he came to know alloy two eighty-eight seventy-four intimately. The transitive properties were every bit as powerful as the initial tests had suggested. The graph resembled most strongly an alloy marketed under the name of Blue Ice Flux but used only a fraction of the orelchium. The mechanical properties were good for industrial use as well, a melting point high enough to take hard use in a gearbox but not so high as to make working it difficult. It was strong enough for most applications—not as hard as steel, but then, it didn't have to be.

MATERIALS SCIENCE

It was photoreactive, but not unduly so. It conducted electricity better than any other transitive substance Leonid had heard of, which was useful in some applications, a drawback in others.

He wondered if whoever eventually manufactured it in quantity would name it after him. Vetch's Metal, after all, was a much better name than Two Eighty-eight Seventy-four. It would look much better in the advertisements.

Manufactured using Vetch's Metal, the new miracle alloy!

Despite his absorption, he made sure to keep a close eye on the clock. He gave himself enough time to summarize his findings on one page, put away his equipment and lock the sample in the hazardous materials safe in his office.

"This is what I have so far," he told Welsh. "It'll take another day to produce a full materials and applications brief."

Welsh nodded and accepted the sheet. He had several books open on his desk, including both volumes of *The Modern Cyclopedia of Metals and their Properties* and Traal's classic (if somewhat antique) *On the Exporting of Ensorcerelled Items*.

"Any thoughts on how it will function in Nivose?"

"Impossible to say for certain, of course, without testing a sample over there," Leonid hedged, "but I think it's likely that the properties will remain constant. Alloys with a similar flux graph tend to keep that behavior in Nivose." He paused for thought. "Probably in Messidor as well, actually, since there is no silver in the mixture."

Welsh studied the sheet. "Very good."

"Now if you will excuse me...?"

Welsh looked up. "Oh, yes, of course. Enjoy your evening. Check in with me here tomorrow before you head into the lab, right?"

"Will do, boss."

Eleanor wore a blue gown trimmed with white fur. She looked like a queen, and Leonid, in a simple black suit that she had bullied him into having tailored, was proud to be her knight. He did not think of himself as a wealthy man, but that night he tipped like a millionaire, and the staff of the Satrap's Yacht treated them accordingly.

He told her about the sample he had discovered—not the technical details, which wouldn't interest her, just that he might have uncovered something valuable.

"Dean Welsh keeps asking about its possible properties in Nivose, so I suppose someone will have to take a sample there for testing. One could replicate the cosmological constants with an apportation field, of course, but that would get dreadfully expensive. Cheaper to simply go there."

"Oh, make them send you!" Eleanor exclaimed. "And I'll go with you."

Leonid laughed. "It would hardly be a vacation."

"It could be!" Eleanor insisted. "We'll have them get you a suite in Hunger City, and while you're puttering about in the lab, I'll go shopping."

"I doubt the board would approve that."

"The board doesn't have to know," Eleanor leaned close. "Please, dearest, I'm ever so ancient, and I've never been abroad. Not once."

Leonid raised his hands in surrender. "I will do what I can. I can deny you nothing." He sighed. "I expect that they'll just send a sample from Ferose and have it worked up in a local facility."

"But moreau can't do magic. They'll need you."

"You don't have to do magic to run bench tests," he pointed out. "And there are plenty of human magi living abroad. I considered it once myself, you know."

She nodded. He meant after his late wife Annalise had died.

"Well, I, for one, am glad that you stayed here," she said. "Have you digested sufficiently to take me to the ballroom? I simply must dance."

"Your wish is my command, my lady."

Later, much later, Leonid lingered on the front porch of her rooming house but declined her offer of a nightcap with real regret.

"I mustn't," he told her. "Not tonight. I have to be in the lab early tomorrow."

"My dedicated man," she said with a smile. "Take me with you to Hunger City; we'll have orange liqueur cocktails for breakfast, and you can dress me all in furs."

"First, I must dazzle the board with my brilliant bench work."

She made a shooing motion. "Off with you then. Be dazzling."

He kissed her—long enough to scandalize the neighbors, if any had still been awake—then got into his car, the sparse traffic on the Quayside Bridge, a quiet neighborhood in Centerburg, and his lonely bed, in that order.

The next morning, he saw Dean Welsh crossing the parking lot.

"Eager to get to work?" The dean grinned.

"I should be able to wrap it up today."

"Excellent. Get me the findings soonest, then?"

"Of course. Have the custodian unlock my lab for the boys, will you?"

"Certainly."

"And could you check in on them sometime this morning? They know the procedure, but..."

Welsh smiled. "I know how students are. I will ensure they are properly monitored to forestall any horseplay."

Leonid locked himself in the Boom Room and, for the next few hours, lost himself in the work. The precision was soothing, and underneath it was the growing excitement of knowing that he was seeing something that no one had ever seen before. The sample had been made in a factory abroad, packaged, sent on a ship, unloaded, put in the back of a truck, unloaded again, handled, and carried by dozens of men and oneiroi, and, at last, delivered to his lab, but now he, Magus Leonid Vetch, was learning secrets that no one else in the Ten Realms knew.

The thrill of hermetic knowledge had drawn Leonid into the study of magic in the first place, so many years ago, but the economic reality of making a living doing magic had leeched the wonder out of the craft. It had become a job—a good job, to be sure, one that provided professional satisfaction and a comfortable living and the respect of his peers—but a job nonetheless.

At long last, he was doing something more than following a procedure that had been worked out by other wizards long ago or shepherding students through an experiment with all the variables controlled and the result known in advance.

This was *basic research*, by the Dragon! And while it might have seemed on the surface that all he was doing was writing down numbers and marking lines on a graph, Leonid felt that he was interrogating the great formless chaos of the cosmos itself and forcing it to reveal its mysteries.

It was a good feeling, and he was rather let down when, by early afternoon, he was forced to conclude that his bench work was complete, and it was time to write up his notes for the dean and Dr. Bink and—eventual—publication.

He ended up retyping the manuscript three times, cursing his clumsy fingers, with the latest edition of the *Handbook of Gnoetic Materials* open beside him so he could be sure to follow the accepted format perfectly. The report came to six pages, three typewritten and three carefully inked graphs. He got up to take it to the dean, then paused and took his earlier attempts out of his office trashcan.

"Can't be too careful," he muttered.

He folded the paper together and wrote a circle of symbols on the blank side of the outside sheet, then set them on his desk. He watched as the paper turned yellow and flaked away into dust, then into nothing at all. Now the only evidence of his work was the pages in his hand.

Welsh was impressed with his findings. "Let's take this to the president."

Dr. Bink studied the report. It was clear that he'd been cramming on materials science, at least enough to make sense of the graphs.

"This is the genuine article, then?"

"Yes, sir," Leonid agreed readily.

Dr. Bink looked over at Dean Welsh, who nodded and said, "Leo, the college would like to send you to Nivose to run the spectrum of material tests on this sample. The Dracoheim Academy maintains a facility in Hunger City, and they'll loan us lab space for a few days."

"Really?" Leonid was surprised. Despite his banter with Eleanor, he hadn't expected them to go that far.

"We think this is significant," Welsh went on. "We can apport you to their facility tomorrow."

"Oh, I wouldn't," Leonid said quickly.

"Wouldn't what?" Dr. Bink asked.

"I wouldn't advise apporting an untested alloy."

"What's the harm in that?"

"Well, it could explode," Leonid pointed out.

"Bosh!" Welsh said. "The risk is minimal."

Leonid ignored him. "It's a matter of altering the exothermic profile," he told Dr. Bink, tapping one of the graphs. "Apportation alters the cosmological constants suddenly, and that can lead to instability on a molecular level. Not always, of course, but it's possible. On a dreamsea passage, the change is gradual, and I can monitor the heat signature for any anomalies." He grinned. "I can dump it over the side if the box starts smoldering."

Dr. Bink looked from one magus to the other, clearly back out of his depth.

"It's like citrus in Verdemaire," Leonid concluded.

"Oh, *that!*" Welsh rolled his eyes.

To Dr. Bink's confused expression, Leonid explained, "Citric acid becomes unstable under Verdemairean conditions. It can be shipped in, but if you apport citrus fruit to Verdemaire, it explodes on arrival." He gave Welsh a glance. "It's a proven fact."

Dr. Bink turned to Welsh. "Is that true? Oranges... *blow up* if you apport them to Verdemaire?"

"Yes, it's true." Welsh gave a deep sigh. "But that's an organic substance with a complex deep structure. A bar of metal is a completely different situation."

"It's a quantity of a transitively reactive material. Until it is tested for native properties it is simply not safe to apport," Leonid said. This was his area of expertise, and they both knew it. "The Ferose embassy didn't apport it here, did they?"

"No," Dr. Bink agreed. "The samples were on a cargo ship."

Leonid turned his attention back to Welsh. "I can take a commercial liner and be in Hunger City in two days. Figure three days in the lab, then the return trip—I'll be back in under a week."

"I don't like this," Welsh said. "That sample is too valuable to risk on a cruise ship."

"I'll lock it in the purser's safe," Leonid assured him. "Besides, nobody will know what it is. Certainly no one in Nivose."

"Make sure of that," Welsh said sternly. "Magical industrial espionage is a major factor in moreau technology. They can't do magic on their own—they have to steal it."

"Or trade for it," Leonid argued. Then he raised his hands in surrender. "I get your point. Mum's the word, I promise. And the sample will be locked up. The ship's safe, and the hotel safe when I get to Hunger City."

"We can assume the Academy's testing facility is secure," Dr. Bink put in. "I think the risk is minimal."

Welsh seemed inclined to argue the point further but nodded reluctantly. "It'll have to do."

"I'll have Mrs. Barden book your accommodations," Dr. Bink decided. "Can you leave tomorrow?"

"Sure, provided someone can ride herd on my students."

"I'll make sure your lab has coverage," Welsh said.

Leonid went back to his lab. There were four of the six students there now, all of them actually getting work done. He explained to them that he was going abroad for a week, but that Dean Welsh would be available to help them and make sure their hours were recorded for the stipend payments.

By noon, he had his travel itinerary from the president's secretary. He had a ticket for the liner *The Luck of Jack Ketch*, registered out of Pluviose, departing from the Marsh Parish docks at 1000 tomorrow. There was a suite reserved for him at The Trapper's Rest, on Telegraph Square in Hunger City. The Nivose Testing Hall of the Dracoheim Academy for Thaumaturgical Studies would be expecting him and make a materials lab available.

Leonid read the paper over several times, unable to quite believe it.

Then he went up to his office to call Eleanor.

"Darling, were you serious about wanting to go to Nivose with me?"

"Absolutely serious." A pause. "Why? Is it going to happen?"

"Tomorrow at 1000."

"Tomorrow!"

"I know it's very sudden, and I'll understand—"

"Where must I be? And for how long should I pack?"

"Well, if you're sure..."

"Leonid Vetch, if this is a prank you will regret it for the rest of your short and agonizing life!"

"I'll need to buy your ticket—they are only providing one. I'll do that now, and I'll pick you up at..." he considered. "800 tomorrow. Pack for a week."

"You wouldn't play with me, would you? You know that would crush me. We are really going abroad?"

"On *The Luck of Jack Ketch*, tomorrow at 1000. Two days each way, then three or four in Hunger City. I'll be busy during the days, testing this damned sample, but we can go out at night. You'll be terribly bored."

"I will not."

"And it won't disrupt your affairs here in the city?"

"It's the intersession, you fool. The only affair I have in this city is you."

"Then I will see you tomorrow at 800."

"Oh, you magnificently clever man. You must have truly dazzled them."

"I supposed I must have."

He left the college, pleading the necessity of packing for his voyage, and headed down to Marsh Parish. He had no difficulty buying a cabin passage for Eleanor and switching his ticket to a dual occupancy. At a luggage shop near the docks, he purchased a small but stout travel case, iron-bound oak and with a solid lock. The sample fit neatly inside, cushioned with a horsehair-stuffed pillow that the luggage merchant also sold him.

Then he packed his best suit, his second-best suit, and some dungarees suitable for lab work. After some thought, he added his formal robe and sash—in Dracoheim, he wore it only for graduation, but as a wizard of the Academy visiting a foreign land, it might be called for. The moreau, forbidden by their nature from working the

179

hermetic mysteries, expected a certain formality from practitioners of the craft.

He slept poorly that night.

He wasn't worried about the job he was being sent to do—that was simple, well within the capability of any competent lab worker. There was no technical reason to send a magus, and he assumed that the president and the dean just wanted to be able to put the name of one of their professors on the articles that would come from the work.

It was Eleanor. He was sure that she would be disappointed. This was, after all, just a business trip. Well, she was a grown woman, and he'd explained the situation. If she was bored, she'd have no one but herself to blame.

She was waiting on the front porch in a smart charcoal suit and a heavy brown traveling cloak, a suitcase beside her. She hurried up as soon as she saw his car, not giving him time to get out and open her door.

"Oh, do let's go," she said, after she leaned over to give him a peck on the cheek.

He glanced back at her suitcase, which she had slung casually into the back seat.

"Is that all you're bringing?" he asked. "You said you wanted to do some shopping."

"I am sure they sell luggage in Hunger City."

Leonid left his car with an attendant, paying the fee and adding a hefty tip. Then they took the trolley to the dock itself. The chaos was impressive, with passengers streaming in all directions, but they managed to find the proper berth with luggage intact and—after some scrutiny of both their tickets and their identification—they were allowed to board.

The Luck of Jack Ketch was a modern Pluviose liner. Below the waterline, it looked like mercury frozen in the act of flowing; but it was a passenger liner, and the upper decks were designed for air-breathers. Leonid and Eleanor followed a human purser to their stateroom to stow their bags.

"I need to store this in the ship's safe," Leonid said, hefting the wooden lockbox.

"Oh, is that the magical metal?" Eleanor leaned forward. "May I see it?"

Leonid obediently opened the box to display the alloy cylinder.

"Doesn't look like much, does it?" he asked.

"No..." she agreed, thoughtfully. "But it could be worth a lot, right?"

"Millions, potentially."

"Best get it locked up, then." She smiled. "I'll be up on deck. This is so exciting!"

It took Leonid longer than he expected to find a ship's officer who was willing to take possession of the sample and give him a receipt, and when he returned to the uppermost deck, the ship was in motion, the alchemical engines leaving a wake of oddly colored bubbles.

Eleanor was on the uppermost deck, watching the city recede. When she saw Leonid, she pulled him close.

"Oh, you clever man. How did I find such a wizard?"

He looked away, blushing. "I'm really just a lab tech. It's nothing special."

Just then an amplified voice sounded across the decks. "Attention passengers. Our navigational magi have determined that we are now cleared to begin our transit. Please be advised that directly observing the interstitial space may cause disorientation. Should you feel confused or overwhelmed sit down where the sky is not in your direct field of vision and the sensation should soon pass. If you feel acute mental distress, signal a purser for relief."

Eleanor's eyes were on the sky—still blue and clear. Quietly she asked, "What do they mean by acute mental distress?"

Leonid shrugged. "It can be disturbing for an unprepared mind. In rare cases, it can cause your brain to explode."

She sneaked a quick glance at him, then faced the sky again. "You're a beast."

He mock-pouted. "I thought I was a clever wizard."

"You're both." She chuckled. "My house mother in school warned all the girls against dating a magus. She insisted that the study of magic inclined men to unnatural passions."

"I don't have unnatural passions," Leonid protested.

"I know. It's been such a disappointment."

Leonid opened his mouth but couldn't think of anything to reply.

Then Eleanor shushed him. The sky was melting.

It was as if the blue—with the faintest scrim of white clouds—had been painted on a pane of glass and the paint was running off, showing another sky. A night sky, a purple so deep that it made black look gray, with pinpoints of brilliant white exploding and fading away.

And it was... bigger. Somehow it seemed to dwarf the Midworld's sky. There was a sense of vast gulfs of space, as if the Midworld itself was just a stage set, a backdrop to some theatrical performance; and that, at long last, the curtain had gone down, and the audience left the theater to see—for the first time—the whole of the world outside.

Leonid leaned close. "What you're seeing is the coruscation of eigenstates as they actualize—" he began, gesturing at the stars winking into and out of existence overhead.

She cut him off. "Oh, be quiet. I don't want to know, and I wouldn't understand it anyway. It's... *magnificent.*"

Leonid shut up. He stood beside her and watched her watching the sky.

After a long time, she spoke softly. "It's not cold. It *looks* cold, but I don't *feel* cold."

She looked over at Leonid. He shrugged and mimed zipping his mouth closed.

That got a laugh. "Let's go inside, wizard, and see if they are serving dinner yet."

Leonid glanced at his watch. "Lunch, maybe."

"Hush."

The found the dining room and their table. They were seated with Chad and Bett, a moreau couple returning from honeymooning in the Midworlds.

Chad had recently been awarded the title of savant from the Royal University and worked as a mechanical engineer in Nivose's infant motor car industry. To Leonid's eyes, they looked like pigs walking upright, with human arms and legs. Or maybe humans with the heads of pigs. But he knew he was doing them an injustice. Moreau weren't a mix of human and beast. Their ancestors had been beasts, given intelligence by the will of the Grimm, Lord of Nivose, tens of thousands of years ago. They were the product of a civilization older than Leonid's.

If Eleanor found their companions strange, she gave no sign. She introduced herself and Leonid, proudly using his title, which impressed the others.

Chad gave him a speculative look. With deliberate casualness he said, "Bett and I toured the Blackstone-Tate Pavilion of Wizardry at Regent's Park."

Leonid smiled. "How was that? I've been meaning to go, but I haven't found the time."

"Not what I expected," Chad admitted with a chuckle. "I guess we've got a pretty, uh, romanticized view of human magic in Nivose."

Leonid waggled his fingers. "Alaka-zoo! Alaka-zam!"

Chad nodded. "Yeah, like that."

"It's changed a lot since I was a kid," Leonid observed. "There were still a few old school practitioners when I was in the Academy, robes and staves and daggers, long white beards, all that. But it's really just another branch of engineering now."

During the meal, Eleanor became fast friends with Bett. By the time dessert arrived, it had been decided that the two would go shopping together in Hunger City. Chad gave Leonid an amused glance over his wife's head, and Leonid shrugged and smiled back. He was amused, but not surprised, that Eleanor had found a native guide so quickly. She was good with people.

Bett advised them to retire early, because of the time change. The ship's clocks showed the time in both Dracoheim and Hunger City, which were currently about six hours apart.

"At midnight, they change official ship's time," she explained. "So, midnight goes straight to quarter past six in the morning. It wasn't so bad the other way 'round, but it's confusing no matter what."

"Especially because it's always night out here between worlds," Chad added.

The next day *was* disorienting. Leonid woke in what his body told him was morning and the clocks claimed was early afternoon, while the sky above insisted it was midnight. He was glad that he would be called upon to do nothing more strenuous than join Eleanor for a lunch that felt like breakfast and a dinner that felt like lunch. Eleanor seemed to adapt to the time change effortlessly, which she credited to working rotating shifts when she had been a nurse at Angel Street Hospital.

Despite having been up for only a few hours, he was ready to retire when the ship's clocks said it was evening. Transition to Nivose would occur the next morning.

Whatever "morning" currently meant.

When the ship's speakers announced that they were cleared for transition, Leonid was on the observation deck with Eleanor and the moreau couple. Again, the sky melted, the deep purple of the dreamsea fading into a pale dawn over the still waters of the Nivose ocean, with the lights of Hunger City glowing on the horizon.

It was breathtaking.

After a long moment, Chad broke the silence. "I'll take you to your hotel."

"Oh," Leonid said automatically, "I wouldn't want to trouble you. You must be anxious to get home."

"No trouble at all," Chad insisted. "It's on our way."

Bett put a plump pink hand on his arm. "He's been dying to show off his car to a real human wizard. It's the very latest model."

Leonid smiled, "Well, in that case, we accept. Thank you."

Hunger City was an architectural kaleidoscope, sprawled across the coastline. Even from a distance the different styles of building—reflecting the different bodies of the builders—gave the impression of a patchwork quilt.

Bett pointed. "That tower there is the Gleamer's Watch. Just past it is Oakshire, where we live."

"Good to be going home?" Eleanor asked.

"Oh, it's been a lovely trip. Dracoheim is an amazing city," Bett said, then looked out over the water to Hunger City. "But, yes. It's good to be home."

"Attention all disembarking passengers. Please ensure that you have collected your possessions. We will be docking in approximately thirty minutes," the speakers announced.

"Time to get organized," Chad said. "Wait for us at the passenger pickup lane. I'll collect the car and meet you there."

"Thank you again," Leonid said, offering his hand. Then he rushed to the purser's office in time to collect the sample from the safe while Eleanor collected their bags.

***

At ground level, the city's patchwork came alive. Leonid and Eleanor came down the gangplank from the ship and into a mad profusion of shapes and sizes. Moreau filled the streets, from fox-faced ones the size of schoolchildren to furred behemoths like bulls on their hind legs. At first glance, every one seemed different, but on closer inspection, tribes or clades became apparent. Leonid forced himself not to think of them as a menagerie. They were all moreau, all *people*, walking upright and wearing clothes and all contributing to the din of mingled voices.

Other species—humans, incubi, chigoes, forged ones—were lost in the mix.

The traffic on the street was mostly drawn by animals, yaks and dogs and horses and great lizards, which was fortunate for Leonid because it made it easy for him to see the sleek bulk of Chad's motor car when it arrived. The metal was painted an iridescent blue, garnished with gleaming chrome. Chad tapped the horn, but Leonid was already hastening towards it with their luggage and Eleanor in tow.

The car was impressive. The passenger compartment was roomier than human-made vehicles, which gave it a feeling of luxury. Each leather seat was independently adjustable. In the short drive from the docks to Telegraph Square, Chad managed to demonstrate all the amenities. There was a tape player—no radio, of course, since the Nivose cosmological constants didn't allow for radio transmission—with studio-grade sound quality. Air conditioning and heating, although neither was needed on such a fine day. The windows, including the windscreen, folded down by means of an ingenious system of cranks. The headlamps and running lights had three settings, daylight, nighttime, and fog. That last was an innovation that Leonid wished his own car back in Dracoheim had.

"Any of your designs in this car?" Leonid asked.

Chad laughed. "Not this model. I'm in drive train and transmission. We're running about three years from drawing board to production."

"He's only been with the company for about a year," Bett added.

At the hotel, a uniformed bellman—a hulking brute with a wrinkled gray hide—collected their bags and ushered them in, with Bett demanding that Eleanor call her to set up plans for lunch. She asked, "You won't forget, will you?"

The suite was on the third floor and had a bedroom, a sitting room, and a huge bath. Leonid didn't take time to investigate it; he simply left his bags, made sure Eleanor was happy with the accommodations—she took her eyes off the picture window that overlooked the street to tell him everything was wonderful and to collect a quick kiss—and then he headed back to the lobby to have the doorman call him a cab.

The Nivose Testing Hall of the Dracoheim Academy for Thaumaturgical Studies turned out to be somewhat less impressive than its name. It was a brick building with thin slit windows. Through the heavy front door was a small antechamber with a large sign reading, "Warning: Thaumaturgically Active Materials. No Unescorted Visitors Beyond This Point."

Once he'd proved his identity and been provided with a graduate student to escort him, though, he was ushered into the familiar bustle of a research facility. Most of the staff was human, with a handful of moreau working as assistants. The materials lab that had been set aside for him was small, but the equipment was well-maintained. He thanked his hosts and got to work.

The transitive curve was similar, but not identical to the curve

186

he'd traced in the Boom Room in Leeshore. As Leonid performed his calculations and plotted the results, he felt again the thrill of discovery. It was not simply discovering the properties of this metal but catching a glimpse of how those properties changed as the cosmological constants changed. There was a structure here, unknowably vast, that ran the length of the Ten Realms, through the dreamsea. Understanding that structure, seeing it in its totality, would lay bare all the secrets of the universe. He was counting grains of sand on a beach on the edge of an infinite sea of knowledge. The bits he had hinted at a grace and majesty that moved worlds, the music of the spheres.

At one point, the graduate student opened the door to ask about lunch, and Leonid grunted a negative without looking up from his graphs. Later on, when he was running current through the sample, increasing the voltage incrementally, the student came back to tell him that he was very sorry, but they had to close the institute for the day.

Leonid stared at him like a man awakened from a dream. He looked at his watch, realized that he'd neglected to set it for local time, and tried to do the conversion in his head, gave up, and asked, "What time is it?"

"Nearly 1800," the student replied. "We have to be going."

Leonid hastily shut down the grid and removed the sample, placing it in his case. "Of course, I'll just grab this. Could someone call me a cab to take me back to the hotel?"

Eleanor was lounging in the sitting room when he returned, wearing a new brown dress and leafing through a local magazine. She got to her feet and smiled. "How did it go?"

"It's the genuine article," Leonid said. "It's going to be just as valuable here as back home."

"Wonderful." She came forward to give him a hug. "My clever man. Now, I have some recommendations for dinner, if you're not too worn out from the lab."

With his arms around her, he felt her dress, and it wasn't fabric but thin leather, clinging to her delightfully. "Not too worn out at all," he said, pulling her tight. "But maybe we could skip dinner?"

She laughed and pushed him away. "I insist on dinner, first—and a quality meal. Maybe even a drink as well."

"As many as you'll let me buy you," Leonid agreed. The dress was extraordinary, and she must have had it tailored to fit. "That looks like it cost a fortune."

"I had some pin money put aside," she said. "You like it?"

"I love it," he said honestly. "I don't know if you'll be able to wear it at home."

She ducked her head and grinned coquettishly. "I can wear it for you."

"Any time you want," he agreed, reaching for her.

She pushed him away, laughing. "Dinner first, you brute. I need a steak—and I bet you never had lunch, did you?"

Leonid thought back. "No," he admitted. Now that he was thinking about it, he was ravenous. "Lead on, and let us murder some steaks."

The next day, he finished the electrical series and ran through the light sensitivity tests. Again, the curves were similar to the results he'd obtained in the Midworld, but not the same. All three curves rose more sharply, and then leveled off sooner. He began to itch to run a series in Messidor, but there was little chance that the college's resources would stretch that far.

He finally set his watch to local time, and even went out with some of the staff mages for lunch. They had savory sausage rolls and talked about the news in Dracoheim. None of the humans assigned to the institute stayed long, nor wanted to.

"The money's good, and it'll be a nice entry on my resume," one admitted, "but I wouldn't want to emigrate."

"Why not?"

He looked around nervously. "Most of the locals are great, but—" He broke off and lowered his voice. "It's nothing to worry about if you're still a Midworld citizen. Even the bad ones won't risk an international incident."

"Bad ones?" Leonid was confused.

"You hear things," the mage went on, looking uncomfortable,

"about some of the locals. Look... we're not supposed to say it, but they're still beasts, down inside. And some of them, well, they see humans as *prey*."

Leonid nodded gravely, but he didn't believe it. It sounded to him as if the man was just uncomfortable being around moreau and looking for a justification for his prejudice.

After lunch, he started in on the thermal properties test and was pleased to see that it also showed a sharper rise and flatter top than the Midworld curve. He wanted to finish up in the morning, so he found the grad student, who assured him that he could leave the sample in the freezer overnight.

"Once we lock up for the night, this is one of the most secure locations outside of the Bone Fortress."

That was good enough for Leonid. He left his notes in the lab and the sample in the freezer, two floors up. He waited while the last mage locked up and set the alarms, then flagged down a cab. For a long moment, he couldn't remember the name of his hotel, then it came to him. Two days of intensive bench work—after the disorienting transit across the dreamsea—left his brain feeling wrung out.

He needed a good meal in the company of a good woman, in a place with hot music and cool lights, a few turns around the dance floor, and a good night's sleep. In the morning, he would wrap up the material series and make arrangements for the return trip.

He found himself humming "On Blue Dolphin Street" in the elevator to his floor. He wondered if Eleanor had gone shopping again, and what exotic skins she might have found to wrap herself in. He opened the door of the suite, still humming.

The song died on his lips. There were two figures in the suite, neither of them Eleanor.

The one in front was a massive brute with a doglike face, covered with thick black fur. He was dressed in a cheap imitation of a human style suit, with a blade the size of a machete on his belt.

The other was Chad.

"I'm so sorry, magus," the pig-man said. He showed signs of a beating: his face was bruised and his clothes were torn. Blood spotted the front of his shirt.

"What is the meaning of this?" Leonid asked. He felt cold.

"Just hand over the metal," the big dog-man said, "and everything will be fine."

"Metal?" Leonid raised his empty hands. "If you're talking about the Ferose sample, I don't have it. It's at the Testing Center."

"What?" Chad cried.

The dog-man backhanded him, and he crumpled.

"That's gonna be bad news," the dog-man growled. "Bad for you, and bad for the ladies."

Leonid felt rage overcoming his fear. "If you've hurt Eleanor—"

The dog-man drew his blade. "Ain't hurt her yet, wizard. But we will, if you don't come across with that metal."

"But..." Leonid thought furiously. "I can't get it until the morning. It's locked up."

"So unlock it."

"I can't! I don't have keys for that place. I'm just a visiting technician."

"Who does?"

"It would be the staff from the Academy." Leonid tried to think. "Magus Anton Draker is the operations director. He'd have access afterhours if anyone would."

The dog-man gestured at the phone on the sitting room desk. "Call him."

"I don't have his home number," Leonid argued. "I'm just here to use a lab for a few days. I've got the address of the testing center and a couple of contact names. That's it."

The big moreau worked his jaws as if he was literally chewing that over. He came to a decision and picked up the hotel suite's phone. He gestured with his blade. "No funny stuff, now."

Leonid spread his hands placatingly.

The moreau dialed an outside line, waited while it was answered.

"We gotta problem. The ape doesn't have it. He left it at that testing place."

A pause. Leonid looked over at Chad, who was sitting very still on the floor.

190

MATERIALS SCIENCE

"Right."

Another pause.

"He'll cooperate as long as we got his woman."

A long pause.

"You gonna send a couple of the boys, just in case?"

A short one.

"Got it."

The dog-man hung up the phone and turned to his captives. "We gonna sit and wait, real civilized, until my friends get here. Then we're all going to go see the boss."

"Go *where*?" Leonid demanded.

"To see the boss," the dog-man said slowly.

Leonid gestured towards Chad. "Let me help him clean up."

"Leave him."

"You really want to take him through the lobby looking like this?" Leonid let some of the anger he felt come out in his voice. "You don't think anyone will notice?"

The dog-man growled, then nodded and gestured towards the suite's bathroom. "Okay. But remember we got your women."

"I haven't forgotten."

Leonid went to Chad, moving slowly, and offered his hand to the pudgy moreau. "Come on," he said gently. "Let me help."

Chad looked up warily, then took the proffered hand.

In the suite's bathroom, Leonid started the tap running, adjusted the temperature. Very softly he asked, "Who is this goon?"

"He's a buck-cutter," Chad whispered.

Leonid didn't know the term. He soaked a washcloth and started gently washing the blood from Chad's face. "Is that a gang?"

Chad nodded, wincing at the roughness of the washcloth.

"And they really have Eleanor and Bett?"

Another nod, then Chad looked away.

Leonid pulled his face back and kept washing him. "If I give him the sample, do you think they'll let them go?"

"*No, you mustn't,*" Chad whispered.

Leonid shrugged. "Why not? It's just a chunk of metal. It's the manufacturing rights that are valuable, and some forged one in

191

Ferose owns those."

The dog-man came up and banged on the door frame. "Time to move."

Leonid shut off the water and passed Chad a hand towel. "Dab the water off. You don't want to open any of those cuts."

There were two more of the hulking dog-men in the suite. To Leonid, they all looked identical, even to their crude suits. They all wore long knives on their belts. Leonid had noticed that a lot of moreau carried blades, but these seemed well used.

The five of them squeezed into the elevator together, the dog-men keeping Leonid and Chad separated. Just before the elevator reached the lobby, one of them said softly, "One word and your woman spends a week dying."

Leonid believed him. The threat had been delivered in a calm, even tone. It was a promise.

There was a big cargo van parked at the curb. One of the dog-men opened the rear door and pushed Chad in, then Leonid. Two of the dog-men followed, then the third got up front to drive.

The van was an import, manufactured in Dracoheim for sale in Nivose. The back was a windowless box and pitch dark when the doors were closed. Leonid took the opportunity to go through his pockets by feel. His late wife, Annalise, had always complained about his habit of sticking oddments of his profession in his pockets, particularly as he often forgot to empty his pockets before dumping his clothes in the laundry.

It was a habit that he'd never been able to break, though, not even for her. In the dark in the back of the van, he inventoried two scribes, an athame, a pocket slide rule, an object that confused him until he worked out that it was an ocular monocle that he seldom used and only packed to save space, a screwdriver with the odd crescent-shaped head that moreau favored. The last object he had borrowed to adjust a locally manufactured bit of equipment and really should have returned to the lab assistant before he left.

In addition, he had his pocket watch, a ballpoint pen, a small but extremely sharp knife, his wallet, his key ring, and the key to his hotel suite.

MATERIALS SCIENCE

How this collection of objects would help in his current predicament, he had no idea. If the dog-men were telling the truth and would let them go once they had the Ferose sample, then all he had to do was keep calm and cooperate.

He doubted that was the case, though. What these "buck-cutters" were doing had to be against local laws. Criminals back home were known to make inconvenient witnesses disappear, and Leonid suspected that was a tradition that transcended Realm borders.

The van stopped and the dog-men opened the back door, letting in weak artificial light.

Leonid waited for them to beckon him to leave the van. There were more of them waiting outside, not just dogs but also tigers and bears. All predatory animals.

Chad moved slowly, and Leonid helped him climb down to the floor of the garage. The pig-man was terrified. Leonid's suspicions hardened into certainties. These were killers and had no intention of letting any of their captives live. As long as they hadn't hurt Eleanor—and Bett, of course—yet, then there was still hope he could come up with something.

If they had harmed the women, then Leonid would make them pay. He was a middle-aged academic, a teacher at a trade school, a widower who drank too much and got out of breath climbing the stairs to his apartment.

But he was also a wizard, and he was armed.

The time wasn't right yet. He could wait and see what they had planned, get a feel for the lay of the land. They would keep up the pretense that they would release him unharmed until the morning, to gain his cooperation getting the sample when the testing center opened.

The group of moreau formed up around them like a military unit. The garage was large—some commercial building—and seemed to be underground. It was filled with pallets of crates. Some kind of depot, then, for goods wagons to be loaded. It was old, built from brick and timber. The strings of electric lights were recent, with soot staining the walls from old gas fixtures. It stank of damp and mold.

They reached a wooden door, and a tiger and a dog escorted them through it. The office was big, but cluttered, filled with ledgers stacked haphazardly. At a desk sat a big moreau, a tiger-man who must have weighed four hundred pounds. This had to be the boss.

"Magus," he began, his voice low and reasonable. "I'm sorry—"

Leonid interrupted him. "Where are Eleanor and Bett?"

The tiger looked annoyed. "They're safe."

"If you want my cooperation, you'll let me see them."

"If you want to ever see them again—"

"This is not negotiable." Leonid used his lecturer's voice, speaking over the tiger without shouting. "Show me that Eleanor and Bett are safe. Let me talk to them. Then we can discuss how to get you the metal sample you want."

Leonid waited while the tiger-man glared at him.

The boss waved to the dog-man. "Get the women."

The dog-man left, and Leonid looked around the office, feigning indifference. In fact, he was studying the room. The place was a mess. He glanced down at the floor. It was filthy. Idly, he scuffed the toe of his shoe across the tile and observed the line he left in the dirt.

He shifted his weight from foot to foot, careful not to move far. Two more short lines and a longer curved one. *Rho.*

He glanced at the tiger-man. The big moreau was glaring at him, but in annoyance, not suspicion.

Leonid stretched and used the movement to scuff a loop, then crossed it with two slanted arcs. *Kesh.*

The door opened, and two of the dog-men entered, pushing Eleanor and Bett before them. The women's hands were bound behind them, but they didn't seem injured.

Leonid took a step towards them, dragging his foot in the dirt. *Ascending arc.*

The other tiger waved him back angrily. "Stay put."

Leonid took a step back, drawing another short straight line in the dirt.

"Eleanor, I am so sorry," he said. "I promise, I'll do whatever they want. Whatever it takes to get us out of this."

He looked down, shuffling nervously. Short line, circle, two crossed lines. *Aleph.*

MATERIALS SCIENCE

"It's okay," said Eleanor. "They haven't hurt us."

"Good," Leonid said. "We'll get through this."

He looked down again. Swept his foot around. *Completion arc.*

The light in the room turned red.

Leonid crossed the floor to the desk. The boss sat frozen. Leonid was moving at sixteen—no, wait, recalculate for Nivose values of rho—*eighteen* times as quickly as the ambient timestream. He slid his pen out of his pocket and scrawled a pax invocation on the tiger's shirt.

Then he went to the other tiger and did the same, then both dogs. He moved as fast as the thick air would allow. The effect wouldn't last long.

He had just started sawing at Eleanor's bonds with his pocketknife when the red faded out of the light. The buck-cutters all slumped to the floor, deeply asleep. Leonid breathed a sigh of relief. He hadn't been entirely sure how the pax charm would work on moreau, but they were all asleep. Maybe they wouldn't wake up ever again, but he wasn't much concerned about that.

"What?" Eleanor stared around the room. From her perspective Leonid had just blurred out of sight.

"We're getting out of here." Leonid said. "Chad, grab one of the goon's knives and cut your wife free."

He had Eleanor free. She turned and threw her arms around him. "I knew you'd come for me," she whispered. She was shaking.

He held her tight. "I had to," he whispered back. "I can't get a refund on your return trip."

She gave a ragged laugh. "Bastard."

He gently disengaged himself. "We're not out of danger yet."

Leonid turned to Chad and Bett. The two moreau were embracing, both crying.

"Bett!" he ordered. "There's a phone on the desk. Call the police."

She obeyed meekly, picking up the phone, then looking at him, stricken. "I don't know the address here."

"It's a freight depot," Leonid said patiently. "It's bound to be written all over this paperwork."

She nodded and shakily began to hunt through the papers on the tiger-man's desk.

Leonid had spotted something. "Chad, get me that walking stick."

Chad fetched it, and Leonid got out his scribe and got to work. As he scratched runes into the wood, he said, "These goons won't be quick to interrupt the boss, but they won't wait forever. We have to be able to hold them off until the cops get here."

He looked at Bett. She had found a bill of lading and was talking on the phone. Her voice was tense, but she wasn't hysterical. She told the story clearly.

Leonid reviewed the Nivose cosmological constants in his mind, then added another series of runes to the walking stick.

Chad held the knife in a two-handed grip, looking at the door.

"Give me the knife for a minute," Leonid said.

Chad passed it over, and Leonid scribed symbols on the handle with his pocketknife, then held the knife carefully, watching the blade. The metal shimmered, then a corona of blue fire formed around the blade. Leonid carefully offered it back to the moreau, who stared and made no move to touch it.

"The handle is perfectly safe," Leonid said firmly. "Just don't touch the blade."

Gingerly, Chad took it. After a moment, he swung it carefully, testing the feel of the weapon.

"With any luck you won't have to use it," Leonid said. "It's just supposed to scare them."

"It's scaring me," Chad said. But he was grinning.

"Do this one," Eleanor said, holding out another blade.

Leonid studied her a moment, then nodded and took the knife. He scribed the runes and handed it back as the metal began to flame.

Then he bent to the cane again. As he was working through another series, there was a knock at the door.

"Mr. Frenck?" The voice was tentative. "Everything all right in there?"

Leonid held up a hand for the others to wait and completed his sequence.

MATERIALS SCIENCE

Another knock. "Boss?" The voice was insistent. "What's going on?"

Leonid crossed to the door and put his hand on the knob. He waited for another knock, then slammed it open. The force of the swing would have knocked a man off his feet, but the great bear-like moreau on the other side just staggered back a step.

Leonid stuck his cane through the opening and unleashed lightning.

Over the crackle of electricity, he heard moreau screaming. All the lights went out.

Not what he'd intended. He must have messed up a constant in his sequence. Oh, well, it couldn't be helped now. He activated one of the other sequences, and the end of the cane flared into light, brilliant as an arc lamp.

He used the end of the cane to push open the door. In the light of the flare, he saw moreau crowded around the door, most of them on the floor, some twitching weakly.

"We are leaving," he announced to the ones who could still hear him. "You will not stop us. If you try, you will die."

He stepped over the twitching bodies. Eleanor and Chad, both armed with flaming blades, followed him. Bett brought up the rear.

No one tried to stop them. They heard the approaching sirens before they reached the door to the street.

In the end, they only had to stay an extra two days in Hunger City. Leonid had expected more, but the Grimm's guard assured him that his recorded testimony would be sufficient, and there was no need for him and Eleanor to be present at the trial of Kaizer Frenck and his associates.

He was concerned for Chad and Bett. They seemed to trust the local authorities' ability to protect them from any reprisal from the gang. Leonid hoped they were right.

There was a long meeting with a nervous human from the Midworld consulate who was concerned about possible negative repercussions from the incident. Leonid and Eleanor reassured them that they had no intention of causing trouble and agreed not to talk to the press of either Realm.

DRACOHEIM CONFIDENTIAL

Leonid had already had more than enough publicity after the Summerisle Ferry fire. He rather hoped this entire incident could be decently forgotten.

He finished up his work in the testing facility and wrote up his notes. The facility had a facsimile translator—a very expensive piece of specialized hardware that Leonid had read about but never seen. They were able to send photographic images of his notes directly to the corresponding device at the Dracoheim Academy, who would forward them to Magus Welsh.

Leonid kept his own copy of the notes. He didn't trust modern technology.

Their last day in Hunger City they spent with Chad and Bett. Chad apologized—again—for his part. He'd been talking to a coworker about Leonid's presence in Nivose and the reason for it. One of the cleaning staff had overheard and passed on the message to a relative who was a buck-cutter, who passed it on to Frenck.

Leonid told him not to fret about it. The whole affair was stupid in any event. Yes, the metal was potentially very valuable, but it was not as if that sample could be sold for millions. It was the manufacturing techniques that would arise from use of the metal that would make someone rich.

They toured the Grimm's gardens in the shadow of the Bone Fortress, then had a long lunch in an open-air steakhouse off the square. It was a beautiful city, all things considered.

Still, he wanted to get home. Eleanor probably would have been happy to stay another month, and he had to promise her that they would come back next summer—on a real vacation this time. Chad and Bett said they would be happy to have them stay with them, and if they had time, they could tour the countryside around the city.

At last, it was time to go. They returned on a Ventose liner, crewed by chittering chigoes. The accommodations were suitably luxurious, if a bit odd by human standards.

They stood together on the rail as the ship left the harbor, waiting for the spectacle of transit.

"You never told me you could make flaming swords," Eleanor said, her body close to his.

"You never asked," Leonid said reasonably. He slipped his arm around her shoulder.

She cuddled close. "Would you make me one when we get home?"

"Well, sure," he said. "If you want one."

"Silly man," she said. "What woman wouldn't want a flaming sword?"

And she kissed him as the sky melted into a wilderness of alien stars.

Against the Midnight Currents

Currents

Case:03-SBR-373//CI#373-0851

Yesterday had been the Autumn Tide Festival, and today the Autumn Tide sales were in full swing. The Century Orchard Shopping Plaza was packed. I was working with a young magus named Engles, watching the door of a small alchemist shop through the bustling crowds.

Earlier I had made the mistake of mentioning that I was considering buying a multi-band radio, since my old console had been made before the high frequency bands came into use. It turned out that Engles was something of an expert in home electronics, having worked in his uncle's shop while he was in school. I was treated to an exhaustive lecture on the principles of high frequency radio broadcasts and why the sound quality was far superior, and what each tube in a radio did, and why I should make sure my radio had the latest and most expensive tubes.

I hadn't realized that mages could be that excruciatingly dull when they were discussing something other than magic.

Fortunately, the Century Orchard operative came out of the shop with her purchases before Engles could produce a chalkboard and start drawing diagrams.

The local constable's office had received complaints of bum alchemical preparations being sold out of that shop. Century Orchard constables had requested CPS assistance. They sent in their operative—a pretty young dispatcher who looked nothing like a cop—to buy a list of compounds. Once she had them, Magus Engles could examine them to see if they were really what was on the tin.

I was there to make the pinch if they weren't.

We went around the corner, out of sight of the shop. There was a coffee shop with outdoor seating and a pair of Century Orchard uniforms holding a table for us.

AGAINST THE MIDNIGHT CURRENTS

I took a statement from the operative and sealed her receipt into an evidence envelope while Engles got his tools out of his briefcase and went to work on the bottles from the shop.

In about a half hour, he had compiled his report. Of the eight bottles of alleged alchemical reagents, four of them were completely inert—just colored water. Three of the others were diluted to a lower concentration than the labels said.

Engles told the dispatcher that she had done a good job and sent her on her way. Then he packed up the samples and his gear, and we went to go make an arrest, with the two constables as backup. I sent one of them down the alley to watch the back door.

Before we got to the shop, though, a man staggered out of it, looking shocked. He saw the constable and pointed back towards the shop.

"He's dead!"

"Get his statement and keep him here," I ordered the constable and trotted to the door. Engles looked confused, but followed me.

I got my gun out and pushed open the door with my elbow. It was a small, brightly lit shop. Rows of colorful bottles were across one wall, the others had pictures of flowers. It was the kind of shop designed to appeal to hobbyists, middle-aged women who read *Alchemy for the Modern Housewife* and decided to try their hand at home remedies for upset stomachs.

The clerk was young and handsome, in a nice suit. He lay in the middle of the floor, his body twisted. The carpet around his head was wet.

I scanned the room. One back door, closed, with a window showing that it led out into the alley. Another door, ajar, showing a combination storeroom and office.

"Stay here," I told Engles.

I crossed the room and took a quick peek into the storeroom and behind the counter, didn't see anywhere a man could be hiding, then knelt beside the body.

Dead. His chest was distended and water filled his nose and mouth, dripping out to soak the carpet. He'd been drowned in the middle of a perfectly dry shop on a busy street in a shopping center.

I put on my gloves and patted the body, pulled his wallet. Marcus Sweetgrass, with a local address.

"Murder by means of magic," Engles said softly, sounding sick.

"You think?" I asked him. I waved him to the office. "Call this in, I'm going to talk to our witness."

The witness turned out to be one Mr. Cleave Rockwell of Freebooter Park. About forty, balding, in a cheap suit. He was rattled by what he'd seen, and I offered him a cigarette, which he took.

"I didn't touch anything," he said. "I went into the shop, and he was on the floor like that. I went right back out and saw you."

"You didn't try to help the victim?"

"I'm no doctor."

"How did you know he was dead, then?"

A blank stare. "He was just lying there. Not moving. He *looked* dead." A quick glance to the door of the shop. "He *is* dead, isn't he?"

I nodded. "Yes, he's dead."

He swallowed hard, looking away.

I changed the subject. "What were you shopping for?"

He looked away and grew even more nervous. "Uh, nothing. Just, you know, looking."

I turned slightly so that my body language excluded the constable from our conversation and lowered my voice. "Something personal?" I suggested. "Something for men's health issues?"

He reddened and looked down at his feet, but nodded.

I gave him a reassuring smile. "That doesn't need to go into the report."

"Can I go now?" he asked in a near-whisper.

"Soon," I promised him, and held out my hand. "Can I see some ID, please?"

He fumbled through his pockets and came up with a wallet. I copied down his address.

"Rugar," Engles called. "Blackwell wants you."

I turned. The young magus was in the doorway of the shop, still wearing his ocular. I saw him react to something he saw through it. Something right beside me. I turned to look at my witness.

"Sir—" and that was as far as I got before Rockwell bolted.

202

AGAINST THE MIDNIGHT CURRENTS

I headed after him and ran straight into a lightning storm. It blinded me and threw me on the ground. Through the convulsions I heard the constable approaching me. I tried to tell him to leave me and go after Rockwell, but I couldn't unclench my jaw.

The constable and Engles dragged me out of the middle of the plaza and to the wall of the shop. The electrical charge left my body aching all over but wouldn't have done any lasting damage. If an attack like that doesn't kill you right away, you can usually shake it off in a few minutes.

Rockwell was gone. In the wind.

"We've got his ID," the constable told me.

"It'll be false," I said, and got to my feet, leaning against the wall.

Engles was fumbling in his briefcase. "You've had a bad shock. You need to—"

I cut him off. "What I need to do is call the boss," I told him, and went into the shop to the phone.

"All right," Blackwell said when I finished my report. "You've got lead on this."

I thought for a moment. I hurt all over and I wanted to lie down and take a long nap. Later. There was work to be done.

"Get a county-wide fugitive bulletin on Rockwell," I said. "And get Freebooter Park to check out that address."

"Roger that," Blackwell said. "Start the initial on the scene. The lab boys are on the way. Have the locals secure the area, I'll square it with Century Orchard."

"Thanks."

A pause, and then Blackwell asked casually, "How do you read it?"

"Sweetgrass runs the shop, moving somebody else's product. The supplier gets wind that the law is moving in and sends Rockwell to silence him, which means our victim knew something. Rockwell wouldn't have had time to do any thorough search of the shop, so I figure that's our best shot at moving up the chain."

"I agree," said Blackwell. "Century Orchard coroner's coming for the body. Have Engles do a full scan before they get there."

"I think he already did."

203

"Check his work. He's new."

"Right."

"Keep in mind," Blackwell said, his voice carefully casual, "whoever sent Rockwell knew there was an investigation ongoing."

He wouldn't say that he suspected a mole in Century Orchard, not out loud over the phone, but I had been thinking the same thing.

"Copy that, boss." I hung up and went to check on Engles.

"Okay, what have we got here?" I asked him.

"Sir?"

"Have they got a lab on the premises?"

He shook his head. "They barely have a shop on the premises."

"What do you mean?"

"That"—he pointed at the shelves full of bottles— "should be showing residuals. There's scarcely enough to register."

"How far off is it?" I asked.

He frowned. "Uh, well, for example, blood orchid distillate has a passive gradient of ten to twenty talents. Those bottles there register as flat. That's not blood orchid distillate."

"What is it?"

"I don't know. Raspberry jam, maybe? Tomato sauce? Taste it and find out."

"I'll pass. You figure they've been running a scam the whole time?"

Another frown. "Residuals don't last forever. Technically, these shelves could have held legitimate product a month ago and I wouldn't be able to pick it up. But I doubt it. You run a shop like this, even if you're careful and follow all the lab procedures—which nobody does—you have accidents. Asynchronous mixing, product overconcentration, somebody's going to spill something. That kind of thing leaves lasting traces—that's why alchemical labs cost so much to sanitize. There's none of that here."

I nodded and turned towards the late Mr. Sweetgrass. "What about him?"

"That was one *vicious* spell." He shuddered. "Targeted transformation. Turned all the air within the confines of his body into water. An ugly way to die."

I considered that. "He wouldn't die instantly," I mused. I'd come close to drowning more than once, screwing around in the sea. Even with a lungful of water you had minutes to reach the surface. This man hadn't been submerged, he should have been able to cough it out and breathe fresh air.

"Shock, probably," Engles shrugged. "The coroner can tell for certain."

"There's residual on him, though, right?"

"Oh, yes. High residuals." He consulted his paperwork. "Four hundred talent range. That Mr. Rockwell had to have been carrying a massive focus. You're cursed lucky that he depleted it in here before he hit you with the electrical discharge."

"That's what you saw through the ocular, right? Rockwell's focus?"

"Yes," he said, then looked down at his feet. "I tipped him off, didn't I? I shouldn't have reacted like that."

"Don't worry about it," I said. "He would have rabbited anyway. You forced his hand—now we know for sure it was him."

"I almost got you killed."

I shrugged. "It's a dangerous job."

"But—"

"Drop it."

Engles started to argue, then just nodded. "What do you want me to do?"

"You've got all your..." I waved my hand at his briefcase, "...charts and stuff filled out?"

"Full site workup," he assured me.

"It's got to be letter-perfect," I pressed him. "In a criminal case involving magic, the defense always attacks the department's findings. If they can disallow it, they will."

He looked serious, but nodded. "I've checked it."

It took almost four hours to tag and pack everything, put seals on the products, load everything into a department truck, and unload it into a situation room at Government House.

By then I was dead on my feet. I left Engles to handle the alchemical samples and told the night crew to leave the desk contents for me to sort through in the morning.

At home, I had a bottle of honey liquor that I'd picked up on my vacation to Nivose. I took a couple of medicinal shots and went to bed. In the morning, I was still sore, but no more than I would be after a hard workout at my health club. It hadn't been the first time I'd been sucker-punched by a freecaster, and it wouldn't be the last.

When I got to Government House, I asked the desk officer to let Blackwell know I was here and went straight to the situation room. The boxes of bogus product had been moved to a lab, so I had plenty of room. A case like this is like a jigsaw puzzle. I dumped the contents of the desk on a table and started sorting paperwork.

There was a ledger for operating expenses like rent, utilities, Sweetgrass's salary—he was well paid for a shop clerk, but not near enough for the risks he'd been taking. He'd probably been drawing a second, larger salary, in cash. Unless he really was so simple that he didn't understand what he was selling. Unlikely, but possible.

I wrote "victim bio" as the first action item on my to-do list.

There were regular deposits made to a bank in the city. Merchant's Consolidated. It was a financial giant that did business in tens of millions, perfect for a small business that wanted to be unnoticed. The process of getting the account ledger would be arduous.

I wrote a note to pass that up to our legal department.

Blackwell dropped by when I was going through the materials documentation for the product.

"How's it going?" he asked.

"Have you ever heard of an importer called Black Rose Investments?"

He thought it over. "No."

"How about a distribution company called Five Dials?"

Another pause for thought. "No."

"A bonded transport firm called Park Coastal?"

He shook his head. "Those names are from their paperwork?"

"Yeah, and a couple of others. None of them exist."

"Color me shocked," Blackwell said dryly.

He held out his hand and I passed him the sheaf of documents.

206

He paged through the stack slowly and I waited.

"This place could never have survived an audit—or even a spot check—from Licensing," he said at last.

"Which means," I finished for him, "that they were pretty sure they'd never be audited."

Frowning, Blackwell looked over at the closed door, then nodded again.

Then he changed the subject. "What do you have on our victim?"

"A bit of a slob," I said. "That desk was a mess. He's got a telephone memo book, but it's only first names. I'm going to send a request to get the numbers identified. Most of the numbers seem to be women."

"He was a handsome young man." A sigh. "His next of kin are parents in Leeshore. The locals notified them yesterday. Interview them."

"Right."

"And there's an address for him in Century Orchard. An apartment, nice building. Go check that out after you talk to the parents."

"Anything on the Rockwell ID?"

"It's a phony. A high quality one, would have fooled me. The address is a Manning & Goodstone's. Freebooter Park has no records of anyone with the name Cleavus Trent Rockwell. I've got a county-wide request on the name, I'll let you know if anything comes in."

Then he sighed. "Okay, Rugar, I'll follow up on the paperwork. There are still some men in Licensing I trust. You dig up everything you can on Marcus Sweetgrass. Give me a report by end of day. In person."

"Right, boss."

I headed out.

The senior Sweetgrasses lived in a modest townhouse in a quiet working-class neighborhood. I knocked on the door and a big man in clean work clothes answered it. He looked to be about my age. I lowered my voice and showed him my badge, asked if I might talk to Devin and Essie Sweetgrass.

"I'm Devin Sweetgrass," he said. "But I assume you mean my father."

He led me inside.

"I'm here investigating the death of Marcus Sweetgrass," I said. "Your brother?"

"Little brother, yeah."

Just inside the door was a low shelf with a row of books displayed on it. I didn't have to read the titles to know what they were. *The Keys to The Cosmos. Thoughts and Prayers. Opening New Doors. Love and Its Manifestations.* My parents had kept the same set of books in our front hallway.

He led me down a narrow hallway to a bright kitchen. A man and woman in their sixties sat at a wooden table, a three-handed card game in progress.

"Mr. and Mrs. Sweetgrass, I am Erik Rugar of the Comittee for Public Safety. I am investigating the death of your son."

Mr. Sweetgrass rose to his feet but didn't offer to shake hands. "He was killed by magic? That's what the constables said."

"We believe so, yes."

"When can we see him?" Mrs. Sweetgrass asked, still seated.

"That's at the discretion of the Century Orchard coroner." I got out my notebook and found the number, then wrote it on the back of one of my business cards and put it on the table. "They'll be able to answer your questions."

Then I flipped my notebook back to a blank page and asked, "What can you tell me about your son's job?"

Not much, as it turned out. Marcus hadn't been very forthcoming about his life after he'd moved out of the house. From the way they talked around the subject I got the impression that there was bad blood between Mr. Sweetgrass and his youngest son. I listened and made sympathetic noises and doodles on my notebook while Mrs. Sweetgrass told me that Marcus had always been such a good boy, clearly trying to convince herself rather than me.

I got out of there as quickly as I could without being rude.

Devin junior walked me out to my car.

"Something to add?" I asked casually.

AGAINST THE MIDNIGHT CURRENTS

"Marc fell in with a bad crowd," he said. "He's the baby, and I guess mom kind of spoiled him. He never was one for working if he could figure a way around it. Me and Jake—my other brother—got him a half-dozen jobs at least, but he couldn't ever keep any of them."

I nodded sympathetically for him to continue.

"Then, oh I guess it's been two and a half years, maybe three, he shows up in a sharp suit, flashing a roll of cash, talking about his new friends and how much money they were all going to make. Some sales opportunity, with big investors.

"We all knew there was something wrong. A twenty-five-year-old kid, no experience, no real skills, making that kind of money—it *had* to be illegal. And Dad..." A sigh. "Dad tried to set him straight. Marc couldn't see that we were all concerned about him.

"Instead, he gets irate, says we're all just jealous of him, and storms out of the house. I don't think any of us have seen him since. Maybe Marji, our sister, but she's busy with her own family."

I thanked him for his time and got his contact information, gave him my card in case he remembered anything else. I also got the married name and address of sister Marji. Brother Jake was out to sea and not expected home for three weeks.

Then I drove back to Century Orchard. Marcus Sweetgrass's apartment was in a very modern building of turquoise tile and glass brick. The manager had been told of his tenant's death and was expecting me. He unlocked the door and left me alone.

My first impression was that this was an apartment designed to be admired rather than lived in.

Opening the front door was like the curtain going up on a stage where the script called for The Home of a Modern Successful Bachelor.

The furniture was matching, all in black leather with brass accents. Above the couch was an abstract tapestry that might have been an import from Messidor. Against one wall was a steel shelving unit containing a component stereo system in brushed chrome, neat cables connecting the gleaming cubes.

The kitchen contained all the latest gadgets, the refrigerator was stocked with party food—cheese, cider, fresh fruit, sliced sausages. One could make quite a feast without needing to turn on the gleaming stove. The glass-fronted liquor cabinet was better-stocked than the pantry.

The condition of the tile floor and the counter tops suggested regular visits from a maid service.

The bedroom was just as neat. The bed was polished dark wood with fur throws and a wealth of pillows. The sort of bed a single man makes when he anticipates overnight visitors.

The toiletries in the bathroom were all the finest quality. The shaving set looked like surgical instruments.

Nowhere did I see any personal touches. There were no pictures except for abstract art. The few books were the newest best-sellers, dust jackets pristine as if they'd never been opened. His clothes hung with department store precision in his closet. The apartment was a showplace, a stage set designed to impress... whom?

I dug deeper.

I didn't find anything under the mattress, and under the bed itself there was only a matched set of leather luggage, all empty. There was a small collection of creams and lotions in one bedside table, all in unlabeled jars. The other was empty.

I checked all of the obvious hiding places without finding any of the money I was sure he had stashed someplace. He was spending far more than his modest salary at the alchemical shop. It was possible that he had a hidden bank account, but I didn't believe it. He seemed the sort who would want his cash nearby.

I was looking absently at his stereo setup when I noticed something odd. It had the usual components, high band receiver, tape deck, rack for holding tape reels, and an amplifier.

But it shouldn't have needed an amplifier. Thinking over my recent lecture from Magus Engles, I examined the receiver and tape deck. Both had built-in amplifiers. The speakers were big—polished wooden cabinets with black fabric covered fronts—but not so large that they needed an additional amp.

The amplifier wasn't connected to anything else, not even a power cord. I lifted it out and turned it over. There was only one screw holding the back cover on.

There was a lot of money in there, rolled up and wrapped in rubber bands. Most of the bills seemed to be twenties and fifties. In addition, there was an envelope full of photographs.

The last thing in the phony amplifier was a book of tickets. They were well-printed on heavy paper with perforations so they could be torn out one at a time. About half of them were gone, presumably used or sold.

Good For One Passage On The Graveyard Island Ferry. Sevenday Evening, 2100. Day and time, but no date. Curious. I'd never heard of a Graveyard Island Ferry. Graveyard Island sounded familiar, but I couldn't place it.

I stuffed everything back in the amplifier and put the cover back on. This had to go back to Government House to be entered as evidence.

My first stop was the property locker where me and the clerk counted the cash—eighteen thousand, four hundred, sixty dollars— and he sealed it in an envelope and gave me a receipt.

Then I checked my desk and found that the telephone exchange had produced a list of names to go with the numbers in Sweetgrass's memo book. I stopped in the reference office on the way to see Blackwell.

"Talk to me," he said.

I started with the receipt from property. "Sweetgrass had cash stashed in a fake stereo amp."

He glanced at the total and nodded. "We figured he was getting paid off the books."

"He also had these," I laid the envelope of pictures on his desk.

There were eight of them, high quality prints, nearly identical. They showed a man and a woman sitting together in a booth in a posh restaurant. A romantic dinner for two, with candles on the table. In all of them the man and woman were touching, in a few they kissed. The angle was the same in every picture, high and a little to one side, an awkward angle, but one that afford a very clear view of the couple.

The man in all the pictures was Marcus Sweetgrass.

The women were all different, all older than him—some by a comfortable margin—all wealthy.

Blackwell studied the pictures, giving nothing away, although I was sure he must have recognized some of the women.

"Blackmail is a little out of our jurisdiction," he said at last.

"I don't think it was blackmail, at least not directly. I think he was being paid by his bosses to collect insurance for their operation. But this is too much work for just that little shop. The question is, what else are they doing?"

He thought that over and picked up a photo to study it. The woman in it was the wife of a Century Orchard magistrate, and their home number was in Sweetgrass's little black book.

"I don't suppose you recognize the restaurant?"

I shook my head. "There are a lot of places that look like that," I said. "There isn't much to go on."

"No." A long sigh. "We'll find it, in time. Probably too late. They'll know Sweetgrass is dead soon, if they don't already, and they'll assume we found those. That camera will end up in the river. Maybe the photographer, too."

"And then there's this," I put the ticket book beside the envelope of photographs.

He picked it up and studied it, frowning.

"There isn't any Graveyard Island Ferry," I told him.

"Is there even a Graveyard Island?" he asked.

"Yes," I said. "It's a Pluviose treaty zone. They have one of their refineries on it." That's why I remembered the name—it was marked on the charts as Do Not Approach.

"So... is this for employees?"

I shook my head. "The only humans employed there are administrative workers, and they're only there during normal business hours. The non-native workers live on-site."

"And undines wouldn't need a ferry in any event," he observed.

"Right."

"Did you get anything from the parents?"

"Not much." I outlined what I'd learned from talking to the Sweetgrass family.

AGAINST THE MIDNIGHT CURRENTS

Blackwell laid the evidence out on his desk. "So, we have a kid from a strict Theosophist family. He's bright, he's handsome, and he's a sucker for a promise of easy money. He gets a gig selling fake alchemicals and his bosses set him up with a sideline in romancing the wives of influential politicians and getting incriminating photographs. When the shop is about to get raided, those same bosses send in a freecaster hitman to snuff him before he could talk."

I nodded.

"Once we get the bank records, we'll start tracing the money. The boys in the lab are working on the fake product, hammering out where it came from." He picked up the photographs, leafed through them again. "I have to think about what to do about these. If we're lucky, maybe nothing. Maybe we won't need to pursue that particular angle of inquiry."

He set the photos back down and picked up the ticket book. "Which leaves this. Tickets for a ferry that doesn't exist, to an island where no one has any business going. Tickets that are important enough that our victim kept them in his hidey-hole with his cash and his naughty pictures."

"Right," I agreed. "So how do we follow up on this?"

He flipped through the remaining tickets to the end. On the inside of the back cover was stamped, **Printed By Jittlov-Kaye Graphics** with a business address in Anders Parish. He tapped the stamp. "You might want to start there."

I wrote the name and address in my notebook and picked up the book. I hadn't thought to check for the printer.

"I'm an idiot, boss," I told him.

He didn't comment on that. "Check in when you know something."

I got on my way.

Railroad Avenue in Anders Parish once ran alongside railroad tracks, but the main Anders Depot was shut down years ago and the rails pulled up and sold. These days, it runs alongside a low-rent industrial park. I met a patrol car with a pair of constables at the corner and followed them through a maze of dirty alleys and unmarked buildings. I might or might not need them for backup, but

I definitely needed them as guides.

We walked in together, and I laid my badge on the desk of a startled receptionist.

"Uh," she said, looking up from her radio magazine. "Can I help you?"

"I'm here to see the boss."

Her eyes flicked nervously to one of the two doors that led out of the reception area, then picked up a house phone. "I'll, uh, see if he's available."

"Don't bother," I told her, "I can see myself in." I walked to the door she'd looked towards and the constables followed me.

Darius Kaye turned out to be a fat balding man in a cheap suit. He was smoking a cigar and paging through a supplier's catalog when I barged in. He dropped both when I held up my badge.

"Erik Rugar, Department of Public Safety, Criminal Investigation Division," I introduced myself. "I need to ask you some questions."

His eyes went wide. With shaking hands, he picked up his cigar and stubbed it out in the ashtray.

"Wha—" he began, then sputtered to a halt.

There was a chair across from his desk. I pulled it out and dropped into it. Then I reached into my jacket and took out the ticket book, glanced through it, and laid it on his desk.

"Let's talk," I suggested.

He looked down at the ticket book and shook his head. "I got nothing to say."

"Then I'll start," I said. "I found that in an apartment rented to a man named Marcus Sweetgrass. You know him? No? Well, he's dead now. He drowned. Somebody cast a spell on him that filled his lungs with water. Pretty grisly, huh? The gunner who did it tried for me, too. Lightning, but it wasn't enough to kill me. Still, you can see why I want to get this guy, right? It's kind of personal now."

I reached out to tap my fingers on the words on the front of the booklet. He flinched back.

"There's no Graveyard Island Ferry, but I bet you already knew that," I said. "I looked up Graveyard Island, and it turns out that it's owned by the Pluviose government. They have a refinery there, and

214

it's a no-go area for civilian traffic."

"I don't know anything," Kaye managed to mutter.

"You know who ordered these tickets," I said. "You didn't print them just for fun. Somebody paid you, and somebody picked them up."

Kaye looked scared now, and not of me. "They'll kill me," he said in a near-whisper.

I nodded sympathetically. "That's the problem with working with gangsters," I agreed. "The money's good, but then they kill you before you can spend it. And these guys—I think they'll kill you whether you talk or not. They're clearing up loose ends—like Marcus Sweetgrass. And you, well, you've got to be on their list."

He dropped his head into his hands.

"I think your only chance is to cooperate with me. Tell me what you know, and these officers will take you into custody. Or you can sit there and wait for them to get to you." I sat back and lit a cigarette. "Your choice."

It took him twenty minutes to spill all he knew.

The tickets had been ordered in person and paid for in cash. Mr. Kaye wasn't a sailor and hadn't thought anything strange about the name, but the money was too good for it to be strictly legal. The first order had been for fifty books of twenty tickets each. That one had been picked up, but later orders had been delivered.

The address was a law office in Centerberg. It wasn't much, but it was something to go on.

The receptionist wasn't at her desk, so I used her phone to call in, making sure that Kaye heard me tell Blackwell that he was a cooperative witness and should be assigned a protective detail.

"I'll have Centerberg meet you at the address," Blackwell told me. "Don't go in until the locals are there."

"Copy that," I said. "I'm on my way."

They hit me on Division Avenue.

I was pulling out of the industrial park headed to the Outer Belt Loop. I had a glimpse of movement outside my passenger side window and then the air was full of flying glass.

As I struggling to make sense of what happened, someone jerked open my door and dragged me out. I was tangled in my seat belt, but a hand holding a blade slipped in and cut it.

I hit the ground hard and had the wind knocked out of me again. Hands pulled open my jacket and removed my gun. There were three, maybe four of them.

I could see the wreck now; a heavy goods truck had pulled out of a blind alley and hit my cruiser broadside. My head was clearing, and I was able to struggle.

It didn't do me any good.

I was rolled over, and my hands were cuffed behind my back. Someone else pulled a black bag over my head. Then I was hoisted and jammed into a small, cramped space.

A car trunk, I realized.

We drove off.

It had happened so fast. Lying in the doubled darkness of the black hood and the car trunk, I tried to reconstruct the events in my mind. It had taken a half-dozen men, I figured. One to drive the truck, one to drive the car, and three or four others to jump me while I was disoriented from the crash.

A very slick operation. It had taken some planning, guts, and a good guess as to my probable route. Even if they hadn't figured on me heading to Centerberg, Division Street was the best way to get to the highway. That time of day, traffic would be light—most of the truckers were already on the road and that wasn't a retail shopping area.

I considered the absent receptionist. She could have made a quick phone call before she left for parts unknown. *Who did she call, Agent Rugar?*

Cursed good question.

I felt like an idiot. I was always careful to make sure I had local backup, but it didn't occur to me that I was vulnerable on the road. But that was the past; I needed to figure out what to do next.

I stretched my muscles as best as I could in the cramped space. Nothing felt broken, but I would be plenty sore tomorrow, if I was still alive.

They had gone to a lot of trouble to take me alive. It would have been easy to just shoot me in the head when I was stunned and lying on the pavement. They wanted me for something—but that didn't mean they had any intention of leaving me alive once they had it.

The car stopped, and I heard movement in and around it. Then the trunk lid opened. I lay very still.

"We're at a private dock, Agent Rugar," a man said. "We're going to get on a boat now. If you try anything stupid, you'll get on the boat with a broken leg."

I gave an exaggerated slow nod to show I understood.

They pulled me out of the trunk, one man on each side. There were others moving around me. The hood was thin, and I could smell the air. Brackish, rather than salt. Somewhere on the river, then.

I was pretty sure the car had never gotten onto the highway, so we must still be on the west side of the river. Leeshore, maybe, but I was betting on Quayside Parish. There were blocks of warehouses that had their own river docks, and it was late enough in the afternoon that most of them would be closed for the day.

I was led up a metal gangplank and onto the deck of a boat, then into a small cabin. Not a cargo space by the smell, and not loud enough to be an engine room. A crew lounge. I was probably on a tug.

"There's a seat here," one of the men leading me said, not unkindly, and they guided me onto a bench. A man sat on either side of me, and I heard the others moving around the cabin.

We headed off. Downstream, I was sure, to open water.

I sat quietly, listening, trying to get a feel for our progress. The engine ran smoothly. Above it, I could hear the occasional bells and whistles of a working river.

Another half hour passed. I wondered my car had been found yet. No, they had probably towed it out of sight—I didn't think it could be driven, but it was clear that whoever was behind this had resources to spare. Centerberg would have reported when I didn't show up at the law office, but that would take time.

So, I'm no-show in Centerberg, and by now Blackwell knows it. They know what time I left the printers in Anders Parish, but that wouldn't help. I would have to assume I was on my own.

I felt the ship pull up to a dock, and a minute later someone opened the door and said, "We're here. Bring him out."

The two men beside me got to their feet and helped me up. One of them said softly, "There's nowhere to run to. We're on an island."

I gave him the exaggerated nod again and walked between them, one holding each elbow.

I already knew we were on an island, and I already knew which one. The air smelled of salt, but more strongly of elixir and alchemical preparations. In the distance was a low rumble of machinery I could feel through the ground. It was a refinery.

It turned out there was a Graveyard Island Ferry after all.

Which meant that this had become an international case. There was no way that anyone human was on the island without the undines knowing about it. I was in very deep waters, and the only boat was in the hands of my enemies.

And it was still their move. I walked between the two men, head down under my hood, meek as a piglet. I could see my feet moving over the ground, a smooth path carved from the rocky surface of the island by the undines' acid.

I didn't have many dealings with undines. They produced the combustive elixir we burned in our cars and other machinery, but Licensing or Import/Export dealt with that. No doubt back in Pluviose, the enforcers of Queen Chuz's court dealt with as much crime as I did, but here in the Midworld, the undines seldom left their enclaves. They were fully aquatic creatures, after all.

The sound of the machinery grew irregular, and I realized there was another noise competing with the throbbing pumps. The roar of a crowd. It sounded like fight night at the arena.

"There are stairs here."

I nodded to show I understood and felt with my foot. Metal staircase, leading up. I could feel both the pounding of the machinery and the excitement of the crowd. There was a cheer. I guess somebody won.

We went slowly up the stairs, then through a door. The sound of the crowd was muted when the door closed behind me. I was guided to a chair, and then the bag was taken off my head.

I blinked around, getting my bearings.

It was an office, built for humans. Panoramic window overlooking a large space lit by firelight. Five people aside from me, four men standing, a woman seated at a desk. Mid-forties, handsome, in a red evening gown, and I recognized her.

I glanced around the room. Kept my mouth shut. It was still their move.

Outside the room, someone shouted and the crowd roared in response.

The woman in red leaned back in her chair, looking me over. She seemed disappointed that I was just sitting there. Maybe she'd expected something more dramatic, like a scene from a melodrama. My line would be, *You'll never get away with this!* or something like that.

I sat still and looked back at her calmly, quietly. She'd have to do her arch-villainess monologue solo.

"Do you know who I am, Agent Rugar?" she asked at last.

"Marilisa Mabuse," I answered obediently. She was the wife of a Centerberg Member of Parliament and the subject of one of Marcus Sweetgrass's romantic snapshots.

She nodded, then turned to one of her troops. "Take the cuffs off, Pietr."

The man crossed the floor, and I leaned forward on the bench to let him get at the cuffs. Then I leaned back and flexed my arms. Carefully, in as non-threatening a way as I could.

"Come here, Agent. I want to show you something."

I stood and crossed the room slowly. I swung my arms as much as I dared, feeling the blood returning to my cramped forearms and hands.

The office overlooked a freight yard of some kind. There was a wide gravel yard surrounded by a high chain-link fence. Two men faced each other in the yard, bare-chested, in dungarees and boots.

The crowd stood on a catwalk that surrounded the yard, looking down on the men through the fence. The fence was oddly decorated, with white strips of fabric woven through it.

219

One of the men gestured, and blue light flared, turning the figures momentarily into silhouettes. Startled, I stepped back from the window as the crowd roared.

Mrs. Mabuse laughed. "A wizards' duel, Agent Rugar. Ever seen one before?"

I shook my head and stepped back to the window. The strips woven through the chain-link were containment runes, I realized, to protect the crowd. They were pressed against the rail of the catwalk now, straining to watch the action. Men in suits, women in evening gowns.

Light flared in a half-dozen colors from the pit, too fast to follow. Then one of the men was down, stunned, but trying to roll to his feet. The other combatant posed above him, fingers dripping lightning.

"Two hundred fifty dollars a head," Mrs. Mabuse continued. "And tonight, we have..."

She glanced at one of her men and he said, "One hundred seventeen, Ma'am."

She turned back to me. "Figure a hundred tickets at two hundred fifty each. That's twenty-five thousand dollars."

There was another brilliant flash from beyond the window, and she glanced down into the courtyard and nodded. "We have four fights on a card, with a progressive purse totaling eight thousand dollars distributed to the winners. Operating expenses are about five thousand—mostly for the boat crew. That leaves in the neighborhood of twelve thousand dollars profit. Every week. That's a very rich pie to share."

She paused and waited for me to ask how big a slice she was going to offer me. I didn't. I said nothing.

Her eyes narrowed. I wasn't playing along. After a moment she said, "Five hundred a week. In cash. Delivered to a place of your choosing."

I looked back at her, kept my face blank. Five hundred a week was a lot of money. At my current pay grade, I was clearing three-twenty a week.

"Well?" she demanded. "Say something!"

"What's the undines' cut?" I asked.

Annoyance and confusion warred on her face. "What?"

"For use of the island," I explained. "This *is* Graveyard Island, isn't it? It's a Pluviose treaty zone. You couldn't be here without the consent of the refinery administration. How much do they get?"

"We have an arrangement," she said smugly. "Undines care nothing for human laws."

That was far from the truth, but I could tell she believed it.

"I'm not asking for much," Mrs. Mabuse went on. "Just your cooperation. You're a senior field agent, you know how to steer an investigation."

"All by myself?" I asked. "Or do you have someone else in CI?"

She didn't like that question. Her eyes narrowed and she said, "You'll be working alone."

"I'm used to that," I assured her.

She relaxed a bit.

"Of course," I said, pretending to think it over, "we'll have to come up with some explanation for where I am right now..."

She was ready for that, and I could tell that she liked that I had used *we*. "You're in a private hospital in Freebooter Park," she said easily. "Your car was struck by a truck leased to a shipping company with no traceable connection to me. The owner of the company felt responsible and had you treated for your injuries. You've been unconscious all afternoon."

"You have a doctor who will attest to that?"

She nodded.

Outside in the yard, a new bout was starting. There were flashes of light, and the crowd roared in response.

That story about me being hurt in an accident and not being able to call in wouldn't fool Blackwell for a minute, but that was okay. I just needed her to think that I bought it.

"Okay," I said. "The sooner we get back to shore the better. I'll give your courier the spare key to my locker at my athletic club. You can leave my cash there."

She raised her hand with a smile. "There is one final detail."

I braced myself. "And that is?"

She turned to one of her men. "Fetch Stefen, please."

He got up and went out the door, but that still left three men, probably armed. I didn't like those odds, but they might not get any better. I tensed myself to act, but before I worked up the nerve the door opened again and the man returned, with Stefen.

"Hello, Mr. Rockwell," I said.

He glowered at me. "That's not my name."

"Obviously," I agreed. "Not your address, either, unless you're bedding down at night in the linens aisle."

He ignored that and looked to Mrs. Mabuse. She smiled and told him, "Agent Rugar has agreed to work with us."

The magus—Stefen Something, not Cleavus Trent Rockwell—turned a smile on me. It wasn't a nice smile.

"Welcome to the family, *agent*," he said. He held out his hand to one of the men and was passed a metal briefcase. Opening it, he added, "Lose the shirt."

"Excuse me?" I asked, stalling for time.

Stefen ignored me and laid out the contents of the briefcase. A philosopher's egg, a brass cylinder the size of a can of soup, the sides showing graduated markings. It would contain the magical energy to power his working. Next, an isolate flask, a glass bottle covered with warding symbols, half full of a thick black liquid.

Lastly, a tattoo needle.

I stared at it and made no move to remove my jacket. "What is this?"

"Simply a precaution," Mrs. Mabuse said, her voice sounding reasonable. "All of my employees have them. It prevents problems with loyalty."

"You want to put a geas on me?" I shook my head. "I work for CPS. You don't think they scan us for spellwork?"

"It's a passive constriction," Stefen said, in that bored schoolteacher tone that mages—even gangster mages—use when talking to the unwashed. "There's no telemetry effects. It won't show up on an isinglass test. As long as you don't undress at work you'll be fine."

"This is not optional, Rugar." The mask was off. She no longer sounded like a society wife. This was Mabuse the crime kingpin.

AGAINST THE MIDNIGHT CURRENTS

Her men, who had been starting to relax, stood straighter and every one had a hand in his pocket.

I lifted my arms slowly. "Okay," I said. "As long as you can guarantee that I won't get burned when I go through the door at Government House."

I shrugged out of my jacket, and the mood in the room eased—just a little.

Then I threw my jacket over Stefen's head and snatched up the philosopher's egg. Only a magus could use the magical energy stored inside it to craft spells.

But anyone could discharge one. It just wasn't safe.

I spun the regulator ring at the top of the cylinder to wide open, and it flared. My hands felt suddenly cold, but I wasn't too numb to toss the egg at Mrs. Mabuse.

Her thugs, under the compulsion of the geas, rushed to protect her, and I bowled over the magus—still struggling with my jacket—and was out the door.

If she had men stationed in the hall outside the office...

She didn't.

I was in a narrow wooden corridor and running. There was a door directly ahead; I hit it without slowing down and it popped open, the frame splintering. Then I was on the catwalk around the yard where the mage battle was still going on. All eyes were on the fight and no one noticed me running away from the block of offices and deeper into the maze of piping that was the refinery proper.

The catwalk ended at a ladder, and I scrambled down it.

At the bottom of the ladder was a pipe four feet thick, with a valve on it the size of a truck tire. I grabbed the valve and spun it closed, then ran on. Mrs. Mabuse's men would be after me soon, and they would know the ground better than I did. I took a turn at random and paused to spin another valve. This one was closed, so I opened it.

There were shouts and running feet behind me.

Some kind of machine like a huge pump blocked my way. I flipped a few switches, then turned left and headed down a narrow alley formed by two massive pipes. At the end of the alley was another enormous pump, this one studded with mixing valves. I

223

started turning and flipping things at random.

"Rugar!"

I turned. The mage, Stefen, entered the alley, two of the thugs flanking him.

A yellow light started flashing on the panel of the pump. A moment later another light, much brighter, started strobing somewhere far up in the tangle of pipes.

"Sir," I told him. "You are under arrest for suspicion of murder by means of magic. Please place all weapons and thaumaturgically active devices on the ground."

He stared at me incredulously for a moment, then laughed. I missed what he said in response, though, because just then an earsplitting alarm began sounding. It was a whistle, rather than a horn.

All three men looked around nervously. Stefen seemed to be trying to say something to the other men over the din of the alarm. More brilliant lights were now flashing high up in the superstructure, the strobes not quite synchronized. The resulting stutter of brightness and shadow made it hard to see. I hoped that if they decided to shoot at me it would make it hard to aim.

Then—at last—an undine appeared.

A sphere of water drifted down from somewhere up in the maze of pipes. It was maybe ten feet across, but the strobing alarms made it hard to see details. Inside the huge bubble, I could see only a suggestion of sinuous limbs, like an octopus.

"What is the meaning of this?" it asked. Its voice sounded like a human voice to my ears, irritated, no doubt, at being dragged out of its watery bed to answer the alarms.

"I am agent Erik Rugar of the Lord Mayor's Committee for Public Safety. I was brought to your island against my will by these men, whom I believe intend me harm. I apologize for my interference in your operations; it was the quickest way to get your attention."

Stefen and his men turned and ran down the aisles of piping away from the undine. I don't know where they thought they were going, and I didn't care.

AGAINST THE MIDNIGHT CURRENTS

The voice from the sphere of water spoke again. "Stand aside, agent. I must return the equipment to its proper functioning."

I did as it asked and took a long shaky breath. At last, I was able to relax. The good guys had won this round.

That's what the papers said, anyway.

Reading the newspaper accounts of what came to be known as "The Graveyard Island Affair" was like watching a musical based on a popular novel. Events were changed, characters left out, and, all in all, one was left with a vague sense of missing the nuances of the plot.

I testified in the trial of Stefen Westin. He was convicted of murder and sent to the gas chamber.

Six other freecasters were eventually charged with unlicensed use of magic and ended up doing time. A dozen others were charged with conspiracy to violate statutes regarding the use of magic.

A number of senior staff members of the Graveyard Island Refinery were quietly sent back to Pluviose, as were two adjuncts in the Pluviose ambassadorial office. The ambassador made a formal statement in which he admitted nothing and claimed not to have known about anything. He was probably telling the truth.

A similar shakeup occurred in the CPS Licensing Department, but Import/Export escaped unscathed. My own name was mentioned only briefly, as part of the "also appearing" credits on page six.

The names Kevin and Marilisa Mabuse were conspicuous by their absence. Nor did any of the other subjects of Marcus Sweetgrass's photographs come into the public eye. I heard that there were some hearings held in camera, but my testimony was not required. The deposition I made—all five hours of it—was sealed and, so far as I know, locked away in a file cabinet, never to see the light of day.

Devin Sweetgrass Junior asked me if I was going to attend Stefen Westin's execution. I told him I never attended executions. I wondered how much he knew. Probably all he knew was that the man who'd killed his brother was going to pay for it with his life.

Probably that was all he needed to know.

I went back to work, at three hundred and twenty dollars a week.

DRACOHEIM CONFIDENTIAL

In the spring I rented a boat and took Darla from Miss Kitten's out for a day's fishing. We went close enough to Graveyard Island to see the pipes and tanks of the refinery. Darla asked me about my role in the affair, and—after swearing her to total secrecy—told her some lies about what a tough guy I was, and she pretended to believe them.

Then I caught us some dinner and cooked it there on the boat, on a little built-in grill.

"You should have been a fisherman," Darla told me after dinner.

"Yeah," I agreed, thinking about what we'd caught on Graveyard Island, and what we'd had to throw back. "I should have been."

Solvable Games

"**G**ood evening, gentlemen," Leonid said. "I am Magus Leonid Vetch, and I'll be introducing you to magical notation. I know that your course catalog lists Magus Schuyler as the instructor, but there has been a change."

He looked around the room. They were first year students, most of them just out of high school. To his eyes, they all looked the same, just boys really. There were seventeen names on his class list and he counted seventeen heads.

"It looks like everyone is here," he went on. "In time I'll learn your names, I promise, but today I'm using the cheat sheet. Please respond by raising your hand."

Automatically he read the roll, glancing up at each one to see who responded. Inwardly he wondered if he really would learn their names. His classes seemed to be getting younger every year. He'd be lecturing in a nursery soon. The uniforms didn't help, either.

"All right," he said when he'd made a neat check mark beside every name. He sat down on the edge of his desk and lit a cigarette. "The first thing you have to realize about magic is that you can't see what you're doing, only what you've done. The *effects* of magic are visible, but the thaumic flux—the force behind the magic—cannot be perceived by any human senses. If we were norns, we wouldn't need all this rigmarole because norns sense thaumic gradients the way that human eyes see light.

"But we're not norns. We have to use specialized equipment and complex calculations to determine what is going on, and then we make adjustments with more equipment, all without directly perceiving the workings of what it is we're tinkering with. We're like blind men trying to rebuild a car's engine—while the car is driving in rush hour traffic.

"Taking this course is mandatory. *Passing* this course is mandatory. Until I am satisfied that you have a solid understanding of how to measure, record, and calculate changes in thaumic flux, you will not be allowed to step foot in a working laboratory, because you would be a danger to yourself and to anyone in your general vicinity."

He paused to finish his cigarette and put it out in the ashtray. Then he hopped off the desk and went to the blackboard at the front of the room. He quickly wrote a list of terms, saying each one out loud as he wrote.

"Amplitude. Frequency. Resonance. Magnitude. Vector."

He put down the chalk and turned to face his students. "These are the coordinates for charting the thaumic flow. Before any working is begun, these five attributes must be determined by direct mechanical observation and the working calculated for these attributes. To do otherwise is to court disaster."

He turned back to the board and drew an arrow beneath each term. "Then there is the time element. These attributes describe a static equilibrium"—he paused to look over his shoulder at his class— "which you never find outside of an isolate chamber." He turned back to the board. "All of these are constantly changing. Sometimes gradually, sometimes with catastrophic rapidity. You *must* know not only the current values, but also how those values are changing over time."

He finished with the arrows and from memory he wrote a long, complex calculation on the remainder of the board. When he was finished, he went back over it, double checking each term to ensure that he had transcribed it accurately. He tapped the board and turned back to his class.

"This is the base thaumic flux equation—what we call the Itherton/Jymes equation. You will find it on page seven of your textbook." He broke out of his stern lecturer's bearing to grin at them. "It's somewhat neater in your book."

Then he put his serious face back on. "You will learn this equation. You will learn how to apply it, how to modify it, how to adjust it for environmental factors, and how to use it to calculate and predict the effects of a particular working on the existing flux.

"Or you will not be sitting here at the end of the semester."

SOLVABLE GAMES

He paused to look slowly around the room, meeting the students' worried eyes with his determined ones.

"Now. Get out your workbooks, and let's begin."

Two hours later, he was crossing the empty parking lot to his car. The problem with evening classes, he reflected, is that it always took him so long to wind down afterwards and get to sleep. He wouldn't call Eleanor, she had a full schedule this term and would be lecturing on Advanced Anatomy at 0800 tomorrow. What he should do, he knew, was head straight home and start in on the stack of alchemy textbooks that Magus Simmons had given him.

Over the last few years, some gnoetic manufacturers had begun experimenting with alchemical techniques, and the results had been encouraging. Now the president of the college, Dr. Bink, wanted Leonid to sit on a committee tasked with creating a dual Artificer/Alchemy program.

"Old dog," Leonid muttered as he started the car, "meet new trick."

He almost made it home. A few blocks away from his lonely house with its waiting copy of *The Foundations of Alchemical Conjurations* he was waylaid by the pink neon sign of Mitzi's.

One drink, he told himself. *Just a few minutes detour, then on to the books.*

Mitzi herself, a retired actress who had been a leading lady in numerous second and third string productions but had never quite made the big time, was behind the bar and she had his setup waiting by the time he crossed the floor. A shot of top shelf absinthe and a glass of ice water with a twist of lime.

He threw back the shot and sipped the water. Just the thing.

"How's the wizard biz?" Mitzi asked.

Leonid shrugged. "Just started the new semester," he said. "No one's blown up a lab yet, but give it a couple of weeks."

She laughed and gestured at the empty shot glass.

Why not? He nodded for her to refill it.

"Haven't seen you around much lately," she said when she set the new shot on the bar.

"They gave me tenure," Leonid explained, lifting the shot. "Now

229

they think they own me. Spent all summer in the lab, doing research."

He threw back the second shot and then deliberately put the glass on the bar upside down.

"Magus Vetch!" The voice was cheerful. Leonid turned.

The young man was in a decent jacket and open-necked shirt without a tie. His blond hair was close-cropped. Leonid cast his mind back and came up with a name.

"Mr. Kent." He stuck out his hand. "You're looking good."

Kent grinned. "You remember."

Leonid grinned back and pointed to an imaginary row of seats. "You sat right there for six semesters. So what are you doing with yourself now?"

"Iron Logic Imports," he said. "In Century Orchard. I write spec for user applications."

Leonid considered. "I don't think I know that company."

"We're new to the Midworld market. They've been selling calculating engines in Nivose and Verdemaire, mostly for business applications. I'm helping them break into Dracoheim."

"Impressive."

"Mostly I tell customers that what they want isn't practical without actually using the words, 'a stupid idea'."

Leonid laughed and reached to turn his shot glass back upright and wave to Mitzi, who gave him a quick nod and took the glass.

"Have a seat," Leonid said. "It's good to see you."

The young man did, then asked, "Did you hear about Shotwell?"

Leonid winced. "No. What happened?"

"He's back in Ventose."

"What?"

Kent nodded.

"As a prisoner?"

"Oh, no," Kent assured him. "He's working for an importer. The chigoes are just mad for Dracoheim music, and this company was looking for an import agent. Evidently it's hard to find humans willing to live in Ventose."

"They know about his record?"

SOLVABLE GAMES

A laugh. "Sure. That's why he applied. He was going through the want ads and found one looking for anyone with experience in Ventose. He applied as a joke, and they hired him."

Leonid sipped his new shot. "And he's happy there?"

"He seems to be. He's written a couple of times. There's a human expatriate community in Stiger, and he met a girl over there."

"That's good to hear," Leonid said. He'd always felt bad about Thodd Shotwell's arrest and his own part in it. "I'm glad he's doing well."

"And you've got tenure now," Kent said with a smile. "It's about time."

Leonid sighed heavily. "It's a lot of extra work. I'm on a dozen committees now and..." He broke off as an idea occurred to him. "You remember the career speakers series, right?"

"Of course."

"I don't suppose you'd be willing to give a guest talk?"

Kent laughed. "About what?"

"Oh, just tell them what you do. Dr. Bink wrote out a sample format sheet I'll send you, but you don't have to follow it. The idea is to let the students know what kind of jobs are available out there, get them all excited about staying in school and earning a certificate. You remember."

Kent nodded, thinking it over. "Well, I'll have to run it past the coordinators. They're very concerned with how humans see the company, but I think they'll approve."

"I can have the secretary send them a letter," Leonid offered.

Kent nodded. "That might be best, yes."

"Got a business card?"

Kent dug through his pockets and came up with one.

Leonid took it and looked longingly at the empty shot glass. With a sigh he got to his feet.

"I need to get going, but I'm going to hold you to this."

Kent smiled. "I'll come up with something to say. Heck, if we keep expanding, we'll probably have openings soon."

"Mention that during your talk."

The next day—between Thaumic Properties of Materials and

231

Indeterminate Calculus—Leonid gave Kent's card to the department secretary with a request that she send a formal request for Vladimir Kent to speak at Leeshore Technical College, at a time of his convenience. He'd be back to sign it after his next class.

His schedule wasn't particularly onerous this term. He had two first year lectures, NOTE101 and LAB001, three intermediate classes, MAT204, MAT210, and CAL205, one graduate class, LAB400.

Then there was his advanced research fellowship lab, limited to ten students. Over the next week, he would be meeting with the students one-on-one to discuss their projects. It was a new program, and he hoped that the students could come up with ideas on their own because he had no idea what Dean Welsh expected. "Directed experimentation in student centered independent practical projects" could mean almost anything.

Well, he'd nix anything that sounded too dangerous, and Welsh would disallow any project that was too expensive. Once the projects got underway, all he had to do was be available to answer questions and put out fires. Hopefully only in a figurative sense.

It was the committees. They'd started two weeks before the first day of the term, and he could already see they were going to be a problem.

He'd been on the distribution list for the minutes of the monthly Thaumaturgy Department meetings since he began teaching, but now he was expected to attend them in person. He was on the Steering Committee, which turned out to be Dr. Bink and Dean Welsh telling everyone else what was going to happen and pretending that it was a group decision. The Textbook Committee. The Operations Committee.

The Joint Curriculum Committee. He still hadn't managed to get more than a chapter into any of the alchemy textbooks he was supposed to be reading. The problem was that alchemy was so cursedly subjective. The text was full of phrases like "forces in congruence" and "proper proportions" and short on hard data.

That wasn't magic, that was mysticism. Sure, it worked, but even alchemists would admit it was more art than engineering. Leonid wasn't an artist, didn't want to be an artist, and was too old to be fiddling around with "contingent states of understanding," whatever they were.

He wanted to sweep Eleanor off her feet and run away with her to some fishing village in the islands and spend his days lying on the beach with her.

No, no, he really didn't. He loved teaching, and he knew Eleanor felt the same way about her students. It was just the cursed committees. Maybe he could have his research students craft a simulacrum that could attend meetings in his place.

Eleanor's suggestions over lobster salad and cocktails were more practical.

"You're a very straightforward man," she said. "It's really very sweet—everybody likes you because everybody knows that you're exactly what it says on the tin. You always say what's on your mind." A giggle. "Which is why you don't talk much."

Leonid paused with his fork halfway to his mouth. "I think I'm insulted."

"Oh hush," she went on. "The point is that's not how academic politics work. I've been chairing the stewardship board of the Quayside School of Nursing for twelve years now and not once in that time has the board ever decided anything. That's not what board meetings are for. The decisions are made before the meeting starts."

Leonid nodded. That's the conclusion he'd come to, at least as far as the Steering Committee was concerned. "So why bother with the meetings?"

"That's where the factions count heads. The different groups get together, and everyone gets to show what side they're on."

"I'm not in a faction," Leonid complained.

"You should be," Eleanor countered seriously. "You'll make everyone nervous if they don't know whose side you're on."

"I don't even know if we have sides."

"Of course you have sides. Every organization has factions." She had some more lobster, considering. "Spend some time with Dean Walsh. Something outside of work."

"He has asked me to his gaming club," Leonid admitted. "But I don't have time for that."

"Make time," Eleanor urged him. "Look, it's not like you're going to be part of some conspiracy to take over the school. It's just how business gets done. Let yourself be seen with Walsh, speak up every now and then to agree with him. That's all. You can't avoid the politics, and you'd never learn to play the game at your age. Being part of someone else's faction is the, uh, 'low impact course of treatment.'"

"Okay," Leonid frowned. "But why Walsh?"

"Because he's got legitimate avenues of power, so he won't need anything from you but your prestige."

"My prestige," Leonid snorted. "Right."

"You're one of the most senior instructors." She sighed. "Modesty is a virtue, but darling, you do overdo it."

"Any other instructions, Matron?"

"Order us dessert. And cognac."

In the middle of the next week, Leonid received a phone message from Clever Hammers, of the Iron Logic Company. He called back at once, and the forged one was available.

"Magus Vetch, I read with great interest your article regarding the properties of my nation's new metal for the export trade. We are securing a quantity of it for use in our manufacturing facilities." The forged one's voice was mechanically produced and sounded odd even over a phone line.

"I am pleased to hear that. I find the metal's properties fascinating, myself," Leonid replied.

"We will, of course, be pleased to have young master Kent speak at his former school. We have no doubt that he will represent himself as a credit to both of our businesses."

"He's a bright young man."

"Would it be permitted for me to tour the campus? The request is purely from my own curiosity regarding the instruction of young humans."

Leonid hadn't expected that, but he couldn't think of any reason why it would be a problem. The administration was always shepherding possible donors around the place.

234

SOLVABLE GAMES

"Well, certainly. I'd be happy to show you around myself, class schedule permitting."

"Excellent."

They made an appointment for two days hence. Leonid was free that day, except for the research fellowship lab. He could introduce the forged ones to his advanced students, they'd like that.

Leonid expected a truck to pull up at the appointed time, but Clever Hammers arrived in an ordinary taxicab. The forged one was constructed from brass and steel, polished to a mirror shine. It was as tall as a human being, but delicately built, with a central torso not much larger than a fire extinguisher and spindly arms and legs of jointed metal. Its head was a sphere with no attempt made to mimic a human face, just a dozen or so tiny lenses in a circular array.

Shaking hands with the forged one was like grasping a bundle of screwdrivers, but Leonid smiled warmly and introduced himself, welcoming Clever Hammers to the College.

"The president would like to see you before the tour," Leonid said.

"I would be honored."

Mercifully, the meeting with Dr. Bink and Magus Welsh was brief, an exchange of pleasantries. Mindful of Eleanor's advice, Leonid made sure to introduce Welsh as "my master" and used his full title, which the dean seemed to appreciate. Then Leonid started with the classrooms.

"We have no such facilities in Ferose," the forged one said.

"No, I don't suppose you would," Leonid said slowly. "I have heard of your wisdoms—printed cards that contain the skills for using magic. I suppose your 'school' would be a library of such cards?"

"There are many such libraries, beginning, of course, with Thirty-Nine Dire Wisdoms scribed by Xor the Unliving."

"I've heard of those." There were rumors that the Blackwater Street Market riots of a few years back were somehow connected to the Dire Wisdoms.

"They have great power. The lesser wisdoms that we use for ordinary matters contain only minute fragments of the Dire patterns."

"It must be convenient to learn a new skill that way," Leonid said, thinking of his struggle with the alchemical texts. "I rather wish humans could."

"Is it true that memory in humans is activated by repetition?"

"I suppose you could say that," Leonid said slowly. "Practice is certainly important to the process." He considered, then went on. "Well, we like to think that comprehension of the material is as important as repetition for our students. Hence the combination of lectures and copybook work."

The bell rang then to signal the end of the class period and the hall was full of students. The boys, Leonid was pleased to see, took the unusual visitor in stride, just as they would if one of their instructors was guiding a human around the campus. Leeshore was a cosmopolitan school.

Clever Hammers in turn greeted the students as they passed in the hallway. It had no face to read, but Leonid sensed that it enjoyed watching the bustle of the young men.

The bell rang again and the hallway emptied out.

"I'd like to show you our labs next," Leonid said, heading for the stairs.

The forged one obediently followed. "I was in Verdemaire before," it said.

"I've never had occasion to visit there," Leonid replied. "It's closer, cosmologically speaking, to Ferose, so I imagine it's more like your home."

"In many ways, yes. Yours is a sexually dimorphic species, unlike the incubi and ourselves."

"That probably seems strange to you."

"I find it interesting how it shapes your social customs. For example, it seems that only the males are educated here?"

"If you mean this school, yes," Leonid said. "There are other schools for young ladies who wish to pursue a trade. A close friend of mine works at one such school, for medicine."

"The sexes are kept apart."

Leonid sighed. "It's easier that way. Young men would find the

236

presence of young women distracting. But they mingle outside of school hours." He hoped that the forged one wouldn't ask him to explain dating and courtship. His own grasp on the subject was tenuous.

Clever Hammers seemed willing to let the subject drop and toured the school's lab facilities with a polite interest that Leonid felt certain was entirely feigned. He was painfully aware of how primitive human artificery was compared to the wonders the forged ones were able to produce.

His mood lightened when they reached room 317, his independent study boys. Here was something he could be proud of. He introduced them to Clever Hammers and explained the purpose of the seminar.

The forged one shook each young man's hand and then went to the blackboard at the front of the room. It wrote quickly—and with the precision of a typewriter—and filled the board with a dozen lines of dense mathematical notation.

Automatically, Leonid followed along. It was a material frequency calculation, but not one he was familiar with. The forged one put down the chalk and turned to the students.

"Analyze," it said.

Several of the young men glanced nervously back at Leonid. He kept his face neutral and gestured at the board. It seemed clear that Clever Hammers had set the problem for the students and not their instructor.

"What's $t_{(f[m/C])}$?" one asked, pointing.

"Time adjusted for cosmological constant," another one answered him.

"It's on both sides," a third pointed out. "Does that mean it cancels out?"

"Maybe.... But only if it's the same constant on both sides. It doesn't specify that."

"That's a material flux array." A pause. "It's also on both sides."

"And also adjusted for cosmological constant."

"For theta and rho. But lambda's inverted."

"Plus or minus... that sequence. Looks like a limit function of rho sub zero divided by rho sub prime?"

"That's the limit? Boy, that's a lot of uncertainty..."

Leonid smiled as he listened to the boys dissect the strange equation. This is what he loved about teaching, seeing that spark of comprehension dawning in their eyes.

At the same time, he was running his own silent analysis. The notation was standard, although the format was different than Midworld ordinal. It was, he decided at last, a matrix for calculating the etheric equipotential between two realms based on the cosmological difference in the properties of the same material in both environments.

Very elegantly done, too. It would have taken him several pages to produce the same outcome. He studied the symbols, making mental notes on how the arrays were collapsed. Unorthodox, by human standards, but it looked as if it should work. He wanted to run his data from his recent journal article through it and see whether it yielded the proper constants from the Midworld and Nivose.

Later. The boys were still talking together in low, excited voices.

"Is it?"

"It's got to be."

"But the inverted lambda?"

"Doesn't matter. It's inverted on both sides."

"So... it's the difference in scales rather than additive?"

"Yes! That's why. It's to calculate the difference instead of the congruence."

"Got to be."

"We're sure?"

"I'm sure."

"Yeah."

One of the students—Kush, a self-possessed Territorial who had become an unofficial class leader in his years at the school—said formally, "Artificer Clever Hammers, is the purpose of this computation to determine cosmological constants as a function of observable material qualities?"

The forged one bowed its spherical head, and its ring of eyes narrowed and widened their irises in a complex pattern. Leonid wondered if that was the Ferose equivalent of a human facial expression and, if so, what it signified.

"Precisely so, young humans," it said. "We call it the Traveler's Map. It was of very great utility during the early days of pathfinding."

"Can it be reversed?" Tompkins blurted out. Then he looked around and grew embarrassed. "I mean," he said softly, looking at the board, "Could it be used to predict changes in material qualities across realm boundaries?"

Leonid had already considered the same question. He waited to see what Clever Hammers would say.

"Can it?" It gestured at the board.

"No," spoke up Miller. "I mean... yes, but no." He looked around for confirmation.

Koynes took up the explanation. "The uncertainty factor. It would be, uh, twice, uh, four, no—*sixteen* times as great a margin. Right?"

"Like Samuel's Law," suggested Kush.

"I do not know that," Clever Hammers said.

"The Law of Exponential Decay," Leonid supplied. "Here, it was formulated by Ivor Samuel."

The forged one nodded. "You have taught these young ones well, Magus."

Leonid grinned. "They're smart boys. A year from now, they might be working for you."

"We would be honored." A pause while the forged one turned its gaze to each student in turn. "But now I must go—I have business matters to attend to."

Leonid escorted it out to the front office and asked the school secretary to call a cab.

While they waited, Clever Hammers said, "With your permission, Magus, I would like to send your class a gift. It is a tradition of my nation, to mark significant events."

"That would be very much appreciated, I'm sure."

Clever Hammer's gift arrived three days later.

One of the custodians was waiting in the hall for Leonid after he wrapped up his Intermediate Properties of Gnoetic Metals lecture.

He had a hand truck with a wooden box about three feet on a side, stenciled with Iron Logic Imports. In place of a packing slip, an envelope addressed to Magus Vetch was taped to the side.

Magus--

Thank you again for the opportunity to visit Leeshore Technical College as your guest. During the brief time I have been in the Midworld, I have learned to appreciate human culture, so different from my own nation, but so welcoming to the stranger to your shores.

I trust that you will enjoy seeing your students solve the enclosed puzzle box in order to claim their gifts as much as they will enjoy delving into its mysteries. Such devices have a long history in my nation, and I am delighted to be able to share this tradition with your young human scholars.

I do hope you will keep me informed of their progress and let me know when they reach the center,

Clever Hammers, Business Planner, Iron Logic Imports.

"Could you take that up to 317 and put it on one of the lab tables?" Leonid asked the custodian. "It's not too heavy to lift, is it?"

"Not too bad."

While the box was being delivered to the lab, Leonid checked out a camera and a tripod, an ocular filter for the camera, and a case of film.

He set up the camera and loaded it with film, then took two pictures of the box sitting on the lab table, one with the filter and one without.

Then he made himself leave it alone until his students arrived.

Once they were all assembled, he read them his letter from Clever Hammers and added, "You're on your own on this one, boys. If you need me to check out any equipment, let me know. Other than that, it's all on you."

Then he added, "I do want to get a picture of you all together before you open it, though."

SOLVABLE GAMES

Miller had already taken a small prybar from the tool chest. He stood poised over the wooden crate and the others clustered around him.

"Perfect," Leonid said, and took the shot.

Then Miller opened the crate, moving slowly and carefully, with the other boys clustered around him. Under the wooden box was a metal box, and Leonid made the boys stand back so he could get a clear picture. It was ornate in the distinctive Ferose style, covered with small hatches and enigmatic projections, all of it showing the brilliant edges of precision machining.

A second envelope was taped to the metal box itself.

Kush reached for it gingerly, as if he expected it to explode when he touched it.

Mr. Bates, Mr. Brinker, Mr. Elder, Mr. Evovitch, Mr. Koynes, Mr. Kush, Mr. Miller, Mr. Placid, Mr. Tompkins, Mr. Wilson, was written on the outside of the envelope. Kush opened it and withdrew a single sheet from the inside.

I am the box of metal, locked up tight,
A challenge to the students standing near,
Intricate twists and turns they must ignite,
To solve the puzzle, conquer any fear.

My secrets hidden, waiting to be found,
A labyrinth of locks and doors to breach,
The students gather, with their minds so sound,
To open me up, a prize within their reach.

With skill and wit, they twist and turn with care,
Each step they take must lead them to the key,
A test of patience, focus, and repair,
A journey to the answer they must see.

So take the challenge, let your mind unfold,
And solve the puzzle that is locked up, bold.

After he read it aloud he presented it to Leonid, who took a picture of the poem.

"Okay..." Brinker said slowly. "Now what?"

Elder started forward, then paused and turned to Leonid. "We should get a picture of each side before we do anything. Including the bottom."

Leonid nodded and gestured for him to turn the box.

"Whoa!" Tompkins said suddenly. "Have you got a filter on that camera?" He was wearing one of the class oculars. "That thing has a got a wicked flux."

Elder pulled his hand back quickly and went to put on a pair of containment gloves, stitched with the metal thread of wards.

Leonid didn't believe that the forged one's gift would be dangerous, but handling potentially active material with containment gloves was standard lab procedure. Elder should have put them on without being prompted.

They turned the box so that Leonid could get detailed shots—one standard, and one with the ocular filter—of each of the cube's six sides. There was no obvious bottom or top, all the sides seemed equally detailed. There was no writing on the box, either.

"They're not quite the same..." Evovitch said. "The sides."

Placid was leaning back and forth, studying two of the adjacent sides. "No," he announced. "Close, but there are differences."

Koynes began making drawings on a pad of graph paper.

Leonid checked the counter on the back of the camera. Nearly through the first roll. He snapped the last few quietly, catching the boys in conversation, then popped the roll out and put a new one in place.

"I'm going to develop these," he told the students. "Then you can work from the pictures."

Koynes looked up, but went back to his sketch. Leonid approved. It was good lab practice.

This photo lab was mostly used to document experiments and was empty this early in the semester. Leonid was able to use all of the equipment at once which let him run the entire roll in two batches. Still photochemistry took time and it was over an hour before he returned to the lab with the set of prints, all on 32-inch sheets.

The box sat serenely on the lab table in the center of chaos. The boys had moved two of the rolling chalkboards together and covered them with scrawled notes. More notes covered papers scattered everywhere. Placid and Evovitch were wearing oculars, Tompkins had the Tillinghast Resonator set up next to the box and was arguing with Koynes over where to attach the leads. Kush, Miller, and Elder stood at the chalkboards, annotating each other's calculations.

"Going well?" Leonid asked cheerfully, setting down the sheaf of prints.

There was an awkward moment of silence, then Evovitch said sadly, "This thing doesn't make any sense at all."

"These might help," Leonid suggested, gesturing at the prints. "At least they'll give you more to argue about."

He went back to the camera and snapped a few shots of the cluttered lab as the boys started checking out the prints, Koynes frowning as he compared them to his sketches.

That done, he announced, "I don't have any morning classes tomorrow, so I'm willing to keep the lab open until, say, 2100. You're welcome to stay until then, if you like."

The boys looked over at him, nodding and checking their watches.

"But for now, I'm going to run down to the corner diner. Don't burn the place down while I'm gone."

Leonid ordered dinner, then called Eleanor from the payphone while waiting for the food.

After he explained the forged one's gift and his students' reaction to it she asked, "Do you think they'll work it out?"

"Hard to say," Leonid hedged. "Ferose metaclockwork is far more advanced than anything we can do on our own. I'm sure Clever Hammers dumbed it down for human students, but even so, he may be overestimating our capabilities."

"You'll help them if they get stuck, won't you?"

"No! Of course not. This is a puzzle for them."

A laugh. "Like you'll be able to help yourself."

243

Leonid felt a flash of annoyance. He did want to try his hand at the alien mechanism, but he intended to leave it alone. It was a matter of his professional pride. "It's their puzzle, not mine."

Eleanor was contrite. "Of course, darling."

After dinner—and a stop at his office for a nip of absinthe—he went back to the lab.

One of the hatches on the box was open.

Leonid came forward to look inside. There was a collection of meshed gears. Stamped on the face of each gear was an arrow. They were all pointing up.

"Wonderful. Did you document this?" Leonid asked, gesturing at the camera.

"We got pictures," Kush assured him.

"And notes," Koynes added.

"Placid got it open," Evovitch said. "He pried it with a screwdriver."

Leonid looked sharply at Placid, who rolled his eyes.

"Did not," Placid shot back. "You have to press each hatch in sequence. Then this one pops open."

"And the gears?" Leonid asked.

"They were pointing in all directions when we got it open," Tompkins explained. "Took some figuring to get them all lined up."

"I think we have to close the hatch to activate the next puzzle," Kush said. "We were waiting for you."

Leonid took his position by the camera. "Go ahead, let's see what happens."

Placid reached out—all the boys were now wearing containment gloves, Leonid noted with approval—and pushed the hatch closed.

It clicked home and stayed shut. Inside the box, things whirred and clicked, then another hatch popped open, this one on the top. Leonid took a picture, slipped the ocular filter over the lens, and snapped another one.

That evening, the students solved the puzzles under a total of three of the hatches—the gears with the arrows, then a maze of clear glass tubes filled with colored liquids, then a lock with a key that had to be manipulated into a different shape in order to work.

SOLVABLE GAMES

At last, Leonid had to force the students out of the lab so that he could lock up and go home. They would have been happy, he was sure, to keep messing with the thing all night long, but one had to draw the line somewhere.

The next morning, Kush and Bates were waiting for Leonid when he unlocked his office at 900. With a sigh he escorted them upstairs to 317 and unlocked that.

"Get pictures of everything," Leonid reminded them. "There's a whole case of film on my desk."

Then he went on to his first lecture, Organic Gnoetics. As soon as the bell rang, he went back upstairs.

There were four students clustered around the puzzle box in 317. Dean Welsh was standing by the camera, watching them.

Leonid joined him.

"I sent three rolls down to be developed," the dean said softly. "They managed to get another one of those hatches open. Evidently they have to solve each puzzle in order?"

"As near as we can determine, yes," Leonid agreed. "It didn't come with an instruction manual."

"We can use some of these shots in our next brochure. And maybe we could get an article in the Leeshore Courier."

"Oh, the boys would like that," Leonid grinned. "Something for their scrapbooks."

The two men watched the students studying the latest puzzle and discussing theories in low, intense voices.

Leonid took a deep breath and steeled himself. "Look, Kravitz," he began, "is that invitation still open for your gaming club?"

Welsh grinned broadly. "Oh, certainly. Sevenday evenings at the Sun and Steel Club in Fort Charle. Dinner around 1800, and we get to the tables about 2000."

"Eleanor would like to go." It was her idea, after all.

"That would be great," Welsh said with genuine enthusiasm. "This week? I'll call the club secretary and have you listed as my guests."

"If that's okay."

Welsh stuck out his hand.

245

"We'll see you there." They shook on it. "You've met Marjorica, of course. We can play girls against boys—if Eleanor plays."

"She was part of a club when she worked at Angel Street," Leonid said.

"Perfect."

"I've got to go set up my next lab."

"Yeah," Welsh sighed. "I've got things to do, too. It's rather captivating, this Ferose puzzle."

"That it is."

Leonid fled to his office and called Eleanor at the school. She was in class, but he was able to leave a message with the secretary.

"Tell her that I've got reservations for us at the Sun and Steel Club in Fort Charle for 1800 on Sevenday."

"Will do."

Then he called Iron Logic and told the—human sounding—receptionist to let Clever Hammers know that Magus Vetch's students had solved five of the puzzles so far, and that they were having the time of their lives.

They'd solved seven by the end of the week, and Leonid had to be firm. There would be no access to room 317 over the weekend. They could play with their toy again on Oneday morning—and any student of the fellowship lab discovered skipping his assigned classes would be barred from the lab.

On Sevenday, Leonid picked Eleanor up at 1700. She was wearing the brown leather dress that she'd bought in Hunger City and had her hair pulled back in a tight braid. She looked spectacular.

He found the Sun and Steel Club easily, although he'd never been there before, and they were in the lobby at quarter to 1800. The club clerk took their names and invited them to have a seat in the bar while they waited for their hosts.

Kravitz and Marjorica Welsh showed up a few minutes before the hour, and while Leonid was introducing Eleanor to them, another couple arrived.

"Dave and Jenna Higgins," Welsh explained. "Dave is head of personnel for Amber Elixir's Marsh Parish refinery."

Over excellent steaks, Leonid explained to Higgins about the puzzle box from Clever Hammers.

"They've solved seven puzzles, you say? How many do you think there are, altogether?"

Leonid shrugged. "There is a total of forty-four panels, but I don't imagine there's a puzzle behind every single one. They'll just have to go through the sequence and find out."

"Fascinating. This is a Ferose tradition?"

"That's what Clever Hammers said. We still don't know much about the forged ones' culture."

"Not much tourism," Jenna Higgins observed. "It's so far, and the pictures don't look inviting."

"I don't know about that," Kravitz objected. "Extraordinary architecture. The city of Xor is an incredible work of engineering."

"Yes, but the landscape is so bleak outside the city. Nothing grows there," his wife argued.

"No local cooking to sample, either," Eleanor observed wryly.

The conversation turned to travel, then. All of them had been to Nivose, and the Higgins had been to Verdemaire for a week.

Then the waiter came to tell them that their table was ready in the gaming room.

The set up was a simple one, with three armies on one side of the table and three armies on the other. The terrain was mostly flat, cut by a few rivers, with a single hill in the center of the board and a small fort atop the hill.

"Thirty turns," Kravitz said. "The team that has possession of the fort at the end of turn thirty wins."

Leonid nodded. The small armies didn't seem to be labeled by player, so he picked up the token for the blue army and took a chair on that side of the table. He had a squad of longbows and two squads of pikemen.

Eleanor studied the armies on the other side of the board before settling on purple, which was four knights supported by two squads of light infantry. The other players picked their armies.

Dave Higgins lifted the dice that would determine the turn order. "Okay, girls," he said, "who wants to roll?"

Eleanor picked up her team's dice but paused before rolling. She slid a folded ten dollar bill out of her purse and set it in the fort on the center of the board. She looked challenging across to the men.

Kravitz laughed. "I'm in," he said cheerfully, and took a bill out of his wallet.

Jenna Higgins looked worried. "I'm not very good at this," she admitted to Eleanor.

"Just do what I tell you," Eleanor assured her. "We'll be fine."

Leonid put a ten-spot from his wallet on the other bills. All of the others did likewise.

"Now let's roll," Eleanor said.

The men's team won the first roll, and Dave and Kravitz elected for a cautious advance, with Leonid placing his supporting troops where they suggested.

Eleanor, in contrast, ran her knights straight to the center hill, leaving the non-mounted troops to catch up as best they could. It was a risky strategy, and the men's archers peppered the knights as soon as they were in range.

The knights held out for two more turns, giving the rest of the women's forces time to move into position to flank the men's armies with a crossfire.

What followed was a bloodbath. Since Eleanor's pieces had been the last ones to occupy the center fortress, all the women had to do was prevent the men's armies from taking that position. The men, however, had to advance into the fort and hold it for an entire round to turn over possession.

Leonid lost his entire force of pikemen in suicide runs, none of them successful. Dave managed to move a few of his heavy infantry into the fort itself, but they didn't survive the round.

At the end of the thirtieth turn, Eleanor's initial mad dash was still the last occupation of the fort, and Kravitz laughed delightedly as he handed Eleanor the flag that symbolized victory.

"I really didn't think you'd get away with that," he said.

She smiled and accepted the flag, "I wasn't sure myself. It was a calculated risk."

"Well calculated," Kravitz said. He scooped up the bills from the middle of the battleground and handed them over.

SOLVABLE GAMES

Dave Higgins was clearly unhappy with the loss, but managed to be gracious about it.

"We'll have to try this again sometime."

"Absolutely," Eleanor agreed. "But not tonight. Kravitz, Marjorica, thank you ever so much for inviting us." She distributed the winnings to the other women.

Leonid picked up the hint. "We really should be going."

In the car on the way back to Eleanor's boarding house she said, "I think that went well, don't you?"

"I'm not sure that beating the dean advanced my cause any."

"Oh, bosh. He loved it." Eleanor grinned at him. "Oh, dear, I didn't bruise your fragile male ego?"

"My fragile male ego is not bruised by war games, dear." Leonid considered. "It may have bruised Mr. Higgins a bit, though."

"Mr. Higgins should learn how to rank his missile fire better, then."

He parked at the curb in front of her building.

"Are you coming in, magus?" she asked.

"I don't know. What will the neighbors think?"

"They'll think you're about to become the luckiest boy on the mainland."

On Oneday morning, his entire advanced research class was waiting for him outside his office when he arrived.

"All right, all right," Leonid raised his hands in surrender. "Come on."

"I figured out the sequence for the beads," Koynes said excitedly.

"*We* figured out the sequence," Evovitch corrected.

Leonid unlocked the door of 317. "Pictures, boys," he reminded them. "Get pictures of everything."

Leonid went back downstairs for coffee in the teacher's lounge before the day's lectures.

He saw Kush and Bates waiting in the hallway while he was wrapping up his 1400 class, Intermediate Matrix Transformations. The young men were nearly dancing with excitement.

"Problems 1 thru 6 at the end of the chapter for next class, and show your work," Leonid said. "Dismissed."

249

He left the room while his students were gathering their books. "Well?" he asked.

"It's open," Kush said.

Leonid was out of breath when they reached 317.

The box had unfolded on the table. In the center was a stack of velum envelopes.

Leonid looked around, counting heads. "Who's missing?"

Before they could answer, Evovitch and Miller hurried in.

"I found him," Miller said unnecessarily.

For a moment they looked at each other and the box, then Kush stepped up to pick up the first envelope. He handed it to Bates, who examined it, but didn't open it yet.

"Maybe it's a hundred-dollar bill," he said with a smile.

"Too thick for that," Kush said and handed around the rest of them quickly.

"Hold them up," Leonid said. "I want to get a picture to send Clever Hammers. Big smiles, now!"

As soon as he clicked the pictures the boys opened their envelopes.

He took several more pictures as they removed the cards from their envelopes. They were like playing cards, but a bit larger than a standard deck.

The boys studied the cards. Leonid could see the backs of them, black and gray in a diamond pattern.

"So, what did you get?" Leonid asked.

No answer. The boys stared at the faces of their cards, not moving.

"Boys, you're scaring me," Leonid tried a laugh. It didn't come out right. Something was wrong.

Brinker fell to the ground, convulsing.

Leonid rushed to him. The card had fallen from the student's hand, and Leonid glanced at the face of it. On it was a pattern of intersecting lines, detailed and impossibly complex. He tore his eyes away with an effort. Another boy hit the ground, then another.

Leonid rushed to the door. The hallway was empty. He ducked into the next classroom. Magus Tellman was lecturing.

SOLVABLE GAMES

"Get the dean up here, now," Leonid shouted. "And call an ambulance—a bunch of them. I've got ten students who need help!"

Then he ducked back into 317. All of the boys were on the floor now. They were twitching gently, eyes wide and staring at nothing. Leonid collected the cards, careful not to do more than glance at the faces, and stuffed them in his pocket. He was crawling under a bench for the last one when Tellman came in the room.

"What's going on?"

"Where's Kravitz?"

"I sent a student to get him and call the hospital. What's wrong with them?"

"Ferose wisdoms," Leonid said acidly. "Clever Hammer's gift."

"What?" Tellman stared at the boys.

Just then the dean came into the room, out of breath. Behind him Leonid could see the hallway filling with curious students.

Leonid explained what had happened.

"Where are the wisdoms now?"

Leonid patted his pocket.

"Is there anything we can we do for them?" Kravitz asked, gesturing at the students. They had stopped shaking and lay still, staring blankly upwards.

Leonid scrubbed his face with his hands. "I... I don't know," he said miserably. "I took away the foci, but other than that... I don't think so."

Kravitz nodded, then glanced at Tellman. "Oskar, you go down to the front and wait for the medics."

Tellman looked startled, but nodded and obeyed.

Once Tellman had gone, Kravitz glanced at the door and spoke quietly. "The college has got your back on this, Leo, but I have to know—did you have any idea that the Ferose artifact contained optical spellwork?"

"No—" Leonid started automatically, then stopped himself and thought hard. "No," he repeated slowly. "I knew Clever Hammers wasn't very familiar with humans, but it never occurred to me that he would try *this*."

Kravitz sighed. "I'm not up to date on the research, but what I

251

know about human exposure to the wisdoms isn't encouraging."

Leonid looked down at the students—*his* students—lying still on the floor and couldn't reply. He remembered the offhand remark he'd made to the forged one.

I rather wish humans could.

Was that why Clever Hammers had given the boys the cards? Was this in some way his fault?

The first ambulance crew arrived with folding stretchers. Leonid tried to help, but Kravitz took him by the elbow and led him away.

"Leo, go home. I told Mrs. Barden you'll be taking few days off and to arrange substitutes for your classes," Kravitz said. "Look— you understand that this will have to go to the board, don't you? It's nothing for you to worry about, but, well, something like this..."

Leonid nodded, feeling empty. "Where are they taking the students?"

"Fort Charle. Progress Central," one of the medics said without looking up. "It's closest."

"They'll get the best care available, believe me," Kravitz said.

"I should tell Clever Hammers."

"No," Kravitz said quickly. "We need to handle that through legal. You go home. I'll call as soon as there is any news."

Leonid left, pushing through the milling students trying to ask him for information. He made it to his car without speaking or looking anyone in the face. Then he drove home automatically, trying very hard not to think about anything.

He poured himself a drink and sat, holding it in his hand for a long moment before taking the first sip. Then he called the Quayside School of Nursing. Eleanor was available.

"Something terrible has happened," he told her.

"What?"

He outlined the situation quickly and almost dispassionately. It was easier to treat it as a technical problem. Easier not to think about the boys, their pride in solving the puzzle, their excitement at earning their prize.

"Fort Charle," Eleanor said when he had finished. "No, Dr. Benway's team at Dracoheim Major has the best neurosciences department. I'll call over there and get someone to consult on this. The head of department knows me."

"What's going to happen to those boys?"

"Impossible to tell. How long were they exposed?"

"A minute, maybe?" Leonid tried to reconstruct the horrifying moment when he realized what had happened. "Less. I moved as fast as I could to get the cards away from them."

"That's good. They'll probably need the cards, to determine the course of treatment. Are they still at the school?"

Leonid felt in his pocket. "No, I have them with me." He counted them by touch. All ten.

"I'll call a service and have them messengered to the hospital. Do you have an isolate envelope for them?"

"I should. Around here someplace."

"Put them in there and seal them. Make sure the messenger knows how dangerous they are."

"Right." He felt on the verge of tears.

"Listen to me, darling," she said, "this isn't your fault. You couldn't have predicted what that forged one would do. It was criminally irresponsible, putting those things in the puzzle box for the kids to find. You did everything you could."

He didn't answer. He didn't believe that.

She sighed. "I need to get busy. Seal up those cards and wait for the messenger. I'll be over as soon as I can. Don't do anything stupid."

He laughed bitterly at that. "Yes, Matron."

"Good boy. We'll talk when I get there."

He was drunk by the time she arrived, but not as drunk as he could have been. Not drunk enough to do something stupid. Instead, he went through his library and read everything he could find on Ferose wisdoms.

"The optical spellwork of artificial beings is intrinsically abhorrent to any living mind," Leonid said to Eleanor as she came in the door, reading from *The Runic Paths to Power,* "leading inevitably to madness, imbecility, and death."

"Have you eaten?" she asked him.

"The course of decay is inescapable," he went on from the book, "once the first steps upon the cursed path of inhuman knowledge are taken, all hope is lost."

"Eaten," she repeated slowly. "It's when you put food in your mouth. Have you done that today?"

Without waiting for a reply, she bustled into the kitchen.

He was brooding silently over the book when she returned with some bread and cheese. "You've got thirty seconds to start eating, or I feed you."

He looked up, his face grim.

"I'm not bluffing," she went on. "I used to work in the mentally incompetent ward."

That got a bitter laugh, and he took a bite of bread. Once he tasted food, he realized he was starving.

Eleanor watched him wolf it down and said, "I'll make some soup."

In the morning, they went to the hospital, after a brief stop at Eleanor's apartment for her to shower and change.

"Be quiet and let me do the talking," Eleanor whispered as they crossed the lobby to the registration desk.

Leonid had no desire to speak. His chest was a cold knot of guilt and dread.

Eleanor chatted easily with the staff and got them a private consultation with the doctor in charge of the ward.

"It's too early to make any firm predictions, of course, but I don't anticipate any lasting harm from their exposure."

"Really?" Leonid felt hope for the first time since the awful moment he saw the boys collapsing to the floor.

"The wisdoms themselves are minor ones, what they call fourth order derivations, and I understand that an instructor acted swiftly to limit the contact."

"That was me."

"You did exactly the right thing, block the line of sight and call for an ambulance."

"What happens now?" Eleanor asked.

"We have the boys on low doses of a sedative that suppresses cognition. You see, the malmeme does damage by setting up a mental loop—rather like having a catchy tune stuck in your head. By keeping the brain from being able to follow the higher order reasoning inspired by the images, we break that loop. In a few days, they won't remember what they saw on the cards."

The doctor smiled reassuringly at Leonid. "We know a great deal more about the physiological effects of magic on the human brain now than we used to, and we have techniques to mitigate them."

"Can I see the boys?"

The doctor's smile was replaced by a worried expression. "That's not a good idea right now. Perhaps in a few days."

Leonid nodded. "All right."

The doctor seemed relieved that Leonid agreed so readily. Kindly, he said, "It's not *you*, you understand. But it would be best to avoid any associations that might remind them of the wisdoms. Insomuch as that's possible."

"I do understand," Leonid said. He took what felt like his first full breath since the incident, let it out slowly. "I'm just glad they'll be okay."

"We'll want to keep them under observation and schedule regular follow up visits for a few months, but like I say, it's unlikely that there will be any permanent damage."

Leonid stood and extended his hand. "I'm sure you're a busy man. Thank you for your time."

"Your office will receive regular updates."

Eleanor stopped Leonid in the lobby and pointed to the bank of pay phones. "Call your office."

He looked at her, confused. "And say what?"

She took his arm and led him towards the phones. "Tell them that you have visited the hospital and heard the good news and that you will be available to the inquiry committee at their convenience."

"They can call me at home when they want me," Leonid muttered, but he was already digging in his pocket for a coin.

He got the school switchboard and asked for Mrs. Barden. After a suitable pause she came on the line.

"This is Leonid Vetch," he said, then paused, unsure how to

proceed.

He didn't have to. "Magus Vetch," she said brightly, "I'm glad you called. Dr. Bink would like to see you in his office at 1300, if that's good for you."

"1300? Certainly. Can you tell me what this is about?"

"Dr. Bink will explain everything then," she assured him.

He hung up the phone and looked over at Eleanor. "I think I'm fired," he said miserably.

"What did they say?"

"I'm meeting with the president at 1300."

"Did they tell you to bring your keys?"

"No."

"Then you're not fired."

They went out for brunch, but Leonid wasn't able to do more than play with his food, despite Eleanor's attempts to lighten his mood.

"Darling, suppose the college lets you go—they won't, but suppose they did," she said softly. "What of it? You certainly don't need the money. We could go traveling. I'll take a term's sabbatical and we'll book an outrageous cruise. We can stay with Chad and Bett in Hunger City, and cruise Pluviose, and see the Garden of Heart's Desire in Verdemaire. I've got money put away, and I've always wanted to see the realms..." She reached across the table to put her hand on his. "I've just never had anyone to see it with until now."

"I might lose my license over this." His words were almost a whisper.

"Oh, now you're being melodramatic," she chided him. "Honestly, on what grounds? Because you couldn't foresee what that horrid little mechanical man would do? Did Magus Welsh anticipate it? He saw that box, too."

"No," Leonid agreed. He gave a long sigh. "I should have... Those boys trusted me."

"You did everything you could," Eleanor said firmly. "What you are going to do now is go to your hearing or inquiry or whatever it is this afternoon and get yourself back in the classroom. When those boys get out of the hospital, you are going to be there for them and make sure they graduate at the end of the term."

Leonid nodded. "I can do that," he admitted, and stood.

Eleanor pointed at his untouched food. "And eat something. At least your toast. I am not going to let you go to see Dr. Bink on an empty stomach."

Leonid sighed, then picked up the toast and crammed it in his mouth. He chewed messily, then swallowed. "Satisfied?"

"Well, no," Eleanor said, standing. "But I suppose it will have to do."

Halfway across the parking lot Eleanor stiffened and grabbed his arm. He looked up and saw a bright slim figure standing beside his car.

Clever Hammers.

"The nerve of that thing!" Eleanor muttered, starting forward.

Leonid put up his hand to hold her back. "Allow me," he said.

Striding forward he said loudly, "Artificer Clever Hammers, I have been instructed by my masters at the college not to speak with you until such time as all legal issues are resolved."

"As have I," the forged one replied. "I am in disobedience being here."

That took Leonid by surprise. The forged ones' loyalty to their superiors was legendary.

"I will not be permitted to speak with you again," Clever Hammers continued. "I could not make my departure without telling you that I meant no harm in what I did. Please believe me."

Leonid nodded slowly. "I believe that you acted without malice. However, it was an act of carelessness and ignorance. It may be that no permanent harm has been done, yet the risk was unconscionable."

The forged one did not reply directly to Leonid's accusation. Instead, it rotated its head slowly, the ring of lenses focusing in sequence. "This is such a strange world to my eyes, and also a very beautiful one."

And then it turned and walked away.

Leonid watched it until it was out of sight, lost in the crowd of colorful Dracoheim pedestrians.

"I suppose it was talking about being sent back to Ferose,"

Eleanor said.

"Perhaps."

He opened her door and then got in behind the wheel. He wanted a drink, badly. But he knew that he would not have *a* drink—if he started, he wouldn't stop until the bottle was empty and he went staggering out in search of another.

At a quarter to 1300, he was still cold sober, standing awkwardly in front of Mrs. Barden's desk, feeling like a schoolboy who had been caught smoking in the locker room. He'd left his car parked in the faculty lot and Eleanor at the corner cafe with a magazine and a chocolate malt. The doors of both the president's and the dean's offices were closed.

Mrs. Barden looked up and smiled warmly. "Good," she said, "you're here. They're all down in the board room."

Leonid hesitated, unsure if that was an invitation or not.

"Go on." She waved. "They're expecting you."

Despite her smile, he wasn't reassured. He went up the stairs to the boardroom, casting a furtive glance down the hallway that led to his own office.

Will it still be "my" office this time tomorrow?

The door was closed, and Dean Welsh answered his tentative knock.

"Leo, great, come on in," Welsh said. "Let me introduce you to Clarifier."

Leonid stopped and stared before he regained his composure. Clarifier was, of course, a forged one. But this one was a type he'd never seen before. Its massive body was nearly featureless, gleaming with the bluish tint of a steel high in cobalt. Its face was dominated by a single lens protected by a thick pane of glass that was reinforced by a wire mesh.

Other forged ones were tinkers or builders or engineers. This thing was a war machine.

"Thank you for meeting with me," it said. Its voice was soft and uninflected. It didn't offer a handshake, which Leonid appreciated. It looked like it could punch a hole through a bank vault door.

"Of course," Leonid said. "Anything I can do to help."

SOLVABLE GAMES

"Clarifier, this is Magus Vetch," Welsh said. "Magus, Clarifier is from the Export Instrumentality. It has some questions regarding the conduct of Clever Hammers."

Belatedly, Leonid realized that he wasn't the one on trial here. He looked around. In addition to the president and the dean, there was a man he recognized as being one of the college's solicitors and another man in a suit who looked like a cop of some kind.

No one made a move to introduce them, so Leonid turned back to Clarifier. "Tell me what you need to know."

It was more of a conversation than an interrogation. Despite his intimidating appearance, Clarifier had an informal manner and Leonid found himself relaxing. Idly, he wondered if there were calming harmonics built into the investigator's voice box.

Clarifier quickly ran down the events leading to the students receiving and opening the puzzle box. It obviously knew the specifics already and was only asking for confirmation. Only once did an answer seem to trouble it.

"You, yourself, did not observe the box opening?"

Leonid shook his head. "No, it was open when I came into the classroom. The envelopes were sealed, though."

It paused, then turned its ponderous head to face the solicitor at the back of the room. "If he is willing, I would like Magus Vetch to be present at the inquest. His testimony should not be required, but it could save time if he was in the building."

"You will permit me to be there as well?" the solicitor asked.

"Of course. And Magus Welsh and Dr. Bink, if they choose."

"Leo?" Welsh asked.

"If I can help, I'll be there."

"Good man."

Clarifier turned ponderously towards the door. "Unfortunately, my transport has no provisions for passengers."

"Wait," Leonid said. "Do you mean now?"

"Is there a problem?" Dr. Bink asked.

"It's just... Eleanor is downstairs. At the cafe. I hadn't expected..."

"I'll have one of the staff run her home," Welsh offered.

Eleanor, once Leonid explained the situation, was having none of it.

"Of course I'm going with you."

"Darling," Leonid tried, "I think this is an official proceeding under Ferose law. They're only allowing me to attend because I might be a witness."

"So find me another cafe. They do eat in Century Orchard, don't they?" She held up her magazine. "I'm only halfway through Stage Door Secrets—I haven't gotten to the spicy bits yet. I'll be fine."

"It might take a while."

"They also sell magazines in Century Orchard." She was firm. "I'm going with you."

Leonid sighed and gave in.

Twenty minutes later, he left her at the counter at a diner around the corner from Iron Logic, with his solemn promise to collect her as soon as he could. She waved him off airily, studying the menu. "Oh, the egg and cheese sandwich looks good," she said to the counterman. "And is your coffee fresh?"

The trial—if that's what it was—of Clever Hammers was swift and brutal. Clarifier asked a series of questions and then pronounced sentence. Leonid expected the guilty forged one to be sent back to Ferose, but instead Clarifier produced a card and held it in front of the other's ring of eyes.

The eyes whirred and focused and for a long moment nothing else happened. Then Clarifier lowered its arm and put away the card.

"What is your name?" the inquisitor demanded.

"I don't know."

"Your name is Copper Tradesman."

"My name is Copper Tradesman."

"Go with these workers. They will equip you with your necessary skills."

That was it. Clever Hammers was gone. The forged one who had visited Leonid at the college and constructed the puzzle box for his students no longer existed.

Eleanor looked up with a smile when he returned to the diner. "All finished?" she asked. "That didn't take long—" She broke off,

260

seeing the look on his face. "What happened?"

"They *erased* it," he said softly. "Erased its mind. Deleted its personality somehow. Clever Hammers is gone—there's something else living in its body now."

Eleanor got up and walked with him back to the street. "Oh. I didn't know they could do that."

"I didn't either."

"I suppose..." Eleanor began. "I suppose it was a mercy."

"No." Leonid's voice shook, and he felt like he was about to be sick. "Nothing merciful about it. They just wanted to reuse the body."

"Let's get you home," Eleanor said. "You've had a long day."

The next day he returned to the classroom. The routine soothed him. By the end of the week all ten of his advanced research students were back, seemingly none the worse for their experience. Leonid scheduled time to meet with each of them individually and conduct his own informal assessment of their condition. To his relief, he determined that they were all fit, mentally, and hadn't seemed to have any problems remembering the material.

"I recommend that we graduate them as planned," Leonid told Kravitz at the gaming table the next weekend.

The dean grunted. "Good to hear. It's not as if we have any choice—can you imagine the publicity if we denied a student a certificate because of an accident that occurred as part of a class? It'd be an absolute nightmare."

Leonid hadn't considered that.

In the middle of the next week, he was called into the office to talk to the event coordinator.

"I called Vladimir Kent's employer to confirm his appointment for the Career Speaker's Series, and they informed me that he is no longer employed at Iron Logic," she said. "I supposed we'll have to cancel?"

"Yes, I suppose we should," Leonid agreed.

The news troubled him, and he went next to the registrar's office and looked up Kent's address. There wasn't any update card from the alumni office, but that didn't mean anything. No one ever filled out those cards. Well, if his family was still there, they would know where he was living now.

Kent's mother was home, and was pleased to see her son's former instructor.

"Vlad doesn't live here now—he has a rooming house in Freebooter Park—for a little while longer. He's packing to move, of course."

"I was wondering about that," Leonid said. "I'd heard he was no longer with Iron Logic."

"It was rather sudden," she admitted. "And so far out in the colonies, of course. But the money is good." She gave a sad little smile. "He's promised to write—but you know how boys are."

"I'd like to visit him before he leaves town," Leonid said, then added, "I'll remind him to write."

The small boarding room was nearly empty, just a few packing crates that were being used as temporary furniture. Vlad Kent answered the door and smiled when he saw Leonid.

"Magus," Kent said, opening the door wide. "I guess you heard."

"The school called Iron Logic to confirm your speaking engagement," Leonid said. "I wanted to know... is this my fault? You getting let go?"

"I wasn't let go," Kent said. "I quit. It's a better job out in Green Mountain anyway—they are desperate for magic workers out there and not all that concerned with credentials. They'll sponsor me for full certification—if I can do the work, of course."

"Oh, you can do the work," Leonid said quickly. "That's great. Magus Kent—that has a nice ring to it."

Kent laughed. "We'll see. It's a company town—the coffee plantation owns pretty much everything and I'll be working for them. I haven't actually been there. The interviews were all in town, at the importer's office. But the pictures are beautiful."

"Sounds good," Leonid said, relieved that the boy seemed to have landed on his feet. But he still had questions. "I'm sorry about what happened to Clever Hammers."

"Copper Tradesman," Kent corrected automatically. He sighed. "I know it looks bad to human eyes, but it's not all that unusual. It's

262

not like dying, it's more like getting a fresh start. Some forged ones have a dozen different personalities during their operating life."

"It seems terribly harsh for a simple mistake, though."

Kent looked out his window into the street for a long moment, lost in thought. Then he came to a decision and turned back to Leonid.

"Magus, I don't have much in the way of food here—you want to go grab a sandwich and maybe a couple of ciders? There's a great little place down the road."

"Sure," Leonid agreed quickly.

Kent grabbed a topcoat, and they headed out into the street. Once they were on sidewalk, Kent spoke softly, not looking at Leonid.

"Did you know that Ferose produces wisdoms calibrated for chigoes?"

"What?"

"It's not very well known—the Iron Council is avoiding publicity for the time being. But they work. Only fourth-order, so far."

Leonid was struggling with the concept. "I thought the wisdoms could only work on mechanical minds. All the literature on the subject..."

"Is wrong," Kent said. "At least as far as chigoes are concerned. There have been some experiments on incubi as well, but... the results are not encouraging."

"Are you saying that my students were exposed to those wisdoms deliberately as some kind of experiment?"

"No," Kent said quickly. "I am absolutely not saying that. There is no evidence that this was anything other than a tragic mistake made by an employee who was not properly briefed on human physiology."

Leonid nodded slowly. "But you suspect..."

"All I suspect is that a change of scenery would be nice right now, and there are standing offers for territorial thaumic workers."

They walked in silence for a while.

"Do you think it's possible?" Leonid asked quietly. "That humans might—someday—be able to learn new skills through wisdom imprinting?"

Kent stopped walking and looked down at his feet. "Yes," he said at last. "I think it's inevitable. Someday. Fourth-order certainly, maybe third-order as well."

Leonid digested this slowly as the two started walking towards the corner again.

"Well. That would change everything."

"Yes. Everything."

At the door Leonid stopped Kent with a hand on his arm. "Before I forget, your mother made me promise to tell you to write."

Kent smiled. "I will. I promise."

End Notes

"Lab Day": Like many of my stories, this one began with me questioning the tropes of a particular sub-genre. An author I know was putting together an anthology with the theme of Fantastic Schools and I took it as an opportunity to write a counterpoint to a particular series of novels about a school for wizardry. Leeshore Technical College is solidly blue collar and Leonid Vetch is the kind of instructor that you'd find at any trade school, a man with a practical background and more than his share of rough edges. At the same time, I wanted to play around a bit with the Realms of Nightmare that I had laid out, but not really explored, in the Rugar stories.

"In the Forests of The Night": This one was written specifically for Baby Katie Media's *Sidearm & Sorcery* anthology. This one also involves a trip into Nightmare, and Erik working closely with an oneiroi, specifically a moreau. I couldn't resist making the agent of the Grimm a catgirl—I leave to the reader to decide just how close their working relationship becomes at the end of the story.

"The Last Night of Summer": This is my follow-up to "Lab Day", written for a Fantastic Schools collection on the subject of school holidays. I had introduced the idea of the Autumn Mixer and Matron Eleanor in the earlier story, so it seemed a good event to craft a story around.

"That Summer's Evening Long Ago": This was the first Erik Rugar story I wrote after wrapping up *Bad Dreams & Broken Hearts*. I wanted to play with a trope I usually abhor, the detective investigating a case where he is personally involved with the victim. I think I pulled it off, Rugar being able, for the most part, to keep his personal and professional life separate. There's also a bit of cautionary tale there—there's a reason why it's best not to investigate a friend. You could find out something that you'd rather not know.

"Better Off Dead" Back when I wrote the first Erik Rugar story, I included the Pickmantown Ghoul Squad as a bit of background information (and a joking Lovecraft reference). Since then, I have fleshed out the existence of ghouls in Dracoheim, and I wanted to find a way to get Erik to work directly with the ghoul squad on a case.

"Materials Science": I went back to Nivose in this story—of the Realms of Nightmare it is probably my favorite. Kind of Richard Scary's *Busytown* all grown up. I also wanted to show a concrete example of a technological breakthrough, and while the implications are only hinted at, I think I made it clear that "Vetch's Metal" would cause an upheaval in magical manufacturing.

"Against the Midnight Currents": I return to a theme that runs throughout the Rugar stories here, that of corruption in high places. This story went through a number of revisions while I was writing it. The idea of bare-knuckle boxing matches, but with magic, came to me in a dream and pulled everything together.

"Solvable Games": This story is sort of a companion piece to "Cards for Sorrow" in *Bad Dreams & Broken Hearts*. I've always found the idea of "instant learning" by some kind of technology fascinating. I just took the cyberpunk style memory chips and made them magical cards. The ending of the story implies a major change to the Dracoheim universe, at least in potential. I'm not sure if I want to take things in that direction, though. That may be a technological change I don't care to deal with. As Leonid says, "That would change everything."

More Misha Burnett From Cirsova Publishing

Misha Burnett's Endless Summer: Twelve Strange Tales of Mankind's Future (2020)

Bad Dreams and Broken Hearts: The Case Files of Erik Rugar (2021)

An Atlas of Bad Roads (2022)

Small Worlds (2023)